Seven Mile Bridge

Seven Mile Bridge

Michael Biehl

Pineapple Press, Inc.
Sarasota, Florida

Inquiries should be addressed to:

Pineapple Press, Inc.
P.O. Box 3889
Sarasota, Florida 34230

www.pineapplepress.com

Library of Congress Cataloging-in-Publication Data

Biehl, Michael M.
  Seven mile bridge / Michael Biehl. -- 1st ed.
    p. cm.
  ISBN 978-1-56164-451-3 (alk. paper)
  1. Adult children--Fiction. 2. Parents--Death--Fiction. 3. Family secrets--Fiction. 4. Wisconsin--Fiction. 5. Domestic fiction. I. Title. II. Title: 7 mile bridge.
  PS3602.I34S48 2009
  813'.6--dc22
                                        2009023029

First Edition
10 9 8 7 6 5 4 3 2 1

Design by Shé Hicks
Front jacket photo courtesy of the State Archives of Florida

To my son

The hardest thing in life is to know which bridge to cross and which to burn.

— David Russell

I

The House

1

The House, Day One

AS I START TO CLEAN OUT THE HOUSE where my mother spent the last fifty years of her life, it occurs to me that in a half century the woman never got rid of anything.

Except my father.

Wandering through the forlorn rooms where I spent most of my childhood, I see that my mother has left the house in such a state of disrepair that the piles of old clothes, stacks of paper, and mind-boggling mass of memorabilia might be all that's holding the place up. I have never seen a house with so much deferred maintenance. In fact, you couldn't even call it deferred. It has been *denied* maintenance.

The roof has apparently been leaking for years, with the result that the drywall is so rotted with mildew that in places it has acquired the appearance and texture of Roquefort cheese. The Thermopane picture windows all lost their seals so long ago that they are milky white and nearly opaque, while the wooden frames around them are black with mold. All the doors are warped, all the floors squeak, all the faucets drip. The wallpaper is stained and faded, and in some places it has peeled off and curled into scrolls that hang on the walls like sconces. The fuse boxes are plugged with pennies, a hazardous temporary means of restoring power that apparently became a permanent solution for a woman so worn out that she chose to risk a house fire rather than make a trip to the hardware store. The whole house smells musty, with hints of rotted vegetables and urine.

The condition of the house speaks volumes about how much my mother's faculties deteriorated in the last few years before her death. It seems to me it also indicates that the neighborhood has changed a lot since I left thirty-four years ago. The neighbors I remember were as nosy as foraging warthogs, and obsessed with property values in their middle-middle-class subdivision. They would have reported anyone to the police who let knee-high weeds flourish in the lawn and had seed-bearing trees growing out of the gutters. Perhaps, as the Glen Oaks subdivision of Sheboygan, Wisconsin, matured, its occupants became more tolerant and easygoing. Or maybe they just don't give a damn anymore.

Merely contemplating the Herculean task of clearing out this cataclysmic clutter and getting the dump in any kind of shape to sell wearies me like a long hike up a steep hill. It also frightens me more than a little, and I know why. Lurking in the heaps of junk are undoubtedly countless mementos of the events that led to the death of my father, damaged the rest of the family beyond repair, and ended my youth on the sourest note imaginable. I think of the archaeological dig portrayed at the beginning of the movie *The Exorcist* and wonder what demonic icons I might unearth in this excavation.

The inevitability of uncovering buried souvenirs along with buried memories is what has kept my younger brother away and left me to handle the job alone.

"I, um, I, uh, can't do it," Jamie had told me on the phone a week earlier.

"But there might be some stuff in there you want," I said.

"No, uh, not enough to face all that shit. I can't."

I understood. Jamie knows his own limitations better than I do. He was four years younger than me, only thirteen, when it happened. I always thought that was why it had affected him more profoundly. Unlike Jamie, I have never spent time in a psychiatric hospital.

"You want me to keep anything for you?" I asked.

"Just my old record albums, if they're still there."

I have no doubt that Jamie's LPs — a comprehensive collection of Wagner and Mahler that seemed totally bizarre for a thirteen-year-old boy to own — are still here. Like I said, my mother never got rid of anything.

I decide that a good way to start the project is to go into the kitchen and see if there is anything potable in the liquor cabinet. Sure enough, the humble cupboard over the refrigerator is pretty well stocked, as it always was. Mostly cheap crap, American blended whiskey in a plastic bottle and vodka with a fake Russian name. But I manage to dig out a couple of airline bottles of Old Crow that look about forty years old, wipe the thick dust out of a water glass, and make myself a drink. It smells safe, and tastes fine.

Is there anything in this house worth anything? I wonder. Sitting in the kitchen, which has not been redecorated since the early '60s, I think of my mother scurrying about in her favorite frilly yellow apron, cooking dinner, and I remember she had a set of bone china she only used on holidays that she claimed was worth plenty. She would have a fit every Thanksgiving and Christmas, yelling at us, "Be careful with my grandmother's china! It's irreplaceable and it's worth a fortune!"

I find the china in the same place she used to keep it, the built-in cabinet in the dining room. The pieces are all cracked and chipped. Every single plate, saucer, cup, bowl, and serving piece, cracked and chipped. Worthless. The china cabinet also holds her set of cracked and chipped crystal. A bunch of Hummels and other figurines, as well, and a couple dozen vases. All of it damaged. It seems as if everything the least bit fragile that was in this house for long got damaged.

Everything and everybody.

Her sterling silver tea service is in here, too, pitch-black with tarnish and dented like a junked car. I realize there is slim chance I will find anything in the place that could be turned into enough cash to make it worth the time and trouble. From a practical standpoint, it would make more sense to pay someone to haul every last scrap to the dump, and raze the house or abandon it to the taxman. Or burn it to the ground.

But I didn't travel from Marathon, Florida, to Sheboygan, Wisconsin, and close my dive shop for three weeks because I thought I would find valuables or money in the house on Foxglove Lane. I came because I thought I might find answers.

It will be painful and exhausting to sort through this dismal mess and the vestiges of a fairly happy family that failed, but I have a feeling that I might find something here that I have been looking for for a long time. Something tells me this is my last chance to finally figure out what really happened to my father.

○

I'm draining the last precious drops of bourbon from the glass when I hear a clicking that sounds like a fingernail tapping on glass coming from the direction of the front door. I open the door and find our neighbor from across the street, Agnes Atkins, standing on the doorstep. My brother and I used to call her "Old Lady Atkins" even though she was only a few years older than our parents. She was the kind of fussy sourpuss who would yell at us if our ball rolled into her yard. I haven't seen her in three decades, but I must have been subconsciously aging her because I recognize her immediately and am not surprised by her appearance. She's diminutive and slightly hunched. Her face is pale and crinkly, and she holds a brown wool coat that's way too big for her closed in front of her neck with an arthritic-looking, purple-veined hand. Behind her, a herd of dry brown leaves stampedes down the sidewalk, driven by a stern wind.

"Mrs. Atkins, nice to see you."

"I tried the doorbell," she says, wagging a swollen finger at the button. I test it.

"It's broken," I say. "Probably has been for years."

She squints at my face for a moment, then widens her gray eyes.

"Jonathan?" she says. Her head moves slowly down and up. "Look at you! I almost didn't recognize you. Don't you look nice."

A polite lie. I have gained at least thirty pounds since she last saw me, have lost a lot of hair, and am dressed in a faded black sweatshirt and blue jeans with holes in the knees. My face is probably flushed from bourbon. It often is.

"You, too," I lie back. "Please, come in. It's cold out there."

"Not too bad for November," she says. She has to put both hands on the door frame to boost herself up the four-inch step into the house. A candied, floral smell accompanies her into the small foyer. "I saw the car and wondered who was in Louise's house." She glances around like a furtive bird. "Is Jamie with you?"

"Nope, just me." I'm relieved that someone in the neighborhood cares enough to snoop. Given the appearance of the house, I had thought that my mother could have dropped dead on the front lawn and been there long enough to attract vultures before anybody noticed.

"Where is Jamie now?" she asks. Apparently she and my mother haven't communicated much. Jamie has been in the same home for at least ten years.

"He's living at a place down in Port Washington," I explain. The "place" is an assisted living facility run by a private charity that houses adults who need help either staying off drugs, or, like my brother, staying on them. "He has a view of Lake Michigan."

"Oh, how nice. Are you still living in Florida?" She says "Florida" like she has something against the place, which I suppose she does. That was where her husband Tom ran off when he left her, back about the time I was in college. I recollected that my mother had told me another woman figured in Tom's exit. Tom and Agnes were childless, so she was alone after he split, and presumably still is.

"Yeah, I'm down in Marathon, at the east end of Seven Mile Bridge, if you know where that is."

"Still scuba diving?" Again, a hint of poorly concealed scorn in her voice, as if she thinks it deplorable that a college boy ended up as a scuba bum.

"Yep."

"Your dad got you into that, didn't he?" Her eyes move in the direction of the garage. It seems that for her, like everyone else, the memory of my father is inextricably linked to that garage.

"Yeah, he did."

She tilts her head and gives me a coquettish glance that makes her wrinkled face look sort of adolescent. "Ever get married?"

She reaches out and puts her hand on my forearm, making me aware that I have crossed my arms in front of me in response to her personal questions. I repress a subtle urge to tell her it's none of her goddamn business if I ever got married.

"Nope. Still batchin' it."

"Oh, Jon," she says, "your mother was always so proud of you boys."

Another lie. My mother stopped being proud of me when I dropped out of college. As far as I could tell, she was never proud of Jamie, not for ten minutes.

"I know," I say, returning the lie. "Can I offer you something? A soda, something to eat?" As soon as I say it, I wonder if I can back up the offer. The putrid smell that hangs in the house is particularly strong in the vicinity of the refrigerator. God knows what fetid refuse is in there.

"No, nothing, thank you," she says, to my relief. "I'm sorry I missed Louise's funeral. Her obituary didn't say anything about a service."

"It was very small," I reply. In fact, there has been no service. Jamie couldn't handle it, my mother's siblings and second husband all predeceased her, and I don't know who her friends are anymore, if any. She never expressed any wishes on the subject, except that she thought embalming and open caskets were hideous. As I speak to Mrs. Atkins, my mother's cremains are resting in peace in the trunk of my car.

"You take care now, Jonathan," she says, turning toward the door. "Let's get together for lunch or something before you leave town, okay?"

"Okay," I say. The biggest exchange of lies in the conversation. I can tell neither of us wants to get together, for lunch or anything. I figure I will never have any reason to speak to Agnes Atkins again for the rest of my life.

About that, like so much else, I am wrong.

2

I DECIDE TO START THE PROJECT by tackling what used to be my bedroom. The house is a Cape Cod, and my room, a second-floor dormer, has one of those ceilings that slant down to meet the wall, so designed in order to carve a few extra square feet of living space out of an attic. Once I hit puberty I was constantly bumping my head on the slanted part, and on the even lower ceiling in the gable, where the room's only window affords a view of the backyard.

The room now appears to be used exclusively for storage, like much of the rest of the house. My old bed is still there, with brown cardboard boxes stacked up on top of it. The desk I studied at in high school is piled high with stuffed manila folders. Bundles of papers and magazines tied with twine cover much of the floor. The closet is packed tight with clothes, some of them mine, most of them my mother's, all of them ludicrously out of date. Madras and paisley shirts, bell-bottomed corduroys, tartan wrap skirts with giant safety pins, rust-colored polyester pants suits. You wouldn't want to let go of any of that good stuff, would you, Mom? I expect I'd find my old Davy Crockett coonskin cap in there if I looked.

One item I want to get out of the way first. I don't want to stumble across it three days into the project when I might be feeling sentimental. I suspect it is somewhere in those manila folders where my mother kept important documents. Given the chaotic condition of the house, I am surprised to see that the folders are labeled and alphabetized, sort of, which should make finding things a whole lot easier. Or so I think until I start looking into the folders and find that the logic of my mother's filing system was entirely her own. The contents of the folders are, as far as I can tell, completely haphazard. I see no discernible order or organization regarding which papers are in what folders.

Yes, the "A" folders include one labeled "Auto Insurance," and there are a bunch of car policies in there. But they are on cars my parents owned in the '50s and '60s, and the same folder also holds recipes, newspaper clippings, Book-of-the-Month Club mailings, and a coupon for 25 cents off on a can of Alpo.

That starts with A, but my mother never owned a dog.

The more recent auto policies are in a folder labeled "Insurance," which also contains several life insurance policies, every one of them surrendered or cancelled for failure to pay premiums. The policies are mixed up with personal correspondence, business cards, and pages of advertising ripped from old *Newsweek* magazines.

The folders labeled "Taxes" each have a year on them — 1975, 1992, 1956 but they are not in numerical order, and the most recent one is for five years ago. It looks like my mother has not filed a return for the past five years, and I wonder what kind of headaches that will inflict on the executor of her estate. She has kept hundreds of bank statements from dozens of accounts at different banks, but a quick flip-through reveals that they are sown like wildflowers across folders from "A" to "Z" and it is impossible to tell which accounts are still open and which aren't.

Another hassle for the hapless executor.

One of the folders is labeled "Jamie," and it is adjacent to one marked "Jonathan." That makes me think the item I am looking for might be under "D," for David, my father's name. While shuffling through the "D's," I come across my mother's will. Not under "W," nor "L" for Last Will and Testament, not "T" for Testament, nor "E" for Estate Plan. Why "D"? For Death? Who knows? I check her will, not for the bequests (that can wait), but just to see who she has named as the executor of this hopeless mess.

It's me. Thanks, Mom.

There is no "David" file, but there is one labeled "Dad." This strikes me as odd, even though it seemed perfectly natural that my mother continued to refer to my father as "Dad" even after she remarried, since she had no children with her second husband. I open the folder.

The scrap of paper I am looking for, my father's obituary from the *Sheboygan Press-Gazette,* is right on top.

Local Man Found Dead in Garage

David H. Bruckner, a lifetime resident of Sheboygan, died Tuesday. He was 50.

His body was found in the garage of his home in the Glen Oaks subdivision. The cause of death was carbon monoxide poisoning. Police have ruled the death a suicide.

Bruckner worked for the past 15 years at Falls Dieworks, Inc., in Sheboygan Falls. "He was a loyal employee who will be missed," said Falls Dieworks corporate president Leon Bridette.

Bruckner is survived by his wife, Louise, 48, and by two sons, Jonathan, 17, and James, 13.

The obit hits me like a faceful of scalding water, the words evoking the same mix of anger and mortification they did the first time I read them.

Local Man, they called him. Not "doctor" or "professor" or "business executive" or "journalist" or "philanthropist." Not "corporate president" like that bastard, Leon Bridette. Just "local man." I was angry that they tagged him with that insultingly commonplace epithet. I was mortified because, at that point, that's about all he was. The statement that he was 50, which seemed sad and strange at the time, seems all the more so now that I am over 50.

Found Dead. They didn't say by whom he was found dead, which was a relief.

But after three decades I can still remember the shame rising in my cheeks and behind my eyes at the word *suicide*, and I feel it again. The first time I saw it, I couldn't believe the *Press-Gazette* would do that to us, to me. Didn't they (I say "they" because there was no byline, which I, in my wrath and ignorance, interpreted at the time as cowardice on the part of the reporter) have any idea how it would affect me and Jamie socially? *I* did. I knew immediately we would henceforth be the worst thing you could be as a teenager: different. We would be the oddballs whose spooky weirdo dad offed himself in the garage. The tainted apples that could not have fallen far from the bent, sapless tree.

I was furious that they quoted Leon Bridette, after all the trouble that asshole had caused us. At the time I thought they should have said that it was Bridette's fault my father was dead. The quotation had made me want to rip the article to shreds, since it was my father's loyalty that Bridette had misused to screw him, and because the words were so outrageously phony. Bridette had fired my father months before he died.

Survived by. Now that phrase was good. Succinct, accurate, complete and, with the benefit of over thirty years' hindsight, almost clairvoyant. If you want to describe what my mother, Jamie, and I did after my father died, "survived" sums it up pretty well.

A drinking buddy of mine in the Keys once suggested that I enhance the sign over the door to my dive shop by appending a piece of driftwood to it with "Jonathan Bruckner, Proprietor" painted on it. Typical Keys kitsch. I found a piece of driftwood that was actually a plank from an old skiff, weathered smooth with a few splotches of marine paint still clinging to it, something naive tourists might think came from a shipwreck. I shellacked it and dangled it from my sign out front, but what I put on it was: "Jonathan Bruckner, Survivor."

The clipping of my father's obituary is only about three inches long and two inches wide, so I can see what is directly underneath it — a yellowed, dog-eared letter addressed to David H. Bruckner on Bank of Wisconsin letterhead, dated April 5, 1971, which was about half a year before "local man" was "found dead in garage."

That letter was a grenade lobbed into my family's foxhole.

∘ ∘

April, 1971

The letter arrived on a Tuesday. I don't remember what the weather was like but it must have been either cold or rainy because Jamie and I were both in the rec room watching television after school. I was stretched out on the sofa. Jamie was sprawled on the floor, insensitive to the cold hardness of basement linoleum.

We were not much alike in appearance. He was quite tall for thirteen and husky, while I was only average height for my age and thin. Jamie was blue-eyed and sandy-haired, like our Polish-American mom, while I had brown eyes and almost black hair, like Dad. I had a flat pie-face; Jamie had a foxlike face with a high-bridged, pointy nose. We had the same mouth and chin, though — thin lips, slight underbite, lopsided grin — so that people often told us we looked like brothers.

"Wow! Look at those guys go!" Jamie yelled, wild-eyed with enthusiasm. "Dynamite! Those guys are dy-no-mite!"

We were watching footage of the Chinese men's table tennis team. It was in the news that day that Mao Zedong, whom we then called Mao Tse Tung, had invited the U.S. team to visit China, one of the opening moves in the diplomatic ping-pong that led to Nixon in Beijing, which we then called Peking.

"They're gonna kick our butts," said Jamie. "Chinks are amazing at ping-pong. They must all play it like, all day, every day."

The Chinese team *was* amazing. The ball moved so fast it was almost impossible to follow it. Still, I couldn't let Jamie's stupid remark pass.

"Chinese people can't afford ping-pong tables, Jimbo," I said, as snidely as possible. "Those guys are an elite corps selected and trained by the government, like Russian gymnasts. And don't say 'Chinks,' you Polack-kraut."

"Chinks, Chinks, Chinks," said Jamie. I flung a sofa cushion at his head. "Greet for me Valhalla!" he shouted.

Jamie would do that when he got excited, just suddenly yell something that made no sense. I was compelled to needle him about it.

"What did you say?" I asked superciliously.

"Never mind."

"You said, 'Greet for me Valhalla.' What does that mean?"

"Don't blame me if you can't figure it out." Jamie would never give an inch.

"It doesn't mean anything," I said.

"It means I saw you in the quarry with Lori."

"You're nuts. You're bonkers."

I knew Jamie was sort of peculiar and annoying, but I never seriously considered the possibility that he was actually mentally ill. After he was diagnosed I stopped telling him he was nuts, but I never stopped feeling guilty about having said things like that to him. I probably said it this time because I was afraid Jamie might actually have seen me at the quarry, which was the neighborhood teen make-out spot, with my girlfriend, Lori.

"It means," said Jamie without missing a beat, "that any Chink could kick your butt at ping-pong."

"Maybe, but *you* can't."

Jamie gave me a look out of the corner of his eye and a crooked-mouth grin that said, "You're on." Without another word, we leapt to opposite ends of the ping-pong table our dad had set up in the basement, grabbed our paddles, and started whacking the little white ball back and forth across the smooth green tabletop. Ordinarily, Jamie gave me a run for my money in spite of our age difference, but on this occasion he ill-advisedly tried to employ the grip used by the Chinese players, with the thumb in front on the forehand. He had never practiced that way, so I was beating him handily when my mother's voice rang down the stairs.

"What about homework?"

"All done," I shouted. Jamie didn't say anything, and I suspected his wasn't done. He struggled in school, but it didn't seem to bother him.

"Dinner's ready in ten minutes. Jon, set the table. Jamie, bring in the mail. Pronto, pronto!"

"Whoever loses the last point," I said to Jamie, holding the ball out in front of me 'twixt thumb and index finger, "gets the mail *and* sets the table."

He assumed the pose of a shortstop with men on base, up on the balls of his feet. I served conservatively, and he struck like a cobra. He had switched back to his usual grip without me noticing. I dove ineffectually at the spiked ball. Jamie whooped and danced around the basement with unreserved joy.

I know that I had no premonition about the white business-size Bank of Wisconsin envelope mixed in with the regular bills and junk mail, because when my mom asked if we got anything interesting, like she always did, I said, "Nope."

My dad was sitting at the kitchen table, wearing wrinkled chinos and a plaid flannel shirt with the top button buttoned, reading the newspaper as I set the table. He had a softly constructed face, with low cheekbones and thin, tentative lips.

The table, which had a fake marble laminate top and tubular steel legs, is still in the same place where I would drink a glass of Old Crow thirty-six years later, and it still seems way too big for the room. Back then, the Formica was gray and flat, not yellowish-brown and curling up in the corners.

My father had just recently begun using reading glasses, and I thought they made him look old; the black frames brought out the gray at his temples, and the lenses exaggerated the puffiness around his thoughtful eyes.

"How was school?" he asked, with a sing-songiness that mocked the triteness of the question.

"It was fine," I said, echoing his cadence.

"What did they teach you today?"

"English and math and social studies."

"What social things are you studying?"

"The war."

"Did you talk to Lori today?"

Naturally, I had no appreciation for my father's bland, predictable questions, his attempt to show interest without being intrusive. I didn't disdain his efforts, but I was never aware of how the gentleness and regularity of his mealtime inquiries contributed to my equilibrium, the safety there was in the expectation that no matter how perfunctory my answers, he would keep asking. I suppose nobody appreciates this sort of thing about their parents at seventeen, or even notices it, unless it suddenly stops.

I don't remember what we ate for dinner that night. Other than the Chinese table tennis team I don't remember what we talked about. I wish I did. I wish I had a clearer recollection of the countless dull, normal, placid dinners my family had before my father opened the envelope from the Bank of Wisconsin. I wish we'd had a video camera back then and I had taped some of those family suppers before the letter, suppers that I now recollect only vaguely in the soft focus and pastel colors of old faded snapshots.

I remember that my father would make corny jokes that elicited gentle scolding from my mother and giddy laughter from my brother, but I don't remember the jokes. My father would often over-compliment my mother's cooking, and she would accept the praise with the patently false modesty of an Oscar recipient. But I don't remember what my parents said, what their exact words were. I wish I did.

I remember thinking that we were happy, but I don't remember what it felt like.

After dinner that night, my father took the mail and sat down in his red and gold striped overstuffed easy chair in the living room. He read by the light of a brass floor lamp. My mother sat cross-legged on the sofa, knitting. Most evenings we were all in the same space reading, knitting, studying, playing games, whatever, always with the television blaring the whole time. We had an obsolete black and white Philco console with a cabinet the size of a washing machine. I was on the floor reading the sports page of the Milwaukee *Journal* and half-watching *The Mod Squad* when I heard my mother say, in a tone of voice that alarmed me, "What's wrong, David?"

I looked at my father. He held the Bank of Wisconsin letter in one hand, while with his other hand he squeezed the side of his face so hard it looked like it must hurt. Behind the black-rimmed reading glasses, his eyes had an expression of terrible agitation. Jamie was glued to the TV set, unblinking and oblivious.

My mother put down her knitting and asked again, "What is it? David, what's the matter?"

○ ○

My hand is shaking as I put the letter down and look again at my father's obituary. The item is accompanied by a tiny black and white photo that the *Press-Gazette* must have gotten from my dad's employment file at Falls Dieworks. The portrait is barely an inch high, less that an inch wide, and grainy, but even so I can see that my father has optimism and confidence in his eyes, that "young man looking to the future" expression. Maybe the photographer posed everybody that way, I don't know. I do know that I never again saw a look like that in my father's eyes after he opened that letter.

3

I DECIDE TO TAKE A BREAK from the manila folders and go down to the kitchen for that other airline bottle of Old Crow. It's the only decent booze left in the house, so I want to nurse it. I take my drink out to the living room and sit down in the red and gold striped easy chair where my father was sitting when he opened the letter from the Bank of Wisconsin. The arms of the chair are worn through the fabric to the white stuffing, and in one spot through the stuffing to the wood frame. The chair smells like stale cigarette smoke, and the fabric is stained orange in several places. The brass floor lamp next to it is encrusted with tarnish, the harp is bent, and the pull chain to turn it on is missing.

"Did it have to be that big a deal?" I say, out loud. In the silence of the empty house, the kitchen faucet answers, *"Plop . . . plop . . . plop."*

The living room drapes that used to be white but are now yellowish-brown are open a crack, and through the milky fog in the window I can see a snow flurry astir outside. I realize my fingers and toes are cold. A small pile of firewood is stacked on the hearth. Probably sitting there gathering dust for years, it should burn robustly. I wonder how long it's been since the chimney was last cleaned. If I opt to burn the place down, a fire in the fireplace might be all it takes to do the job.

I look down at the glass in my hand. It's empty. I set the glass down on the coffee table, which is embellished with ring-shaped stains that form Venn diagrams and Olympic symbols on its nicked surface, half expecting to hear my mother say, "Use a coaster."

○ ○

My father didn't get out of his chair and carry the letter over to my mother, who had three balls of different colored yarn on her lap. She was working them into a sweater that Jamie got for his birthday that year. When she said, "David, what's the matter?" with that dire tone in her voice, my father just looked down at his lap and held the letter out, as if it were too heavy and he was too deflated to carry it over to her. My mother stood up and took it from him, then sat back down to read it.

She had a nervous habit of picking at her fingernails with her thumbnail, which made a clicking noise. As she looked at the letter, she clicked like she was playing castanets.

"What does this mean?" she asked.

"What it says," replied my father.

"It's a mistake, right?"

"No."

There was a long pause, during which my mother stared at the letter and clicked her fingernails furiously. The normally smooth, even features of her face were pinched into a scowl of equal parts fear and anger. I was curious as hell as to what was in the letter, but I didn't think they'd tell me if I asked. They were acting guarded and deadly serious. I pretended to read the sports page while I listened surreptitiously.

"Who's this Newley?" my mother asked.

"Customer of the Dieworks," said my father. "Friend of Leon Bridette's."

Leon Bridette was my father's boss. From the tone in my parents' voices whenever they spoke his name, I had the sense that they both mildly disliked him, and less mildly feared him.

"Where is he?"

"I don't know."

"What happened to the money?"

"I don't know."

"Why would you do such a stupid thing?"

"Bridette made me."

"How could Bridette make you? Did he put a gun to your head?"

"He might as well have!" he thundered. My father rarely raised his voice, almost never when he was sober. He caught me peeking at him, and said, "Not in front of the children, Lou."

I don't remember my parents arguing or even discussing grownup matters around me and Jamie very much while I was growing up. For people with so little experience fighting in front of the kids, they sure got good at it towards the end.

My mother stood up suddenly and walked to the staircase, which descended from the upstairs right into the living room. She turned at the landing and glared at my father for a moment, then made a show of stomping up the steps. In my memory she has on a purple ski sweater with pink snowflakes on it, black stretch pants and black suede lace-up shoes, but that may be because we had several snapshots of her in that outfit. My father tried to salvage a little dignity by waiting long enough to make it seem like he wasn't scrambling after her. Then he shuffled over to the stairs and slowly ascended, without saying a word to me or Jamie.

I could hear them through the ceiling, could hear anger and anguish in their voices, but I could not make out their words. I turned the volume down on the Philco. Jamie turned it back up. I turned it down, he turned it up again. He wasn't about to yield, so I went over to the stairs and crept halfway up on all fours, being careful to avoid the squeaky fifth step. There, I could make out some words, snippets of the exchange going on in my parents' bedroom, but I couldn't quite get the gist of the conversation, just that it scared me.

My mother's voice: " . . . end up on the street *with two children!*"

My father's voice: " . . . never let it come to that. I will take care of my family!"

Mother's voice: " . . . *man* wouldn't let his boss push him around."

Father's voice: " . . . don't understand how these things work."

There was a lull in the action on *The Mod Squad,* and I heard one sentence from my mother clearly: "I am not going to let the rug be pulled out from under me now, not after everything I've had to put up with!"

I had never thought of my mother as spoiled. On the contrary, she was sturdy, practical, what we now call "low maintenance." So I was baffled by her exclamation. What was this "everything" she was claiming she'd had to "put up with"?

We weren't well off by anyone's standards, at least not anyone American. I knew my parents were perpetually strapped, hanging on to modest suburban home ownership by their fingernails. Whatever we did, money was always an issue, whether it was a vacation up north or a trip to 31 Flavors for ice cream cones. Sometimes an unexpected expense like a furnace repair would cause my father to miss a mortgage payment. Once the well pump went out and we couldn't afford to get it fixed until my father's next paycheck. We had to go to the bathroom in a plastic bucket and bury our feces in the backyard for five days. Maybe this was what my mother was talking about, but she had not made much of a fuss about it at the time. If she was that dissatisfied with the way things were, I had never noticed it.

My father opened the bedroom door suddenly, and I scurried backwards down the stairs like a startled crab. I forgot to skip the fifth step, and it let out a squeal like fingernails on a chalkboard, announcing to my father that I'd been eavesdropping. He appeared at the top of the stairs and we locked eyes. His face was flushed and he looked more embarrassed than I was.

"Go to bed, Jonathan," he said. "Tell your brother to go to bed, too."

I turned the TV off. Jamie yelled at me that the show wasn't over and turned it back on. "Dad says we have to go to bed," I said.

"Forget it," said Jamie.

We argued for a minute, but it was obvious Jamie wouldn't budge. Taking the opportunity to demonstrate how much better a son I was than Jamie, I went upstairs, stopping to tell my father, "Jamie refuses to go to bed." My father just stood there while I went to wash up.

When I came out of the bathroom my father was still standing at the top of the stairs, frozen, as if he just couldn't decide whether to go back into the bedroom and face his indignant wife, or go downstairs and deal with his stubborn, disobedient son. So he just stood there, a guy with no place to hang out in his own house.

I went to bed, but I didn't go to sleep. I lay on my back staring at the long, meandering crack in the ceiling and wondering what was in that letter, who "Newley" was, what was the stupid thing my dad's boss made him do, and how it all might result in us ending up on the street. An hour later the noise from the television stopped. Then Jamie clumped back and forth between his room and the bathroom for a while, brushing his teeth with the same exasperating deliberation as any other night, and finally the house quieted. Out of a combination of self-protective vigilance and morbid curiosity, I had left my bedroom door ajar. I was still awake when my parents' voices started back up, from the direction of their bedroom. Barely audible whispers at first, then agitated but still hushed tones, then anguished declarations loud enough I could make out the words.

"I *will* take care of it. I'll talk to a lawyer tomorrow."

"And pay him with what? Lawyers don't work for free, you know."

"I'll work it out."

"How, David? If you file bankruptcy again, our credit is finished."

Again? What was she talking about? When had my father filed for bankruptcy? I wasn't even sure I knew exactly what bankruptcy was.

"Perhaps *I* should be the one talking to a lawyer."

"Don't talk nonsense, Lou. This isn't grounds for divorce."

"Nonsupport is grounds in this state. Besides, I read Wisconsin might be no-fault soon."

I heard some shuffling around coming from their bedroom, then the squeal of the fifth stair tread, followed by a door slam that sounded like the report from a cannon.

I lay awake for another couple of hours, replaying the events of the evening in my mind and trying to decipher my parents' remarks. My stomach ached and I couldn't seem to take a satisfying breath of air. The crack in the plaster over my bed looked threatening, like it might spontaneously start spreading and cause the ceiling to collapse on me.

I was picturing what my mother looked like tramping angrily up the stairs, her blonde flip bouncing up and down, when I realized something. Her hands had been balled into little fists, with nothing in them. She was not holding the letter. I thought of my father on the stairs, slinking after her, head down, pulling himself up with the banister. His hands were empty, too.

I got out of bed and shuffled quietly to the stairs. The uncarpeted wooden treads were cold on my bare feet. Halfway down I could see my father passed out on the sofa in his bathrobe, gently snoring, one slippered foot on the floor, one draped over the arm. The room reeked of whiskey and cigarette smoke. On the coffee table, next to an empty bottle of Early Times and a brass ashtray full of Tareyton butts, was a tri-folded sheet of white paper. I stepped over the squeaky fifth step and moved as quietly as I could to retrieve the letter. By slipping in behind the drapes I was able to read the letter by the light of the streetlamp in front of our house.

o o

I pick up my empty glass and go back in the kitchen, just to make sure there isn't another little bottle of Old Crow or something else palatable hiding in the cabinet over the refrigerator. There isn't, so I pour two fingers of the sorry-ass blended whiskey into my glass. It's as bad as I expected, but better than nothing.

Back in my old room, I read the Bank of Wisconsin letter again. It doesn't scare or confuse me anymore, like it did when I was seventeen. It just makes me feel sad, and a bit queasy. Below the date, my father's name and the address of our house on

Foxglove Lane, it says, "Re: $80,000 Promissory Note dated June 1, 1970."

Dear Mr. Bruckner:

The loan made by the Bank of Wisconsin to Philip J. Newley of Oostburg, Wisconsin, is in default. Mr. Newley has not made payments as required by the Loan Agreement of even date with the above-captioned Promissory Note for the past nine months. We have been unable to locate Mr. Newley.

Under the terms of the Loan Agreement, the entire principal amount of the Promissory Note and all accrued interest, together with default penalties as provided in the Loan Agreement, are due and payable on demand. As guarantor of the Note, you are liable for the amount due, $108,715.87.

Demand is hereby made for payment of the said amount. If full payment or other arrangements satisfactory to the Bank of Wisconsin are not made within ten (10) days from the date hereof, this matter will be turned over for collection with instructions to commence immediate action.

Very truly yours,
Frank T. Shriner
Vice President, Business Loans

After thirty-six years and with three stiff drinks in me, I think I can finally see that the letter *did* have to be as big a deal as my parents made of it. If the same thing happened to me now as happened to my father then, I could just give up my equity in the dive shop and my boat, move to the mainland where the cost of living is lower, and drive a forklift or do odd jobs. But I don't have a wife and kids.

I stare at the letter, remembering how it alarmed and

disheartened my father. Perhaps witnessing the effect these three paragraphs had on him is the reason I don't have a wife and kids. I think acknowledging that possibility is what is making me queasy.

I hoist a couple of large corrugated cardboard boxes off the bed and onto the floor so I can lie down for a moment. The bed sags like a hammock. The crack in the ceiling is still a meandering river across the room, but it is wider now and has developed tributaries. In the stillness of the house, I imagine I can still hear my parents' argument that night escalating down the hall, the plaintive wail of the squeaky stair tread roused by my father in retreat, and the punctuating slam of a bedroom door reverberating through the house with an ominous finality, like the concluding chord of a Beethoven sonata. One of the grim ones.

4

I WAKE UP TO WHAT SOUNDS LIKE A SNARE DRUM rat-a-tat-tatting
in the room. I'm cold and my back aches from napping on the
sagging mattress. My eyes and nose are full of dust and I sneeze
repeatedly.

The snare drum turns out to be the window in the gable,
rattling violently in the harsh wind. I check to see if the window
is latched. It is, but the sash is loose in the frame and no one has
bothered to put up the storm window, this late into November. No
wonder it's so damn cold in the room. I pull a couple of magazines
from a nearby bundle and jam them in around the window sash
to keep out the worst of the gale. Outside, darkness is gathering in
the bare tree branches and along the ground.

On my way back to the desk, I notice that the top of one of the
boxes I moved off the bed is open, and some of its contents have
spilled. I must have popped it open grabbing the flaps to lower it.
It's a large box that once contained a microwave oven. Pouring out
of it onto the floor are more than a dozen old photographs. Three-
by-five and four-by-six color prints, typical family snapshots.
The box is packed to the brim with pictures, hundreds, maybe
thousands of them.

I go downstairs to turn up the thermostat, and the furnace
comes on with a resounding roar. How many decades has it been

since that decrepit dinosaur was last serviced? I realize I am hungry, so I head to the kitchen and rummage around for something to eat. Spilled beverages, dark mold, and something green and sticky coat the inside of the refrigerator. Nothing in there looks bacteriologically safe; I'm surprised my mother didn't die from food poisoning a long time ago. An off-brand can of pork and beans in the pantry looks like it won't kill me, so I heat it up on the stove and eat from a pink plastic plate that dates from the '50s.

The cheap plastic plates she wasn't able to chip.

Down in the Keys I usually follow dinner with a couple of snifters of Curaçao. Here the best I can come up with is a slug of cheap vodka, which I take straight from the bottle. Thus fortified, I venture back upstairs to poke around in that box of pictures.

The photos are a jumble without even the chronological or subject matter grouping one might expect would occur naturally. It is as if the contents of the box have been spun in a clothes dryer for an hour. Snapshots of my mother gray-haired and holding hands with my stepfather Ray are mixed in with those of her young and holding my brother and me as babies, and with dog-eared black and white pictures of her as a baby herself, being held in the arms of my grandparents next to a shingle-sided bungalow and a car with running boards. Regardless of age, she has strong cheekbones, a short, straight nose, a broad, rounded forehead, and a penetrating, dramatic look in her eyes.

Decades of vacations, weddings, holidays, school portraits, and family get-togethers are all shuffled together, as if inside this box, linear time has unraveled and everything is happening all at once.

As a dive master and PADI scuba instructor I have had to learn rudimentary photography in order to take underwater shots for tourists and ID portraits for certification students. I can't help but chortle at how consistently terrible the photography in these pictures is. So many shots centered on the faces, so the subjects are cut off at the waist and half the picture is empty space above their heads. Sunbursts in windows or mirrors from reflected flashbulbs. Overexposures, underexposures, jittery, cockeyed Polaroids. People with their heads or half their bodies cut off, out of focus, or lost in shadows. Fingers over the lens.

The most consistent blunder I see is the photographer standing too far from the subjects, so the people are tiny and their faces have no discernible expression. This is especially true of the vacation pictures, where presumably the excuse is the photographer wanted to get a lot of scenery in the shot, as if they really needed to have a permanent record of that particular beach. But it is also characteristic of the really old pictures from the time my grandparents were young and photography for the masses was a novelty. Some of these old photos are black and white, some are sepia. Virtually all of them are group shots with a whole lot of people lined up, as if at a company picnic. Even though the faces in these pictures are no bigger than match heads, just eye sockets and tiny hyphens for mouths, I can recognize my grandparents, great aunts and uncles, and my mother and her siblings as small children.

Here is photographic evidence that these folks all got together with some regularity back then. Now, the idea of assembling a group that size from either of my parents' families seems ludicrous, as they are scattered across the continent, estranged, divorced, too busy to write each other, let alone assemble for a group photo. In this respect I think my extended family is fairly typical, and this strikes me as a change the last seventy years has wrought that is more significant than space travel or personal computers.

Near the bottom of the box I find a sealed envelope, yellowed, with "Lake/Audrey" handwritten on it in black ballpoint. It opens easily. Inside are a couple of black and white negatives. I hold one up to the light and see tiny black-faced minstrels standing on a granite slab in a sea of milk. As small as they are, I can recognize my mother and father. They are on a swimming raft in a lake. My mother's blond hair is black as ink. She's wearing a two-piece suit; she has a good figure, a little thick in the ankles. My father's black hair is white, his baggy trunks riding low enough to reveal love handles and a slight paunch. Both are smiling, showing a lot of black teeth.

The other negative is of a foursome, in front of what looks like a small log cabin. My mother is in the same swimming suit, holding a baby. My father has his arm around her waist. At his side, a child whose head does not reach my father's hips is holding onto his index finger possessively with one hand and grasping a small object in the other.

There is a Lake Audrey in western Sheboygan County, in the Kettle Moraine State Forest. My father took me fishing there when I was eleven. I sat on the grassy shore angling for bluegills with wax worms and a cane pole, while my dad waded in with hip boots and tossed a fly around. I remember it was a sunny day and the lake was weedy. We didn't catch much, but we talked a lot and I don't recall my father saying anything about having rented a cabin there when I was little. If Jamie was a baby, I must have been at least four. Old enough to have retained a few mental images, but I don't remember it at all. This gives me a strange, hollow feeling, like I've lost a piece of myself and have no way of knowing how to get it back, or what else I may have lost. Maybe if I had prints made from these negatives, with a clearer image of the place I could dredge up a memory.

Just beneath the envelope with the negatives I find a picture from a day I do remember, and vividly: the day Sheboygan got ten inches of lake-effect snow on the seventh of April.

○ ○

April, 1971

School was cancelled, and my brother and I dashed to the quarry with our skis. One of the quarry walls was collapsed and it made a challenging, if brief, downhill ski run. There was no lift, of course, so after trudging up the hill ten times with our skis on our shoulders, we were worn out and went home.

Snow shovels awaited us, planted imperatively in a deep drift at the end of the driveway. We made short work of the task and then employed the shovels to hastily build opposing forts in the backyard for a snowball fight. My brother threw harder than I did, and more accurately. He laughed more, too, and louder, and went absolutely wild with glee whenever one of his missiles found its mark.

The snow was the sticky, good-packing kind, and after twenty minutes we looked like ambulatory snowmen. My father stepped out on the back porch with no coat or gloves and took this picture of me and Jamie, white-coated like powdered doughnuts, our faces red, wet, and raw. Then he called us in for hot chocolate.

Jamie and I stomped the snow off our boots and hung up our ski jackets in the mud room, both of us punchy from fresh air and exhaustion. My mother placed steaming mugs on the table. The kitchen was warm and smelled of chocolate. My father wasn't there. I had almost shaken off the malaise from the sleepless night I had just spent worrying about my parents and the letter from the Bank of Wisconsin. The stricken look on my mother's face brought it back.

"Jamie, hang up your coat. It's on the floor." Grief in her voice, as if the jacket were a dead infant.

"So what?"

"You have to make that jacket last another year."

"Forget it. I hate that jacket. The sleeves are too short already."

My mother stood at the kitchen sink, pressing the tips of her fingers against her forehead. "You have to take better care of your things." Her jaw muscles clenched. "Hang the jacket in the closet."

"I'm tired. I'll do it later."

Jamie held his mug in both hands and blew on his hot chocolate. My mother whirled around and yelled, "Pick it up!" Jamie ignored her. I couldn't decide whether he was being valiantly defiant or just obtuse. With Jamie it was hard to tell the difference. Either way, I thought he was about to catch hell, which was always a guilty pleasure for me.

Before my mother said another word, Jamie took a sip of his hot chocolate and spit it out in a spray. "The cocoa's too hot!" he snarled. "I burned my mouth! Gah!" He banged the mug down, slopping half its contents onto the table, and bolted from the room.

My mother started to mop up the spilled brown liquid with a dishcloth, then slumped down in Jamie's chair and leaned forward with her brow resting on the heel of her hand. Her hair, which she usually wore in a Jackie Kennedy flip that sentenced her to sleep in large rollers, was shapeless and hung over her face. The bright sunlight that streamed through the kitchen window illuminated the gray in her hair and wrinkles around her mouth and eyes that I hadn't noticed before. Her shoulders shook. She was crying.

Until that morning, I had never seen my mother cry, except a couple of times when we were watching the Hallmark Hall of Fame on television. I'm sure she wept plenty of times, like the day Dr. McNulty called to report that an x-ray showed Jamie had bone cancer (three days later he called back and told her a specialist overread the x-ray and said it was just a minor stress fracture, sorry to have worried you). But she never let us kids see her cry, and I felt sort of honored that she was showing me her emotions in this crisis, like in some way it elevated me to adult status.

I didn't know what to do. We didn't hug much in my family. I considered saying, "It'll be all right, Mom," but I didn't know if that was true and was afraid it might sound juvenile. So I said nothing.

"Jonathan," she said, and sniffed deeply. "There's something I have to tell you. I'm going to need your help to get through this."

Gosh. I was getting more grown up by the second.

"Jonathan." She heaved a long sigh. "We're in trouble. Your father has done a very stupid, stupid thing. This is hard for me to tell you."

I felt guilty for not confessing that I had snuck a look at the letter and knew all about it already. It hurt to hear her call my father stupid, while at the same time it gave me a weird little boost in the dark recesses where I felt I was in competition with him for my mother's esteem. That made me feel even guiltier.

She went on to explain why the Bank of Wisconsin was demanding that my father pay $108,715.87, which was more than seven times his annual income and over ten times our entire net worth. Philip Newley, the guy the bank couldn't locate, was a friend of my dad's boss at the Dieworks, Leon Bridette. My mother said Newley was an "entrepreneur," saying the word like it was synonymous with "con man" or "thief." Newley had once served on the school board, and with school lunch programs on the upswing, he decided there was easy money to be made selling lunch trays to school districts. He formed a corporation and signed a couple of contracts to supply trays. Problem was, Newley needed a bank loan to start the business. He had a bad track record with the local banks, having started businesses before that had failed.

"So," she continued, "he asked Leon Bridette to get someone at the Dieworks to co-sign for the loan. Do you know what that means?" She sipped the dregs of Jamie's hot chocolate. Her eyes were clearing and she seemed to be regaining her usual starch.

"Yes." My mother waited while I chewed on this. I asked her, "Why would Bridette make Dad the guarantor?"

She glanced up from the mug and shot me a suspicious look. My remark disclosed that I had listened in on the argument the night before. Worse than that, while she had said Bridette got someone to "co-sign" for the loan, I said he made Dad the "guarantor," the word Frank T. Shriner used in his letter. I was trying to sound sophisticated, but I think she caught on that I had seen the letter.

"Bridette told Dad that Newley's company was going to hire the Dieworks to stamp the thousands of lunch trays he was going to sell. Newley had contacts all over the state and your dad's company was supposedly going to make a whole lot of money." She waved her hands up and down like she was dribbling invisible basketballs. "Big deals, big deals. But they never made one lousy tray. The loan came through and Newley took off with the money, eighty thousand, leaving David holding the bag." Her jaw slid into an underbite and her lip curled. "Him and some other patsy."

"Why did Dad go along with it?" My father's title was Manager of Product Design, which sounds distinguished but at a low-tech, mid-sized company like Falls Dieworks was a modest job. He was not one of the big shots, not by a long shot.

"You'll have to ask *him* that." She put the mug down and began clicking her fingernails. "Some baloney about it being a test of loyalty to the company. He and the other patsy were in line for the same promotion, and your dad would lose out if the other

31

guy went along and he didn't." Click, click, click. "David says he would have looked like a milquetoast if he didn't do it. If you ask me, he did it *because* he's a milquetoast." Click, click. "But," she sneered, "*I* don't understand how these things work." Click.

Anger and contempt wafted in the air around her, souring the smell of the hot chocolate. I couldn't blame her. She had good reason to be angry and contemptuous. What I didn't appreciate at the time was that she used anger and contempt as anesthetic, so she wouldn't feel the fear.

I felt the fear, though, in my chest and neck, hard and cold. "Will this other guy pay the loan?"

"David says no. He's like us, no money." She looked off to the side and seemed absent for a moment. "Years and years. No money."

"What happens if we can't pay the loan?"

She got up and walked to the sink, rinsed out the mug, drenched the dishcloth, wrung it out. I thought she wasn't going to answer my question. Then she leaned on the counter, her face pale and furrowed.

"I don't know, Jonathan. We might lose the house. We might lose everything. I may have to get a job. You'll have a lot more responsibility around here. I don't know if David and I will stay together. I just don't know."

I looked out the window. The sun was melting the snow fast and the gutters dripped as if it were pouring rain. Elevation to adulthood suddenly didn't seem so peachy.

"And Jonathan," she added. "Don't tell Jamie about any of this. He's a lot more fragile than you."

Jamie? Fragile? Strong, stubborn, obtuse Jamie? I thought of him as about as fragile as a block of wood.

"Promise me, Jonathan. Promise me you won't tell Jamie."

○ ○

I look at the photo my father took of Jamie and me in the backyard, coated with melting white snow, our wet faces smiling, our eyes squinting against the glaring sunlight. My high school graduation portrait, taken less than a year later, is lying on the floor at my feet. In it, my hair is shaggy and my face has the same expression as the guy with the pitchfork in *American Gothic*. I look like a different person.

I kept my promise. I never told Jamie. As I lie down on the sagging, musty mattress, I wipe dust from my lips with the back of my hand, and say, "You shouldn't have told *me*."

5

The House, Day Two

WHEN I WAKE UP, SUNLIGHT IS STREAMING through the flimsy, rattling window in the gable. I have slept the entire night uncovered, in my clothes, sharing my old bed with a half-dozen cardboard boxes. Pictures are scattered over the bed and on the floor. The envelope with the negatives of the photos of my parents, my brother, and me at Lake Audrey is on the pillow next to my head. Thinking I might have prints made from the negatives, I shove the envelope in the back pocket of my jeans and head downstairs to forage for breakfast.

There are about twenty cereal boxes in the pantry, all of them opened, none of them with the liners properly folded. Stale Wheaties, rancid corn flakes, raisin bran from the Pleistocene era. Unless I want another can of beans for breakfast, I must venture out. I have fond memories of the ham and eggs at the counter in Wischki's Pharmacy on 7th Avenue.

No one in the Keys keeps an ice scraper in his car, so I have to use an old spatula to clear some of the frost off my windshield. The heater in my '91 Dodge, irrelevant in the Keys, fights a losing battle against the raw Wisconsin morning. I don't own a winter jacket, and my teeth are chattering as I drive past rows of small Colonial homes and '50s-era brick ranches. The trees in the yards

34

are bare and the houses have a battened-down appearance.

Sheboygan is colorless in November, even on a sunny day. It is a small, hard-scrabble city that achieved most of its growth in the early part of the last century making furniture, shoes, dairy products, and sausage. Sheboygan is enormously proud of its sausage. Its sole tourist attraction is the annual Bratwurst Festival. For two days in August each year, thousands of people from all over converge on Kiwanis Park to assail their arteries with grilled pig intestines stuffed with fat, batter their eardrums with excessively loud music, and pickle their brains with prodigious quantities of beer.

Wischki's Pharmacy is gone, a victim, I assume, of the big chain drugstores. The dingy brick building on the corner now houses a nameless tavern with a neon Pabst Blue Ribbon sign in the window. Will it and the others like it be driven out someday by giant chain taverns?

Wal-bar.

Down the block is a clean, modern storefront with a new sign: "Photo-Phast – Prints in 1 hour." I give the Lake Audrey negatives to a very young, pretty Asian woman with straight black hair, rimless glasses, and a somber demeanor. Behind her, several young black-haired, white-coated techs are diligently developing and earnestly enlarging. I don't remember there being any Chinese-Americans in Sheboygan thirty years ago, but there appear to be quite a few of them now, at least at Photo-Phast.

I manage to wolf down a couple of dry pancakes at McDonald's, together with coffee in a Styrofoam cup covered with grave warnings about the coffee's hotness, but none about its insipidness. I avoid the sausage entirely, shaking my head that they would try to pass off these venomous little globules in a city that treats sausage like a religion.

On the way back I realize I can't face another day of the deplorable liquor selection at the house on Foxglove Lane, so I stop to pick up a decent bottle of bourbon. Do I have a problem? Such things are relative. In Utah, I would be considered an alcoholic, whereas here in Sheboygan I am well within the norm. In the Keys, I am the very soul of moderation; if the tourists are included in the sample group, I am practically a teetotaler.

When I get back to the house it is noticeably colder; the furnace is out. I risk a fire in the fireplace and warm myself by it. I'm not ready to spend the money or the time to bring in a furnace contractor at this point. I want to get right back to those cardboard boxes on the bed.

My old room is chilly, so I rummage around in the packed closet and come up with my high school letter jacket. Its white leather sleeves, cracked with age, come to about the middle of my forearms. Not because my arms have gotten longer, but because the rest of me has gotten larger.

The next box I open has "L.L. Bean" printed on it. It is full of books, and I get a whiff of library smell when I pull it open. The books have a consistent theme. Personnel directories from Falls Dieworks, family albums, high school and college yearbooks. Books with pictures of people we once knew. Here is my high school graduation yearbook, covered in fake maroon leather with a gold bas-relief Viking head. Sheboygan North High School. Raiders, 1972.

I flip immediately to the pictures of the seniors whose last names start with the letter H, and there she is. Delores Ann Hagen.

Lori.

She is wearing a black sweater and has a scarf tied dramatically around her neck. Her body is turned to the side and she is looking over her shoulder, her head slightly tilted. A half-smile, a dimple, and a look in her eyes that tells you she knows exactly the effect she has on boys, and takes pleasure in it. Even in a black and white photo you can tell she is that rarest of colorations: a genuine brown-eyed blonde.

I usually think of myself as slightly ridiculous. For the moment, I have passed beyond slightly. I am fifty-four years old, sitting on a dusty, saggy old bed, shivering, wearing an old jacket that's about four sizes too small for me, looking down at a tiny picture of an eighteen-year-old girl I haven't seen in decades and it's giving me an erection. The picture is only her head and shoulders, she is fully clothed, and the image is not more than an inch and a half wide by two inches high, yet Lori is able somehow to reach out from that page and across thirty-plus years, and get to me just like she always did. It triggers a memory of a warm day in late October.

oo

October, 1971

The temperature was up in the '70s, rare in Sheboygan at that time of year. By third period they had opened the windows at North High and the feel of summer with the smell of autumn leaves wafted into the classrooms and through the halls.

The fresh air seemed to animate everyone and there was near pandemonium between the bells. I had English third period; so did Lori.

"Indian summer," she said, smiling at me, her eyes twinkling. She was wearing a lime-green sleeveless top and a pleated skirt that was hemmed about four inches above her knees, which was about as revealing as girls' clothes got at North High back then. Now I see teenage lasses waiting for the school bus with bare midriffs and their thighs exposed nearly to the hips. Imagine trying to pay attention to algebra surrounded by that. It strikes me as cruelty to animals.

"Why do you suppose they call it 'Indian summer'?" she asked.

"The origin of the term is not known," I said with an exaggeratedly authoritative air, having read an item in the news-paper about it that very morning. "One theory is that European settlers saw Indians hunting during warm days in fall."

"How do you know stuff like that?" She wrinkled her little nose. "You're too smart. No wonder you're wrecking the curve."

Her observation about my effect on the curve was obsolete. By the fall of my senior year, my class rank was tumbling. With what had been going on at my house for the last six months since the letter came from the Bank of Wisconsin, it was almost impossible to study, or even care about exams or grades. The only curves I cared about were Lori's. But one's image in high school is a fairly sturdy thing, and my classmates still thought of me as a top student.

I fumfered around for something to say, anything to hold her attention until I could find a natural opportunity to firm up the tentative plans we had made the day before. Had to be cool about this.

"Have you heard the new James Taylor album? *Mud Slide Slim?*"

"No. Is it as good as *Sweet Baby James?*"

I shook my head. "Not even close, but what is? It's got a couple of good songs."

The bell rang. To hell with cool. "Do you need me to carry your books after school today?" This was our code. It meant I would get on her bus after school and we'd get off at the stop nearest the quarry.

"Oh, yes." She pretended to lift the two slim volumes in her hands with great effort. "They're sooo heavy."

We laughed and took our seats. Most of the rest of that school day is lost in a fog. I remember that in English class we read John Keats' poem "On First Looking into Chapman's Homer." Mr. Osbourne in Physics chided me for not paying attention.

During lunch my friend Bill Sorenson also remarked on my absence of mind. He guessed correctly that I was anticipating a rendezvous with Lori and made obscene hand gestures and mouth noises that drew snickers from the other diners at our table. Most of what passed for conversation among the guys at North was to some degree malevolent, but at least by senior year the cruelty was usually just for laughs. There were still a few social rejects in the class who took some serious flak, but I was not one of them at that point. "Local man" had not yet been "found dead in garage."

I must have gone to see the cross country coach to get excused from practice, but I don't recollect what lie I told. Mostly, I remember my head swimming, my face burning, and the time passing like a tortoise on Quaaludes until Lori and I got off the bus.

To get to the quarry you had to walk across a large field of waist-high weeds, crawl through a hole in a barbed-wire fence, and ignore a menacing black and yellow "No Trespassing" sign. The quarry was no longer in operation; the fence and sign were there for safety's sake. When I was in grade school a kid in my class had drowned there.

The quarrymen had hit groundwater, creating a twenty-acre lagoon that looked as blue as a sapphire when the sky was clear. The walls were striated limestone, notched with coves that afforded privacy. On the floor of the quarry there were piles of crushed stone, mixed gravel and powder, saffron-colored like beach sand.

In keeping with the custom, I removed my shoes as if I were entering a Japanese home and left them outside the cove we had selected as a "Do Not Disturb" sign, confident that this would be respected by any others making use of the quarry. Teenage pranksterism and spite always gave way to the conspiracy of "us against them" where romance was concerned.

"Want to take a dip?" I asked. It was calm and warm in the quarry and a haze of autumn mist and limestone dust hung in the air. A flock of seagulls that had strayed over from Lake Michigan languidly circled the sun-dappled lagoon, which looked intensely inviting. Still, my question was a joke. The water in the lagoon was icy cold in late October, Indian summer or not.

"You first," said Lori, settling herself on a soft mound of loose scree. She had a businesslike air about her, less playful than she normally was when we were alone together. I assumed this was because of the plans we had made. We had been to the quarry before, but all we had done previously was neck, pet, and smoke cigarettes.

"Have you been to the drugstore?" she asked.

"Yep." I had a three-pack of Trojans in my pocket, the first condoms I had ever seen, let alone purchased. Buying them had not embarrassed me, but I hadn't gone to Wischki's for them, where the pharmacist knew me. I had practiced with one of the Trojans the night before, so I wouldn't be awkward with it.

"Me, too," she said. She opened her purse and pulled out a little can with a pink top and a plastic tube about the size of a small panetella. A bit of white fabric edged with elastic emerged from the purse. I realized a moment later that Lori had already removed her panties and stuffed them in her purse. When did she manage that? I observed the deftness with which she filled the plastic tube with foam, its plunger rising like a meat thermometer, and the agility with which she laid back and tilted her pelvis, her dainty hands and the foam-filled tube disappearing under her pleated skirt. I knew then that Lori had not merely practiced the night before, as I had. She had done this many times before.

What a load off my mind *that* was.

Plenty of other worries still plagued me, though. Self-consciousness about my inexperience, furtiveness about being seen, fear of getting Lori pregnant in spite of our precautions, concern about one of us getting injured on the jagged outcroppings of limestone poking through the gravel around us, insecurity about what was happening to my family, just to name a few. It had been six months since the Bank of Wisconsin letter had come and an undercurrent of anguish had become chronic for me.

Having completed the injection, Lori pulled her top off over her head, slipped off her pleated skirt and looked at me with impatience. I stripped down to my white T-shirt and unfurled the condom onto myself with minimal dither. We lay down on our sides, facing each other. I remember she had on her "special occasion" Jean Naté perfume, a pink bra, and startling dark blue fingernail polish, but many of the subtler traits I usually found so intoxicating about Lori — the silkiness of her hair, the sweetness of her voice, the softness and sheen of her skin — were obscured by the smog of my own anxiety until Lori took matters into her own hands. Literally. She put her little hand on my chest, rolled me gently onto my back, got on top and guided me into her.

Her eyes closed and her head rolled back. She wasn't nervous at all. She was . . . *intent.* Whether this was from desire for me, or just desire to get the clumsy first time with me out of the way, I didn't know, and I didn't care. Once penetration had been accomplished, I caught a wave that lifted me up and carried me away from everything that had been bothering me that day, and for days and weeks and months before, and suddenly, for the first time in memory, the whole world felt good. The weight of Lori's body on mine, her hands, her skin, the still, hazy air around us, the blood moving in my veins, even the hunk of limestone poking me between the shoulder blades felt good, and it all just kept feeling better and better until the wave broke. Then a low moan that sounded nothing like Lori came from this golden-haloed angel hovering over me, the same sound coming from me, then a delicious flash in my face and from the base of my spine, and an absolute conviction that this was without a doubt the single finest moment of my life, accompanied by the bubble-gum sweet taste of Lori's mouth and the exotic squawks and squeals of seagulls on the lagoon.

In the aftermath I thought about the Keats poem we had studied in English that day, and had new appreciation for it, especially the part that goes, "Then I felt like some watcher of the skies when a new planet swims into his ken." We remained motionless, I don't know for how long, until Lori said, "I'm cold," and I realized it was getting dark. It took a long time to brush the limestone dust off our clothes.

As we were leaving the cove, Lori said, "Isn't that your brother?" I looked in the direction she was pointing. About two hundred yards away an athletically built male was scrambling down the collapsed wall of the quarry, kicking up a cloud of dust behind him. Even in the dim light I could tell Lori was right, it was Jamie. He was moving swiftly down the steep slope with the power and grace of an NFL halfback. Jamie had teased me many times, claiming to have seen me with Lori in the quarry, and I wondered, how long had he been up there? What had he seen? What had freaked him out so badly he was sprinting through the dusky quarry like he had a pack of hounds at his heels?

Lori and I waited until Jamie was out of sight around a corner on the far side of the lagoon, then we crawled out of the quarry and through the hole in the fence. Halfway across the field, Lori stopped and gave me a kiss. We were hip deep in prairie grass.

"You better not walk me home," she said. "I told my mom and dad I was going to Denise Janacek's house to study after school. They might see you."

Smart girl. Her cover story was better than mine. I was supposedly at cross country practice, which would have had me home before dark, and I had more than a mile walk back to the house ahead of me. Over an hour late. But I wasn't worried about it. I wasn't worried about anything. No matter what repercussions I had to face at home, it was worth it.

"Want to do this again sometime?" said Lori. She batted her eyelashes facetiously.

"How about tomorrow?" I said, although I was thinking, How about right now?

"My, my." She put her hand on my face. "How am I going to handle you?"

That was a laugh. Lori could handle me with both hands tied behind her back, and we both knew it.

"All right, sure," she said. "Weather permitting. Call me after dinner, okay?"

I was in mid-season condition and could easily have run all the way home, but I didn't. I strolled, and savored the rare, sweet evening air and a feeling of satisfaction that was rarer and sweeter still. Oak leaves descended in seeming slow motion from the night sky, and Venus beamed like a signal fire above the dark horizon. The only thought I gave my parents was to wonder how they could have done for twenty years what Lori and I just did and end up hating each other over money. It seemed the most foolish and pathetic thing I could imagine, and I swore it would never happen to me and Lori.

I was surprised to find the house dark when I got home.

"Mom? Dad?"

My mother had been working as a checker at Piggly Wiggly for three months. She was always there by the time I got home from school on days when I took the late bus. My dad was out of work and was usually puttering at his desk in the basement before dinner. I knew where Jamie was.

The kitchen showed no sign that anyone had even started preparing dinner. I decided to check if my mother's car was in the garage and went out the side door. The garage was closed, but from twenty feet away, I could hear a car engine rumbling and could see exhaust billowing out from under the door.

6

A TEAR PLOPS ONTO THE GLOSSY YEARBOOK PAGE. I quickly brush it off with the back of my hand, but it leaves a stain. Luckily, it landed not on Lori's picture, but on that of some kid I barely knew in high school, Jim Hecht. I knew him better in grade school, but the only thing I remember about him is that he liked to eat library paste.

I set the yearbook aside and head downstairs. Didn't think I'd need a drink this early in the day. When I step on the fifth stair tread it brays mockingly. Hee-haw.

I use the wall-mounted telephone in the kitchen to call Photo-Phast, having neglected to ask when my prints of the Lake Audrey negatives would be ready while I was in the store. A polite, efficient female explains that the " 'Prints in 1 hour' not apply to special aw-duh." Tomorrow before noon. Photo not so phast after all.

Jim Beam and a ceramic coffee mug with bunny rabbits on it accompany me back upstairs to my room. Good bourbon is wonderfully versatile. On the rocks, it's perfect in hot weather; straight, it warms you in the winter. It is sweet enough to drink as a *digestif* but is not too sweet to enjoy before dinner. Or, as in this case, before lunch.

The next thing I pull out of the L.L. Bean box is my mother's college yearbook from the University of Wisconsin, where she and my father met. The yearbook is from her senior year, so my father would have graduated two years earlier. I flip to my mother's picture and am surprised at how dramatic her pose is. Body turned, chin lifted high. No smile at all, but instead a theatrically intense stare and slightly parted lips, like you'd see in a publicity still for a '40s film actress. Her extracurricular activities are listed under her maiden name, Louise Warchefsky. Drama Club every year, president of the club senior year. A list of titles of plays and musicals, some of which are familiar to me: *Our Town, MacBeth, Show Boat*. On the Drama Club's two pages in the yearbook are pictures from several productions, and it looks like Louise Warchefsky had the female lead in every one of them. I remember somebody telling me my mother was in some plays as a student, but I had no idea theater was such a big deal to her.

Beneath her college yearbook is one from Oshkosh High, 1943. It looks amazingly similar to Sheboygan North, 1972. The index lists all of the pages on which my mother appears, and I peruse them. She looks about twelve years old in her graduation picture, but no question about it, she was a pretty girl. She's in the Drama Club again, and there's one candid shot of her in a hallway. She's carrying a stack of books in front of her and laughing cheerfully at the camera. Her hair is up and she is wearing an oversized white cardigan sweater with the sleeves pushed up to her elbows. Her books partially conceal the big blue varsity-size "O" on the front of the sweater.

Oddly, the next item I remove from the box is a duplicate copy of the 1943 Oshkosh High yearbook. Can't have too many of those around, can you, Mom?

The next layer in the box includes my brother's high school yearbooks and my college freshman class book. Beneath those I find a brown vinyl album with the words, "Our Wedding" in gold script on the cover. Inside are snapshots from my mother's second wedding, when she married Ray. What a cheesy-looking reception. Paper plates, paper cups, plastic forks for the cake. I remember it was in a rented hall that was part of a tavern and drunks from the bar staggered through on their way to the restrooms. I'm in some of the pictures, dressed in a cheap polyester suit, hair to my shoulders, refusing to smile for the camera and affecting the look of a communist revolutionary, or perhaps a mad poet.

The wedding took place in June after my freshman year. It was only the second time I had met Ray. The first time was the previous December when I came home from Madison for Christmas.

o o

December, 1972

"So this is the college boy, eh?" Ray gripped my hand so hard it brought tears to my eyes. He was short, about five-eight, stocky, and muscular. His crew-cut was gray on the sides and black on top. He pumped my hand up and down like he was using a cross-cut saw.

"How do you do," I said.

"I do great." He looked at my mother. "Hey, honeybunch, what say we get your boy here a haircut while he's home. He looks like one of them hippies."

I had prepared myself to like Ray. When my mother told me on the phone that she was dating a man she had met at work, I was happy for her. Ray delivered fruit to the Piggly Wiggly store. The checkers who smoked, like my mother, usually took their breaks in back of the store, on the loading docks. One day, she explained, Ray had lit her Tareyton and one thing led to another, "so maybe smoking's not as bad as they say."

My father had been dead for over a year. It was time for my mother to move on. She needed companionship, affection, and help with the house and my brother. I was determined to accept Ray, to appreciate whatever there was to appreciate about him, and above all, to get along with him.

"You're not one of them hippies, are you, son?"

Son? Jesus Christ. I hated the guy instantly. "No, sir."

"I hope not." Ray tossed my suitcase into the trunk of his car and slammed the lid. "These peaceniks with their pot smoking and their war protesting make me sick."

I smoked pot and had attended several anti-war rallies, but I held my tongue. My mother was giving me a look that said "lay off," so on the way home from the Greyhound bus depot I talked about sports, college courses, and no politics. I remember feeling painfully drowsy in the car.

It felt odd returning to my room after three months. Everything was just as I had left it. My mother had not even dusted. Yet it was not exactly as I remembered it. The desk was smaller, the ceiling was lower and the window was closer to the bed. My memory had distorted the room's dimensions.

That was the strangest Christmas Eve of my life, even stranger than the previous one, after my father died. My brother seemed different, unusually quiet, distant, and fatuous. Ray dragged us to his church for a candlelight service, which had never been part of my family's traditions. It was an evangelistic, Jesus-freaky church out in a rural area, and the congregation did a lot of amen-ing and hallelujah-ing. My brother kept giving me goofy looks and I was fighting the giggles through most of the service. Right in the middle of "Silent Night," Jamie got to me with his wavering falsetto, fluttering eyelashes, and the mockingly exaggerated expression of piety on his face. At "'round yon Virgin," I let out an audible snort. Ray looked at me like he wanted to kill me on the spot.

Coming out of church I enjoyed the crisp, clean air on my face. The pipe organ was playing "Joy to the World," and a gentle snow was falling. For a moment, I had a slight hint of Christmas feeling, something I hadn't experienced in two years. Then just as I was about to get in the car, my mother looked at me sharply and said, "You embarrassed Ray." The only thing Christmassy about the ride home was that it was silent and cold.

Back at the house, we all drank spiked eggnog, even Jamie, while we watched an unbelievably corny Christmas special on the Philco. My mother went into the kitchen to wash dishes when the ten o'clock news came on.

That was the year of the infamous Christmas Bombings. For a week, American pilots had been flying thousands of sorties, dropping bombs day and night on cities in North Vietnam. The reporter said it was the first time B-52s, which were imprecise area bombers, had ever been used against cities.

When the report ended, I said, "So much for Peace on Earth."

"You got a problem with it?" said Ray.

"Yeah," I said, taking advantage of my mother's absence from the room. "I have a problem with carpet bombing civilians on Christmas Eve."

Ray waved his hands in the air. "Oh, here we go. I mighta known, with the long hair. Tell me, Joe College, how else we gonna get the Gooks back to the bargaining table?"

"We don't need to get them back to the table, we should just pull out. The war is lost, why are we still killing people?"

Ray downed an eggnog in a single gulp. A creamy drop trickled from the corner of his mouth. "Those aren't people," he said. "They're inhuman beasts."

"I don't believe that."

"That's because you don't know what you're talkin' about." He thumbed his chest. "I fought in the Pacific in World War Two—*I* know. And the Gooks are worse than the Japs." He poured another eggnog, spilling some onto the coffee table. "Just pull out. What about our POWs? You think we should just abandon them? What it if was you over there rotting in a bamboo cage? Or your brother?"

He pointed at Jamie, who had a blithesome grin on his face and a goggle in his eyes. I guessed he was feeling alcohol intoxication for the first time in his life. He raised a wobbly index finger in the air and said, "Fighting for peace is like fucking for chastity."

Ray's lip twitched. He stared at Jamie. "Mind your language, son."

"Fuck, fuck, fuck," said Jamie.

Roy flushed. "How'd you like me to wash your mouth out with soap?"

Jamie gave Ray the same look he always gave me when I challenged him athletically. Ping-pong, snowballs, whatever, Jamie had tremendous confidence in himself physically, and he did not even remotely understand the concept of backing down.

"You and whose army?" sneered Jamie.

Ray glowered. His face was beet-red. Then, he smiled amiably.

He stood up and pushed the coffee table aside. "Okay, tough guy," he said, waving a hand toward himself, "let's go. Ten bucks says I pin you in two minutes."

I did nothing to stop it. My brother was going to get in trouble and Ray was going to get his clock cleaned, and both of those outcomes were fine with me.

Jamie stumbled when he stood up, but only as a ploy. Dropping to his hands, Jamie swung his legs around in a quick, smooth arc, catching Ray off guard and taking his feet out from under him. Ray went down shockingly hard on his elbow, and I thought he might be hurt badly enough that it would end the fight right there.

"Son of a bitch," said Ray. He shook his head like he was clearing cobwebs. "Nice takedown, son. Here, help an old man up."

Ray reached out a hand. The elbow of his shirt was soaked with blood. Jamie gripped Ray's wrist and pulled him to his feet. Ray spun around and dropped to the floor immediately, taking Jamie down with a fireman's carry and putting a hammerlock on him in one smooth movement. It was obvious Ray knew what he was doing. He grimaced, and veins bulged in his neck and forehead as he strained to press Jamie's shoulders to the floor.

Jamie went absolutely berserk. He kicked out furiously with his legs and thrashed his arms wildly. One of his kicks caught a bough of the Christmas tree, and sundry glass ornaments fell to the floor, one of them breaking, a couple of them rolling into the field of battle. In desperation, Jamie went for Ray's face with his hands, clawing at Ray's eyes. A cut opened up on Ray's temple.

That seemed to make Ray even more resolute. He spread his legs out for leverage and twisted his body such that his forearm slid across the front of Jamie's throat in a ruthless chokehold.

My mother appeared in the room, a look of horror on her face.

"What on earth?" She looked at me. "For heaven's sake! Jonathan, stop them!"

Fat chance I was getting anywhere near those two. "It's almost over, Mom," I said. And it was. With the chokehold applied, Jamie would either be pinned or unconscious in a matter of seconds. Ray hooked an elbow under Jamie's knee and rolled his shoulders flat against the floor.

"One . . . two . . . three," grunted Ray. He released his hold and wiped a hand across his sweaty forehead. "Whew! That's a strong boy you got there, honeybunch."

"He's not moving, Ray." Click, click, click.

Ray got up and straddled Jamie, whose face was as purple as a plum. Ray grabbed Jamie's belt and lifted it a foot off the floor. Jamie sucked in a breath of air and coughed.

"He's all right," said Ray. "Little rasslin' won't do a boy like him any harm."

My mother put her fists on her hips. "No more roughhousing around here. It's Christmas Eve, for heaven's sake. Oh, dear . . ."

She walked over to the Christmas tree and looked down at a shattered ornament, distress in her eyes. "That was one of my grandmother's ornaments, from Poland. Those are irreplaceable, and they're worth a fortune."

Jamie got up on all fours and looked at Ray with fierce hatred. For a second, I thought Jamie was going to attack. Instead, he sprang toward the front door and bolted out of the house. My mother yelled, "Not without a jacket! Jonathan, take your brother his jacket."

I fetched both of our jackets and stepped out onto the front porch. Ray called after me, "Tell your brother he owes me ten bucks!"

I heard my mother say to him, "You can't get Jamie so excited, Ray. He's on medication." I had not known about that. Maybe it explained why Jamie seemed so different to me.

Across the street, Tom and Agnes Atkins' house was lit up like a tavern, with colored lights strung along the roof line and around the windows, same as every year. My brother's footprints in the fresh snow led down the street and around the corner, but he was nowhere in sight. I put on my jacket and followed the footprints, even though I knew there was no possibility I could catch up to him. I had just started smoking regularly, and I took a pack of Marlboros from my shirt pocket, tapped one out, and lit it. It was a frigid night, and I couldn't tell when I exhaled what was smoke and what was my breath. The sublime lightheadedness achieved by combining alcohol with nicotine was still new to me at that point and still an effective treatment for short-term anguish.

As I strolled the quiet, snow-covered streets, I wondered: Why was Jamie on medication? Would he run all the way to the quarry for solitude? Why had Ray picked a fight with Jamie instead of me? How soon could I get the hell out of here and go back to Madison? Did Lori, to whom I had not spoken in over two months, have a date for New Year's Eve?

Mostly, I wondered how a woman who had married a man as gentle and thoughtful as my father could stand to be around that asshole.

○○

Little did I know then that six months later my mother and Ray would be having their picture taken shoving cake into each other's mouths. As I set the wedding album aside, I realize it is so cold in the house that I must do something about the furnace. It takes me two hours to figure out that the problem is with the thermostat. Somebody, probably Ray, has installed a cheap, do-it-yourself automatic setback thermostat that uses a nine-volt battery. The battery from the smoke detector in the kitchen fits, and the furnace comes to life like an awakening giant.

It occurs to me that I will not have to scrape frost off my windshield in the morning if I put my car in the garage overnight. I get the opener out of my mother's old Chevy, which has not been driven in so long that it is covered with dust and all four tires are flat. The opener doesn't work, but the hard-wired button on the wall does. The garage door sticks a couple of times on the way up.

There is room for my Dodge next to my mother's car. When I pull in, I am in the exact spot where I found my father on that warm evening in October thirty-six years ago.

7

October, 1971

SOMEBODY ACCIDENTALLY LEFT THE ENGINE RUNNING. That was what I thought as I walked around to the access door on the side of the garage. I had no premonition that I might find anyone in there. Or if I did, I have erased it from my memory.

The access door was locked, which was odd, because we all knew it was pointless. The door was so warped that only about a quarter inch of the latch bolt penetrated the hole in the strikeplate, and a good push popped it open. I held my breath as I found my way through the clouds of exhaust to the button that opened the overhead door. Then I went outside to let the air clear a little before I went back in to turn off the engine.

My father was in the driver's seat, pitched over on his side. His face was flaccid and cherry-red. The passenger compartment reeked of alcohol and an unpleasant, ethereal odor I had never smelled before but assumed was from some kind of liquor. I remember feeling a clutch of shock in my face and chest, but I don't remember feeling anything else except the urgent desire to get my dad out of there. I knelt down on the garage floor, got one arm under his knees and the other under his back, and carried him out of the garage in the same position a groom carries a bride over the threshold.

I lowered him to the lawn next to the driveway as gently as I could. An hour later I would feel the pain from the muscle I pulled in my back, but I did not feel it at the time.

His body was limp and his skin was stone cold. I had no training in CPR, but I had once seen it illustrated in a medical pamphlet. Could I remember how it went?

Just do your best.

Tilt head back, listen for breathing. Pinch nose and cover mouth completely with yours. Blow until you see the chest rise. Repeat. If he doesn't start breathing, do chest compressions. How many? I forget. Try five. No, try ten. Repeat mouth-to-mouth and chest compressions. This time, try fifteen. Continue until help arrives.

Realize you've fucked up already, help is not going to arrive because you stupidly started CPR before calling for it. Run to the kitchen, dial the operator (there was no 911 in Sheboygan back then), say you need an ambulance, it's an emergency. Get to the brink of screaming with frustration at the ambulance dispatcher.

Run back outside. Rip your shirt on the door handle. Continue CPR until you hear a siren on your block, then use your torn shirtsleeve to wipe your tears and snot off of your father's red, lifeless face, collapse on the lawn and sob like a baby.

Sad to say, that, apparently, was my best. One of the paramedics was nice enough to tell me that, from the looks of things, my delay in calling and poor CPR technique "probably" had not made any difference. That "probably" haunted me for years after, but not nearly as much as the belief that my father might not have perished if I had come home on the athletic bus when I was supposed to, instead of fornicating in the quarry.

The paramedics must have shot everything they had in the ambulance into Dad before they gave up trying to revive him. They left behind scores of plastic hypodermic needle sheaths, scattered on the lawn like confetti. They did not, however, leave Dad behind. Obvious as it was, he had to be hauled to the hospital so a physician could pronounce him dead. He was later autopsied and then cremated. I never saw him again.

The police showed up a little while later and asked me

questions about how, where, and when I found my father. Then they snooped around in the garage for a while. I started to feel sick, so I went into the house and sat down at the kitchen table. The police were still there when my mother got home. She had on her work uniform, a pink cotton dress that had her first name embroidered on the front and "Piggly Wiggly" in big letters on the back.

Two cops escorted her into the kitchen, a short one in a uniform and a tall one in a trench coat. One of my parents had turned the heat off for the unseasonably warm day, and it was getting chilly in the kitchen. It was also dark, because two of the three lightbulbs in the fixture over the table were burned out.

The cop in the trench coat, who introduced himself as Detective Adams, did all the talking. He had a deep, raspy voice, and when he wasn't talking he made little saliva bubbles between his lips.

"You just get off work, Mrs. Bruckner?"

"No, officer. I get off at three. So I can be here for my two sons when they get home from school. What's the problem?"

"Please sit down, Mrs. Bruckner."

"What's all that junk on the lawn?" She looked around, her eyes settling on me. "Jonathan, what's the matter? Where's Jamie?"

I shrugged. I figured I could tell her where Jamie was after the cops left. She didn't ask where Dad was.

She looked at the detective. "Did something happen to my son? Where is my son?"

"I don't know, ma'am. Please have a seat."

My mother sat down and the detective broke the news to her. She did not cry or become hysterical; she just stared blankly and clicked her fingernails. Every so often she looked at me with a sad expression in her eyes.

"You say you get off work at three?"

"Yes."

"You work at the Piggly Wiggly?"

A regular Sherlock Holmes, this guy.

"Yes."

"What time did you leave the house again?"

"I haven't been home since this morning. I went to my sister's house after work."

My aunt Melanie lived two blocks away. She was two years older than my mother. Her husband, my Uncle Stan, was disabled in World War II and used a wheelchair. My mother rarely went over there straight from work.

"Mrs. Bruckner, does your husband have any serious health problems?"

Click, click. "He had a kidney removed awhile back. He's allergic to pollen. He hasn't exactly been robust for years." Click. It seemed to me my mother was volunteering a lot of irrelevant information.

"Has he been depressed lately?"

"Oh, yes. Definitely."

"Anything in particular making him depressed?"

"Yes." She proceeded to tell the detective the whole story of my father's colossal blunder, saying he had suffered "severe financial reverses," like he was some sort of distressed capitalist. She said, "David incurred a large debt as part of a business transaction at Falls Dieworks," which had "resulted in litigation and the termination of his position with the company." I could not understand why she was putting on airs. Surely the detective could look around and see that we were of extremely modest means, and had been for a long time.

"David has been attempting to start up a new enterprise, but his ventures have not met with any success," she said.

It boggled my mind to hear her describe it that way. After my father got fired, he looked for a job for a few weeks and then he seemed to give up. He started drinking more heavily and spent a lot of time puttering at his desk in the basement, ostensibly working on inventions or ideas for new businesses. I snuck down to spy on him a few times and more often than not caught him playing solitaire. Our neighbor Mr. Atkins also fancied himself an inventor, and sometimes he would come over and the two of them would get drunk in the basement and talk about their ideas. My mother derided this activity in the harshest possible terms, saying my dad and Tom Atkins were down there "baking pie in the sky," "living in fools' paradise," or "looking for the pot of gold at the end of a rainbow of crap."

Now she described it to the detective as "attempting to start up a new enterprise." La-de-dah.

"I would say he has been despondent lately."

"Has he been drinking alcoholic beverages?"

"Yes. Quite a bit."

"To excess?"

"Sometimes."

The short cop in the uniform was taking it all down. When he wasn't writing he was clicking the push button on his ballpoint pen. Between that and my mother's fingernails, the kitchen sounded like a typing pool.

My father was dead, beyond helping or hurting. I didn't know why it bothered me so much to see them making a record of his weaknesses, but it did. It revolted me.

"Is there any history of mental illness?"

"What?" Her eyes darted around, over to the door, up to the ceiling. It occurred to me she was looking for Jamie. "Oh, you mean David? No."

"How about his parents? Siblings?"

Click, click, click, click. A look came into her eyes like she had just had an epiphany of some sort. "Yes," she said, relief in her voice. "I think he once told me his grandfather died in a sanitarium."

"Uh-huh. Well, thank you for your cooperation, Mrs. Bruckner. I'm sorry for your loss."

After the police left, my mother poured herself a drink, lit a cigarette, and sat down in the living room. Jamie came in through the back door about five minutes later and headed straight for the stairs.

My mother questioned him. "Where have you been?"

I thought it was obvious. His clothes were covered with quarry dust.

"Out."

"Where, out?"

He goggled his eyes. "Far out. It's none of your business."

She raised her voice. "Jamie. Tell me where you went."

"Forget it." He bolted up the stairs two at a time.

I thought we would talk about what had happened that night, but we didn't. I had told Lori I would call her that night, but I didn't. Instead, I went straight to bed and lay awake all night, sweating, staring at the crack in the ceiling, and replaying the evening in my mind. My heart raced, my mouth was incredibly dry, and I felt nauseated. Around half-past four, I heard my mother step on the squeaky tread as she came upstairs. She came into my bedroom two hours later and sat at the foot of my bed.

"Are you all right?"

"Yeah."

"Jonathan, I want you to keep an eye on Jamie for me. I don't know how he's going to handle this."

"Okay. How about you, Mom? How are you doing?"

"Don't worry about me." She paused and put her hand on mine, a rare gesture. "Jonathan, I know you haven't ever seen me cry very much."

That was true. Just the once, actually, when we got the letter from the Bank of Wisconsin.

"And I know it probably hasn't looked lately like I care much for your dad."

Man was *that* true.

"But you should try to understand that he was still my husband and the father of my children, and it wasn't so long ago that I loved him very much. So don't be upset if you see me crying a lot for the next few weeks."

But I didn't. Not even once.

○○

The House, Day Three

The sun streaming through the window in the gable awakens me. Sitting up, my head reminds me that it took more whiskey than usual to put me to sleep, probably because I took that detour down the dark alley off Memory Lane.

Now I am getting earnestly, gut-gnawingly hungry. If I am

going to spend even one more day here, I must buy groceries.

The Piggly Wiggly where my mother worked is still on the same corner. It has gotten much bigger and now has a strip mall attached to it. I pick up a frozen pizza, a couple of frozen dinners, a bag of chips, some cans of soup, a sixer of beer and, for the sake of my health, an apple. I put the groceries in the trunk of my Dodge, right next to Mom.

On the way back I swing by Photo-Phast to pick up the prints I had made from the negatives in the envelope labeled "Lake/Audrey," the pictures of my parents, my brother, and me in front of the lake cottage. The bright sun of the early morning is gone and the sky is now paved over with concrete-gray stratus clouds. A few snowflakes wander restlessly over the potholed street.

The Asian woman behind the counter has her black hair pulled into a sprightly ponytail today. She gives me a friendly smile as she hands me my prints, and I feel desire stirring. Too young, I tell myself, don't risk making a fool of yourself. Besides, she's probably just smiling because you look slightly ridiculous in your high school letter jacket. I return a minimal smile and retreat to the Dodge with my pictures.

The snow has picked up and it is starting to accumulate on the windshield and moonroof. I open the Photo-Phast envelope and pull out two four-by-six black and white glossies. The first shows my mom and dad standing on a wooden raft buoyed by oil drums, floating on a large, weedless lake. Behind them in the distance, a tiny motorboat pulling a skier churns a long, white wake.

In the second print, my parents are standing in front of a tidy cabin with window boxes full of geraniums. My mother is holding a baby and my father is holding the hand of a child who looks about two or three years old.

The child is not me. It's not even a boy.

I look at the baby in my mother's arms. When I looked at the negative, I thought the baby was my brother. In the print I can tell that he isn't. I have seen enough family pictures lately to recognize myself as an infant.

There is something familiar about the little girl holding my father by his index finger. The mouth, the jaw, the contours of the forehead. No wonder I mistook her for myself in the negative. There is a resemblance. But I don't know who she is.

I feel a flutter in my gut and an urgent need to take a drive out to the Kettle Moraine State Forest, to Lake Audrey. The Dodge hesitates before it turns over. Time for a new battery if I intend to hang around Sheboygan much longer. The tank is almost empty, not enough to get me out to the Kettle Moraine and back.

The attendant at the Amoco station is so covered with grease I hesitate to take change from him. He's heard of Lake Audrey, but doesn't know how to get there. A map costs me $4.98. They used to be free.

The snow is really coming down by the time I get on Highway 23, heading west. Even so, I can't seem to hold my speed down. Traction is poor and visibility is worse. But the road is flat and straight, there is no traffic, and the freshly flocked trees fly past me on both sides until I see the sign for the Northern Unit of the Kettle Moraine Forest.

Here, the road starts to rise and fall, and several times I almost slide into the woods on narrow, hairpin curves. Much of eastern Wisconsin is so flat that it looks like God came down on it with a gigantic iron. In school I was taught that the reason for this is that a glacier came through during the last Ice Age and scraped the land smooth. But in some places the retreating glacier left behind humps and ridges of rock, sand and gravel in various characteristic forms. They gave the humps and ridges cute little names like eskers, drumlins, kames, and kettles. At some point they figured out that glacial detritus made for lousy farmland but nice scenery, and the Kettle Moraine units were set aside for tourism and recreation.

I don't remember anymore what the difference is between an esker and a drumlin. I know it's a bitch to drive through them with six inches of snow on the road and not enough tread on your tires. But I press on.

The wind is whipping the snow hard across the road, and I almost miss the small, brown wooden sign for Lake Audrey. At the end of a quarter mile of gravel road there is a deserted parking area and a small boat ramp. The lake is frozen and white as a wedding cake.

Wet snow sticks to my face and hands and invades my shoes as I walk out on the lake and look around. The lake is so small I can see the entire shoreline through the blizzard. I turn 360 degrees, wincing against the brutal wind.

So that's why my father didn't mention a vacation home on Lake Audrey. There are no homes on Lake Audrey. No log cabins, no cottages. No one would waterski on a lake this small.

A blast of snow accompanies me back into the car. My face and hands are raw, my feet are soaking wet. The yellowed envelope in which I found the negatives is crumpled on the passenger seat.

"Lake/Audrey," it says. That slash between "Lake" and "Audrey" bothered me, but I'd ignored it. I look again at the picture of my parents with the two children in front of the log cabin, and now I know.

Audrey is not the lake. Audrey is the little girl. Who looks like me.

Who is she? Why is she in this picture with me and my parents, in front of a vacation cabin, grasping my father's finger as if he were her daddy?

8

TO GET OUT OF THE PARKING LOT I must dig gravel with my hands and pile it under the tires for traction. My knuckles bleed, turning the cuffs of my jacket pink as I coax the Dodge back onto the paved road. The plow has been through and the curves and hills are sanded, which is good, because I am eager to get back to the house, eat, and resume excavating. Twice as eager now that I have opened up a two-front war: my father's death, and Audrey. I glance down at the photo resting on the passenger seat — could this be a sister I never knew I had? If so, what happened to her?

The clouds break up; midday sun on fresh snow overwhelms my retinas and reminds me I am a bit hungover. My sunglasses, a constant necessity in the Keys, are clipped to the sun visor. The visor comes down and the shades go on.

In the Keys, one day is as bright as the next. Here, it is blinding today, while yesterday was so dark that when the sun set, the difference was negligible.

The road back to Foxglove Lane takes me past Sheboygan North High School, a cluster of flat-roofed, brick Bauhaus-boxes that looks the same as every other suburban high school I have ever seen. A few additions have been tacked on since I graduated. The flagpole out front looks taller, the flag itself larger — an indication, perhaps, that these are more patriotic times.

I wonder if I would feel nostalgia if I wandered through those halls. Might it be rejuvenating? How familiar would it be? I decide to pull in the front drive and stop. School is in session; the front doors are unlocked.

The lobby is smaller than I remembered. It smells slightly sour. One wall is lined with glass cases filled with athletic trophies and plaques commemorating teams that won championships. Our cross-country team took the regional title my junior year and my name was on a plaque in one of those cases. Tarnish has dulled many of the trophies and plaques, indicating antiquity. I wonder if I'm still in there somewhere.

I am bent at the waist, squinting at inscriptions, when a voice says, "May I help you?"

I turn my head and see a fat belly drooping over a thick black belt. My back twinges as I straighten up to face a heavy-browed, slack-jowled security guard in a dirty gray uniform.

"Uh, no thanks," I say. "I'm just looking around." I turn my head this way and that as if to demonstrate. My nose is running from the cold; I sniff.

"Do you have a visitor's pass?"

This is new. We didn't have security guards when I was in high school, and visitors came and went freely. A legacy of Columbine, I suppose.

"No, I just stopped in. You see, I used to go to school here. Class of seventy-two." I point to the patch on the shoulder of my jacket that designates my class. This feeling *is* reminiscent of my youth, and associated with this place. Awkward, mortifying insecurity when confronted by authority. Very familiar.

"You have to leave. Visitors aren't allowed in the building without a pass."

"Can I get a pass?"

"What's the purpose of your visit?" He looks me up and down with a severe, skeptical expression. What's the matter, never seen a fifty-four-year-old guy in a wet letter jacket with bloody cuffs wandering around the high school before?

"I'm, you know, reminiscing. I'm an alumnus. Go Raiders." I give a feeble little fist pump. Slightly ridiculous.

"Let's take it outside," he says. He makes a move for my forearm and I pull away, palms raised. No need to give me the bum's rush. I can take a hint.

As I look back at the door swinging shut, I have another feeling I associate with this place.

Rejection.

○○

November, 1971

My mother kept me out of school for two weeks after my father's death. I felt ill for the first couple of days, then numb. My face broke out, especially my chin. I came down with a wicked head cold and lost ten pounds. Sleep eluded me, but I seemed to be in a trance while awake, phlegmatic and hollow. The strongest emotion I felt at the funeral was head-pounding rage when my dad's boss, Leon Bridette, showed up. Smug bastard in his pin-stripe suit, smiling and shaking hands, probably cooking up deals and exploiting people right there at the gravesite. I wanted to point at him and scream, "There he is! There is the son-of-a-bitch who drove my father to kill himself!" But I didn't say a word. Not even when he clasped me on the shoulder, said I was the man of the house now, and told me I should get a haircut.

I felt sheepish about seeing Lori third period in English on my first day back at school. Not only had I not called her the evening after our rendezvous at the quarry, I had not called for the entire two weeks I was out. Inexcusable. She would be angry, I assumed, if not freaked out.

"I'm sorry about your dad," she said, the first words spoken to me by a classmate all morning. Her brown eyes were full of concern, soft and warm as the cashmere sweater she wore.

"Thanks."

"How're your mom and brother doing?"

"Good. Jamie is crazy as ever." I wish I hadn't talked about my brother that way, but I didn't know, yet.

"Did you ever ask him why he was running through the quarry?"

"No." Given the sequence of events that evening, Lori's curiosity on this point was understandable; I shared it. But Jamie had made it clear on his way in that he wasn't going to discuss his whereabouts, and I didn't want to explain what I was doing in the quarry either.

"We can do something Saturday, if you want," she said.

"Okay. Maybe."

"I miss you."

"Um. Yeah." I may have shuffled my feet.

She smiled and squeezed my hand. The bell rang, and I sat down. Lori pulled a small package from under the books she held, and placed it on my desk. It was the size of a paperback, wrapped in pink tissue paper. I didn't open it until I got home that night, after the cross-country meet.

At lunch, my friend Bill Sorenson greeted me with, "Hey, Pizza Face. Do you still go to this school?"

"Unfortunately," I replied.

"Well, I'm glad you're back. We need every man we've got if we're gonna make regionals."

Bill was tall and rangy, a regular human gazelle. He was easily the best cross-country runner in the conference. It took a lot of nerve for him to call me "Pizza Face." He had the worst case of acne in the school.

"I'm not suiting up," I said.

"Aww, come off it, Bruckner. Don't be a *leaker*." He feigned a couple of left jabs at my face.

"I've missed a bunch of practices."

"Yeah, the first one you missed for quarry time with Hagen." He made a smooching, slurping noise. "So tell me, Bruck-eroo, didja score with Lor?" He mimed Groucho Marx flicking his cigar and bobbing his eyebrows. "Didja hump Hagen? Didja handle Hagen's humps?"

This was high wit for the jock table, and Bill got a good laugh for his efforts. I didn't even pretend I thought it was funny.

"I'm not kidding. I'm not ready to run."

Bill's eyes narrowed, and he jabbed a finger at my chest. "Well you better fuckin' *get* ready, you wuss. I can't get us to regionals by myself."

Cross-country had been the last thing on my mind for the past two weeks. I had forgotten about today's regional qualifying meet. We were defending champs, but two of the best guys from last year's team had graduated. It would be an uphill battle for us to repeat, but not impossible.

When the conversation at the table turned to other topics, Bill leaned toward me and spoke quietly, so only I could hear.

"Look, Jon, you gotta do this. You got your grades, you got Lori, you got it made. All I've got is cross-country. If we take regionals again, and I do well at state, I can get a scholarship even with my shitty grades."

"Nelson can take my place."

"Nelson's a wuss. Come on, man. Don't leak out on me. *Please.*"

Cross-country is a sport that rewards one's willingness to accept pain. Not just during the race itself, but day after day, week after week. Conditioning means working to near exhaustion as a matter of routine. Any letup in the routine is paid for in the race, with interest. In November, running on the hard earth gives you shin splints and the cold air sears your lungs.

The weather for the meet that afternoon was chilly and overcast. A mass of gangly teens in shorts and T-shirts stretched and ran in place on the frozen field, awaiting the gun. Because of my cold, I left my sweats on as long as possible before the start of the race. My head felt like it might explode. Bill trotted up to me, blowing on his hands, his breath visible.

"I gotta watch out for number twenty from Kiel," he said. "That's Schmidt. He's got a kick like a fuckin' mule." He socked me on the arm. "Hey, thanks. You're not a leaker."

The gun went off and we separated, Bill up with the cream, me back with the pack. Having missed those practices I planned on running conservatively. I didn't need to do much. Bill would probably take first. We had a couple of other guys who would be up there. Any points from me at all and the team would move on.

My emotional numbness actually seemed to help me for the first mile and a half. Striding over the hard, brown turf, I went on autopilot and fell into a rhythm. As the pack attenuated, I was not that far off my usual pace. Then, about a half mile from the finish line, a fortnight of stress, sleeplessness, and viral infection caught up with me, and I awoke to my pain. My lungs seized up and my diaphragm cramped. My legs simply gave out — they absolutely refused to take instructions from my brain to keep moving. I slowed to the pace of someone jogging through neck-deep water. It took everything I had just to stay on my feet. The other runners passed me, first one at a time, then two at a time, then in bunches. Then one at a time again, until there was no one left behind me.

It was dark by the time we got on the bus. The team was unusually quiet. No one sat with me. Coach Rather got on and walked halfway down the aisle, clipboard in hand, silver whistle bouncing on his chest. He was an ex-pro football player, with a noticeable metal tooth and a nose that appeared to have been broken multiple times.

"We failed to qualify by one point," he said, working his jaw muscles. "First time in eight years. Nice going, ladies." He looked down at me. "What happened to you, Bruckner?"

I shrugged.

"I know you've got problems, but that's no reason to hurt the team. If you weren't ready to run, you should've told me. Nelson would have picked up at least one point.

"I'm sorry."

"You're sorry. The best harrier in the conference doesn't get to go to regionals, and you're sorry. Get a haircut."

Once the bus got rolling, the usual chatter kicked in. I turned my face to the window and hoped my sniffling was not audible over the rumble of the school bus. The sniffling was from my head cold, but I feared it would be misinterpreted. It may have been, because Guy Williams leaned across the aisle and said to Bill Sorenson, "Maybe he's gonna go kill himself."

Bill said, "I'd be glad to let him use my garage."

o

When I got to the cafeteria the next day, all the seats at the jock table were mysteriously occupied. I crossed the gender barrier and sat with Lori from then on. Coach Rather was neither surprised nor disappointed when I quit the cross-country team that afternoon and told him that I did not intend to go out for track in the spring.

My social status plummeted like AOL stock after the Time-Warner merger. Lori was the only one of my classmates who did not throw in with the prevailing view that I was now a loser, and she paid a huge price for her loyalty. The previous year she had been a shoe-in for junior prom court and had been homecoming queen earlier that fall. By the time of senior ball in January, her stubborn refusal to stop dating me kept her off the court. How cool could she be? She was going steady with the quitter who ruined the cross-country team's chances to repeat, the outcast who barely talked to anyone anymore, the freak whose dad offed himself in the garage. So the prettiest and most poised girl in the class became a pariah because she hung with me.

Lori's sacrifice perplexed me to no end. For months after my inauspicious return to school, I was moody and withdrawn — not even good company, let alone someone deserving of such devotion.

I had it easy compared to Jamie. Freshmen were much more overtly cruel than seniors. They did not merely ostracize Jamie, they openly taunted and ridiculed him. Jamie could not suck it up and take it the way I did. He fought back, and from time to time came home with a split lip or a shiner. Worst of all, Jamie's illness became increasingly manifest as the year wore on. It is one thing to have the kids call you a psycho when you know you're not one. It is quite another to have them do it when you're hearing voices in your head.

Some older brothers might have jumped in and tried to protect their sibling. I did not, and my dereliction made me ashamed. All I offered him was advice.

"Who gave you the bloody nose?"

"Hunding."

"I don't know him. Is he a freshman?"

"He's a son of a bitch." Jamie wiped his nose with his shirtsleeve, smearing blood on it.

"Why don't you just ignore those idiots? Why do you let them provoke you?"

"Hunding intends to kill Siegmund."

"What are you talking about? Who the hell is Siegmund?"

"The son of Woton." He hugged a pillow to his chest, daubing red splotches on the pillowcase.

"The son of . . . Oh, I get it. That's from one of your Wagner operas, isn't it?"

"The forces of evil *must* be stopped." He had a frenzied look in his eyes. Blood glazed his chin and cheeks. I felt a twinge of fear.

"Jamie, you better lay off the Wagner. It's making you a little bonkers."

"So greet for me Valhalla!"

○ ○

A hot shower, dry clothes, and a bowl of Campbell's tomato soup work wonders. I feel warm and sanguine as I settle in for my third evening in the house on Foxglove Lane. It seems the exercise and fresh air I got digging out of the parking lot at Lake Audrey were quite salubrious. Three fingers of bourbon and everything is copacetic.

There is an item I want to find before I continue rooting through the boxes in my old bedroom, an item my visit to my old high school has brought to mind. I am fairly sure it is in a set of bookcases in the cellar, so I get a flashlight and descend into the belly of the beast. The basement is damp, musty, and poorly lit. I wend my way through a maze of boxes and rotting furniture to the dilapidated bookcases in a dark corner, next to my father's desk. The desk is piled high with coiled plastic tubing, remnants of one of his failed inventions. I smile and shake my head, remembering the Opuba.

The flashlight dies. Before I quit smoking, I always had a book of matches handy.

After twenty minutes of eye strain, I find what I am looking for and bring it back upstairs to the striped chair under the brass floor lamp in the living room.

I look down at a crumbling, mildewed paperback book of poetry that has a scrap of pink tissue paper attached to it with Scotch tape, the gift Lori gave me on my return to school after my father's death. These poems are not like the challenging, abstruse verse we studied in school. They are simple ditties with sing-songy rhyme schemes, meant to be inspirational — the literary equivalent of Frank Capra movies. When Lori gave this book to me, the day I returned to school after my father's funeral, I was unimpressed, far too absorbed in my own failure and too busy constructing defenses to appreciate sentimentality.

A thin cloth ribbon marks a poem by someone I never heard of, John Robert Quinn. Lori's feminine hand has carefully drawn a frilly frame around the first verse, in red ink.

Grief, being private, must
be borne alone,
And though I cannot share
your sorrow, still
Your anguished tears are
mingled with my own,
I walk unseen beside you —
up the hill.

9

August, 1971

ON A HOT AUGUST AFTERNOON about four months after he got the letter from the Bank of Wisconsin, my father unveiled the Opuba. Of all his best-laid plans of that summer, the unveiling of the Opuba was the one that ganged most agley.

I was in the kitchen getting a drink of water when the front screen door banged shut and my father announced, "Louisie, I'm home!" This was what he used to say when he got home from work every day, before Leon Bridette fired him, thereby revoking his status as breadwinner. After my dad got canned, he would slink in quietly and head for the basement.

"Good heavens, what in the hell is all that?" said my mother, in a sharp tone. Then her voice softened. "Oh, hello, Tom. How are you? How's Agnes?"

Tom Atkins spotted me through the archway as I smelled the smoke from his pipe, a mixture of ripe cherries and vanilla. "Hey, Jonnie." Tom was the only person who called me "Jonnie." "Go outside, see what your old man got you and your brother. You're gonna love it!" He chortled.

Tom was a stocky man with disproportionately large forearms, like Popeye the Sailor. He had a square jaw, a wide, rectangular smile and deeply grooved cheeks. With his wiry, salt-and-pepper hair and horn-rimmed classes, he resembled Vince Lombardi — a good man to resemble, more beloved in Wisconsin at that time than Santa Claus. Tom stood in the foyer behind my dad. The men were both wearing Bermuda shorts and short-sleeved shirts that buttoned up the front; their faces were flushed and sweaty. My mother had on white pedal pushers and a blouse that resembled a sailor's shirt.

My father had coils of plastic tubing slung over both shoulders and a cylindrical metal tube in one hand. Tom carried a box of what looked like machine parts.

As I sidled past the three of them in the foyer, I smelled alcohol. My mother sniffed loudly, announcing that she knew the men had been drinking and she did not approve.

Outside, the hot sun glittered in the spray from the sprinklers on the Atkins' lawn across the street. Our grass was brown and parched. In the driveway, trailered behind my dad's Chrysler, a white and turquoise fiberglass runabout shimmered like a mirage. The boat sported a racy windshield, shining chrome fittings, and a fifty-horsepower Evinrude outboard motor.

Man was I surprised.

I popped back inside. "Whose boat is that?"

"It's ours," said my dad. Tom Atkins laughed heartily.

"Boat?" said my mom. She hurried to the front window. Her brow furrowed as she looked out, and her fingernails clicked like a Geiger counter in Chernobyl. "Have you lost your mind? We can't afford a boat."

"It's not an expense, Lou," said my father, "it's a business investment. We need it to test the Opuba."

My mother put her fists on her hips. The corner of her mouth drew up and her cheek dimpled. She had a good sense of humor, and for all her efforts to put on a show of disapproval, she could not hide her bemusement, and her curiosity.

"Pooh-bah? What in heaven's name is a Pooh-bah?"

"Not Pooh-bah," said my father, raising an index finger didactically. "Opuba. Sit down and I'll show you. Tom, want a beer?"

"I thought you'd never ask."

"Help yourself, and snag me one while you're at it. Lou?"

"No. Oh hell, why not?"

Tom went to the kitchen, quite at ease helping himself to our beverages. My father put the plastic tubing on the coffee table and unscrewed the lid from the metal cylinder. He pulled out a rolled-up set of papers about a yard long. For the first time in months, he seemed energetic and jovial. Animation had returned to his eyes; he seemed more like his old self. I realized I missed this guy.

"Now, you know what the name 'SCUBA' stands for, don't you?" he asked.

"No," said my mother.

My father looked at me. I said, "It's an acronym for 'Self-Contained Underwater Breathing Apparatus.' "

"Right! And what is the alternative to a self-contained apparatus?"

"Surface air supply. A compressor in the boat pumps air down a hose to the diver. Also known as hookah diving." I was merely repeating back what my dad had taught me. My mother eyed the tubing and the rolled-up documents. A veneer of skepticism and worry glazed over her bemusement.

"Are there any advantages to diving with a surface air supply?" asked my dad.

"Several," I said, good little parrot that I was. "Unlimited air supply, longer down time. Less training needed. Lower cost. But you have less mobility, because you're tethered to the boat. Plus, you have to carry a motor on the boat to power the air compressor."

My father gestured dramatically with his hands, as if he were a cabaret singer putting a big ending on a song. "You did, until now." He unrolled the sheaf of documents to reveal a page of mechanical drawings, the largest of which looked like a multi-tentacled sea monster.

"Why carry a motor on the boat," he continued, "when you already have one mounted on the stern? Behold the first Outboard-Powered Underwater Breathing Apparatus — the OPUBA!"

Tom Atkins slurped a Pabst right from the can. He nudged me with an elbow. "Your old man is a smart guy, ain't he?"

My father launched into an explanation of how the Opuba

worked. A device "no bigger than a breadbox" was bolted to the transom, next to the outboard motor. An arm extended from the box and attached to the outboard's driveshaft. With "the flick of a switch" (actually it looked more like a lever, about three inches long), power could be transferred from the propeller to the box, which contained an air compressor. In the drawing, the compressor looked like a bell pepper. Four plastic air hoses emerged from it, "so a whole family can dive together. No certification needed, and a child can't stray farther than the length of the umbilicus."

"Wow," I said. It really looked like fun. Why wasn't hookah diving more popular? I couldn't wait to try it. "How long are the tubes?"

"A hundred feet," said my dad.

"So you could use it for wreck dives in Lake Michigan?"

"Absolutely," he said. His eyes lit up, and he leaned forward. "The *Niagara* is a spectacular wreck, only a few miles offshore, in fifty feet of water. This time of year the water is comfortably warm at that depth, with good clarity."

"Wait a minute," said my mom, her bemusement rapidly fading. "You're not planning to actually go under water with that contraption." Click, click, click.

"That's what it's for, Lou." My dad chuckled. "We gotta test 'er."

"You're not testing it with my baby boy, I'll tell you that right now. It's too dangerous. What happens if the motor dies when you're at the bottom?"

My dad looked at me. "Jonathan?"

"One person always remains on the boat with surface air diving. If he can't restart the motor, he tugs on the hose to signal the diver."

My mother's forehead furrowed like corduroy. She clicked her fingernails so furiously I feared they would split. "The compressor is right next to a stinking outboard motor. You're going to poison yourself with carbon monoxide."

My father dismissed her prophetic comment with a wave of his hand. "All taken care of. Notice the fifth tube doesn't run to a diver. That's the air intake. It runs along the gunwale, to draw air several feet away from the motor." He popped the top on his beer, toasted in Tom's direction, and quaffed. "Ah," he said. "Nothing like a cold beer on a hot afternoon."

"Where did you get all this crap?" My mother gestured at the huge coils of tubing.

"I got it from work, from Northrup's Plastics Division," said Tom. "Practically for free."

"Well, I'm sorry, but the boat goes back," she said. "We can't make payments on a boat now. With what the Piggly Wiggly pays checkers, we can barely make the mortgage."

"No payments," said my father, wiping foam from his lips with the back of his hand. "I paid cash."

My mother's eyes opened wide. "What? How?"

"I'm not without resources, Lou."

She rose suddenly and scurried into the dining room. Tom, Dad, and I discussed the ingeniousness of the device's design, particularly the small clutch that shifted power to the compressor. When she returned, my mother was somber.

"Tom, David and I need to discuss something privately." Her lips tightened against her teeth.

"Oh, sure," said Tom, "you probably want to talk about how you're gonna spend your millions." He finished his beer. "See ya around."

As soon as the door clacked shut, my mother said, in a deep, solemn voice, "David. The *Waterford.*" She had to get rid of Tom Atkins before she started this argument, which from the sound of her voice was going to be a doozy, but she didn't dismiss me. Kids are around all the time; I suppose parents have to become hardened to fighting in front of them or they would barely get the chance to fight at all.

"My *family's* Waterford," rejoined my father.

All trace of bemusement, curiosity, skepticism, and worry had vanished from my mother's face, all replaced by simple anger. "We agreed we would hang on to the good crystal, unless we needed to sell it to pay for Jonathan's college tuition."

"He's going to get a full scholarship," said my father. I crept up the stairs quietly, until the traitorous squeaky tread drew attention to me. "Aren't you, Jon?"

Please leave me out of it. Please.

"Then, Jamie's tuition," said my mother.

"Um, dear," said my father, with a forced patience bordering dangerously on condescension, "Jamie's admission to college is contrary to all reasonable expectation."

"We agreed!"

"Lou, you don't understand how these things work. You have to spend money to make money!"

I was in my room now with the door closed, but I could hear their raised voices clearly.

"But you don't have to waste money on a bunch of nonsense!"

"Tom doesn't think it's nonsense. He thinks it's brilliant."

"What does he know?"

"He's an engineer with an advanced degree."

"He's a drunk and a fool!"

Few human faculties are as elastic as one's memory of one's own pronouncements. My first year in college, one of Tom Atkins' inventions would hit big and my mother would write me a long letter about it. Tom's clever design for a parking meter that could be made with plastic internal parts promised to make metered parking much more affordable for small municipalities. The Midwest Meter Company paid him $400,000 for the invention, which seemed like an incredible sum at the time. My mother had no difficulty recalling that she "always knew Tom Atkins was a really smart guy." She said she envied Agnes, a pronouncement that itself would be conveniently forgotten two months later when Tom took most of the four hundred grand and ran off to Florida with a younger woman.

"How can you talk that way about Tom," said my father, "after what he did for us? After his generosity saved us from bankruptcy."

There was that bankruptcy allusion again. In a previous argument, I had heard my mother imply that they had *filed* for bankruptcy before. From my father's remark I gathered they never actually went bankrupt. Tom Atkins had "saved" them.

"It wasn't Tom's generosity that saved us," said my mother. "It was his rose-colored glasses."

"Whatever it was, it was lucky for us," said my father. "No bank or credit union would have loaned us the money *then,* and nobody else would give me a loan to get the Opuba off the ground *now.*"

"No." The volume of her voice increased dramatically, her tone bristled. "No! You are *not* borrowing money to flush it down the toilet on that silly gizmo. For heaven's sake, David! We're over a hundred thousand in debt as it is. Instead of borrowing more, you should be working on a way to pay what we owe."

"This *is* the way. I could never raise that kind of money with a salaried job."

"What are you doing about tracking down Newley?"

"I'm working on it. Day and night."

"Good. Work on that, and don't waste any more time or money on that stupid Pooh-bah."

"*O*puba."

"What were you planning to do? Build a factory?"

"No. We just develop a prototype and apply for a patent. Then we sell it to a company in the aqua sports business. Like Dacor."

"No way." She snorted derisively. "It won't happen."

"Why not?"

"No big company is going to be interested in a product that idiots would kill themselves using. They'll take one look at it and see nothing but lawsuits."

"You're always so pessimistic." The joviality and zip had left his voice completely, replaced by dejection, coupled with a grim resistance. "For once, couldn't you get behind me?"

"I would, but I might step in the shit back there."

My parents proceeded to sustain the longest non-stop quarrel I ever heard. It went on for the rest of the afternoon, during dinner, and right through the evening until past midnight. From my room I could hear them returning again and again to the refrigerator for beers. They also returned again and again to the same topics. You sold the Waterford crystal. You have to spend money to make money. The boat goes back. You never get behind me. Find Newley. You don't understand how these things work.

You let Leon Bridette push you around.

Waterford. Spend money to make money. Boat. Newley. Bridette. Waterford. Boat. Get behind me.

Waterford.

Eventually they segued into more personal attacks, running down each other's character and their respective parents and siblings. By this time Jamie was in bed with his door closed. I assumed he was sleeping. My parents' ability to control their volume had ebbed as the evening wore on, and their tone got harsher and more nasal with each beer. It was like listening to a carpenter push pieces of lumber through a circular saw.

"And that brother-in-law of yours. That's one greedy sum-mo-bitch."

"Oh, sure, attack a guy in a wheelchair."

"Greedy, avaricious bastard."

"At least he didn't ruin *his* family financially."

"No, he just tried to ruin ours, the sum-mo-bitch."

"It wasn't him, it was the shyster lawyers."

"Thank God Tom helped us. And he'll come through again. *He* gets behind me."

"You are *not* borrowing from Tom Atkins again. Absolutely not."

"Have it your way. I'm not without resources."

"You sold the Waterford. What else do *you* have that's worth anything?"

My father's voice became high and sing-songy, almost playful. "I can come up with fifteen thousand with my signature, just like *that*." He snapped his fingers.

"How the hell . . ." There was a lull — the first one since the argument began. My mother was apparently chewing on my father's assertion. She knew that, no matter how much he had to drink, my father never made an idle boast. When she spoke again, her voice was grave and shaky.

"Your Little Sisters of Benevolence policy."

"Um-de-dum."

"Listen, David. Don't even *think* about cashing in your life insurance. As of now, that's all you're worth to this family."

"Other than its surrender value, the policy isn't worth anything while I'm alive."

That was where the fight ended.

10

AS IT TURNED OUT, MY MOTHER WAS RIGHT about the Opuba. It failed to draw any interest from Dacor or anyone else. Just as she had said, too much risk of liability.

On the other hand, the boat purchase worked out. The Little Sisters of Benevolence initially refused to pay anything on my father's life insurance policy, because the cops had ruled his death a suicide. The policy contained an exclusion for suicide. My mother shrewdly used the proceeds from the sale of the boat to make a donation to Holy Family Church. The priest there was grateful for the contribution and willing to pretend he believed that my mother, fallen away though she was, sincerely feared for my father's immortal soul. The priest arranged for the local diocese to issue a finding that the death was accidental. Faced with the official church finding, the Little Sisters benevolently coughed up fifty cents on the dollar, enough to keep my mother in her house until she married Ray and he bought in. So my father's rash purchase of the boat kept my mom in the house. Had my dad not bought it, my mother undoubtedly would have held on to the Waterford crystal, and it would have inevitably ended up chipped and cracked.

∘ ∘

I do not return the book of poetry Lori gave me to the basement. There is room in my car to take a few small items from the house back to Marathon with me. I decide to hang on to the poems, and to my high school yearbook, which contains the only picture I have of Lori. A whistling in the chimney tells me I need to bundle up for even a quick trip to the garage.

The jacket with the blood-stained cuffs remains soaking wet, and the dampness has kindled in it an offensive barnyard odor. There must be something else in those stuffed closets that I can wear to keep warm in the Wisconsin wind.

The front hall closet is packed so tight with coats, jackets, and sweaters that when I yank on Ray's old olive-drab parka, the entire agglomeration explodes off the rod and lands in a clump on the floor. My mother had osteoporosis and broke her wrists a couple of times during the last few years before her death. She probably broke them getting coats in and out of this fucking closet.

Rays' parka looks absurdly short on me, and it has fake fur trim around the hood; perhaps I can do better. Here is an old camel's hair coat so mottled with dirt and stains it looks like it came off an actual camel. How about a plaid wool car coat with no buttons? Or the ski jacket my brother refused to hang up the day we had the snowball fight?

My mother has a cloth coat in here that is probably identical to Pat Nixon's described in the "Checkers" speech. And another that looks like what Jackie wore in Dallas. When did women stop wearing fox stoles on which multiple beady-eyed, black-nosed heads are perched, baring their sharp little teeth?

Glad you hung onto the fox stole, Mom. Probably worth a fortune.

Near the bottom of the heap I come across an item in fairly good shape — a large, well-made cardigan sweater. Densely woven white wool, it has miraculously survived with only a small moth hole near the label and some yellowish discoloration. It feels soft and comfortable. I hold it up by the shoulders and give it a shake.

A big blue "O" made of boiled wool adorns the front. The O encircles a small "W."

The cardigan is vaguely familiar. I am quite certain I have never seen it before, yet it triggers recognition. Why? I try to place the memory in time, but it seems equally rooted in the near present and the distant past. How can that be? Then I realize that although I have never laid eyes on the sweater, I recognize it because I have seen a picture of it, quite recently.

The fingers of my right hand cover two boiled wool numerals — a four and a three. This is a varsity letter sweater that belonged to someone in the class of 1943. I remember now where I have seen it. My mother's high school yearbook. The candid shot of her in the hallway.

I dash up the stairs, too quickly in the sharply expressed opinion of my fifty-four-year-old knees. It takes a minute to relocate my mother's high school yearbook and find the right page.

There she is, eyes nearly closed in laughter, her hair up and pulled back along her temples, very '40 s. She is wearing the white cardigan with the big "O" on it. The sweater is too large for her and she has pushed the sleeves up so that they bunch at the elbows. Obviously, she is wearing some boy's letter sweater. No doubt, that meant the same thing in 1943 as it did when I was in high school. She was going steady with a letterman.

In the picture she is carrying a stack of books in front of her that conceals the little "W" inside the "O." What does the "W" stand for? Was her school Oshkosh West? No, the cover of the yearbook says, "Oshkosh High School."

I look around for other pictures of students wearing letter sweaters and jackets. There are several, with different letters inside the "O." B, F, T, W.

Eventually, I get it. Oshkosh High had a tradition Sheboygan North did not. The sport in which the letter was earned was identified by a small letter inside the "O." B, F, T, W: Basketball, Football, Track, Wrestling.

I flip to the picture of the varsity wrestling squad. Ha. One of these goofballs in the ear guards and tights went steady with Louise

Warchefsky. Can I figure out which one? I read the caption, "L to R: Anthony Busacca, William Mohr, Edward Brosky, Raymond Moldenhauer . . ."

Raymond Moldenhauer? Jesus. I look at the picture.

It's my stepfather, Ray. Ray went to high school with my mother. Can that be? She told me she met him on the loading dock at the Piggly Wiggly. Didn't she? No, now that I reflect on it, all she said was that he walked up and lit her cigarette. She never expressly said that she had never met him before. That would not be a grievous omission if she barely knew him in high school. It would be something else entirely if they had gone steady. Does the fact that the sweater was in the front hall closet tell me anything? Maybe Ray moved it in. Maybe not. She might have kept it since high school. She never got rid of anything.

As I put the yearbook back in the L.L. Bean box, I notice the second copy of the same yearbook that I had observed before, and it gives me a skittish feeling. I had thought that it was nothing more than an example of my mother's tendency to collect redundantly, but there is another possibility.

Sure enough, inside the cover the blank pages before the title page are filled with faded inscriptions, "To Ray," "To Rasslin' Ray," and "To Moldy."

So, the duplicate yearbook belonged to Ray.

If any of the inscriptions are signed "Louise," it might tell me if that sweater was Ray's. No one signed Louise, or Lou, but the handwriting of one of the inscriptions looks like hers.

To Ray – What a wonderful year it has been. You were the best George Gibbs ever! I will never forget the rowboat on Lake Winnebago. Please don't ever change. I know it won't do any good for me to tell you to reconsider your decision about the Marines, so I'll just say be careful "over there."

—Me

Fairly typical stuff. I figure George Gibbs was a character in a play — further evidence that my mother wrote this. Based on yearbook inscriptions, high school seniors are nearly unanimous about not wanting each other to change, which I do not understand. Change could only have improved most of the kids I knew at Sheboygan North.

Ray apparently was set on being a Marine while he was still in high school. There is nothing about the inscription that suggests a romantic relationship, except that very last word. She signed it, "Me." A casual friend would not do that.

The inscriptions in my mother's yearbook have a consistent theme. To Louise — the next Garbo, the next Dietrich, the next Joan Crawford, and so on. One says, "Hollywood or Bust!" with a loopy rounded "W" next to the word "bust." It is signed, "Yours 'til Sheboygan Falls." This was the humor of the time, I guess. What do you want, there was a war on.

On the inside of the back cover a paragraph in a bold, angular hand answers my question about the sweater.

> *Honeybunch,*
> *I know you are the one for me! You Rhyme with Everything that's Beautiful. Go to college and get smart, but not too smart! I will dream of you while I am helping Uncle get the Japs off our pond. I will write every day. I will be true to you. When I come home I will make you mine forever. And I ain't just bumpin' my gums!*
>
> > *All my love,*
> > *Ray*

I set the yearbooks down and head to the kitchen for a drink. A good stiff one. The ice cubes clank in my glass as I sit in the striped chair with my feet up on the coffee table, brooding upon the new data. My mother and Ray were an item in high school. Ray went off to fight in the Pacific, expecting to marry her when he got back. Which he did, but not until my father was out of the way. In the meantime, she had two children. Or was it three? Did Ray write every day, as he had promised? Did he and my mother see each other while she was in college?

The last time I looked at the picture of Audrey, I thought she might have been a sister I never knew I had. Now I wonder. Half-sister?

My intestines gurgle like fermenting beer. The white cardigan sweater and the duplicate yearbooks argue persuasively, *"Wendy was right."* God damn it. She was *right*.

oo

April, 1974

"What's the green stuff?" whispered Wendy in my ear. I could smell her shampoo over the aroma of Easter dinner.

"Mint jelly," I murmured back. "It goes with the lamb."

"You didn't take any."

"I don't like it. You won't, either."

"Do I have to take some?"

"Of course not."

By spring break of my sophomore year, I had been dating Wendy Lehman for six months. In that time, I had never seen her look anything but poised, relaxed, and self-confident, until I brought her home to meet my family. Now, in spite of her tailored suit and tasteful jewelry, she appeared awkward and diffident. I did not understand. Wendy was beautiful, intelligent, and polished. How could she be intimidated by the likes of Ray, Louise, and Jamie? *I* was the one who should have been feeling insecure. A woman with as much going for her as Wendy might have taken one look at my clan and dumped me like nuclear waste.

"Wendy," said my mother, "have some mint jelly."

"Um, okay."

Ray pointed at my plate. "Aren't you gonna salt your potatoes?"

"I like them plain."

"Them spuds need salt," he said. He reached over and salted my potatoes. I would have knocked his hand away, but I didn't want to start a brawl. So I sat there, embarrassed, while my stepfather salted my food.

Jamie had gained about twenty pounds since I last saw him at Christmas. I'd warned Wendy about his peculiarity, but I had understated it. He slumped in his chair and chewed languidly with his mouth open, smiling asymmetrically as he overtly ogled Wendy.

Easy, boy.

"What does your father do?" asked Louise.

"He's a professor of anthropology at Brandeis."

"Mmm, I see. How nice. My father was also an educator."

I clarified. "Grandpa taught shop at a junior high school."

Ray pointed at me. "Hey!" I never had a good counter-argument for Ray's "Hey!"

"My father studied at Columbia," said Wendy, "with Franz Boas."

My mother looked perplexed, so I helped her out. "He was Margaret Mead's mentor."

"Ah, yes, of course. You must have grown up in a very intellectually stimulating environment."

Holy moly. They went on like this for the whole meal, locked in a contest to see who could do the clumsiest job of trying too hard to impress. Ray was equally clumsy at playing the patriarch. Jamie leered and remained silent, except a couple of times for no apparent reason he smiled lecherously at Wendy, bobbed his eyebrows, and said, "Frrrranz Boas."

After dessert Louise and Ray washed dishes in the kitchen and Jamie disappeared up the stairs. When we were alone, Wendy glowered at me.

"Your mother doesn't like me."

"Come on. Of course she likes you. What's not to like?"

"There's plenty for a blue-eyed Prussian not to like."

"Her eyes are not so blue as yours, my sweet."

Hardly anyone's were. Intentionally or not, I had found in Wendy the opposite of Lori. Lori was blonde and brown-eyed, Wendy had jet-black hair and eyes the color of lapis lazuli. Lori was soft and curvaceous. Wendy was svelte, taut, and angular, like a fashion model. Their dissimilarity did not end with the physical. After Lori's homespun simplicity and warmth, Wendy's New York sophistication and coolness charged me like an injection of pure caffeine.

"Besides," I added, "she's not Prussian. She's Polish."

"Did you see how she reacted when I said my father was at Brandeis? She doesn't like me because I'm Jewish."

Now I suppose somewhere in the back of my mind I was dimly aware of Wendy's religion, but I had never paid any attention to it. My parents were of different religious backgrounds, and neither practiced as an adult. As a result, religion played little role in my childhood. Wendy and I had never discussed our ethnicities. Making any kind of an issue of religion or ethnicity was quite out of fashion at the University in Madison at the time.

"You're wrong. My mother has her faults, but she's not anti-Semitic."

"Why am I surprised?" she continued, as if I hadn't spoken. "Mit all ze Bruckners und Moldenhauers around hier."

I put a hand on her shoulder. "Now settle down."

Man, was that a *faux pas*. Wendy crossed her arms in front of her and shrugged my hand off. She went silent and scowled. We could hear Ray and Louise conversing in the kitchen, in insufficiently hushed tones.

"Look at the mint jelly she left on her plate. Such a waste."

"Didn't even offer to help with the dishes."

"I don't believe her father studied with Franz Boas."

Wendy glared at me with tears in her eyes and a look that said, *"See?"* She headed for the front door.

"Wait," I said, scrambling after her. I caught up to her in the foyer and hugged her from behind.

She tried to pry my fingers loose. "Unhand me, you son-of-a-Nazi."

"Ach," I said. "You Jewish fräuleins are zo bootiful ven you are ankry."

She laughed, and I thought I had salvaged the situation. Then, a loud crackling noise that seemed to come from all directions at once filled the house, followed by an acrid odor.

Ray burst out of the kitchen, his face crimson. He stood at the landing to the stairs and sniffed.

"Jesus H. Christ," he said. "Jamie is fucking around with gunpowder again."

85

11

IF I HAD ONLY LET WENDY RUN OUT OF THE HOUSE, she would have been spared the scene that ensued. My mother came out of the kitchen, wringing a dishtowel in her hands.

"Oh, dear," she said, looking up in the direction of Jamie's room. A loud *zizzzz-bang!* rattled the walls.

"Gunpowder?" I said. "Jamie's playing with gunpowder?"

She glanced nervously at Wendy and tried to compose herself. "He . . . he likes to experiment. One of those boys with scientific curiosity."

My mother, the spin doctor. "Where did he get the gunpowder?"

"He figured out how to make it himself, with saltpeter, sulfur, and charcoal. He has a knack for chemistry." A pretense of pride in her voice. Incredible.

The next sound we heard from upstairs was Ray's deep, gruff bellowing mingled with Jamie's incomprehensible shrieks, followed by the sound of blows being struck. A *whump!* on the ceiling rattled the cups and saucers on the dining room table.

"Mom, you told me Ray was laying off Jamie."

She draped the dishtowel over her shoulder, which freed her hands for fingernail clicking.

"Sometimes it's the only way to control your brother." Her forehead wrinkled. "It's for his own safety. Ray has never injured him."

Thud! Crash! They were busting up Jamie's room. Wendy looked horrified. She grabbed onto my arm like it was a tree trunk and she was hanging off the edge of a cliff.

"I thought Jamie was on medication," I said.

"Dr. Patel is trying a new drug. Sometimes Jamie doesn't take it."

"Dr. Patel is a psychiatrist?"

My mother's eyes darted to Wendy and back. "Yes. A specialist. He did a residency at Johns Hopkins."

Leave it to Louise to make it sound like having a loony kid was a status symbol. Wendy gazed at my mother's clicking fingernails, imagining, I supposed, what neurotic children she would have with me.

"What does Dr. Patel say about Ray using corporal punishment on Jamie?" I asked.

"Ray doesn't use corporal punishment, for heaven's sake."

Whump! Smash!

I cleared my throat, and my mother said, "We haven't discussed it with the doctor."

Wendy's appalled gaze moved to my face. Was she having doubts about whether I could possibly be worthy of her further affections, given what she was discovering about my background? I felt on the spot, under pressure to demonstrate more nobility of character than I actually possessed, to distance myself from this tribe of savages in which I was apparently raised.

"I want to talk to Dr. Patel," I said. Here I am, the smart, rational, caring member of the family capably stepping in to help his ailing younger brother.

"Why?" said Louise. "You're fine."

"Not about me. I want to talk to him about Jamie."

"What for?" Her eyes looked frightened. "What good could that possibly do?"

"I might be able to help," I said. "I've had a semester of psychology."

My mother made a derisive sound like spitting air. *"Ptuh."* I took Wendy by the arm and announced we were going for a walk.

The day was unseasonably warm, but, as is usually the case whenever it's warm in Wisconsin in April, gusty. The trees were budded out, a lacework of chartreuse tingeing the branches. Wendy's shoulder-length hair blew into her eyes, as did my shoulder-length hair into mine. I was searching for a graceful way to apologize for my screwed-up family when Wendy surprised me with a question.

"How did your real father die?"

I had told her my father was dead, but that was all. I had worked for months to put the suicide behind me and had just that spring managed to make it through a day now and then without thinking about it. It put me back on the rack to say it, but I felt I owed her a straight answer.

"Suicide," I said. "I found him in the garage with the car engine running."

"Were they sure it was suicide?"

I stopped walking and looked at her. The question irritated the hell out of me.

" 'They' who? The police? Yeah, they were sure. So was everybody else."

Wendy countered the annoyance in my voice by lifting her chin defiantly and brushing the hair from her face with a dramatic sweep of her hand.

I thought I knew why she was bringing up my father's death at this point in time. "What, you think Jamie had something to do with it? Because he's under psychiatric care?"

As soon as the words left my mouth, I realized why I was peeved. Even though I was crazy about Wendy, I still wasn't over Lori, not by a long shot. For nearly a year after my father's death, Lori had been my only real friend, and much more. She had also been my only hobby, my refuge, and my sole source of pleasure. Whatever she got out of our regular visits to the quarry, for me they were necessary medicine, the morphine drip that made the pain bearable. If not for her, I might have followed in my father's footsteps.

The last time I saw Lori was in the autumn of my freshman year at the University of Wisconsin. She came for a weekend while my roommate was out of town at his uncle's funeral, and she stayed in my dorm room. We went to Camp Randall Stadium on a sunny Saturday afternoon and watched the Badgers lose to Michigan State. Lori, who worked full-time as a secretary at an accounting firm in Sheboygan, appeared to feel out of place with the college crowd. She probably guessed that I had dated other women in the month since I had last seen her. Our conversation and our sex were awkward, and we got almost no sleep for two nights, crammed onto my narrow bed.

We may have gotten past all of that if Lori had not asked me over Sunday morning coffee if I had ever figured out why my brother was running through the quarry at dusk on the day my father died. She had asked the same question before, on my first day back at school after the funeral. A natural question, since she had personally witnessed Jamie's desperate dash across the dusty scree. But its implications — that my brother may have had something to do with my father's death, and that I should have been looking into that possibility — threatened and angered me.

We quarreled in the way two insecure, sleep-deprived people can, both of us defensive and cranky. I don't remember anything Lori said, but I remember I called her "stupid" and I have wished ever since that I had swallowed that word right back down my throat before it came out. How could I have said that, after all the times I'd had to reassure Lori that it didn't matter to me that she was not as school-smart as I was?

When she got on the bus that afternoon, neither of us said we were breaking up. But afterward, neither of us called the other.

So I suppose I was a bit raw when Wendy appeared to be raising the same implication Lori had. Couldn't they just drop the damn subject? How many girlfriends was I going to lose defending my brother?

"Just because Jamie needs a little psychiatric help doesn't mean he's capable of patricide, Wendy."

She pulled a strand of hair from the corner of her mouth. "You misunderstand. Your brother is an odd duck, but he doesn't scare me. Actually, he's kind of cute. *He's* not the one who raises *my* suspicion."

I saw where she was heading, and I would not let her go there.

This was even more absurd than accusing my mother of being a Prussian Nazi. For some reason I could not fathom, Wendy and Louise had become instantly locked in an intense competition, and it was making them both irrational. In spite of my semester of psychology I didn't see that what they were competing for was me; if I had understood that, it would have embarrassed the living crap out of me, but I may have handled the situation better.

I changed the subject to the weather. Wendy and I didn't speak of my father's death again, until a month later.

o

"By the turn of the century, it'll be all over. The polar ice caps will melt, raising sea level enough to flood all the coastal cities in the world. New York, L.A., Miami, New Orleans, Rome, Rio — all *gone.* The Midwest will be a fuckin' desert. There'll be worldwide famine and panic. The whole social order will collapse. We're all doomed."

Luke Willever sat across from me and Wendy at a picnic table on the terrace at Memorial Union, holding forth on global warming and downing his third Budweiser. Global warming was a brand-new topic of conversation at that time, one that was bound to be popular on a college campus. It was sinister and apocalyptic, but best of all it gave students an opportunity to feel superior to the older generation that was ignorantly ruining the Earth. The cool breeze from Lake Mendota carried the scents of duckweed and dead fish, but not even a suggestion of warming, global or otherwise.

I suspected that Luke was a bit blotto, as he often was, and exaggerating, as he often did. Luke had a tendency to get carried away with bleak prophesies and conspiracy theories. I challenged him. "Says who?"

"Professor Obanion in my geology course. Nat Sci 201."

"Rocks for Jocks," said Wendy. "The ultimate authority on the future of the planet." God, she looked amazing in that sleek black turtleneck sweater.

"Let me try to explain the greenhouse effect to you, Lehman," said Luke. He held up the brown Budweiser longneck. "Imagine the air inside this bottle is the earth's atmosphere. Then, assume that the bottle is made of special glass that allows radiation from the sun to enter the bottle, but not to escape it. What do you predict will happen?"

"The coastal cities," I said, raising an index finger earnestly, "will be flooded with beer."

"And Luke Willever," said Wendy, "will split for the coast."

"Okay, smartasses," said Luke, polishing off the Bud and slamming it on the table. "But when the world is plunged into chaos and we're all as dead as Paul McCartney, remember — I told you so."

Luke Willever was my roommate freshman and sophomore years. He was a burly, rosy-cheeked country boy from Wabeno, a small town in northern Wisconsin, and it is likely that his sandy hair covered his forehead and ears even before rock bands made that look fashionable. The Henley shirts and dungarees he wore were also in style at the time, but I suspected Luke had worn Credence Clearwater–type clothes his entire life.

Luke was incredibly smart; he never studied and yet pulled down decent grades. He probably had ten or more IQ points on me. But he also had the worst drinking problem of anyone I have ever known. Which, since I grew up in Sheboygan, went to the University of Wisconsin, and live in the Florida Keys, is saying a helluva lot.

The first time I met Luke, on the first day of school freshman year, he was drinking a pitcher of Harvey Wallbangers — straight from the pitcher. The first night we roomed together he vomited on the floor and passed out.

Part of the bond between us was that most roommates would have found the craziness of Luke's dipsomania intolerable, whereas to me living with Luke was a step up in stability. In addition, we had both lost a parent. Luke's mother died when he was a toddler and his father was unknown to him. Luke had been raised by a bachelor uncle.

On that cool Saturday afternoon in mid-May of our sophomore year, Luke seemed to be using the greenhouse effect as a reason to get blotto. Hey, if we're all soon to perish in an ecological disaster, why not toss a few back? Memorial Union was a popular hangout, and other students were drinking beer on the terrace. But Luke was the only one using it to chase shots of brandy from an army surplus canteen he carried around.

"Look at Lake Mendota," said Luke, curling his lip and taking a pull off the canteen. "No self-respecting gamefish would be caught dead in that cesspool. I took a carp out yesterday the size of a fuckin' submarine."

"What'd you catch it on?" I asked.

"I didn't catch the son of a bitch. I shot it with a bow and arrow."

"Is that legal?"

"The only good carp is a dead carp." Luke wiped the back of his hand across his mouth and stifled a belch. "They cloud the water and foul the spawning beds."

"I bet there are some nice lakes near Wabeno," said Wendy.

"Awww, man," said Luke. He shook his head forlornly. "There's lakes up there clear as gin." The highest commendation Luke could bestow was to compare something to gin. "By the turn of the century, they'll all be fouled like Mendota with mercury, PCBs, detergent gas, acid rain. Hey, speaking of acid, you guys wanna drop this afternoon?"

"I'll pass," said Wendy. She yawned and stretched, putting the idea in my head that I might be able to sell her on a "nap" back at her dorm room.

"Not really a tripping sort of day," I said.

"Yeah, I guess," said Luke. "More of a drinking sort of day. Wanna hit the Nitty Gritty?"

"Maybe later," I said.

"Okay, Roomie," he replied. "Later."

○

I stayed over at Wendy's that weekend and didn't return to my room until Sunday evening. Luke was out, as he often was. I showered and went to bed.

The telephone jangled me awake at quarter past five. I figured it must be one of my asshole classmates calling at that hour, so I answered with a yawn and a joke.

"King Abdul's Pleasure Palace. Chief Eunuch speaking."

"Is this five-five-five-six-seven-one-nine?" A very serious female voice.

"Yes?" Half asleep, I wasn't sure.

"May I speak to Jonathan Bruckner?"

"Speaking?" Not sure about that, either.

"This is the ER at University Hospital. You're listed as the emergency contact for a student named Lucas H. Willever."

"I am?" New one on me. My stomach knotted. "Has he been in an accident?"

"No, nothing like that. But you need to come to the hospital and take responsibility for him. He'll be ready for discharge in a couple of hours, but he's not safe to leave on his own."

Responsibility? I didn't like that word. My sweating hands trembled. "What's he in the ER for?"

"Detox."

○

A fiftyish doctor with presidential-advisor eyeglasses and thin Vitalised hair met me in the waiting room. A badge clipped to his white coat ID'd him as Edwin Wolter, M.D.

"Young man, your roommate is an alcoholic." His stern tone suggested Luke's drinking was my fault, or perhaps the fault of all young men. "He has to stop drinking completely. Otherwise, he'll be dead before he's forty."

"How did he get here?"

The doctor scribbled on a prescription pad and tore a sheet off. "The campus police found him behind Bascom Hall, unconscious. When he got here his blood alcohol level was point four-o."

"Is that bad?"

"It's enough to cause death in some people. We had to treat him for *delirium tremens*. Tragic in a man that age."

Not exactly comic at any age, I thought. The doctor handed me the sheet torn from the prescription pad and pointed out the room where Luke was sleeping it off. I opened the door and walked in.

A jolt of electricity smacked me in the chest and ricocheted off the backs of my eyeballs. In an instant, I was back in the garage with my dead father, two and a half years before, the sensation of Lori's mouth lingering on my lips.

"What's that smell?" It was like rancid garlic soaked in lighter fluid, and I had only smelled it once before.

Luke rolled his head in my direction and moaned. His face was puffy and blotchy, but he didn't seem to be in that bad a mood.

"Aaaauh. Wuz happnin', Roomie? Could you get this manhole cover off my head?"

I ran out of the room and down the hall, intercepting Dr. Wolter before he got involved with another patient.

"Doctor, Luke's room has this sickly, vaporous smell in it."

"Sure. That would be the paraldehyde. It's an anticonvulsant, a sedative. We use it to treat *delirium tremens*. He chuckled. "He's gonna smell like that for a while. Not too long."

"Is it used for anything else?"

"You mean medically? I don't prescribe it for anything but DTs. Some guys use it for *status epilepticus*." He chortled again. "Vets use it to euthanize dogs."

"Do you inject it?"

"Could. *I* don't. It's given orally, or as an inhalant. Excuse me now, young man, I have to get back to patients."

I grabbed his forearm. "Can it cause unconsciousness?"

"You betcha. More effectively than chloroform. Alcohol multiplies the effect." He pulled his arm away. "But don't worry, it won't hurt you to smell your roommate's breath." He winked. "Just don't French kiss him for a couple hours." He laughed and strode quickly away.

Until the moment I walked into Luke's recovery room, as wrong as it felt, I never seriously doubted that my father had committed suicide. All the grownups said so. He was depressed, financially ruined, and facing divorce. I found him in the garage with the doors closed and the engine running. Open and shut case. But as I watched the back of Dr. Wolter's lab coat recede down the hall, I was absolutely certain that Dad was murdered.

12

"SOUNDS TO ME LIKE YOUR CLUTCH IS SLIPPING. No biggee. We'll have to put 'er up on the lift. It'll just be a few minutes."

The mechanic seemed to know what he was doing. He wore striped coveralls smeared with grease. He had his name, "Frank," in an oval patch on his chest.

Neither Luke nor I owned a car, so I had called Wendy to give us a ride back to the dorm in her VW. It was a stripped-down Beetle — no radio, spindly stick shift, bare metal dashboard as thin as a baloney sandwich — but back then, any kind of wheels was a luxury for a college student. Professor Lehman was indulgent.

A half mile from University Hospital the VW had lost power to the rear wheels and coasted to a stop. The three of us had pushed it into a service station. While we waited for an open bay, Luke curled up in the back seat and went to sleep. There was no place to comfortably sit and wait in the service station, and it was drizzling outdoors, so Wendy and I walked over to a bus stop shelter across the street and sat down. She had her hair pulled back in a barrette and was wearing a yellow rain slicker like the ones kids wear in grade school. Cute as hell.

"So what did the doctor say?" asked Wendy.

"He gave me this." I showed her the sheet from the prescription pad. On it, Dr. Wolter had written the phone number of the local chapter of Alcoholics Anonymous.

"Figures," said Wendy. "I've never seen Luke without a drink in his hand. It's a shame. He's an attractive guy."

Hearing Wendy call Luke attractive nettled me, not because it made me jealous, but because Luke and I were different types. Luke was fair and burly, I was dark and slim. If she liked Luke's looks, I worried, how much could she like mine?

"The doctor said Luke will be dead before he's forty if he doesn't quit drinking."

"Is that why you're so freaked out?"

Wendy could read me better than anybody. She was right, I was very freaked out.

"No," I said. "It was the smell in his hospital room."

She pinched her nose and waived a hand in front of her face. "Peeeyew. I got a whiff of it in the car. What was Luke drinking? Antifreeze?"

"The odor was from an anticonvulsive medication they gave him for the DTs."

A city bus pulled up to the stop. Its front tire hit a puddle at the curb and soaked the pant leg of a street person on the sidewalk. Nobody got off the bus and nobody got on. The bus might not have pulled over and splashed the hapless hobo had Wendy and I not been sitting at the stop. The street person shuffled over.

"Spare change?" The guy looked about mid-thirties, long oily hair, unshaven, bad teeth, filthy clothes. I wondered: Luke in about fifteen years?

I dug into my pocket and gave him what I had, which wasn't much. He thanked me politely and moved on. Madison had such nice bums back in those days. Wendy told me it wasn't wise to subsidize panhandling, and I didn't disagree.

"So you're bummed out by the way Luke smells?"

"Not exactly. It's the odor itself. I recognized it. I smelled it on my father once."

"Your father had DTs?" Dismay spread across her face. She was worrying again, I assumed, about my genetic fitness for mating purposes.

"No," I said. "I smelled it when I found him dead in the garage."

Wendy turned toward me and studied my face, waiting for an explanation. When none came, she asked, "Why would he have smelled like anticonvulsive medication?"

"Because it's also an anesthetic, particularly potent in combination with alcohol." Wendy cocked her head and narrowed her eyes. She didn't quite get it yet. "Somebody used it to knock my father out, so they could leave him in the garage and make it look like suicide."

She shivered like a frightened chihuahua and I put my arm around her. "I told you so," she said.

I removed my arm and rotated toward her on the bench. "You implied you thought my mother did it. Wendy, that's ridiculous and you know it."

Her eyes flashed. "It's not ridiculous. Think about it, Jonathan. Your dad was nothing but a big liability to her. She had a lot to gain."

Rage came on so hard my field of vision darkened. My pulse went berserk. Blood roared in my ears and my head buzzed. I gritted my teeth and tried to measure my words. "I don't know why you hate her so much, but I'm telling you, it's impossible. She's not capable of it. She's a kind, gentle person."

"You only see her that way 'cause she's your mommy." A nasal, derisive twang on the word "mommy." "*I* see a cold, hard woman who could do what was necessary to jettison a bankrupt spouse and hang on to her house. She certainly came up with a new husband pretty damn quick, whom she kindly and gently lets beat hell out of your disabled brother."

I felt like picking up the bench we were sitting on and smashing it to pieces, but instead I just dug my fingernails into it. "Wendy, you don't know what you're talking about. Louise couldn't have done something like that even if she wanted to, even with an anesthetic. She's *squeamish*. Judas Priest, she had to summon me or Jamie to squash a spider for her."

Wendy's face was animated. The topic really stimulated her.

"Maybe," she said, "she had help. Yeah, maybe Ray was in on it with her."

"Now, see, Wendy? Louise didn't even meet Ray until after my dad was dead. So what you're saying is plain stupid."

Oh, yes, I did it again. You would think I'd have learned after alienating Lori. Callow youth that I was, I hadn't learned anything. One of the working women I visit from time to time in Key West is fond of saying that no man under thirty is worth a damn, and you certainly could not have used me to disprove the proposition.

Another bus pulled up to the stop. Wendy snapped her little yellow hood up, obscuring her face. She rose and got on the bus. I couldn't abandon Luke, so I just sat there fuming. It wasn't until the bus was out of sight that I began to comprehend what a royal asshole I was.

Beautiful, intelligent, lively women don't come along every day. Or every decade, or every quarter-century. Would it have been so hard, would it have done any harm to say, "Yes, darling, you're right, my mother is a spousicidal Nazi"? I consoled myself with the thought that Wendy had to see me again, because I had her car. At least I would have a chance to apologize.

But it turned out I didn't have her car. Frank the mechanic was stumped, offering only, "I . . . dunno. You might need a new clutch. You'll have to take her to a VW dealer for that. You're gonna have a long wait for the parts."

We always had trouble getting repairs on Wendy's VW. It might have behooved a car shop back then to bring up some Mexican mechanics from Cozumel. As any serious diver can tell you, for some reason Cozumel is loaded with great Volkswagen mechanics. The island swarms with forty-year-old Beetles traversing its bumpy, unpaved streets without a rattle or a squeak. The island also has the best drift diving in the Western Hemisphere.

Luke and I had classes that morning so we decided to abandon the VW for the time being and hop a bus back to the dorm. The streets were wet, bumpy, and busy. Madison is built on an isthmus between two lakes. It sprawls to the east and west of the narrow neck of land, giving it the shape of a butterfly bowtie and the traffic of a much larger city. Madison regularly appeared on lists such as "The Ten Best American Cities to Live In," which baffled me. Sure, the State Capitol and the University were impressive, but otherwise it looked a lot like Sheboygan, only with worse traffic and smaller lakes.

On the bus, Luke asked what happened to Wendy, so I recounted the argument to him. He was still woozy, but the paraldehyde story seemed to perk him up.

"You're certain it was the exact same smell?"

"When I walked into your room, it was like I was transported back in time to that night in the garage."

"Far *out*," he said. The bus windows were fogged, and Luke was drawing Greek letters on them with his index finger. "Olfactory memory works like that, because it's wired through the reptilian part of your brain. The sense data bypass your perceptual apparatus, so the memory isn't distorted like it is with stuff you see or hear. You get a whiff of mince pie and it's like 'Wow, Grandma's house,' even though you wouldn't recognize the place if you saw it." He breathed on the window to refog it and drew a peace symbol. "So you figure somebody knocked your dad out with paraldehyde, stuck him in the garage with the engine running, and closed the doors."

"Yes."

"And Wendy thinks your mom did it, possibly with help from your stepdad."

"She resents my mom. Wendy thinks Louise is an anti-Semite."

"Heavy. What are you gonna do?"

What the hell could I do? The case was closed. Would the police reopen it based on the "olfactory memory" of some long-haired college kid? Not a chance.

"So don't go to the pigs," suggested Luke. "Investigate it yourself. I'll help."

Our room in Kronshage Hall was a Spartan box, fourteen by twelve, with two narrow beds set at right angles to each other, two plain wooden desks with chairs side by side, a wall-mounted bookcase, and nothing else. By the time we got there Luke was fairly lucid and quite keen on the project. He got out pencil and paper, tipped his desk chair back on two legs, and began to interrogate me.

For a guy who hated the pigs, he would have made a good police detective. What was the estimated time of death? I didn't know. Who was the last person to see my father alive? I didn't know. Where did he go that day? What did he do? Who did he talk to?

Didn't know, didn't know, didn't know. Luke was pretty frustrated with me until he stumbled onto a line of questioning that got his motor running.

"Did he have any enemies?"

"Enemies?"

"Yeah. Anybody hate his guts?"

"Not that I know of."

"Did *he* hate anybody *else's* guts?"

"Not that I . . ."

I hesitated. Luke tipped his chair forward and moistened the tip of the pencil with his tongue, like an eager reporter anticipating a scoop.

"His boss, Leon Bridette, fired him. It was totally unfair."

Luke scribbled a note. "Did anybody owe your dad money? Did *he* owe anybody *else* money?"

Bull's-eye. I told Luke the story of Philip J. Newley of Oostburg, the failed school lunch tray business, the Bank of Wisconsin loan, and my father's ill-advised guarantee. Luke was juiced.

"Fuckin-a," he said. "Corrupt business deal goes down the crapper, grifter makes off with eighty grand, fall guy ends up dead. *Quod erat demonstrandum.*"

"Corrupt?" I said. "What was corrupt?"

"You said Newley supposedly had all these sales wired up 'cause he was once on the school board. It's like the defense contractors, man. All that government contract shit is corrupt."

I thought Luke was going a bit overboard, but he had a good point. The whole deal with Bridette and Newley stunk.

We went at it for hours, cataloguing facts and listing potential perpetrators. Luke didn't drink a drop all day, which was good.

On the other hand, both of us cut all of our classes that day, and the next.

Thus began the obsession that would soon overwhelm my college career, and very nearly cost me my life.

○ ○

My glass is empty and darkness is swallowing the house on Foxglove Lane. I still haven't found anything warm to wear outdoors. I'll be damned if I'm going to put on Ray's letter sweater. The thing lies coiled on the floor like a viper, its fangs dripping with the venom of shame and regret.

Could Wendy have intuited instantaneously truth that I wasn't able to figure out for more than thirty years? Add it up.

Ray and Louise go steady in high school. Ray plans to marry her, but when he gets back from the war she's already married to David. She may or may not already have a daughter, who may or may not be David's. Years later Louise's marriage is on the rocks and David is over a hundred grand in the red, but he has life insurance. Ray still carries a torch for Louise. David's death looks like suicide, but Louise has this very clever scheme all worked out to shake enough dough out of the insurance carrier to pay the mortgage. Soon thereafter, Louise and Ray are married, and Ray moves into the house.

Why wasn't she home at her usual time the day my father died? She said she went to her sister's house straight from work. Who better than your sister to give you an alibi?

Who better than an ex-varsity wrestler and ex-Marine to do the heavy lifting? I remember Ray on Christmas Eve, employing a dirty chokehold to pin Jamie on the living room floor, the veins bulging in Ray's neck and forehead. Only in my mind's eye, it is my father Ray is pinning, and he has a pillow full of paraldehyde clamped over my father's face.

"Shit!" I stand up and hurl my glass against the wall. It's a thick, sturdy glass that doesn't break, but it leaves a big gouge in the flimsy drywall.

I was sorry at the time I had that pointless spat with Wendy about her wild conjecture. How much sorrier will I be now if I conclude after all this time that her theory was on the money. Especially since I have long suspected that the chief reason I became so obsessed with the investigation was to prove Wendy wrong.

Bad to be the offspring of a suicide. Worse to be the brother of a father-killer. Worse yet to be the son of a murderess.

I put on my brother's old ski jacket, pick up my books, and jog out to the garage. A wicked wind bites my ears and hands. I try to shelter my free hand in the jacket pocket, but the pocket is missing. Then I remember that my brother carelessly tossed this jacket on the stove once when the burner was hot, and it left a scar of brown concentric circles on the patch pocket. Rather than buy a new jacket or pay to have it repaired, my mother just removed the damaged pocket and my brother slouched around in a one-pocket jacket for a couple of years. Pitiful.

Okay, we weren't starving or on the street. But good God, money was always such an issue for us. It makes me think that in some way, my father's death must have been about money. At our house it seemed like everything was.

Back in the foyer, I see Ray's letter sweater on the floor. It suggests that my father's death may have been about love.

But what do I really know? It may have been about a little girl named Audrey.

At the age of twenty, with my entire adult life ahead of me, I felt compelled to find my father's killer, to either remove the stain from my family or else establish it once and for all. I needed to know what my parents were, in order to know who I was.

Now, more than half of my adult life is behind me, and where am I? Fearful that the blood of monsters runs in my veins, hoping for vindication, desperate for resolution one way or the other.

Exactly where I was thirty-four years ago.

II

The Chain

13

The House, Day Twenty-One

I HAD THOUGHT MY OBSESSION with my father's death died a long time ago, but I see now that it was merely hibernating. Two weeks into December, the house on Foxglove Lane is just as full of garbage as it was in November, but the garbage has been reconfigured, so that the place truly resembles an archaeological dig.

The random heaps and piles of crap are now organized into orderly ranks and files of crap. The completely worthless junk has been separated from the potentially valuable junk, and from the items known to have value, the precious artifacts. The sole determinant of any object's value is its informational content, its potential for yielding evidence. The upstairs has been completely excavated, and I am about halfway through the basement. I haven't worked this hard in years. The physical labor and the irregularity of my meals are loosening the waistline of my jeans. This, I expect, will improve my BMI, my body mass index, which will be good for my diving.

When I opened my dive business I was so lean that I sank in fresh water and needed only a couple of pounds on my weight belt in salt water, even with a full wet suit. As I gained weight I lost density, with the ironic result that I needed a heavier weight belt to get to the bottom. With the tanks on, when the boat is riding seven-foot swells, my middle-aged knees can't push all that weight up out of a deep squat, so to get aboard I have to flop onto the swim platform like a beached whale. Slightly ridiculous.

Lately I have been staying in whenever the seas are more than four feet. This means lost income, which I can ill afford. I'm a month back on my rent. I live over the dive shop, so if I default on my lease I lose my business and my residence simultaneously. One cannot live long-term on a twenty-four-foot scuba boat with no cabin.

Which is why I have kept up such a feverish pace for the past three weeks. I must get back soon. Christmas is coming, and even though late December is not a particularly good time for reef diving in the Keys, Marathon will be swarming with tourists for two weeks. That means full boats. Diving gear and high-profit-margin souvenirs flying off the shelves. If I miss Christmas season, I will likely join the legions of dive shops along U.S. Route 1 that have ended up with "going out of business" banners draped over their tinted windows.

For three weeks my father's desk has been lurking tantalizingly in one of the dank, dark recesses of the basement. It is a nicely made desk, solid mahogany, real Old World workmanship. It is locked. I have combed the house looking for the key, without success. The crowbar from the trunk of the Dodge, applied to the pencil drawer with all of my strength, chips out a few toothpick-size splinters, but the lock holds. Admirable little lock — it even shrugs off a fusillade of blows from a heavy claw hammer, delivered with that extra oomph a man has when he's losing it.

In another shadowy corner of the cellar I locate a rusty cross-cut saw, and now I mean business. Sawdust falls like a gentle snow onto my face, neck, and shoulders as I slice into the vulnerable underside of the pencil drawer. Although I'm lying on my back on a cold cement floor, I'm sweating like a blender drink in the tropics, and the sawdust is sticking to my skin, clogging my nostrils, and encrusting my eyelids and lips. *Ptui.* The sawdust in my nostrils actually brings relief, as the basement reeks powerfully of mold, mildew, and something vaguely resembling vegetable soup. My mother used to buy onions, kohlrabi, and potatoes in

105

large quantities to save money and store them in the basement until the onions and kohlrabi looked like prunes and the potatoes looked like spiders. I suppose over the years a few of these broke loose and wandered under the stairs and into the wet corners, where they may even have taken root and grown in the sodden loam of grime and decomposing insect corpses.

Breach the center drawer, I figure, and I can disengage the catches that hold all of the other six drawers shut. In one of those drawers might be the mother lode of precious artifacts, the critical clue — the answer. The groove grows imperceptibly, but it grows: quarter-inch, half-inch, inch, two inches.

My right hand is cramping by the time I get through the thick front panel. Past the front panel the wood is thinner and softer, but progress is slowed because I only have about two inches of throw to work with. The tip of the saw blade bumps up against the underside of the desktop rhythmically as I saw in short, jerky movements. *Chchch-chchch-bump. Chchch-chchch-bump.*

Three hours of sawing and my neck and back are screaming at me, my eyes and mouth are clogged with sawdust, and my arm and shoulder are blown out, but I think I have cut enough of the bottom panel to crack it open with the crowbar. *Aaaaargh-uuumph!*

I am wrong. I am starting to hate the sadistic, fascist bastards who made this fucking desk. What did they think people were going to keep in here? Nuclear defense plans?

Two hours later the bottom panel of the pencil drawer splits open like a coconut and a torrent of pens, pencils, erasers, rubber bands, and paperclips rains down upon me. A slide rule jabs me right in the eye. Thank God it wasn't the compass.

The contents of the pencil drawer are a letdown. Nothing but a clutter of implements and a pack of business cards. No potentially precious artifacts.

A few minutes of hacking and prying with the claw hammer and I am through to the center lock. Solid brass shafts extend from the lock in both directions. These, I assume, hook up to a vertical bar with the locking pins that hold all of the other drawers shut. I had hoped with all my heart that the brass bars could be disconnected from the lock with a screw driver, releasing the drawers. No such luck. The bars are attached *inside* the metal housing of the lock.

I cannot bear the thought of more sawing right now, and my cramped, blistered hand could not hold a saw even if I wanted to. Leaning my tortured back against the stone-hard desk, I shuffle absentmindedly through my father's business card collection. One is from an attorney named Stewart Sassoon who, according to the card, specializes in patent law. Or did, thirty-four years ago. Another is that of a Rodney Beeber, the "New Products Development Manager" for Dacor, Inc., the scuba-gear company.

Here is the card of Leon Bridette, my dad's boss, who fired him. Asshole. He gave me one, too, last time I saw him, which was in May of my sophomore year at the University of Wisconsin. I remember tearing the card to shreds and throwing it across his desk.

o o

May, 1974

"Come right on in, Jonathan. Let's have a look at you. Well, aren't you shaping up into a fine-looking young man. But you should get a haircut."

Leon Bridette did not look like the bullying, two-faced slimeball I knew him to be. On the contrary, he looked like a middle-aged choirboy, with smooth cheeks that appeared to scarcely grow whiskers, straight sandy-gray hair, round hazel eyes behind wire-rim glasses, and a broad, froggy mouth set in a disarming grin. John Denver in a business suit. He apparently fancied himself an outdoorsman, as he had decorated his office with knotty pine, gun racks, and mounted game.

"It's been too long, Jonathan. When was the last time I saw you?"

"My father's funeral."

"Oh, yeah, that's right. Terrible episode." He shook his head and gestured in the direction of a brown plaid chair. "Have a seat, my boy."

Your boy? I wanted to tell him to screw himself right then. I didn't want to spend ten seconds in the same room with Leon Bridette. Sitting down in his hideous office with the *faux* wood paneling and the stuffed fish and deer heads on the walls made me want to toss breakfast. The meeting was my roommate Luke's idea. "Follow the money," Luke had said. That meant finding Philip J. Newley, the swindler who ran off with the $80,000 and stuck my father with the debt. Luke suggested that to find Newley, I start with Bridette, my "link to Newley," as Luke put it.

Bridette offered me a Coke, which I declined. He had his secretary, a redhead about my age, bring him a glass of ice water that she set down on a round pressed-paper coaster like the ones they use in country taverns.

"How is your mother doing?"

Like you care. "Fine."

"I heard she remarried."

"Yes."

He interlaced his fingers on the surface of his fake-rustic pine desk and tapped his thumbs together, like he was getting impatient already. Bridette was the kind of guy who got antsy if he had to go three minutes without exploiting someone.

"So, Jonathan, what can I do for you?"

Go to hell and stay there, I thought. "I'm trying to locate Philip J. Newley, formerly of Oostburg."

Bridette jerked back an inch. He wasn't expecting *that.*

"Bud Newley? What do you want with Bud Newley?"

"He made off with eighty thousand dollars the Bank of Wisconsin tried to collect from my dad."

Bridette moved his hands aimlessly, his eyes darting about as if searching for the right place to set them down. "But . . . what concern of yours is that? I mean, at this point." His voice squeaked like a teenager's on the word "point." I had never before seen Leon Bridette rattled. I enjoyed it. "Your father didn't pay that loan back, you know. What, do you think his estate has some sort of claim against Newley? There's nothing there."

Bridette was shook up, much more than I had expected. His hands came to rest on his necktie, one of those Rooster ties, blunt on the end instead of pointed. He petted it like it was a cat.

"I just want to find him, Mr. Bridette."

"The Bank of Wisconsin couldn't find him," he replied.

"Doesn't seem to me they tried very hard. They had my dad and another guy on the hook."

"Well, I think you're wasting your time, and I can't see what the point of it is." His tie-stroking settled into a rhythm.

"I find it interesting, Mr. Bridette," I said, "that with all of your objections you haven't denied knowing where Newley is."

He stopped stroking his tie and pointed at me. His eyes blinked as if he had sand in them.

"I was just coming to that. What makes you think I know where Newley is?"

"I didn't think you did, until you didn't deny it, which you still haven't."

Bridette glowered at me fiercely, a crease forming between his eyes, his ears reddening. "You're becoming a very insolent young man. And you used to be so well behaved. I suppose it's those radicals at the University, stirring you kids up, protesting, you lose all respect. And my taxes pay for it."

"So you *do* know where Newley is."

His eyes opened wide and he threw the end of his tie down. He looked away.

"No, I do not. If I did, don't you realize I would have had to tell the bank? My company does a lot of business with that bank, and I felt responsible because I put the deal together. Like most of you college students, you don't know much about business."

If Bridette did know where Newley was, there was no chance he would tell me, or even lift a finger to help. If he didn't know, and might be willing to help, it was stupid of me to piss him off, as much as I relished the thought of me, the little college boy, getting the big shot's goat. I tried to force myself to play good cop for a while.

"No, Mr. Bridette, I guess I don't know much about business. I'm sorry, I meant no disrespect. I really didn't think you knew where he was, I just thought you might know enough about him to help me get started."

Bridette's posture softened and his gaze drifted back my way. "I don't know him all that well."

"But, like you said, you put the deal together for him, and I noticed you called him 'Bud.' Can you at least tell me what he looks like?"

Bridette shrugged. "Bud's a regular-looking guy. Average height, medium build, brown hair, what's left of it."

Real helpful. "How old?"

"About like me. Roughly late thirties, I'd say."

Bridette was off at least a decade on his own age. Nobody in their thirties has turkey wattles under their chin.

"Have you got a picture of him?"

Bridette glanced off to the right reflexively. "Uh, no, why would I have a picture of him?" He looked back quickly, but it was too late. I checked the spot that had drawn his attention. A black and white photograph in a rough cedar frame hung on the wall between a four-foot-long muskellunge and a fat brown smallmouth bass. I stood up and walked over to it.

In the picture, a group of seven men in flannel shirts and fishing vests sat around a weathered picnic table covered with mugs of frothy beer. In the background, feathery balsams with gracefully curved boughs flanked a rustic tavern with a hand-painted sign: "Brent's Camp." I had seen that sign before, but I could not recall where.

One of the men in the picture was Leon Bridette. Two were Dieworks executives I had met. As bland as Bridette's description of Newley was, it fit only one of the others, a balding guy with an average build who looked to be in his thirties. He was toasting the camera with his beer mug and flashing a gap-toothed smile. "That Newley?" I pointed.

Bridette squinted behind his glasses. "Huh? Huh. What do you know. I forgot about that one. Yeah, that's Bud. Goes back a few years."

So this was the face of the fiend, the black-hearted swindler who took the money and ran, who ruined my father and my family for eighty thousand dollars. Was I imagining the evil in his eyes, the perversion in the off-center cleft in his pointy chin?

I sat back down. "When was the last time you talked to Bud?"

"Couple of years ago, around the time the loan closed. Haven't heard from him since he defaulted."

"Any guesses about where he went?"

Bridette started playing with his tie again, flipping the end of it around as if he were fingering a clarinet. His jaw tightened. "No, I told you I don't know where he is."

"Yes, but you know the guy. What would he do if he had a pile of money and had to lay low? Sail the Caribbean? Hang out in Paris cafés?"

Bridette stood up so suddenly it startled me. "Look, Jonathan, I don't have time for any more of this. I told you, it's pointless. You'll excuse me, I have to get back to work. I'm running a company here."

I found I was desperate to keep the conversation going. I didn't think I had gotten anything useful out of Bridette, and I knew he had a lot more to tell, if I could just figure a way to squeeze it out of him. Maybe it was time to switch back to bad cop. This guy was such a hot-head, I thought I might be able to keep him going with a little provocation.

"I think you owe me a little more consideration, Mr. Bridette. After what you did to my father."

"What are you talking about?"

"You pressured him into signing that guarantee. You ruined his life for the sake of your own greed."

This he took with surprising aplomb. He folded his hands in front of him and smiled. "I offered him an opportunity to participate in a deal, for his own good and the good of the company. There was nothing in the deal for me personally. David was gunning for a promotion. He took a risk because he wanted a raise. If he got in over his head, it wasn't for the sake of *my* greed."

Now I was the one losing his cool. My mother had so firmly asserted that my father got bullied into signing the guarantee because he was a milquetoast, I had never considered it from any other perspective. Bridette's suggestion that my father's blunder was the result of avarice unnerved me. My hands shook. I wanted to jump over Bridette's desk and strangle him.

"No. You forced him. My father wasn't like that." I sounded like a child.

"Like what?"

I struggled to find words. "Pettily ambitious. Venal and money-grubbing."

Bridette grinned smugly and jutted out his chin. He knew he had me rattled now. "Look, Jonathan," he said. "Sometimes a man with a wife and children to support has to claw and gamble, even compromise his principles a little. Someday you'll have a family of your own, and then you won't be so self-righteous. Here," he picked up a business card from a teak holder on his desk, "when you're ready to give up this nonsense about Bud Newley and get a job for the summer, give me a call. We're not union and we can always use another strong boy on the dock. Be good for you."

I looked at him out of the corner of my eye and, without a word, slowly tore the card in half, in quarters, in eighths, and flung the pieces across his desk. An idiotic gesture that made me feel even more childish. But when I looked down at the desk, I saw the paper coaster under Bridette's water glass. Through the water, I could see the simple artist's rendition of the hand-painted "Brent's Camp" sign. *That's* where I had seen it before.

oo

I found a hacksaw and am back to sawing again on the solid brass bars that hold the drawers shut, thwarting me. Sawing, sawing, sawing.

I have learned two things about myself from this project. One is that I am more ambidextrous than I thought I was. With my right hand crippled from overuse, I am sawing left-handed now and doing pretty well at it. The other is that I am also more far-sighted than I realized. I could tolerate sawdust dropping into my eyes, but not metal filings, so I looked around for eye protection and found a pair of my dad's old horn-rimmed reading glasses. My mom never threw anything out. To my surprise, I can see near objects more clearly with my dad's glasses. Turns out I could use a pair of reading glasses, and probably could have for a couple of years already.

Remembering my encounter with Leon Bridette made me realize something else, too. Bridette was wrong when he said that someday I would have a family to support and then I wouldn't be so self-righteous. But his prediction left a mark on me. At twenty, I disdained guys like Bridette who committed their crimes and sinned in the name of wife and family, and was certain I would disdain myself if I ever attempted such self-delusion. I didn't want to claw and gamble and compromise my principles. But I was afraid that faced with real responsibility, I might end up doing just that, afraid I wasn't clever or energetic or lucky enough to find another way. So I let first Lori and then Wendy go without much struggle, let all potentially serious involvements slide through my fingers until I was safely into middle-aged bachelorhood, until it was too late for anyone to depend on me enough, or even care enough, that it would matter what I did.

So eventually I didn't matter to anyone. But at least I could still be self-righteous.

14

WHEN I TOLD MY ROOMMATE about my meeting with Leon Bridette, Luke was much more enthusiastic about what I had learned than I was. That Bridette had stalled before he denied knowing Newley's whereabouts Luke proclaimed to be, "Heavy." That Bridette cut the interview short when I started speculating about what a guy like Newley might do if he was on the lam with his pockets full of hot loot, Luke declared, "Dy-no-mite." But Luke saved his highest accolade for the picture of Newley at Brent's Camp, combined with Bridette's having used a coaster from the same establishment.

"Far fucking out," he declared. Of course, Luke was drinking again and fairly enthusiastic about almost everything.

Luke knew northern Wisconsin like a housewife knows her kitchen. He knew exactly where Brent's Camp was and remarked that Brent's served "the best goddamn cheeseburgers in Vilas County." He proposed a trip north to look for Philip Newley.

So Memorial Day weekend, just ten days before final exams were to start, Luke and I checked into a ten-dollar cabin near Land O' Lakes, just a mile south of the border with the upper peninsula of Michigan, the so-called "U.P."

"The road to Newley," Luke postulated, "runs through Brent's Camp." Of course, Luke brought along his tackle in case the walleye were hitting, and I suspected he was so hot for the trip mainly because he vastly preferred the north woods in the spring to UW during exam period.

I appreciated northern Wisconsin myself, but in May its charm eluded me. It was cold, gray, and foggy, the air was thick with mosquitoes, and the wood ticks were on you every time you turned around. Luke and I pulled the top of our socks up over the outside of our pants in an attempt to keep the ticks from crawling up our legs. But still we constantly found the nasty little buggers with their repulsive heads buried in our flesh. We went through a book of matches the first day burning them out.

The cabin was small and dilapidated, and it smelled like a mixture of ammonia and Sterno. It wasn't even on a lake, just a mucky, weedy backwater of a small river. No majestic pines, just cattails and scraggly tamaracks. A swamp. But to Luke it was the Riviera.

"Isn't this place *great?* I can't believe we got it for ten bucks. Look at that gorgeous slough. If I had my waders with me, we'd have enough trout for dinner in fifteen minutes. Man, what a spot! We should go into town and get us some waders."

"How long will it take to get to Brent's Camp?" It was mid-morning, and I wanted to get down to business. Final exams were looming.

"Fifteen, twenty minutes." Luke pulled a pop-top from a can of Point beer. Back then, the pop-tops came off and became litter instead of diving in and dirtying the beer. "We need to lay out a plan, first."

I didn't ask how long it would take to lay out the plan. The answer was two or three beers. I wasn't about to complain about Luke's attempt to make the excursion enjoyable. I needed his intelligence and his familiarity with the turf. He was doing me a hell of a favor.

Luke proposed that we split up to save time. "One of us should cover the places accessible by car, like Brent's and the other taverns and marinas," he said, "while the other one rents a boat and covers the water. You pick."

Whether he was out in a fishing boat or hanging around taverns, Luke would be in his element. His plan made sense,

115

though. Brent's Camp was located on the shore of Mamie Lake, part of the Cisco Chain of Lakes. The chain had fifteen lakes, over 271 miles of shoreline, and hundreds of islands and bays. We had to split up.

"You take the water," I said. I figured I could get lost on the chain, while Luke could get lost in the taverns. "What cover story are we going with?"

In the car on the way up, we had tried out several fictitious reasons why a couple of twenty-year-old strangers were looking for Philip Newley. Luke said the folks in Vilas County would be outwardly friendly, but protective of a local guy and unlikely to help anyone they thought might be a bill collector or a tax agent. We decided to say that all we could tell them was that we worked for a lawyer in Sheboygan who was administering an estate. We'd let them fill in the blanks.

Luke rented a boat and motor at a marina on aptly-named Big Lake, where he also bought a bucket of minnows and a Michigan fishing license, since the Cisco Chain straddles Wisconsin and the U.P. "Got to make it look good," he said, but I knew he planned to do some serious fishing out there. As he pulled away from the pier, whistling, even his wake looked happy.

Nobody at the marina on Big Lake acknowledged knowing Philip Newley, so I got on Highway B around noon and headed east, driving Wendy's Beetle. We hadn't spoken since the day the VW broke down and she stormed off on the bus. I was hoping that when she cooled off enough to come collect her car, I could report that Luke and I had solved the murder, and Louise hadn't done it.

The road was a snaky two-lane blacktop with solid green walls of towering trees on both sides. A billboard steered me into Brent's Camp, where the same hand-painted sign that was in Bridette's photograph, flanked by the same trees, hung over the same rustic tavern. It was, if anything, even more rustic now than in the photo, with chipped paint and splitting wood around the doors and windows, and punched-out, rusting screens.

I sat down at the bar and ordered a cheeseburger and a Pabst. Inside, Brent's was the authentic version of what Leon Bridette's office was pretending to be. Thick, timbered walls and ceiling, planked floor, truly impressive mounts. In my worn-out jeans, faded flannel shirt with the sleeves rolled, and Milwaukee Brewers baseball cap, I thought I would fit right in. But the barmaid and the two burly gents watching TV at the end of the bar all looked at me in a way that clearly announced: "You're not one of us." I only made eye contact with the woman behind the bar.

"How's the fishing been on Mamie this spring?" I asked.

"Cum si, cum sa," she said, setting my tap beer down on a round, pressed paper coaster identical to the one in Bridette's office. My hostess was a stout woman who appeared to be in her mid-thirties, wore no makeup, and had profound fatigue in her eyes. Black hair in a pigtail poked out the back of her baseball cap. "Lindsley and Fishhawk are hot for crappies now, they tell me. You up fishing for the weekend?"

How could she tell I was "up," that I wasn't from the U.P. or say, Canada? "No, I'm working," I said, hoping for a smooth segue. She glanced up from under the visor of her cap with a questioning look, nonverbally asking what sort of work a wussy-looking guy like me could do up here in the north woods.

"Huh. I thought you was a UW student," she said. Holy moly, was she telepathic? Or did I have my biography tattooed on my forehead? Then I remembered that Wendy's Beetle had a UW decal in the rear window. My hostess was pretty sharp.

"No, no," I said, squirming a little from the lie. "I work for a law firm in Sheboygan."

"Oh yeah? What firm?" she asked.

Shit. Luke and I never agreed on a firm name. Stupid, stupid. Say something fast. "Proctor and Bergman," I said, the first two names that popped into my head, two actors from the Firesign Theatre. Lucky I didn't say, "Proctor and Gamble."

"Never heard of 'em." She narrowed her eyes. "They do family law?"

"Sure," I said, "they do a little of everything. Mostly they do probate. That's what I'm working on, trying to locate somebody for an estate administration. By any chance do you know a man named Philip J. Newley?"

When I said the name, one of the guys at the end of the bar looked over, but the hostess kept wiping the bar, hesitating to answer. I didn't sound convincing to myself at all and I was sure she wasn't buying my story. What a lame imposter I was.

"Whoops, burger's ready," she said. She served it up on a paper plate with fries and a slice of sweet pickle. The meat looked greasy. The bun looked greasy. The fries looked greasy. Even the pickle looked greasy. I took a bite. Juice ran down my hands past my wrists. I had no doubt these were indeed the best cheeseburgers in Vilas County. The barmaid wrote up my tab and set it down on the bar.

"So this guy you're looking for," she finally said, "what'd he do, inherit some money or something?"

"I can't say," I replied. "Client confidentiality and all that, you know? Can you help me locate him?"

Her eyes moved toward the men at the end of the bar. They were both watching now. "Not really," she said. "When you're done eating, feel free to look at our mounts. There's some real good ones."

I sensed she was trying to help me, so I finished eating quickly and perused Brent's impressive collection of stuffed game. Snarling bobcats, noble elk heads, a puma poised to pounce. Many of the fish had inscriptions under the mounts. Beneath one toothy, brown-backed beast was this: *Record Northern Pike for Thousand Island Lake. 31 pounds 8 ounces. Taken through the ice by Philip "Bud" Newley, December 16, 1971.*

Paydirt. The inscription told me that Newley was on the Cisco Chain eight months *after* my father got the letter from the Bank of Wisconsin saying Newley couldn't be located. What an ego he had, or just a lack of caution, to display his big fish while he was skipping on an $80,000 loan. He must have assumed no one was looking for him anymore. Guess again, Bud. This is one pike you should have put back in the lake. While I was reading the inscription, one of the hombres at the bar went out the door in a hurry.

My waitress had earned a big tip. I handed her two tens with the check and told her to keep the change. But it wasn't a tip she was after.

"So you sorta hunt people down for that law firm you work for?" She had a Marlboro going. It dangled on her lower lip as she handled the cash.

"Sometimes," I said. "I serve process and run errands. I'm just a 'gofer.'"

"You ever track deadbeat dads?"

When she said this, I noticed something peculiar about Brent's Camp I had not picked up on before. For a tavern, there was a lot of kiddie stuff lying around. Portable playpen in the corner. Big Bird doll behind the bar.

"Oh, uh, once or twice." Now I was really feeling slimy. Please don't ask . . .

"My ex is eight months back on his child support. A friend of mine heard he was working construction over in Hurley. My divorce lawyer don't care 'cause he's waiting to get paid hisself. But I can't pay him till Cliff pays me."

She looked at me with those tired brown Lady Madonna eyes. Shoot. What a lousy goddamn cover story Luke and I picked. Amateurs.

"Boy, that's . . . not fair." I rubbed the back of my neck. It was hot.

"Can you do anything?"

"I'd have to talk to my law firm. . . ."

"Never mind." She handed me the change I had told her to keep. Oh, what the hell, Luke would probably enjoy a side trip.

"When I'm done here, I'd be glad to head over to Hurley and poke around. Can't guarantee anything."

"Thanks." She leaned over the bar and said quietly, "Northeast corner of Thousand Island Lake. Cabin behind the white boathouse that used to be yellow."

o

As scheduled, Luke met me at the Big Lake marina at 6 P.M. The fog had lifted and the late afternoon sun cast a coat of pink across the still surface of the lake. The water by the pier was glazed with oily rainbows and smelled of gasoline. Luke did not show off the mess of crappies and the twenty-inch walleye he had on a stringer dangling from the oarlock.

"Talked to fishermen all over Big Lake, East Bay, West Bay, Poor, Indian, and Mamie. Nobody knows Philip Newley. I'll cover the northern half of the chain tomorrow. How'd you do?"

When I told him, he caught fire. "Hop aboard, Roomie. Grab a beer. *Andiamo.*" I stepped into the bow. Luke opened the throttle on the stern-mounted outboard, and the light aluminum boat rocketed off at a thirty-degree angle.

Rudder in one hand and canteen of brandy in the other, Luke navigated the winding channels and narrow cuts through Morley, Lindsley, and Cisco lakes without referring to a map. The name "Thousand Island Lake" turned out to be a gross exaggeration, but it was an enormous lake with a profusion of islands and peninsulas and countless cottages and cabins. I was opining to Luke that it would be impossible to find a cabin on a lake this size with the meager description we had, when he said, "There."

He was pointing at a narrow, two-story boathouse cantilevered over the shoreline. Its white lap-siding was clean. The yellow trim around its one window was dirty and faded. It was quite obviously a white boathouse that used to be yellow.

Luke tied the boat up at the pier next to the boathouse and headed up the steep steps to the cabin like he owned the place. I followed sheepishly. The steps were fashioned out of railroad ties. The cabin was made of half logs and had an exposed basement on the side nearest the lake. Luke knocked at the back door.

A black Labrador crashed against the door like a battering ram, emptying my adrenal glands. The dog growled and barked and bared its teeth like it wanted to rip our throats open, which it no doubt could have done if the door had not been in the way.

"Let's get out of here," I said. "We can come back tomorrow."

"*Una momento,*" said Luke. He seemed unfazed by the dog. "What's this?"

Someone had thumbtacked a note to the back door: *If you get back from shopping before dark, I'll be out fishing on Record Lake. Bud.*

"I know where Record Lake is," said Luke. "It's at the north end of the chain. Let's go."

North of Thousand Island Lake the Cisco Chain regressed into true wilderness. No cottages, no piers, no buoys to mark the stumps and rocks that threatened to eat up the propeller or take a bite out of the boat. Nothing but virgin pine forest and primordial tamarack swamp bestride pellucid waters the color of weak tea. As twilight rose out of the dark water and we traversed the long, meandering waterway to the first lake on the chain north of Thousand Island, called Big Africa, we didn't see another boat nor any evidence of human presence. Luke slowed the boat to no-wake speed and the outboard dropped into a *chug-chug-chug* rhythm.

"You're awful quiet up there, Roomie," said Luke. "Something bothering you?"

I swatted a mosquito on the back of my hand. "To tell you the truth, yes."

"Pining away for Lehman, I s'pose. Wuz happnin' with you guys?"

"Nothing," I said. "Wendy hasn't spoken to me since we had that fight the day we . . . came to . . ."

Luke broke in. "Fish me out of the drunk tank."

Whap! I got another mosquito, this one already engorged with my blood. Luke never swatted. "Actually," I said, "what's bothering me is that note. If Newley wanted to leave a note for someone coming home from shopping, why would he put it on the back door? Why wouldn't he put it somewhere inside?"

"I know," said Luke. "One of those guys in the bar tipped him. The note was meant for you."

"So he's expecting us."

"I s'pose."

We took a hard right at the north end of Big Africa and slalomed through a crooked channel into Record Lake. Venus flickered behind a blunt-tipped white pine that held an osprey nest on an island in the middle of the lake. Luke cut the motor and we drifted to a stop.

I had never heard such silence. It seemed that there was not a living soul around for miles. Then I heard a gentle *plish, plish, plish,* and the tip of a boat appeared from behind the island, to the right. As the dark silhouette of a boat, a rower, and a trimmed motor emerged, my palms dampened and my heart pounded at the prospect of finally coming face to face with a man who had become to me a mythological villain. A man I held responsible for the capitulation of my father's spirit and the ruination of my parents' marriage. A man who may have been responsible for my father's death and all of the ill that flowed from it.

As the boat drew near, the rower turned and looked at us over his shoulder, and his mouth opened into a gap-toothed grin.

It was him.

15

I FEEL LIKE CRYING AGAIN, this time for joy. Hallelujah! One finished slice through the brass rod and the activators on both sides of the desk have released the drawers. Lucky break, as I had no strength left to make another cut.

The drawers on the left side of the desk are an empty well. Coils of plastic hose for the Opuba, machine parts, gears, springs, knobs. Likewise the top two drawers on the right side, but the right-side bottom drawer is a treasure trove. Files. Correspondence. Legal documents. All of it undisturbed since the day "local man" was "found dead in garage."

Nice investigation the Sheboygan cops did, leaving all this stuff locked up down here. I understand why they didn't bother to look deeper at the time of the death, since everything pointed to suicide. But it still frustrates me that the police didn't reopen the case after I rubbed their noses in the anomalous finding on the autopsy, and put them wise to the Cisco Chain boys.

o o

"You fellas lookin' for me?"

Luke waited for me to respond. I was tongue-tied. When I didn't answer, Luke did.

"Are you Philip Newley?"

"Who wants to know?" Newley lifted the brim of his felt fishing hat with his thumb. He had a long scar above his right eye that was concealed in the picture. His khaki pants and shirt were clean, and they matched.

"An attorney in Sheboygan," said Luke, "who is administering an estate." This was the plan, draw Newley out with the suggestion there might be money waiting for him, then ambush him with questions about the bank loan.

"What firm?" said Newley.

My mouth was so dry and I was so short of breath Luke answered before I could get the words out. "Stills and Nash," he improvised. I guess Crosby retired.

"Oh yeah?" said Newley. "What happened to Proctor and Bergman?"

Fuck. We were busted in less than a minute. A couple of bungling juveniles playing junior G-man. I made an effort to keep the ruse going.

"That's my firm. We're from different firms coordinating on the same estate. Law firms do that sometimes." Man, did I not know what I was talking about.

Newley lowered his eyelids and flicked the side of his nose with his thumb. "Directory assistance for Sheboygan says there's no such firm. Now what are you kids up to?" His eyes moved back and forth between us, his gaze finally fixing on me. "Do I know you? You look familiar."

"You knew my father," I said.

He peered at me intently for a moment, then his eyes widened and his head jerked back an inch. "You're Bruckner's kid."

"Yes, I am," I said.

"Well I'll be damned," said Newley.

"Yes, you will," I said.

Newley rubbed his thumb on his pointy, asymmetrical cleft chin. "I bet I know what you're after. Here, I got something for you."

He bent down and reached under the bench seat in the stern of his boat, behind a brown metal tackle box. I leaned forward to see what he was getting. Luke grabbed the handle of the pull-starter on the outboard and his elbow came back at me so suddenly and so hard it caught me on the side of the head and knocked me over the seat into the bow of the boat. I tried to get up and the boat took off with such acceleration and at such an angle that I pitched back over the seat the other way and landed on Luke's tackle box, spilling a bevy of lures.

Luke offered a single word of explanation: "Rifle."

A sharp *crack!* like the report from an M-80 firecracker jabbed my ears and reverberated in the dark forest around the lake. Luke moved the rudder back and forth and the boat lunged from side to side, zigging and zagging in evasive action that rolled me around in the loose lures. Another *crack!* followed by a *ping!* and a wicked *fshshup!* in the water near the boat. Then a *crack!* with a *thump!* that sounded and felt like someone hit the boat with a hammer. The smell of gasoline filled the air.

We made it off Record Lake and Luke slowed the boat to maneuver the channel to Big Africa. We were nearly through the channel when we heard Newley's motor start.

I pulled myself up onto the seat. Fishing lures hung all over me like ornaments on a Christmas tree.

Luke said, "Son of a bitch is a good shot. I'm hit."

He took his hand from under his thigh and showed me blood on his palm. I felt shock in my mouth and throat. "Jesus, Luke."

"I'm all right," he said. "But the boat's hit, too. We're leaking gas. Newley's got a forty horse. We can't outrun him on the main channel. We'll have to try to slip out of sight before he gets on Big Africa. There." Luke pointed.

I couldn't tell what he was pointing at in the dusk. The shoreline looked like an unbroken wall of black jungle to me. But a minute later Luke pulled the boat into the narrowest, shallowest, and most serpentine channel we had been on yet. It was not much more than a creek. The dense woods closed in and submerged us in darkness.

"This must be the channel to Little Africa," said Luke. "He might not be able to follow us in here with a forty horse. If we can get through ourselves."

Luke piloted the boat through a series of hairpin turns as the sound of Newley's motor drew closer. Water and gasoline and blood pooled in the vee of the hull. Several times our propeller hit something hard. The water was ink. No way to spot rocks or stumps. By the time we emerged on Little Africa Lake, Newley was almost on us. Luke opened it up and we were nearly to the center of the small lake when the motor quit.

"We're taking on water fast," said Luke. "We might as well abandon ship. She's *kaput*." Luke pulled off his shoes and slid smoothly over the stern into the wine-dark water. I tried to disengage myself from the fishing lures without any success. My hands were shaking and the treble hooks stuck to my clothes like burrs. Newley's boat appeared at the mouth of the channel, so I ditched my shoes and floundered over the gunwale.

"Follow me," said Luke. I didn't argue. He breast-stroked just below the surface, trailing a crimson stain. As I swam, a Hula Popper on my sleeve leered mockingly at me with its goggle-eyes. With every stroke, a barbed hook poked or scratched some part of me. The water was cold but tolerable.

We took shelter behind a beaver nest about twenty feet from the marshy shoreline. The lake bottom was as mushy as pie filling, but I had no anxiety left to spare on such trivialities as leeches or snapping turtles lurking in the muck.

Luke cupped his hands over his mouth and my ear. His breath smelled like brandy. "Well, Stanley," he whispered, "this is a fine mess you've gotten me into."

I cupped my hands likewise and whispered, "Why isn't Newley coming after us?"

"If he does, we could slip past him in the dark. The channel is the only way out. Come daylight, he's got us. Cagey."

"Can we get out through the woods?"

Luke explained that we were hemmed in by marsh, and Newley could pick us off easily if we tried to slog through it. Even if we got through, there were no roads for miles, nothing but swamps and dense forest. That was why he was guarding the channel. I could see a cigarette ember glowing in Newley's hand.

"How deep is the channel?" I asked.

"Dead center, at least two and a half feet."

Just off to my left I heard a loud, deep *ker-plunk* that sounded like a two-hundred-pound man doing a belly flop. I very nearly cried out.

"Beaver," whispered Luke. He looked wan, and he was trembling. I asked him how he was doing. He pursed his lips, which were blue, tilted his head to one side and shrugged. "Not so good. Down about a quart." He quietly unscrewed the top of his canteen and took a pull.

I didn't think Luke would make it until daylight. He had been joking about me getting him into this mess, but there was truth in it. I had to try something.

"Help me get my shirt off," I whispered.

Luke didn't ask why. He disengaged the fishing lures from the wet flannel with ease. The Rapala in the fleshy part of my thumb he examined closely.

"Hook's in past the barb," he murmured. "Can't swim through weeds and tamarack roots with that in you." Luke reached into one of the pockets of his pants and produced a pair of needle-nosed pliers. He looked me in the eye. "Ready?"

I nodded. Luke clamped the pliers on the base of the treble hooks and twisted, pushing the hook farther in until the barb popped through on the other side of the base of my thumb. My eyes watered from the pain. I was bleeding profusely now, too. Luke clipped the barb off the hook with the same pliers and backed the hook out. Then he helped me remove my shirt and white undershirt.

"Okay, scuba guy, do your thing."

I moved out from the beaver nest with just my eyes and nose above the flat surface, like a crocodile. In the middle of the lake, our boat was two-thirds submerged. The crappies on Luke's stringer, in their death throes, flipped feebly on the surface. The indigo sky was speckled with stars and framed by the jagged shadow of the horizon. Reports from fireworks or gunshots sounded in the distance. Apparently, discharging firearms at night was common up here, even though it wasn't hunting season. No wonder Newley figured he could take pot shots at us with impunity.

127

I pondered my task. Because I sank in fresh water, staying down would be no problem. From scuba training and practice, I was fairly confident I could work my way along the lake bottom, under Newley's boat, and find the channel in the dark by dead reckoning. My problem was oxygen. Newley's boat was about one hundred yards away. I would need to stay under at least fifty yards past him to avoid detection. I could swim one hundred and fifty yards under water, had done so more than once. But only in a swimming pool when I was safe and my heart wasn't pounding like buffalo hooves in a stampede. My teeth were chattering, and not from the cold. In the state I was in, I would burn a lungful of air in about five seconds.

My survival and Luke's now depended less on my skill and strength and lack of buoyancy than on my ability to *calm down*. Hard to do by willpower. I didn't meditate; I had no mantra. Was there a thought or an image that would bolster my courage, a place I could go to in my mind that might help me believe I had it in me to carry this off?

I whispered to myself, "Seven Mile Bridge."

∘ ∘

The House, Day Twenty-One
My father's legal correspondence folder, which has been locked in his old desk in the basement for three and a half decades, intrigues me. Does it tell me anything? Here is a letter dated September 15, 1971, from that patent attorney, the one whose card I found in the pencil drawer.

> Re: Our file no. 1748
> Dear Mr. Bruckner,
> This is to acknowledge receipt of your check for $150.00 for our opinion regarding patentability. In our opinion, the device is patentable. Incidentally, I also believe it has significant commercial potential.

As I told you, to begin preparing the application
we will need an additional retainer of $450.00. In
light of the value of your invention, I urge you to
move forward without delay.

Very truly yours,
Stewart Sassoon, Esq.

I doubt my dad could have come up with $450 in September
of 1971, a month before he died. For that matter, I wonder where
he got the one-fifty. As I recall, by then we were living exclusively
on my mother's income from the Piggly Wiggly, which she
stretched by every imaginable device. She brought home produce
and bakery goods the store was about to throw out, and made me
and my brother save our lunch bags and sandwich wrappings and
bring them home from school to be reused. She even milled her
own soap.

If my father couldn't put the $450 together for the patent
lawyer, it probably didn't matter. The New Products Development
Manager at Dacor didn't share Attorney Sassoon's enthusiasm:

Re: Outboard-Powered Underwater Breathing
Apparatus
Dear Mr. Bruckner,
We have thoroughly considered your invention,
which you call the Opuba, and find that it is not
suitable for inclusion in the Dacor product line at
this time. The test market panel scores were fair,
and the Engineering Department was favorably
impressed by the design of the clutch. However,
the Legal Department determined that the liability
risk is too high given the limited profit potential
for the product. Perhaps one of the smaller
manufacturers of surface air diving equipment
would be interested. Good luck, and please let
us know if you have other inventions in the aqua
sports category.

Sincerely,

Rodney Beeber

P.S. You might consider a different name for your invention. The test market panel made fun of it.

Ouch. My father was almost as proud of that name as he was of the design of the clutch. During my parents' day-long quarrel about my dad selling the crystal to buy the boat to test the Opuba, my mother ridiculed the name. So she was apparently right about that, as she was about the liability snag, as she usually was about everything.

In their arguments about the Opuba, my mom always insisted that my dad should be putting the time and effort into locating Newley instead. He was not ignoring the task. I find a letter dated September 28, 1971, from an outfit called Discreet Investigations, Inc.

Dear Mr. Bruckner,

We have exhausted all of our leads in the State of Wisconsin and have not found any evidence that Philip J. Newley has resided or transacted business in the state within the past twelve months. However, one of our out-of-state contacts reports that a Philip Newley was a party defendant in an action filed in Gogebic County, Michigan, in August of this year. To follow up on this, we will need an additional payment of $300 at this time. Please let me know what you want me to do.

Sincerely,

Wayne Wolfschmidt

Licensed Investigator

Wow, he got that close. For another $300 my father would have found Newley. I know this because I came across the same lawsuit at the Gogebic County Courthouse in the spring of 1974, and the defendant was the same Philip Newley. If Dad could have put three hundred bucks together in late September of '71, would he have been dead a month later?

Three more letters from lawyers in here. Two are from a Thomas Pfeiffer. In one he says he has been retained to represent Louise Bruckner in her divorce action. I never knew my mom saw a lawyer. In the other letter Pfeiffer says Mrs. Bruckner has decided not to file for divorce "at this time," but that he is keeping the draft documents on file because, "in my experience, once a woman has been to see a lawyer she usually follows through eventually."

I wonder why she backed off. Did Ray Moldenhauer walk into Piggly Wiggly one day and suggest an alternative to divorce?

The other attorney letter is from a Leslie Rozner Jr. I have seen that name before, but I can't remember where. It's dated February 18, 1956.

> Re: *Johnson vs. Bruckner*
> Dear David,
> I have spoken with the plaintiff's attorney and the attorney for State Farm Insurance, and it looks like the case isn't going to settle. The trial date is March 30.
>
> I know you are resisting the idea, but as we discussed I really think that the only way to put this matter behind you is a bankruptcy proceeding. Enclosed is a form for you to complete and return as soon as you are ready.
>
> Bankruptcy does not carry the stigma it once did. As I explained, you can keep your home and obtain credit again in a couple of years. Don't wait too long.
> Very truly yours,
Les
> P.S. As you requested, I asked about Audrey's clothes and toys. You may dispose of them.

This letter, written when I was two years old, electrifies me. Allusion to both Audrey and to the shadowy bankruptcy my parents argued about. The enclosures Rozner mentions are not here, nor are any documents from the lawsuit or the bankruptcy. Rozner can't possibly be practicing law anymore. But the Sheboygan County Courthouse is only twenty minutes' drive, and it will be open for another hour. If I hurry, I can see the file from the *Johnson vs. Bruckner* case, and possibly the bankruptcy, today.

I dash up the stairs, grab my brother's tattered old jacket, and am out the kitchen door. The ten-degree air stings. On my way to the garage, I come as close to sprinting as my knees will allow. I climb in the Dodge, slam the door, and turn the key.

The Dodge won't start. The battery is dead.

16

May, 1974

PHILIP NEWLEY SAT MOTIONLESS IN HIS BOAT, guarding the channel to Little Africa Lake with the smug patience of a poker player holding four aces. As silently as possible, I hyperventilated to saturate my blood with oxygen, then slipped below the glassy surface of the lake and found the bottom with my hand. Billows of black muck arose from the spot my hand touched. I decided to hover eighteen inches above the muck and use a sideways scissors kick to disturb the bottom as little as possible. Toward the middle of the lake, the deeper water was head-numbingly cold.

The bottom started to rise, and I looked up. Opaque as the water had appeared from above the surface looking down, from below looking up toward the sky it was translucent, and I spotted the glowing ember of Newley's cigarette. It guided me toward the channel like a beacon.

Last I looked, Newley was facing the stern, so when the silhouette of the boat appeared above me I moved toward the pointy end.

In practicing swimming long distances under water while holding my breath, I have learned that, when you think you are finished and must have a breath of air, you actually can go another thirty seconds if you are able to stay calm and tolerate the discomfort. Passing beneath Newley's boat I realized I was at my apparent limit, which meant I had about half a minute to get as far down the channel as possible before surfacing. Then all I had to do was wade through a quarter mile of a zigzagging channel filled with stumps, weeds, and roots without making any sound, swim across Big Africa Lake, and walk two miles at night through dense woods in bare feet.

Daunting. Beyond me. I fought back the rising panic that threatened to steal my remaining oxygen. My lungs lurched in my chest, as if they were trying to get out through my throat in search of air.

My left hand struck something that felt like a tree root. I looked at it. It was a half-inch wide, fibrous, and braided. A piece of rope.

Oh my God, Newley's anchor line. What an idiot, I swam into the anchor line. He must have felt it. I rolled over onto my back and saw Newley's silhouetted face and glowing cigarette as wavy, shadowy forms, lurking above me. A long stick distorted by the rippled water into a black lightning bolt arose over the edge of the boat. Newley's rifle! I pushed off the soft lake bottom and a muffled explosion that came from all directions at once filled my ears.

I surfaced near the bow, hiding behind the curvature of the hull, hoping that Newley wouldn't shoot a hole in his own boat to get me. The rocking of the hull and a clumping sound told me Newley was moving forward in the boat.

The clumping stopped, and the side of the boat where I was hiding dipped slightly toward the water. The top of Newley's head and his right eye peeked over the edge of the boat.

"You're as big a fool as your old man," he said. "And you're gonna end up same as him."

He raised the rifle. I did the only thing I could think of. I reached up, grabbed onto the side of the boat, and pulled down with everything I had. The gunwale plunged to an inch below the surface, and Newley pitched headfirst into the lake a yard behind me.

The only way to get into a small aluminum boat from the

water without swamping it is straight over the bow, which is damn hard, or over the center of the stern. If the boat has an outboard motor clamped on its transom, that leaves the bow. I grabbed hold, pulled myself up, and then pushed, like I was getting out of a swimming pool. The tip of the bow poked into my pubic bone as I kicked my feet, frantic that Newley would grab my ankles and pull me back into the lake.

I flopped face-first into the boat, my chin catching the front bench so hard I saw stars. When I straightened up I observed that Newley wasn't coming after me for the moment. He was treading water and looking down, apparently preoccupied with locating his gun. Good.

The outboard seemed a mile away as I stumbled and slogged through Newley's fishing gear, barking my shin on the middle bench, knocking over a bait bucket, getting my foot caught in a fishing net. Blood streamed down my chest. I felt my chin. The fall on the front seat had opened a gash on my chin that gaped like a second mouth.

My father had once shown me how to start an outboard motor. Could my fear-flooded brain remember? Squeeze the fuel pressure bulb until it's firm. Find the choke — it's a little black knob — pull it out partway. Grab the starter handle. Ignore the blood you're smearing everywhere.

The outboard sprang to life with one pull. I remembered to push the choke back in. I remembered how to put it in forward gear and how to operate the throttle.

So open her up and get the hell out of here. Twenty feet of solid acceleration and the boat slowed to a crawl. More throttle didn't help; it was barely moving. What was I doing wrong? I checked the gas gauge, the fuel line, the choke, the throttle.

Then it came to me. How could I have forgotten about the anchor line, after swimming right into it? There it was, tied to a turnbuckle behind the oarlock. Imbecile. I was dragging the goddamn anchor.

Did I have time to stop the boat and raise the anchor before Newley caught up and followed me into the boat? I looked around. Strangely, he was nowhere in sight. He might have been under the bow, preparing to spring aboard. I figured a forty-horse outboard should be able to pull a small anchor across the lake, at least buy me some time. I opened the throttle all the way. The motor roared.

Almost no acceleration. How could this be?

A dark form ascended from the black water thirty feet behind the boat. Newley. He had hold of the anchor and I was pulling him behind the boat like a wake-boarder.

The boat lurched and stalled, lurched and stalled. Newley was pulling himself toward me, hand over hand on the anchor line. His tackle box was open on the floor. I reached in and grabbed the handle of his fillet knife. Keeping my left hand on the tiller, I clenched the sheath in my teeth and pulled the blade out. I stretched toward the rope as far as possible but I could not touch it with the knife. To cut the line I would have to abandon the tiller.

The unpiloted boat crept along as I hacked and slashed at the anchor line. A fillet knife is a very poor tool for slicing through hemp. I had to cut one fiber at a time. Halfway through, I looked back. Newley had closed to within ten feet. He was winning the race. As he hauled himself forward, he was using his feet like rudders to steer the line clear of the propeller.

I didn't want to do hand-to-hand combat with Newley; I would lose. So I decided to go for broke. I lifted the anchor line off the gunwale and got the blade of the knife under the partially cut rope. Then I grabbed the knife handle with both hands and swiped backwards as hard as I could.

The line snapped. The boat veered sharply to port, and took off like a wild stallion. I tumbled backward into the stern, hitting my head on the tackle box. Minnows from the spilled bait bucket flipped and squiggled around me on the floor. Dazed, I struggled to my feet as the bulrushes swept by on both sides. I looked into the black water ahead and saw the beaver nest, hurtling towards me like a meteor out of the dark night. The boat ran aground on the nest and stopped, but I kept going.

With all of the mistakes I made that night, I will give myself credit only for this: in midair, I had the presence of mind to drop the knife. Otherwise, I would have been eviscerated as I slid and tumbled fifty feet across the lily pads.

The water where I came to rest was barely waist deep, but I could not move. A mass of tangled, snarled weeds bound me to the spot. I struggled for several minutes, managing to free one arm and one leg. I looked back toward the beaver nest and saw Newley wading slowly toward me, holding what looked like a huge mushroom in his hand, just above the water. When he closed to twenty feet, I saw that what he held was the boat anchor. He brandished it like the lethal weapon it was.

"I didn't give you permission to come aboard, mother*fucker.*"

At this point, I felt nothing but physical pain. I was almost ready to accept that it was all over. "You gonna kill me, Newley?" I monotoned. "Like you killed my father?"

He cocked his head. "What? You think *I* killed your dad? Asshole."

The water behind Newley erupted, and he appeared inexplicably to whack himself on the side of his head with the anchor. It took me a moment to realize that Luke had silently approached while staying submerged, leapt up and grabbed the shaft of the anchor, and thrust it into Newley's temple. Newley crumpled into the water and Luke stood in his place.

"How you doin', Roomie?" he asked. His voice sounded feeble.

"I've been better."

"Me, too. You almost ran me down. You're not exactly Barnacle Bill the Sailor, are you?"

"No."

He rolled Newley's limp body over and lifted his head out of the water. The blood streaming down his face looked like chocolate syrup in the dim light. "What are we gonna do with this joker? Want to save his sorry ass?"

I didn't want to save Newley. I wanted to tie him to the anchor and drop him in the middle of the lake. Luke told me the bleeding from his gunshot wound had stopped, but he looked like he needed to get to a hospital, fast. I needed medical attention, too. No time to waste on the likes of Bud Newley.

But back then, I was in the habit of doing what I thought

I was supposed to, not what I wanted to. "Let's put him in the boat," I sighed.

I extricated myself from the weeds and we hoisted Newley into his boat. Luke tied Newley's wrists and ankles so he wouldn't give us trouble when he came to. We moved the boat off the beaver nest, me pushing at the bow and Luke pulling at the stern. I knew it couldn't be good news when I heard Luke say, his voice as close to tears as I ever heard it, "Fuckin'-a. We're up shit creek, Roomie."

I climbed off the nest and he showed me the problem. When I ran aground I sheared the outboard motor's cotter pin on a stump. The propeller was gone, buried somewhere in the thick muck. It would take a strong man all night to row back to Thousand Island Lake. I didn't have the strength. Luke didn't have the strength or the time. We looked around for the propeller for ten minutes, longer than it took either of us to realize the search was completely pointless. We spent another ten minutes hunting for flares, an air horn, or anything else in Newley's boat that might help us. Newley groaned and mumbled, but didn't move or talk.

We found nothing of use in the boat. Finally, Luke handed me the pliers he had used to remove the hook from my thumb. He pointed in the direction of our boat, which by that time had foundered.

"You're on again, scuba-boy," he grunted. He sounded awful.

Flotsam — seat cushions, life vests, and bobbers — guided me to the spot where our rented boat lay at the bottom in about ten feet of water. It took me five dives to locate the motor and remove the cotter pin and propeller. It seems crazy to me now, but I remember going down a sixth time in order to release the beautiful walleyed pike Luke had stringered to the boat. Was I that softhearted back then, or was delirium overtaking me? Maybe both.

Another half hour and I had the propeller from our rented boat jerry-rigged onto Newley's motor. Newley struggled feebly and ineffectually to free his bound wrists and ankles.

Luke held on to consciousness long enough to steer us through the channel back to Big Africa Lake, then he settled himself on the floor of the boat and quietly passed out. By that time Newley was wide awake, making me wish Luke had gagged him.

"You'll fuckin' pay for this . . . fuckin' bastard . . . the sheriff's a friend of mine . . . You're fucked, you asshole . . ."

And blah, blah, blah. Newley had incredible energy for a guy with a concussion and an abrasion on the side of his head that looked like a small pepperoni pizza. I futilely attempted over the noise of the outboard to squeeze information out of him about the swindle and my father's death, but all I got was a torrent of invective all the way to a place on Thousand Island Lake called the Outpost Resort.

The proprietor of the Outpost — a spry, elderly man with a deeply lined face and shaggy white hair — insisted on walking down to the pier to get a look at Luke and Newley before he called for an ambulance. I sat on a wooden bench on the pier shivering, watching a half-moon rise over the treetops, worrying myself to nausea about Luke, and listening to a siren get ever so gradually louder until flashing red lights appeared on the surface of the lake.

Luke spent the night at a tiny hospital in Watersmeet, Michigan, as did Newley. When the one emergency physician on duty was finished with them, he stitched up my chin and examined the rest of my vast collection of abrasions and contusions. He took a blood sample, I assumed to confirm his suspicion that the three of us had all been in a drunken brawl. The doctor bandaged some wounds, wrote me prescriptions for painkillers and antibiotics, and told me to take it easy for a few days.

At this point, a very thin, sleepy-looking deputy from the Gogebic Sheriff's Department sauntered into the ER and placed me under arrest.

○ ○

Sheboygan, Day Twenty-One

Car batteries have doubled in price since the last one I bought for the Dodge. I get some curious looks getting on the bus carrying a DieHard in one hand and a bottle of liquor in a brown paper bag in the other. Or maybe it's the ill-fitting jacket with the missing pocket. I guess I do look slightly ridiculous.

The new battery brings the Dodge back to life, but the courthouse is closed at this hour. I'm glad to crawl back inside the house and get a warm brandy into my cold hands.

The letter from Attorney Rozner that I found in my dad's old desk rests on my lap, more recondite now that I take the time to reflect. There's that caption: *"Johnson vs. Bruckner."* This lawyer was writing to my dad about a lawsuit in which somebody named Johnson was suing him. Do I remember anybody named Johnson from my childhood? Sure I do, a bunch of them. A kid in my class in grade school. My aunt and uncle and some distant cousins. A friend of my mom's from the neighborhood. It's a common name.

Why did Johnson sue him? The letter said the case wasn't going to settle, and Rozner came to this conclusion after talking to the plaintiff's attorneys and the attorney for State Farm Insurance. When I was a kid State Farm ran television ads in which the jingle was played by tooting car horns. My best guess is that State Farm carried my dad's auto insurance, and that *Johnson vs. Bruckner* was a lawsuit about a car accident.

I finish my brandy and go up to my old bedroom, where the files that I thought had no use still sit on my former desk. The "A" folder contains several cancelled auto insurance policies, which I had assumed were voided for nonpayment of premium. Sure enough, State Farm insured David Bruckner's 1950 Oldsmobile until the policy was terminated on August 7, 1955. Six months before the date of Attorney Rozner's letter. They probably cancelled the policy because of Johnson's claim. It must have been major.

Major enough that Rozner recommended bankruptcy. From listening in on my parents' arguments, I know that the bankruptcy was filed but not completed because Tom Atkins helped them out with a loan. My mother had said she didn't want to borrow money from Tom "again" to finance development of the Opuba.

None of the other cancelled insurance policies covered a '50 Olds. But I find one on a '48 Buick written by Union Mutual that commenced coverage on August 17, 1955, at a much higher premium than the State Farm policy. It figures my dad would have had to pay for high-risk insurance after getting dropped by State Farm. Apparently, the Olds was totaled. My dad replaced it with a car that was two years older. Not a sign of a guy sprinting up the ladder of success at the age of thirty-four.

The other lawyers and businessmen who wrote to my father signed their letters with their last names, but Rozner signed his "Les." He and my father were probably friends, which might help me get information if Rozner is still alive.

The most cryptic part of the letter is the postscript. *"I asked about Audrey's clothes and toys. You may dispose of them."* Reading it gives me a prickly sensation on the nape of my neck and a hollow twinge in my gut. For reasons I cannot articulate to myself, I am prompted to go look again at the picture of Audrey with me and my parents in front of the lake cottage.

Her right hand holds my father's index finger. In her left hand she is clutching a small figurine that, even though the photo is in black and white, I know has a red hat, green face, blue coat, and yellow pants. It's a plastic Jiminy Cricket, and I know what it looks like because I have seen it many times, most recently about two weeks ago when I was in the basement. *". . . You may dispose of them."* My mother never disposed of anything.

Weird. I played with that little toy as a child many times. In particular, I remember playing with it in our sandbox in the backyard. Whatever happened to our sandbox? Or, for that matter, to sandboxes generally?

I never realized that I had inherited Jiminy from another child. A little girl I don't remember, who I am starting to suspect died in an automobile accident in August of 1955.

17

Sheboygan, Day Twenty-Two

"WE ONLY KEEP CIVIL FILES HERE back twenty-five years. Before that, they're in storage."

The file clerk at the Sheboygan County Courthouse is a dowdy, horse-faced brunette in an out-of-date cardigan sweater and big-frame glasses that are even more out of date. But who am I to criticize, standing here in jeans with holes in the knees and a forty-year-old jacket with a missing pocket? Her facial expression and nasal twang suggest I'm something of an idiot, expecting to find a case file from the '50s in the courthouse file room. I ask her if I can retrieve a case file from 1955 out of storage and she says it will take a week to ten days. I don't have a week to ten days, but I give her the case name anyway.

"Could you also check to see if there's a nineteen fifty-six bankruptcy filed under the name David H. Bruckner?"

In response she gives me a face that says I'm now a complete idiot. "There are no bankruptcies in county court. Bankruptcies are filed in federal court."

"Where's the federal courthouse for Sheboygan?"

She clucks her tongue and rolls her eyes. If there is a rung below complete idiot, I have dropped to it.

"Federal court for the Eastern District of Wisconsin is in

Milwaukee." She looks me up and down. "You're not a lawyer, are you?"

"No. Do I have to be a lawyer to retrieve a case file?"

A disapproving, skeptical look. Attorneys must enjoy the courthouse, if for no other reason than it is one place where you can get a dirty look for saying you're *not* a lawyer. "No," she replies. "What do you want it for?"

Good question. If I give an honest answer — that I'm searching wildly for clues in a possible murder, possible suicide from thirty-six years ago, and trying to find out what happened to a girl who may or may not have been my sister and may or may not have died at the age of three in 1955 — she will recategorize me from idiot to nut case, and might not get me the file.

"The defendant in the case was my father," I say. "I'm the executor of his widow's — my mother's — estate." Completely irrelevant, but true.

"All right," she says, apparently satisfied because my answer was complicated and legal-sounding. "Leave me your phone number and someone will call you when it's in." Her face softens. "I'm sorry about your mother."

Not a bad sort after all. On the way out I notice how similar the neo-Greek architecture of the Sheboygan County Courthouse is to the courthouse in Gogebic County, Michigan, where I spent some time in May of 1974, after my encounter with Bud Newley on the Cisco Chain. Also similar is the feeling of frustration.

o o

May, 1974

"How's the food in jail? Are you getting enough to eat? Are you all right?"

"The food's fine, Mom. I'm okay." Actually the food in the Gogebic County Jail was indescribably horrendous, I'd had almost nothing to eat, and I was not even close to being okay. My body felt as if I'd spent the night in a cement mixer, and I was thoroughly intimidated by the jailhouse *milieu*. My preconceived notion of what jail would be like was way off. I thought I would

143

have one cellmate at the most and sleep on a single bed. But the Gogebic County Jail had one big cell, where I lay awake all night on a cement bunk covered by a foam pad hardly two inches thick, keeping both eyes and both ears open for threatening movements from any of the other seven men in the cell. I sincerely wished I had been more severely injured so I could have spent the night in the hospital like Luke and Newley.

I was so nervous at my bail hearing that my knees trembled and my teeth chattered. Even standing in the narrow hallway outside the visitor's room talking to my mother on the phone raised my apprehensions, as unsavory characters on both sides of the law brushed past me and a guard eavesdropped.

Oddly enough, what scared me the most was neither the deterioration of my health nor the menacing cohabitants of my cell. Not the gruff judge at the bail hearing, not even the looming prosecution. My biggest fear was missing final exams. But catching hell from my mom was a close second.

"How could you do such a stupid thing?"

Tough to answer that, since I wasn't sure what stupid thing she was talking about — there were so many. I guessed she meant landing in jail, although it seemed to me all I had done to accomplish that was try to stay alive. No one had yet explained the charges to me. I assumed they included assault, theft, and who knows, maybe piracy.

"I don't know, Mom. I'm really sorry. Right now I need twenty-five hundred dollars to get out on bail."

I could hear her fingernails clicking at full speed. "Twenty-five *hundred?* Are you kidding? For heaven's sake, Jonathan, you know I don't have that kind of money lying around." Clickety-click-click.

"Well, okay then," I murmured, choking back my impulse to scream in desperation and revulsion. Could I survive another night in this hellhole?

"What? Oh wait, Jonathan. Ray wants to talk to you."

Whoopie, just what I needed. Ray stepping in to play the stern father-figure.

"So, Joe College managed to get himself tossed in the

hoosegow." He sounded cheerful, as if he were getting a big kick out of my predicament.

"Yes, sir."

"What are you doing in the U.P. anyway? Aren't you supposed to be in school?"

"Yes, sir." This was going to be as aggravating and embarrassing as possible. A perfect end to a delightful day. So glad I called.

"So you what — stole some guy's boat?"

"It's a long story."

He chuckled. "I'll bet. And now you need twenty-five hundred bucks from your mommy to make bail."

I wanted to say, "Shove it up your rosy red rectum sideways." But what I said was, "Yes, sir."

"I'll take care of it," he said. "I can wire it from Western Union first thing in the morning."

Total astonishment. Disbelief. Overwhelming gratitude. "Really? I . . . I . . . thank you, Ray."

"Call me 'Dad.' "

Aaack. Overwhelming gratitude or not, that was a tall order. Could I force myself to call Ray 'Dad'? Would the word stick in my throat? Would it make me ill?

Not as ill as more of the Gogebic County Jail cuisine. "Thank you, . . . Dad," I said to Ray.

Sorry, Dad, I said to myself.

○

Kenneth Kelly, the district attorney for Gogebic County, was about five-three, stout, and had bushy gray eyebrows and pointy ears. He resembled a leprechaun, except that he wore a brown herringbone sport coat instead of a green suit. His office was messy and unimposing — linoleum, metal chairs, and a schoolteacher's desk. After I'd been in the room about twenty minutes, the dust in the air and nervous tension triggered a seven-sneeze spasm.

"Bless you, bless you. Or should I say 'Gesundheit'? Bruckner's a German name, now isn't it?" Kelly spoke in a loud voice throughout the entire conversation. "So, at this point you're in

Mr. Newley's watercraft, Mr. Newley is clinging to the anchor line, and young Mr. Willever is in the lake, having been shot in the bum by Mr. Newley." He chuckled. "Then what?"

I told Kelly about how I hit the beaver nest and my momentum carried me into the weed bed, how Newley threatened me with the anchor, how Luke sprang up and rendered Newley unconscious, and how we used the propeller from the other boat to make it back to civilization.

Kelly laughed heartily. "Well, that is a pretty wild tale, Mr. Bruckner, is it not? And you expect a jury to believe all of that, do you? Haw, hawww."

Insecurity permeated every cell of my body, muddling my brain, knotting my stomach, and sapping what little was left of my strength. I had been so naive that I'd waived my rights to counsel and to remain silent, believing what the D.A. said, that if I had nothing to hide the fastest way to get this over with was to simply tell him what happened. Now he was laughing at me. Goddamn, was I stupid at twenty.

"It's the truth," I said.

"Heh, heh, heh. And you swam the entire length of Little Africa Lake under water in the dark. That's a good one, that is."

Jolly fellow. Enjoyed his job, had a sense of humor. Why did I hate him?

"Yes, I did. I'm a certified scruba driver."

"Scruba driver? Haw, haw, haw."

I would have blushed, had I the energy. "I meant scuba diver. I haven't slept in two nights."

Kelly wiped tears from his eyes with his thumb and index finger. He smiled broadly.

"Well, Mr. Bruckner, your story is preposterous. It only has two things going for it. One, the Sheriff's deputies have been up to Little Africa. They found the rifle, the sunken boat with the hole in it, everything exactly as you described it. Two, I talked with your friend Mr. Willever at the hospital two hours ago."

It had not occurred to me that the D.A. may already have spoken to Luke. Kelly had made no mention of it during the interview.

"Mr. Willever," Kelly continued, "told me precisely the same story, to the smallest detail. Except he was shot in the back of the thigh, not in the ass. Even Mr. Newley's version, though different in some respects, has the same general outline."

"So you believe me?"

"It so happens I do, but that's irrelevant." He shook an index finger. "By your own admission, you have violated the laws of the State of Michigan."

Uh-oh. What'd I do? I did not see how anything I had done that night could be construed as theft, assault, piracy, or any other crime. "How so?"

Kelly leaned back in his desk chair and raised his bushy eyebrows. I stifled a sneeze.

"Reckless operation of a motorized watercraft. You left the tiller while the boat was under motor, endangering yourself and others. Plus, disorderly conduct."

Kelly explained my options. Plead guilty to two misdemeanors or be prosecuted for a list of offenses "as long as an elephant's wazoo." I asked what the penalty would be if I pled out. He leaned forward and cleared his throat.

"Time served," he said, "and a fine of," he lifted his chin, "twenty-five hundred dollars."

Ah. I got it. I was startled again by my own naivete, but I recognized that at least in this instance the mercenary character of the system worked in my favor. Kelly knew I got the Western Union wire from Ray. Why do all the work of prosecuting me if he could shake me down for a quick $2500? The point was not to enforce the law, it was to enhance the bottom line.

"What about Luke?" I asked.

"Mr. Willever has already pled guilty to operation of a motorized watercraft while intoxicated and disorderly conduct."

"And Newley?"

"Disorderly conduct. And hunting out of season." Kelly smiled wryly. I couldn't tell if the part about hunting out of season was a joke or not. "Bud's on his way home now, which you can be too, if you're smart."

Anger flashed in my cheeks and bile rose in my throat. "He shot Luke. He tried to shoot me."

Kelly shrugged. "Bud's story differs on that. He says his firearm accidentally discharged when you tipped his boat. His word against yours and Willever's. There's not enough evidence to prosecute for attempted homicide, that's for sure."

I stood and paced while Kelly sat rigidly, elbows on his desk. He knew this was horseshit, letting the local guy off with a fine for two attempted murders. Sweeping the mess under a rug. "Bud" he called him. Did Newley have that kind of clout around here? I suppose anybody had more clout than a couple of scruffy college students from out of state.

"What about his fraud on the Bank of Wisconsin?" I asked. "They've been looking for him for three years. Aren't you going to do anything about that?"

Kelly placed his palms on the top of his desk, as if he were about to push himself up from his chair. It was intended as a signal that he was getting impatient and I had better make up my mind fast whether I was going to take his deal.

"That's a civil matter, between him and the bank. I'm a district attorney, not a collection agency."

I sat back down and held out my hands imploringly. "Mr. Kelly, as I explained, I have reason to believe Mr. Newley may have conspired to murder my father."

Kelly rose. "You have theories and no evidence. Besides, this office doesn't have jurisdiction. Talk to the police in — what was it? Chee-boy-gone? Now, if you don't want to accept the offer, you'll have to excuse me. I have work to do."

I copped the plea, of course. What could I do? It was the only way to get back in time for exams.

o

Luke spent two more days in the hospital receiving IV antibiotics and blood transfusions. I used the time to pop over to Hurley and track down the ex-husband of the hostess at Brent's Camp. The deadbeat dad had a good job with a construction company, and

I returned to Land O' Lakes with enough information to get the hostess's lazy lawyer interested in starting a garnishment.

So the trip up north wasn't a total waste.

I also had time to poke around the courthouse files to see if I could turn up anything on Newley. That's when I found the lawsuit that my dad's private investigator wrote about. Newley's next-door neighbor had sued him over a dog bite. Actually, according to the complaint, dozens of dog bites, all inflicted in one savage attack by that fiendish black Lab that sprang at me and Luke. The complaint also named as a defendant something called "New Bride, Inc." It alleged that New Bride was the "owner of record" of the property on which "said dangerous animal was negligently maintained."

I went to the county real estate records and found the plat map for the northeastern shore of Thousand Island Lake. The complaint had it right. Newley's lake home and a tract of land behind it were owned by New Bride, Inc.

New Bride was the name of a magazine. Why was Newley living in a house owned by the publisher of a magazine for brides? When I visited Luke in the hospital, he had plastic tubes in his arm and up his nose, and he looked as weak as a newborn lamb, but he figured it out in a flash.

"First three letters of Newley," he rasped, "first five letters of Bridette. The two of them bought the property together, in a corporate name so the bank's investigators wouldn't find it. You can check the conveyance to New Bride in the chain of title at the courthouse, and get information from the corporation's annual report by calling the Secretary of State's office in Lansing." He closed his eyes in fatigue. "Bet you'll nail those suckers."

I was amazed that Luke knew so much about corporate filings and real estate records, not to mention the capital of Michigan. His instincts were dead on. My call to Lansing confirmed that the annual report of New Bride, Inc., listed Philip J. Newley and Leon P. Bridette as directors. The property on Thousand Island Lake was conveyed to New Bride, Inc., by warranty deed on January 1, 1971.

The transfer fee was paid on a purchase price of $80,000. The same amount as Newley's debt to the Bank of Wisconsin that he stuck my dad with and then disappeared.

○ ○

The federal courthouse in Milwaukee is a grand neo-Romanesque castle of carved gray granite, with an ornamental exterior, arched windows, a high square tower, and pinnacles that remind me of a French cathedral. It is located in the highest-rent section of the downtown commercial district. The enormous atrium is toasty warm in the dead of winter, and the sound of my footsteps echoes off the glass ceiling through thousands of cubic feet of wasted tax dollars.

This time I have called ahead to be sure the file I want, the bankruptcy my parents filed for, will be here. I sit in a small carrel in a cavernous room and open a manila folder containing a yellowed document headed "United States Bankruptcy Court, Eastern District of Wisconsin, Voluntary Petition." On the top sheet are my parents' names, address, statistical information, and boxes to check to indicate estimated assets and debts. Estimated assets are "$5,000 to $10,000." No surprise. Estimated debts are "$50,000 to $100,000." High, but still no surprise.

I wade through three pages to the "List of Creditors Holding 20 Largest Unsecured Claims." All twenty spaces are filled. Funny. In 1956, my parents owed money on appliances that are still in the damn house.

Here's a shocker. The largest claim by far is for $50,000. The creditor is "The Estate of Audrey Penelope Johnson, a minor," the personal representative of which is Stanley P. Johnson.

Uncle Stan.

18

THE WIND OFF LAKE MICHIGAN IS BRUTAL. To climb into the Dodge I need to put my shoulder to the door and my foot to the rocker panel. My stomach kicks acid into my throat and my hands shake as I fumble with the keys.

Why am I shocked? I remember my parents' big argument about my father's decision to sell the Waterford crystal so he could buy a boat to test the Opuba. At the climax of the fight, when they were both fairly plastered, my father lashed out that my mother's brother-in-law was a "sum-mo-bitch," who had tried to ruin our family financially. My mother responded that the blame lay with "the shyster lawyers."

Three and half decades later I know what they were talking about. The brother-in-law (Louise had three) was Uncle Stan, my Aunt Melanie's husband. A smiley, placid guy who was confined to a wheelchair, Stan was apparently the Johnson in *Johnson vs. Bruckner.* He sued my parents. It doesn't seem like something quiet old Uncle Stan would do, but it doesn't shock me. If Audrey was his daughter and she was injured in a car crash, his lawyer might have started a lawsuit to get a settlement out of State Farm. Nothing personal.

Was Audrey my cousin? That would explain the entry in the bankruptcy file and her facial resemblance to me. My mother had once told me Melanie and Stan couldn't have children because of Stan's war injury. Is that why my stomach is sour and my hands are trembling on the steering wheel? Because I feel betrayed?

What a secret to keep from me and Jamie. What a deception to perpetrate on your kids. But even that should not throw me for much of a loop. I always knew my mother swept anything unpleasant under the rug. My father even joked once that her name should be Cleopatra because she was "Queen of de Nile."

No, what has jolted me is that I finally know how much I do not know, and I suspect that the hidden cousin is the tip of an iceberg of concealment. I am headed back to the house on Foxglove Lane to continue digging, realizing that I underestimated the hazards of the job.

My brother was smart to stay away.

o o

June, 1974

The only academic distinction I achieved in two years at college is that I probably set the University of Wisconsin all-time record for sophomore slump. I took finals distracted, exhausted, and unprepared. My grade point average dropped from an A minus to a C minus.

Luke, the son of a gun, held on to his B-plus average without cracking a book and in spite of drinking every night of exam period.

Wendy sent me a typed letter on magenta stationery asking me to leave her VW in the parking lot near Bascom Hall and mail her the keys. She enclosed a self-addressed envelope. Luke asked me if I thought Wendy and I were broken up for good. When I said yes, he inquired whether I would mind if he asked her out next semester. I lied and said I wouldn't mind at all.

After exams I took the Greyhound bus to Sheboygan, not to spend the summer with Ray, Louise, and Jamie, but to use the house on Foxglove Lane as a place to stay for a couple of weeks while I continued my investigation. I had arranged for Jamie, who had passed his driver's license test a month earlier, to pick me up.

Instead, Ray pulled up in his hulking V-8 Chrysler.

"Hey, Ray. Where's Jamie?"

"Aren't you going to call me 'Dad'?"

"Oh, sure." Maybe with careful phrasing, I could avoid calling him anything.

"Your brother is at home. His license is suspended."

That was quick. Ray's car had air conditioning, which none of my parents' cars had ever had. They both always insisted air conditioning was unnecessary in Wisconsin if you lived near Lake Michigan. Ray had his air on so high I felt like I was getting frostbite.

"Did he have an accident? Or just get a bunch of tickets?"

"Neither," said Ray. He rolled down his window, hawked, spit, and rolled the window back up. "That turban-head shrink ratted him out."

"What? You mean Dr. Patel, the psychiatrist?"

"That's the one. Doctor Benedict Arnold Nehru. He sent a letter to the Department of Motor Vehicles saying it wasn't safe for Jamie to drive because of his medical condition. Never trust an Indian."

Ray drove with one hand. Not even a hand, only his left wrist draped casually over the top of the steering wheel, his right elbow resting on the console. It made me nervous.

"What, exactly, is Jamie's medical condition . . ." I almost said, "Ray"; then I almost said, "Dad"; then I said, "if you know."

" 'Course I know. Whose health insurance do you think is paying for this horse patootie? Jamie's on medication for schizophrenia."

The word terrified me. I knew a little bit about it from my psychology course, but only that it involved bizarre delusions and auditory hallucinations. And that it was very bad.

"Jamie is psychotic? I've never seen any sign of that."

"Well, actually," said Ray, pausing a moment to spit out the window again, "Dr. Maharajah's letter to the DMV said something about 'prodromic stage.' I guess that means Jamie's only got one foot off the curb so far, but the other one is on a banana peel. If you ask me, what the boy needs is a summer job working outdoors, one that will help him burn off some energy. And a good swift kick in the keester."

Little as I knew, I doubted that Ray's prescription would do Jamie any good. It reminded me of the episode at Easter, when Ray got rough with Jamie for setting off homemade gunpowder in the house. In an effort to impress Wendy I had said I was going to talk to Dr. Patel, which had flustered my mother. There was no more need to impress Wendy, but I was now much more worried about Jamie than before. I resolved to see Patel as soon as I could.

The house smelled as if someone living there didn't bathe, and when I saw Jamie it was obvious he was the source. He sat in "Dad's chair," the red and gold striped overstuffed easy chair in the living room, wearing a bathrobe at four in the afternoon, watching a children's show on the Philco. His hair was tangled, and his face and hands were orange from the cheese curls he was wolfing down. He had gained a lot of weight since Easter.

"Hey, Jamie, how's it going?"

He didn't budge. "Hey! Jamie!"

He turned slowly and stared at me with a blank expression in his eyes, like nothing was registering. Where, I wondered, was the energy Ray thought Jamie needed to burn off?

"Yeah," said Jamie. The slightest trace of his lopsided grin appeared. I was glad to see it.

"Want to hit a little ping-pong?" I asked, miming the act of hitting a ball with my open hand. When he didn't reply, I said, "Bet I can spot you five points and still take you."

To my astonishment and dismay, he did not rise to the bait. "Yeah," he said in a dull tone. "Maybe later."

What had they done to my brother? The fifth stair tread squeaked a snide welcome home as I ascended to my room, which had remained unchanged in the two years since I graduated from high school. I found Louise in what I still referred to as my parents' bedroom. She was putting on makeup.

"Mom. What's wrong with Jamie?"

She smooshed her lips together to spread the crimson gloss. "Nothing. He's much better now. The question is, Jonathan, what's wrong with you?"

"What do you mean?"

"Your grades came in the mail today."

I knew the grades were addressed to me, but there was no point in arguing about it. My mother always opened my mail, no matter how indignant I got. Her position was: if it came to her house, it was her mail.

"Sophomore slump," I shrugged. "Happens to everybody."

"Especially if they spend half of exam period in the clink," she rejoined. "For heaven's sake, Jonathan, have you forgotten the terms of your scholarship?"

I had not. I was painfully aware that my scholarship was conditioned on my maintaining a C plus average. My precipitant plunge had dropped me below the mark.

"It's only one semester. Besides, in-state tuition at UW is so cheap I can make enough at my summer job to cover it." I had already lined up a job at a warehouse in Madison.

She clamped an eyelash curler to the lashes of her right eye and squeezed. Watching it made my own eyelid flicker. She looked at me from under her distended eyelid and said, "You could save more if you got a job in Sheboygan and lived here."

We had already beat that horse to death. My mom couldn't understand why I did not leap at the chance to spend my summer under the same roof with Ray and Jamie.

"The place in Madison will only cost me sixty-five dollars a month, Mom. I'm rooming with four other guys."

"And four thousand cockroaches."

"The warehouse job in Madison pays good," I said.

"Not as good as the job you were offered at Falls Dieworks."

How did she know about the job Leon Bridette had offered me? I hadn't said anything about it to her. She must have been talking to Bridette, which disturbed me. But I let it drop. When my mother argued, I could see where Jamie got his tenacity. That is, the tenacity he had before it was doped out of him.

"Does Jamie have to be on so much medication?" I asked.

She dabbed powder on her face. It made me sneeze.

"Oh, yes. Absolutely. For his own safety. Gesundheit."

"What did he do?"

She raised her chin and turned her face this way and that, checking the finished product in the mirror. I was finally old enough to see her as something other than just a mother, and realize she had exceptional looks for a woman her age. Probably could have been in the movies.

"He tried to set a fire in the garage with gunpowder. We had to call the fire department. He's completely withdrawn, failing in school. He was talking to himself, even during class. Plus, he was starting to have delusions."

"What sort of delusions?"

She stood up and brushed stray powder from her dress. "What's the difference? I told you, Jon, it was very hard on Jamie when your father took his own life. It didn't help when you went off to college. He doesn't have any friends."

Louise would not tell me what Jamie's delusions were, but from her segue to my father's death, I gathered they had something to do with that. She had also said *I* was delusional when I told her I thought Dad may have been murdered. She insisted that my father's death was a suicide, "and that's that."

When she and Ray went out for their regular Friday night fish fry, I got out the yellow pages and looked up my brother's psychiatrist, Prashant K. Patel, M.D. The following Monday I called and made an appointment to see him.

o

"There is no question that the development of this category of disorder is accelerated by stress," said Dr. Patel. He spoke with a pleasant, rhythmic cadence. His face was smooth and dark as mahogany, with small, even features, except for eyes that were slightly buggy. He wore plastic-framed glasses and used pomade in his jet-black hair, which was unusual at the time. He looked about thirty-five and had a somber but soothing demeanor. "No question, the same stress has also had a profound effect on you. How are you managing your schoolwork?"

"Fine," I lied. The point of this visit, which was costing me fifty bucks, was to talk about Jamie, not me. "But I haven't been subjected to the same stress as Jamie. What has he told you about his stepfather, Ray?"

The psychiatrist tented his fingers and drew his dark eyebrows together. "As I have made clear, I cannot repeat to you anything Jamie has said to me in therapy. But you are certainly free to tell me anything you think I should know about his relationship with his stepfather."

"Ray hits him."

A quick widening of his eyes told me this was news to Dr. Patel. How could he have failed to pull that little tidbit out of Jamie? Maybe Ray had cowed Jamie into keeping his mouth shut.

"Would that be bad for Jamie?" I asked.

"I could hardly imagine anything worse," said Dr. Patel. "Do you have feelings of resentment toward your stepfather?"

Back to me again. "I'm not making it up, Doctor. Would Jamie require such heavy medication if he wasn't being subjected to such . . . stress?"

Patel straightened the pencils on his desk, which had been fairly straight already. His small office was quite tidy, clean, and modern. Lots of diplomas and certificates on the walls. No couch.

"As I have said from the outset, I cannot discuss the specifics of Jamie's diagnosis or treatment. I can tell you as a general matter that physical punishments do more harm than good in these cases. But even without them, the disorder is always progressive."

I hadn't known that. My bowels went watery. Dear God, Jamie.

"Current thinking," continued the doctor, "is that early treatment including medication may retard the development of symptoms. Is there anything else I can help you with?"

There was, but how could I get him to talk about it? "My mother said Jamie was having delusions. Has Jamie ever talked about . . ."

"I cannot repeat anything he said . . ."

" . . . in therapy, yes, I know," I said. "But, Doctor, if his reported delusions have anything to do with my father's death, I might have some information that would be helpful. If, by any chance, my brother thinks my father was murdered, and you've been led to believe he's the only one who thinks so, well, he isn't."

Dr. Patel leaned back and placed his fingers together, tapping his thumbs. He looked perplexed. "You also think this?"

Ha. I got Patel to unintentionally confirm it: Jamie thought Dad was murdered. "Yes," I said. "I'm actively investigating it."

He straightened his pencils again. "How is your sleeping?"

"My sleeping? I don't know. I don't need much sleep."

"Do you often feel fatigued?"

"I'm not here to talk about myself, Dr. Patel."

"Perhaps you should be. I am seeing here a young man who is brooding about the past, not getting adequate sleep, failing in school and lying to me about it. You are obviously suffering from either an affective disorder or an adjustment disorder, which is entirely to be expected after what has happened to you."

Goddamn son of a bitch. Who was he to tell me I had a disorder? Okay, a psychiatrist, that's who. Nevertheless.

"I have a disorder because I'm interested in how my father died?"

"But this has happened nearly three years ago." His normally smooth voice squeaked. "It should not be the focal point of your life."

"If he was murdered, I need to know who did it."

The doctor waived his soft, brown hands and shook his head. "This is merely a diversion you are using to avoid facing your grief. What you need is to accept your father's death. With this, therapy could help."

This was not my preconceived notion of what psychiatry was like. What about all the gags on television about shrinks being supremely passive, saying nothing at all except, "Go with that," until you had been in analysis for years? This guy was assertive. But he seemed genuinely eager to help. He had an empathetic expression on his face.

"What if . . ." My throat clutched. "What if someone in my own family. You know."

The doctor took a prescription pad and a ballpoint pen from his desk. "I am going to give you something that will help with your sleeping. Tell me, do you have feelings of sadness or hopelessness on most days?"

"I don't know. I guess I'm not exactly ecstatic all the time. So? It's not like I'm fifteen years old anymore."

Patel put down the pen and pad and leaned forward. He raised his index finger and smiled. "What an interesting comment you have made. Do you see? For some reason, you have associated feelings of joy with being fifteen years old. Think back. What happened when you were fifteen?"

He got me. I didn't have to think back for more than five seconds before I vividly recollected warm afternoon sun on my skin, the taste of salt and beer on my lips, exhilaration, triumph, the sound of my father's voice, the words "unlimited potential," and a magnificent view of the azure water sparkling beneath Seven Mile Bridge.

19

THE DAY AFTER MY CONSULTATION WITH DR. PATEL I drove my mother
to the Piggly Wiggly so I could borrow her car for the day. It was
a hot day and we had the windows rolled down. We both had
pollen allergies and were sneezing up a storm as we shared a box of
Kleenex that sat between us on the front seat.

"And why are you going to the police station?"

"To look at the police report from when Dad died."

"For heaven's sake, Jonathan. Haven't you wasted enough time
on that?"

"No."

My mother pulled a couple of tissues from the box. Another
did not pop up — the box was empty. She carefully separated
the plies so we would not run out. Did that woman have ways to
stretch a dollar, or what?

"David committed suicide, and that's that."

"We'll see."

Clickety-clickety-click-click.

o

I spent most of that day at the police station in the waiting area,
waiting. Waiting for a receptionist to appear on the other side of

the glass partition. Waiting for the receptionist to find a policeman who could help me. Waiting for the policeman to find the forms I had to fill out in order to review the police report. Waiting for the policeman and receptionist to find an officer with authority to approve the request. Waiting for the three of them to find the report.

They stuck me in a tiny interior room with cement-block walls, no windows, a metal table, and plastic chairs. The room smelled like restroom disinfectant. The only document they gave me was two pages long.

> Case Number SD 10/28/71 4091;
> Incident: Death, Probable suicide;
> Reporting officer: Deputy Detective Robert Adams;
> Date of Report: October 29, 1971

> At about 1930 hours on 28th October, 1971, I met with Jonathan Bruckner, age 17, at 5451 Foxglove Lane regarding the death of David Bruckner. J. Bruckner said he was the son of the deceased and was the caller who requested ambulance that delivered D. Bruckner to St. Nicholas Hosp. He said he came home from school at 1900 hours and found D. Bruckner unconscious in car in garage, overhead door closed, engine running. I conducted a survey of the scene but found no items to retrieve. I took photographs of the car, 1962 Buick LeSabre License No. HTB 724.

> I met with Louise Bruckner at about 1945 hours. L. Bruckner said she was wife of deceased. She said she had been at work and at the home of her sister. She works at Piggly Wiggly on 17th Avenue. Her sister lives at 3270 Sycamore Blvd.

> L. Bruckner said D. Bruckner has been severely depressed and drinking heavily. She said D. Bruckner is unemployed and has family history of mental illness.

I obtained a sworn statement from L. Bruckner and provided her with case number and Information Pamphlet 69-SS listing County social services.

A blinding rage overtook me for several minutes, and I didn't know why. Maybe it was because the report seemed so dismissive of my father. It paid scant attention to any but the most irrelevant details. Boiled down, all it said was "local man found dead in garage."

Deputy Adams was careful to state the times of his interviews, but the report said nothing about the time of my call requesting the ambulance. Also, nothing about the medical examination at the hospital. The report mentioned photographs. Where were they? I suspected the police had not given me all the documents I wanted.

"On the form, you requested the police report," said the receptionist, a bleached blonde in her 60s whose squirming mouth kept up a running battle to hold her dentures in place. "That's what you got. You didn't ask for the whole case file."

I fought to conceal my exasperation. "I want the whole case file."

"Please have a seat."

More waiting. More filling out forms. More authorizations. Before they were ready to give me the file it was 3:00 and I had to leave to drive Louise home. She gave me a hard time about having wasted the day and said she needed the car to pick up Jamie from school, where he was in "special" classes now. He had lost his bus pass after some "trouble" on the bus.

I got my rusted old bicycle out of the garage, inflated the desiccated tires, and pedaled, hot and sweaty, back to the police station. It was hard work because the rear tire was out of round and rubbed on the fender.

The case file was waiting for me. In addition to the police report it contained a report of the ambulance dispatch, photographs of my father's car, an "Affidavit of Louise W. Bruckner," and a "Final Report" form from Deputy Detective Adams that unsurprisingly concluded that the death was a suicide. The last document in the file bore the caption "Office of the Sheboygan County Coroner: Autopsy No. 932A-12."

The coroner's report listed my father's name, a case number, a date, and the name of the county coroner, Benjamin Garry. It had a paragraph of "General Findings" that described my father as a "well nourished Caucasian male with a weight of 185 lbs and a height of 71 inches," his mouth as "dentulous" and his scalp as "unremarkable." Hey, no hair loss at all at the age of 50, I would call that remarkable. The pH of his arterial blood was 7.01

There were several paragraphs of "Gross and Microscopic Findings," including that his heart was of a normal shape and size, his lungs were edematous, his testicles were non-fibrous, and his brain weighed 1480 grams. I tried not to picture my father's brain plopping onto a scale like a wet salmon fillet.

The "Toxicologic Findings" reported blood ethanol of 0.30 dL, and a "COHb" saturation of 72%. Under "Blood Drug Screen" it said, "Positive screen – $C_6H_{12}O$ (approx. 0.005dL)."

The "Conclusion" was that "the victim died from asphyxiation due to inhalation of carbon monoxide."

Before I left, I asked the receptionist if Deputy Detective Robert Adams still worked for the Sheboygan Police Department. Yes, only he was no longer "Deputy," he was a full detective. He worked the graveyard shift.

I rode my bicycle to the public library and confirmed what I suspected, that COHb is carbon monoxide and $C_6H_{12}O$ is paraldehyde, the chemical I smelled in Luke's hospital room and remembered from the day I found my father in the garage with the engine running. On the way home, the rear tire of my bike blew out. I was overheated and exhausted and the bike was a worthless hunk of junk that had been gathering dust in the garage for years. So I walked the bike to the nearest grocery store and heaved it into a green dumpster. That left me a two-mile walk home, but at least I didn't have to push the damn bike.

"You're late for dinner," blared my mother. "My God, that boy is always late for dinner! If I had a nickel for every time he was late for dinner."

The last time I had been late for dinner was thirteen years before, when I was seven. "Sorry, Mom," I said.

Ray and Jamie sat at the kitchen table, silently eating roast beef and mashed potatoes. The kitchen was stifling. Ray and Louise wore shorts and T-shirts, Jamie was still in his bathrobe. Sweaty, weary, and irritable, I helped myself and pretended to salt my potatoes, so Ray wouldn't salt them for me.

"See you got the old bike out of the garage," said Ray. "I've been meaning to fix that baby up." He patted his stomach. "I could use the exercise."

"I threw it away," I said.

Ray grabbed the edge of the table and turned. "You *what?*"

"Threw it away. It was a piece of crap."

He gave me the pointed index finger. "Hey!" I guessed that meant he didn't like the word "crap." "Who gave you permission to throw it out?"

"It's my bike."

"No, sireee," said Ray. "You don't live here anymore. Anything you left behind belongs to your mother and me. I was planning to use that bicycle."

The kitchen was a hundred degrees and I was beat and I couldn't take another ounce of Ray's bullshit. For once, I let my thoughts slip out.

"Don't make me laugh. You're not taking up cycling."

"I could do twenty miles a day."

"You're full of shit, *Moldy.*"

Ray got red in the face. "You mind your language." He shot a quick jab to my arm. Dirty fighter that he was, he had the knuckle of his middle finger out, so it hurt like hell.

Anger flared in me. I stood up so fast I knocked my chair over. Ray rose and faced me. We squared off and clenched our fists. This was it. Jamie looked at me with the first sign of life I had seen in his face since I got home. I looked back at him. He clenched his teeth and grimaced. His upper lip twitched. His eyes lit up.

"Kill him!" he implored.

"Oh, for heaven's sake," said my mother. "The food is getting cold. Sit down and eat."

We sat down and ate.

o

Shortly after midnight I got out of bed and sneaked out of the house. It was a balmy night, rare in Sheboygan. A full moon illuminated the long driveway down the side of the yard. To avoid waking Ray and Louise I put the car in neutral and rolled it out to the street before starting it.

The police station was so quiet you could hear doughnuts being dunked. Other than the usual legion of winos applying for positions in emergency detention, nothing much went on in Sheboygan in the wee smalls that made work for the cops. Nonetheless, they had me cool my heels in the waiting area for forty minutes before Detective Adams was ready to see me.

"I remember the case," he said in the same deep, raspy voice I remembered. The sound of it made me queasy and brought a sheen of cold sweat to my brow. Bad associations. "You hauled your father out on the front lawn and attempted CPR. You're a gritty kid."

Adams did not receive me in his office. We sat in the same small room with the cement-block walls and the plastic chairs that I had used to review the case file. Maybe the detective's office had evidence from secret investigations lying around. More likely it was too messy for visitors. Adams himself looked unkempt.

"Have you reviewed the case file?" I asked.

"Not lately." The manila folder I had seen earlier lay on the table in front of him. He tapped it with his finger. "Like I said, I remember the case. Obvious suicide." He produced a couple of saliva bubbles on the tip of his tongue and popped them between his lips. "How are you and your mom doing?"

"Fine. Do you remember if you read the coroner's report before you prepared your final report?"

He straightened up in his chair a smidgen. "Of course I did.

What are you driving at?"

"Look at it. Read the toxicology part."

He kept his eyes on me as he picked up the folder and opened it. I should have expected resentment, that he would interpret what I was doing as questioning the competence of his work. That would have been the correct interpretation.

"What about it?" He flicked the page with his fingernails. "High blood alcohol, trace of something in the drug screen, but it was the monoxide that did him in. You don't get that level of saturation unless you're suckin' it in thick right to your last breath."

"Do you know what $C_6H_{12}O$ is?"

He popped three sets of bubbles on his lips and scratched his chin before he answered. "The coroner told me. I think he said it was some sort of tranquilizer."

"Paraldehyde," I said.

"If you know, why did you ask me?"

He had me there. I was being coy. Might as well come right out with it.

"Detective, I don't think my father committed suicide. I think he was murdered."

Adams rolled his head this way and that, as if to relieve the pain in the neck I was giving him. "I don't blame you," he said. "Tough thing for a kid, his father taking his own life. Probably felt like he was abandoning you."

He was right. It *had* felt like that, until the day I walked into Luke's hospital room and smelled the paraldehyde. That had made me see that my father didn't abandon us. Now I needed to make the detective see.

"Don't you think it's possible that someone used the paraldehyde, in combination with the alcohol, to knock my father out, then left him in the garage with the engine running to make it look like suicide?"

"Anything's possible. It's a lot more likely your father was abusing tranquilizers and drinking because he was out of work and depressed. We base our conclusions on evidence. The evidence pointed to suicide."

"With suicide, isn't there usually a note?"

"Not always. With murder, there's usually a motive. The investigation failed to identify anyone with any reason to kill the victim, except . . ." He paused, scratched his nose, popped some saliva bubbles. "Well, frankly, except his wife. Sorry. But she had an alibi. We checked it out."

I had my own manila folder, and at that point I placed it on the table and opened it. "There were two men who had motive to kill my father. Philip J. Newley, formerly of Oostburg, and Leon Bridette."

The cop put his hands up and waved them. "Whoa, whoa, whoa. You mean Mr. Bridette who runs the Dieworks?"

"That's right."

He put his hand over his mouth, failing to conceal a smirk. Then he tried hard to look compassionate, but vestiges of the smirk distorted his attempt and he looked patronizing. "He fired your dad, didn't he? I don't blame you for hating him. But you better watch it, kid. You're slandering a guy who's got more lawyers than Richard Nixon. And better ones."

I proceeded to show the detective a series of documents, explaining what each one was and its significance. The letter from the Bank of Wisconsin to David Bruckner. A copy of the deed conveying the land in Upper Michigan to New Bride, Inc., with a copy of the transfer tax return showing the purchase price of the land as $80,000, the exact amount of the bank loan. A certificate I had obtained from the Michigan Secretary of State's office showing Newley and Bridette as directors of New Bride, Inc.

"Newley and Bridette were fishing buddies who found a highly desirable piece of vacation property on the Cisco Chain, at a favorable price," I said. "They invented the lunch tray business to get a loan from the bank, and Bridette induced a couple of employees to guarantee the loan. Newley took off with the money and bought the property, in a corporate name to cover his tracks and so Bridette's complicity would be concealed. I heard my father tell my mother he was working day and night to find Newley. He must have been getting too close."

Detective Adams studied the documents. He scratched his

head. He scratched his nose. He surreptitiously scratched his crotch. He was an itchy guy. Finally, he leaned back in his chair and sighed.

"I'm not going to reopen the investigation of your father's death, at least not yet. I am going to talk to the chief about investigating the bank fraud. Thanks for bringing this to my attention."

Detective Adams followed me out to the parking lot. As I got in the car, he said, "You know, Newley is probably long gone by now."

"I know," I said. "But Bridette isn't."

o

I killed the engine at the end of the driveway and coasted into the garage. The light was on in the kitchen as I entered through the front door as silently as possible. Now don't forget to skip that fifth tread. . . .

"Jonathan, where the hell have you been?" My mother's voice, from the kitchen. I went in and sat down at the gray Formica table across from her and her box of Kleenex. She was wearing pajamas and smoking a Tareyton.

"I went to the police station to meet with the detective who investigated Dad's death."

She drew in a lungful of smoke and exhaled it through her nose. Maybe she thought that would soothe her sinuses.

"What did he have to say?"

"He's going to look into opening an investigation of the fraud on the Bank of Wisconsin."

"What about David's . . . suicide?"

"Not at this time."

She stubbed out her cigarette and stood up. "Good. Now I'm not asking, I'm telling you, Jonathan, let it go. Do you hear me? You're ruining everything for yourself with this nonsense. Promise me you'll let it go."

I didn't promise, and I sure as hell didn't let it go.

20

IN MY FATHER'S OBITUARY, the Sheboygan *Press-Gazette* quoted Leon Bridette, even though my father didn't work for him anymore. The local paper ran every press release Falls Dieworks issued, no matter how dull or insignificant the story, and every one included a quotation from Leon Bridette. Any article in the *Press-Gazette* that included comment from anyone about how this or that might affect the business environment in Sheboygan included comment from Leon Bridette.

Why was it, then, that he was not quoted in the squib the paper ran on the 24th of June, in the "Crime Blotter" section, along with the shopliftings, domestic "incidents" and vandalism?

> Fraud charged: Thursday, the Sheboygan County District Attorney issued charges against Leon P. Bridette of Sheboygan Falls for conspiracy to obtain property by fraudulent means. The District Attorney's office declined to comment.

That was it. One of the biggest shots in town was charged with fraud and the local paper didn't run a story. Maybe Falls Dieworks owned a chunk of the paper.

To my sheer delight, however, the Milwaukee *Journal* covered the story, so thousands of people all over southeastern Wisconsin read about Bridette and Newley and the "alleged" scam to cheat the Bank of Wisconsin out of eighty K. I was both distressed and relieved that the story mentioned neither David Bruckner nor his death.

I went back to the police station and talked to Detective Adams. He explained that the police didn't have enough evidence to charge Bridette and Newley with conspiracy to commit homicide, but he was sure that when it came time to sentence Bridette the judge would "take it into account" that the fraud may have "contributed to" my father's death. The phrase "contributed to" angered me — it was such sickening bullshit. What he meant was that the police were officially sticking with their conclusion that my dad committed suicide, but that one of the reasons he did it was the bank debt. Along with his failed marriage and the fact that he was nuts.

Adams also said Bridette was lucky the Bank of Wisconsin was a state bank or he would have been up on federal charges. I didn't understand how that could make any difference. The detective told me that if I wanted to I could pursue my murder theory "privately." It took me a day to realize that he meant talk to a private investigator.

At that point I was as broke as the Ten Commandments. I couldn't afford to hire a P.I. On the other hand, I felt that my own investigation had been pathetically inept, and I was out of ideas. So three days before I was to return to Madison to start my summer job in the warehouse, I met with Herbert Tierney of Gamma Investigations, Inc. I selected him because he had a no-frills listing in the Yellow Pages, which I hoped meant he would be cheaper than the outfits that paid for ads.

Tierney did not look like the ex-police detective I had assumed most private dicks were. He was slight of build, stoop-shouldered, buck-toothed, and he reeked of nerdiness and witch hazel. My hope that he would be cheap was bolstered by his office, which was a ten-by-twelve-foot walk-up over a used furniture store. It reeked of Glade air freshener.

"I dunno, but I got to tell ya, the odds aren't good." For a skinny, wimpy-looking guy, Tierney had an incredibly deep voice. "Three-year-old murders almost never get solved."

"But this one," I explained, "has never been professionally investigated. The police never considered any possibility other than suicide. Besides," I added, "I think I know who did it."

Tierney leaned forward and his swivel chair groaned. Several houseflies flitted about his desktop. His office furniture all looked like stuff the store downstairs had rejected. Tierney wore shabby khakis and a faded blue workshirt pilled around the collar. I don't know how I expected a private eye to dress, but it wasn't like this.

"Who?" he asked. Not patronizing or skeptical, like the police detective, just matter of fact and respectful.

"Him," I said. I handed Tierney a copy of the Milwaukee *Journal* article about the charges against Leon Bridette.

The shamus leaned back. His chair moaned like a water buffalo. He perused the article, then he rolled his tongue over the front of his buck teeth and grimaced.

"You think the president of Falls Dieworks killed your father?"

"Yes." I explained how, in order to defraud the bank, Bridette got my father and another man to guarantee the $80,000 loan, and I described how my father said he was working day and night to track down Bridette's accomplice, Philip Newley. "Then, I find my father dead in the garage, an apparent suicide, but I smell this strange odor on him. Two years later, I figured out that the odor was paraldehyde. It's a sedative. His autopsy turned it up, but the police ignored it."

Tierney chewed on this for a minute, studying me and shooing flies. "The bank investigators and the police couldn't find Newley," he finally said. "Was your dad smart enough to succeed where they failed?"

"He was the smartest person I've ever known."

The P.I. half-shrugged. "Not smart enough not to sign the guarantee. Sorry. Who's this other guy who cosigned?"

"I don't know."

"Think he might have been in on it?"

This had never occurred to me. Why hadn't I tried to find

the other guarantor? Because my mother had dismissed him as a "patsy"?

"I don't know."

Tierney peppered me with questions. Did the police dust for prints? Did you? Where were Newley and Bridette the day of the murder? (Yes! He called it "the murder" — he was taking me seriously!) Does paraldehyde have any industrial uses? Might they use it at the Dieworks? The more questions he asked, the more I realized I needed his help.

"How much do you charge?" I remembered an old movie in which Humphrey Bogart, portraying a private detective, said he got something like 25 bucks a day.

"Fifty dollars an hour," Tierney said. I almost puked. At that rate, if he had any work at all, he would have a better place than this dump.

"Oh, well, thanks for your time." I stood up to leave.

He raised a hand. "Hold on there, Mr. Bruckner." I wasn't used to a grownup calling me "Mr. Bruckner." He lowered his hand and I sat back down.

"The case intrigues me," he said in his *basso profundo* voice. "I must admit, if you turned out to be right about Bridette, the publicity would be worth plenty to Gamma Investigations. It would put me on the map. You got a job for the summer?"

"Yes. In a warehouse, in Madison."

"Too bad. We could have worked something out." He looked around, as if noticing for the first time that there weren't any secretaries or assistants about. He moved his open hands back and forth, like he was juggling horizontally. "You know, trade my services for yours?"

○

"For heaven's sake, Jonathan, don't be ridiculous." Fingernails clicking like knitting needles as we sat at dinner that evening.

"I thought you'd be happy, Mom. You said you wanted me to stay in Sheboygan for the summer."

"Not playing cops and robbers and stirring up more trouble."

Trouble for whom, I wondered. Louise and Ray had both seen the Milwaukee *Journal* article about the charges against Leon Bridette, but neither one of them had said one word to me about my role in the case. They were both conspicuously silent on the subject, but I had not bothered to try to figure out why. That my mother said "more" trouble was her first reference to the fact that my visit to the police station had been effective, and that she wasn't happy about it.

Ray sawed his round steak with vigorous thrusts and chewed like a contented cow. Jamie sat in blank despondency, pushing around pieces of meat that, I was dismayed to observe, my mother had pre-sliced. Doped up as Jamie was, some part of him had to be painfully chagrined at this regression, his mom cutting up his food for him.

"That was a very good job you had lined up in Madison," Louise continued. "You might need that money for school."

Funny, before Gamma Investigations offered me work, my mother had disparaged the warehouse job in Madison. Now it was a "very good job," if the alternative was bartering my services as an errand boy/assistant in exchange for Herb Tierney's professional help investigating my father's murder.

"I still have my scholarship," I said, although I knew that with my plunging grade point average it might be yanked at any time, "and Gamma Investigations is paying me almost as much as the warehouse, minus Mr. Tierney's fees. Plus, I'll save money living at home." Staying at the house on Foxglove Lane was a grievous sacrifice for me, but one I was willing to make to pursue my obsession.

Ray and Louise looked at each other. With a subtle shift of her head and the twitch of an eyebrow, my mother signaled Ray that she wanted him to step in. They had achieved a near-telepathic level of communication, something I had never seen between my parents.

Ray cleared his throat. "Son, I don't think that's such a good idea, you staying here."

"Since when? All I've heard for the past two weeks is that I should live at home for the summer."

173

Ray and Louise looked at each other again, a combination of anxiety and embarrassment on their faces. Jamie took advantage of their distraction to gather up rubbery pieces of round steak from his plate and conceal them in a paper napkin. Ray put his palms on the table and turned toward me.

"What you are doing is irresponsible," he said. "Your mother and I can't condone it. By letting you stay here, we make it possible for you to do this damn fool thing. That makes us party to it."

His jaw clenched, his eyes hardened. My mother's eyes looked sad and fearful.

"What are you afraid of?" I asked. "Are you that scared of that asshole Bridette?"

Ray gave me the index finger. "Hey! Mind your language. It so happens Leon Bridette is a pretty powerful man in this town."

"He doesn't scare me," I said.

Ray took a sip of beer and leveled his eyes at me. "You don't work for a trucking company," he said, "that gets a third of its revenue from Falls Dieworks."

Oh, Jesus, was that it? Again, I felt like I had stumbled over my own naivete. Did the need to make a living drive every damn decision adults made? No wonder Ray and Louise had looked embarrassed. Tossing me out of the house for fear of alienating a customer of Ray's employer. They *should* be embarrassed, I thought.

"Excuse me," I said. I went upstairs to pack.

o

I found a motel for ten dollars a night that also offered rooms for forty dollars a week, but even that was more than I could afford. After two nights at the motel I packed my clothes into a corrugated cardboard box that would not be noticed among the other boxes in the storage closet at Gamma Investigations. Herb Tierney must have thought I was one hard-working young guy, always there at the office when he left in the evening and there again when he arrived in the morning. He didn't know that I was *still* there in the morning, that I was sleeping in the office, either on the floor or in

174

Herb's desk chair, because I had no place of my own. The office had a small bathroom where I could shave and brush my teeth, but I had to take a towel and a bar of soap to a public park and use the showers alongside vacationing campers.

That summer I developed the lifestyle that I would enjoy for many of my post-college years, when I wandered aimlessly picking up part-time, temporary jobs that required no particular skill or training. I ate McDonald's hamburgers, day-old bread, canned tuna, and the 99¢ specials at Wischki's Pharmacy. I washed my underwear in the sink and dried it with an oscillating fan. Having no car, I walked or rode the bus, and soon regretted my decision to abandon my old bicycle. The only clothes I bought were deeply discounted irregular underwear. In my free time I read library books or watched sports on department store floor-model televisions.

You would be surprised how many people put out cigarettes with plenty of good puffs left in them in ashtrays in public buildings. The sand-filled ashtrays next to elevators are a particularly good place to pick up free smokes.

The job at Gamma Investigations was interesting, for a while. I answered the phone and took messages, organized the files and ran errands, but I also got to do some private-eye work, or at least that's what it seemed like to me. Herb used me for long surveillances that he didn't expect to be challenging, and I suspected he billed his usual fifty an hour for my time. Most often, my surveillance work consisted of spying on a married man or woman to see if they were cheating, which they usually were. Wisconsin didn't have no-fault divorce back then.

The strangest such surveillance I handled was for an elderly, disabled woman who was confined to her bed. She was convinced that her even more elderly husband was getting up regularly in the middle of the night for trysts with a neighbor at the far end of the house. She couldn't get out of bed to see what he was up to, and it was driving her crazy.

"Old guy's probably just getting up to pee," said Herb, who had me stake out the house from 9 P.M. to 2 A.M. for three consecutive nights. Having no car, I hid in some bushes behind the house with a can of insect repellent and a camera with a telephoto lens and super high-speed film.

175

At midnight on the third night, a neighbor from three doors down tiptoed across the backyards to the breezeway of my subject's house. I got a nice clear photo of the unfaithful old coot in a welcoming embrace with the neighbor, whose name turned out to be Steve.

Herb also did a lot of "skip-tracing," locating deadbeats for stiffed creditors. He had so many ingenious tricks and gimmicks, I was sure he could have found Newley for my dad. I was upset that my father hadn't hired a P.I. — I didn't know then that he had.

Herb turned up a few tidbits right out of the blocks. Paraldehyde did have industrial uses. It was utilized in the production of synthetic resins. Also, Bridette was in town the day my father died. He attended a meeting at City Hall on lakefront development. The name of the other man who guaranteed the Bank of Wisconsin loan was Abraham Kanter.

Five weeks into the job, the telephone rang at four in the afternoon.

"Gamma Investigations."

"Jonathan, it's Mom. I have some things for you. Where can we meet?"

The tone of her voice was deadly serious, like it was the day she talked to me about the letter from the Bank of Wisconsin. Her fingernails were clicking, she was agitated. For some reason, she didn't want me to come to the house. Maybe I was that much of a pariah.

We met at a park on the lakefront. Even in midsummer the breeze off Lake Michigan was cold and it smelled of dead fish. Louise was made up and she wore a jacket and pants. I shivered in shorts and a T-shirt. We sat down on a park bench with a view of Lake Michigan, whitecapped and dark blue under the late afternoon sun.

"You're not dressed properly," she greeted me. "You look thin. Are you getting enough to eat? Where are you living?"

"I'm fine. What have you got for me?"

She handed me an opened envelope with a return address from the State of Wisconsin University Office of Financial Assistance.

Dear Mr. Bruckner,

The terms of your tuition assistance grant require that you maintain a cumulative Grade Point Average of not less than 2.5. The Registrar's Office reports that your GPA at the end of the second semester of your sophomore year is 1.9. Therefore, you are ineligible for financial aid for the 1974–75 school year. Should your GPA improve, you may reapply for aid next year.

There went the scholarship. I would have to pull the belt tighter. Did they sell two-day old bread?

"Are you satisfied now, Jonathan? What are you going to do? Will you drop this stupid game now and get a real job, before it's too late?"

"No."

"Ray and I have a lot of extra expenses with Jamie. We can't afford to give you money for school."

"I know."

She looked down at her hands in her lap, where she held another white envelope, face down. "Has your . . . investigator . . . turned up anything?"

"Yes," I bluffed. "Mr. Tierney is very good. We're getting close."

The envelope in her hands rattled. Her hands were trembling. She looked up at me, tears in her eyes. "You have to stop this. You have to stop it *now.*"

"No."

Her shoulders drooped and she gave one exasperated sob. I thought she was going to cry, but instead she took a deep breath and shook herself. She closed her eyes.

"I promised myself," she said, her voice grave and quivering, "I would never tell anyone what I am about to tell you. I promised myself I would never lay this burden on you, but you've left me no choice. Before I tell, you must promise me you will never repeat it to a living soul. Promise me, Jonathan."

I promised, and I kept my promise. People who compulsively keep promises should never make them.

21

Sheboygan, Day Twenty-Two

ON THE DRIVE BACK FROM THE FEDERAL COURTHOUSE in Milwaukee, the frozen landscape engenders in me a hankering for a warm brandy. It seems to me I have been drinking alone too much lately. Here's the solution to that problem: a tavern.

To my delight, the tavern has a crackling fire going. It is otherwise a typical roadhouse — seedy, poorly lit, smelling of stale tap beer and urinal cakes. The bartender is gaunt, glum, and vaguely hostile. When I specify that I want the brandy in a snifter, he glowers contemptuously.

I put a chair directly in front of the fire, which warms me outside as the brandy warms me inside. I relax, and as I do so I realize I should not be at all amazed that my mother never told me Uncle Stan and Aunt Melanie had a daughter who died. She kept bigger secrets than that one. I remember the story she told me that evening in July after my sophomore year as we watched the purple dusk spread across Lake Michigan to the infinite horizon. And I remember that ugly little letter in her lap, the one she brought along with the notice about my scholarship.

Now that letter nettles me. I have been through the files upstairs at the house, the desk in the basement, all the drawers and cabinets in the kitchen and living room, everywhere my mother was likely to have left old correspondence, and it occurs to me now that I haven't come across that letter.

The brandy is warm, soothing, delightfully fragrant. It opens my sinuses and clears my ears. The fire dances like a giddy, mad friend.

My mother never threw anything out. Where the devil is that letter? Apparently I have not found all the correspondence. It might be in a box somewhere with a lot of other letters, one of which might be the one with the answers.

○ ○

July, 1974

"The day your father died," my mother said, speaking slowly, her eyes narrowed against the cold lake breeze, "I told the policeman I went to Aunt Melanie's house after work."

"I remember."

She looked at me with a coy, mischievous look, a little girl who got caught doing something naughty. "Well, I didn't. I came straight home, like always."

The wind off the lake seemed to drop ten degrees at once. I knew my mother always came home right after work, so she would be there when Jamie and I got home from school. She prided herself on that. Why had I never questioned the story she told Detective Adams?

"I got home a little later than usual. They picked up a shoplifter at the Piggly Wiggly who claimed to have checked out in my aisle, so I had to stay while they went through my tape item by item. When I got home, Jamie was already there. I was surprised, but later heard that Jamie's school had let out early that day — something about a prank fire alarm, I think."

Her cheeks and forehead tensed, and she pursed her lips tightly. Her fingers gripped the envelope in her lap, crumpling it. Her knuckles were chapped and her red fingernail polish was half gone. "I was coming in the side door to the kitchen," she said, "when I heard Jamie stomping down the stairs to the living room. He came running into the kitchen and froze when he saw me."

She placed a hand over her face and rubbed her forehead with her fingertips, as if the recollection were giving her a migraine. "Jonathan," she said, "Jamie had a look on his face I will never forget. He was wild-eyed, flushed, practically foaming at the mouth like a mad dog. I had never seen him look like that before. He was holding a large brown paper bag in his hands. I said, 'Jamie, what's the matter?.' He didn't answer me. He ran for the door and tried to squeeze past me. I said, 'What is this?' and I grabbed the bag. He let go and ran out the door. I didn't see him again until he came in after the police left."

She paused and waited for me to ask the obvious question. "What was in the bag?"

"I didn't know what it was at the time, only that it terrified me. It was a cardboard box with tinfoil tubes taped to it and a long red fuse. It smelled peculiar. I yelled 'David!' several times but Dad didn't answer me, so I assumed he wasn't home. I got back in my car and drove to Aunt Melanie's. I thought Uncle Stan might know what the damn thing was."

It would occur to me later that I should have asked her if she had parked her car in the garage and, if so, was Dad's car there at the time. But I was too stunned to be that analytical.

"Did Stan know what it was?" I asked.

"He said it was a homemade bomb, and a very good one. With a gunpowder fuse and detonator and a charge of some kind of highly flammable liquid. It was all Greek to me, but I understood enough that I flipped my wig. Stan and Melanie wouldn't let me leave until I calmed down. Then I got home and there's the cops telling me . . . telling . . ." She burst into tears.

The point of her story settled on me like dark nightfall on the lake. For nearly three years my mother had pretended that she had no doubt my father had taken his own life, while all the while actually believing that her son had killed his own father. She had lived with Jamie, fed him, taken care of him, while she must have been living in terrible fear of him. But she kept it all to herself, to shield Jamie from prosecution, spare me anguish, and protect our family from further degradation.

Man could that woman keep a secret. "You never really believed

Dad committed suicide," I said.

She sniffed, bit her lip, and shook her head. "Of course not. Not David. Even when things weren't going so well, he always loved life. Surely you remember that."

I did, and I felt faithless and ashamed that I had let the grownups convince me otherwise for two and a half years, until I smelled the paraldehyde in Luke's hospital room. But I also felt it would be equally faithless of me to be too easily convinced now that my brother was responsible.

"I'm sorry, Mom, but if you're saying Jamie did it, I can't accept that. He's not capable of it."

Without a word, she handed me the envelope that had been resting in her lap. Inside was a carbon copy of a letter addressed to Karl Bauer, M.D., whom I remembered was our family doc. The letter was dated October 1 of the previous year.

> Dear Dr. Bauer,
> Thank you for referring James Bruckner to me. I met with James on September 21 and 24 and interviewed his mother on September 25. I administered the Minnesota Multiphasic Personality Inventory, the Wechsler Intelligence Scale, the Rorschach Test, and the Rosenzweig. Detailed test results and interpretations are in the enclosed report.
>
> As described more fully in the report, the patient history, test results and interview data support a diagnosis of Schizophrenic Disorder, prodromal stage. I recommend that James immediately begin regular, intensive psychotherapy and anti-psychotic medication to be specified after further testing. I believe early intervention is critical.
>
> One matter which I have omitted from the report is James's mother's concern about whether James presents a danger as regards violent behavior. I must warn that this is a valid concern. James's delusional ideation regarding his father's

death tends to confirm rather than ameliorate the concern, underscoring the need for prompt, intensive intervention.

Sincerely,
Prashant K. Patel, M.D.

So the shrink thought my brother was dangerous. So what? Was that enough to make a mother suspect her own child? Of course, Louise had seen Jamie at the house that afternoon, observed the wild look in his eyes. I myself had seen him scrambling down the quarry wall, looking like a maniac. That she had convicted my brother in her mind was understandable, even reasonable, if also pitiable.

"Don't blame Jamie," she said softly. "And don't blame yourself. None of us had any idea how sick he was. He really wasn't responsible for his actions."

She stood up and I handed her back the letter. "You see now," she said, "why you have to call off this investigator. If you don't, you may ruin your brother's life, all our lives. Do you hear me?"

I remained on the park bench for I don't know how long, my head buzzing, while the lake got darker, the air colder and damper. What to make of this bombshell my mother had dropped? I knew now why my mother had looked so frightened when I said I was going to see Dr. Patel, and why she had tried so hard to stop my investigations.

Was there any explanation for my brother bolting down the stairs carrying an incendiary device and acting like a lunatic at the approximate time of my father's death *other* than the obvious one? Of course, I had to consider the possibility Louise was lying. She had been so convincing while telling her story, but she was, after all, a gifted actress. The more I thought about it, the fishier it seemed to me that she had brought her copy of Dr. Patel's letter along with her. Why would she do that, unless she planned all along to spin this yarn, sell me on the idea of Jamie's guilt, to get me to stop Tierney's investigation? Why, if not to protect *herself* from apprehension?

And what about Ray's role in this tableau? He told me to back off on the investigation because Leon Bridette used his trucking company. When did he and Louise cook that one up?

The wind calmed and stars materialized over the pitch-black water. I was exhausted. The buzzing in my head quieted, and it finally sank in that it was not possible for me to conceive, really, of either my mother or my brother killing my father, because I knew these people, *before*. Before my father died, before he lost his job, before the letter from the bank came. For the first time in three years, my fear and anger were so tapped out that I could remember what it felt like not to be alone, to feel the security of a family around me, and the pain of my loss sharpened because I was able to admit to myself that I wanted that feeling back.

I stood, walked to the shore, and sat down in the soft, damp sand. Words came out in a voice that did not sound like me, it was so steady and so full of conviction.

"We did not do this to ourselves," I said. "This was done to us."

On that night, I simply could not imagine my mother or my brother as capable of murder. But myself? Now that was another matter. I could see myself as quite capable of it, if I ever found the person who had done this to my family.

○ ○

Sheboygan, Day Twenty-Two

A tall, bald man with a familiar face strolls into the tavern and sits at the bar. After a moment, I realize he is Bill Sorenson, my so-called friend from high school who turned on me because I lost a race and kept him out of regionals. What a jerk. He is no longer the human gazelle he was in high school. More of a paunchy caribou. His teenage acne is gone, but it has left his face a moonscape. That's what he gets for calling me "Pizza-Face."

Damn, he's noticed me. Damn, damn, he's coming over to talk.

He pulls a chair up and sticks out his hand for me to shake. "Hey, Bruckeroo. Been a long time, man."

"Been over thirty years," I say.

He asks what I'm doing "in these parts" and, to keep it simple, I tell him I came to town for my mother's funeral. I ask him what he's up to these days.

"Workin' at the Dieworks," he says, a bit sheepishly. "I'm on the line. Never got to college, like you. You had the smarts."

There's some symmetry. The guy I resented most in my youth is working for the guy I resent most now. Figures. Even though I hated Bill for his disloyalty, I feel bad for him. He told me the day of the qualifying meet that he needed to do well in cross-country that year to have a shot at college admission. Did my failure in that race really cost him the chance to go to college? If so, he is indirectly another victim of my father's murder.

"I spend a lot of time in this joint," he says with a self-deprecating smile. "How about you, man? I bet you're a doctor or a lawyer or some kind of honcho. Right?"

"I live in Florida," I said. "I've got my own business." It's the truth. Why are my cheeks burning?

"Yeah, you had the smarts. I'm happy for you."

Bill seems to have forgiven me completely. Quite magnanimous, since he could be blaming me that he never had a college athletic career and spent over thirty years on an assembly line. His example and the warm brandy inspire me.

"Bill," I say, "I always wanted to tell you how sorry I was I lost that race and stopped the Raiders from going to regionals."

"What are you talking about?" he says, sipping his beer and foaming his upper lip.

"The qualifying meet, I finished last. We needed one more point."

"That wasn't you," he says. "That was Nelson. That leaker."

Forgive and forget, they say. As Bill demonstrates, if you forget, you don't need to forgive.

"The only stupid thing you ever did, Bruckeroo, was that meet in Manitowoc when there was two inches of snow on the ground. Guy Williams hid your shoes on the bus and instead of scratching, you ran the whole two-point-four miles barefoot. Ha! That was hilarious. Remember?" He feigns a left jab at me.

"Oh, yeah," I say, even though I am absolutely certain that

the clown who ran the Manitowoc race barefoot in the snow was Nelson.

Poor Bill, I suppose thirty years of breathing the fumes from molten metal and spending the rest of his time in a tavern has affected his memory. Or is it my memory that is faulty?

One never knows for sure, does one?

∘∘

Eight weeks into my job with Gamma Investigations, I was flat broke. Herb Tierney hadn't paid me since the first week, and I had to screw up my courage to confront him about it.

"I'm a little behind on my paperwork," he said. "I'll have it for you Friday."

Fortunately I had discovered every bar in town that put out free hors d'oeuvres or peanuts during happy hour or I would have had nothing to eat all week. Friday afternoon Herb handed me an envelope on his way out. The statement inside cured me once and for all of my naivete and firmly imbued me with the cynicism that has so enriched my life ever since.

> *J. Bruckner, 8 weeks misc.svc. @ $150.00/week, amount due $1200.00.*
> *Less Gamma Investigations charges: 19.5 hrs @ $50.00/hour, amount due $975.00; travel expenses $135.00; total charges $1110.00*
> *Net due J. Bruckner: $90.00.*

Herb enclosed a check for $90.00. There was no way he spent 19.5 hours looking up Bridette's schedule on the day my father died and researching the industrial uses of paraldehyde. But I couldn't prove that, and even if I could I didn't have the means to start a collection action, so I was screwed. Herb had swindled me out of my summer. Two weeks before school was to start, I had ninety bucks to my name and no financial aid.

I should have kept the job at the warehouse in Madison. Once again, my mother was right. God, that was aggravating.

Luke Willever and I had agreed to room together junior year. With no way to pay tuition, I would be out of school for at least a semester. The first thing I did after I read Herb's statement was call Luke to let him know he had to find a new roommate. We hadn't talked since I called to tell him Bridette got busted for the bank fraud. I got a little satisfaction out of using Herb's office phone for a personal long-distance call.

"Hey, Roomie, wuz happnin'?"

I explained that what wuz happnin' wuz that I was no longer "Roomie."

"Bummer," said Luke. "What are you gonna do?"

Good question. I told Luke I had no plans, no money, and no place to stay.

"Why not visit wonderful Wabeno?" he said. "I've got the place to myself since my uncle died."

I remembered that the uncle who had raised Luke passed away freshman year. That Luke, still a year shy of 21, had lived alone in his uncle's house for two summers drove home how alone he was in the world. Luke had listed me as his emergency contact. That's why I got the call from University Hospital when they brought him in for detox.

Having no alternatives, I gratefully accepted Luke's invitation.

"I scored some dynamite stuff this summer," said Luke. "It'll blow your mind. You make any more progress on your dad's case?"

"Not much. I got the name of the other co-signer on the bank loan. I found out Leon Bridette was in town the day my dad died. Also, paraldehyde has industrial applications. They probably use it at the Dieworks."

"Motive, means, and opportunity," said Luke. "What's Bridette have to say for himself?"

"I haven't talked to him since last May."

Luke chided me, saying I should put pressure on Bridette, that "he may be ready to crack." Luke also suggested I confront Abe Kanter, the other guy who guaranteed the bank loan, and talk to Detective Adams again.

After talking to Luke I gathered up my belongings and said goodbye to Gamma Investigations, Inc. My conversation with Luke underscored my shortcomings as an investigator. Yes, I should have been talking to Bridette, Kanter, and Adams. I was procrastinating because I knew that it made no sense to talk to any of those people until I questioned someone I should have questioned a long time ago, the one I should have, in fact, questioned first. Someone with whom, due to softness, squeamishness, irresolution, and cowardice, I had entirely avoided the topic of my father's death.

But I couldn't avoid it any longer. The time had come for me to bite the bullet and interrogate my poor, sick brother.

22

THE FIRST HURDLE I HAD TO OVERCOME to question Jamie was to find a time he was alone so that Ray and Louise couldn't interfere. My mother drove Jamie to school and to the doctor and picked him up. Otherwise, he was always at the house, under guard. He never went anywhere alone.

This proved to be no obstacle at all when I remembered that Ray and Louise routinely went out for a fish fry on Friday night, the last vestige of my mother's Catholicism. I headed over to the house, then loitered a block away until Ray's Chrysler pulled out.

Jamie didn't answer the doorbell or my persistent knock. I moved to the side of the house and slipped behind the overgrown junipers to peek through a living room window. Jamie was sitting in the red and gold striped easy chair in his bathrobe, eating cheese curls and watching television. The Philco had apparently given up the ghost and was now being used as a stand for a portable TV. Wow. They finally got color.

I tapped on the glass and waved. Jamie didn't appear startled in the least. He carried his bowl of cheese curls over and pushed the window open, leaving an orange palm print on the sash. He looked huge, closing in on 300 pounds. Apparently, the medication was slowing his metabolism. Of course, giant bowls of Cheetos aren't exactly on the Scarsdale diet.

"What are you doin' out there?" he asked.

"Let me in the front door, Jamie."

"Okay."

Jamie walked towards the front door, stopped in the foyer, then, having apparently forgotten what he was doing, went back in the living room and sat down in the striped chair again. Geez, this was not going to be easy. I tapped and waved again, figuring that if he came to the window and asked me what I was doin' out there, I would give up. To my relief, Jamie got up and let me in the house. We sat down in the living room, Jamie in "Dad's chair," me on the couch.

"How's it going?" I asked.

He reflected on the question. "Slowly," he said. Jamie's facial hair growth was about a year ahead of where mine had been at his age, but he hadn't started shaving. His wispy moustache and goatee were orange, like his fingers.

"How's school?"

"The kids aren't mean to me anymore."

Good. I supposed they kept the special-class kids away from the bullies and jocks. Plus, it had been almost three years since local man was found dead in garage. Taunts, like jokes, grow stale over time.

"Are you following the Brewers?" Milwaukee's five-year-old baseball franchise had yet to have a winning season, but I knew Jamie listened to every game on the radio like it was the seventh game of the World Series.

"Yeah. They stink."

So did Jamie. I had observed what it took for Louise and Ray to get Jamie to bathe, and I didn't fault them for slacking off.

"How are you getting along with Ray?"

Jamie didn't answer. He fidgeted and looked around furtively, so I changed the subject. We talked about sports and mutual acquaintances for a while, then I finally got around to asking him if he ever thought about Dad.

"I miss him," he said.

"Me, too. Ever wonder if he really killed himself?"

His eyes popped open and he scanned the room. I had raised a taboo subject.

"No, I never wonder."

"You're convinced he did?"

He squirmed and rubbed his hands on the chair arms. "No. I know that he didn't." He continued searching the room, as if for spies.

"How do you know that?"

Jamie stopped moving and fixed his gaze on me. A trace of his lopsided grin appeared, then faded. "I saw him," he said.

My stomach knotted and my palms got wet.

"You saw him? You saw Dad before he died?"

He stared past me, trancelike. "No. He was already dead."

Man had I screwed up. That I had never asked Jamie about this before nauseated me. What had I been so afraid of? "You saw Dad dead in the garage? When?"

"Not in the garage," he said. "In the basement. I saw him in the basement."

Jesus. That caught me by surprise. "When?"

"I got home from school. Mom wasn't here. I went downstairs to see if Dad was at his desk." Jamie looked down at his feet. "He was on the floor. He smelled funny. He was dead."

"Are you sure he was dead?"

"His spirit was gone. My father dwelleth in Valhalla." Jamie's eyes widened and his hands gripped the arms of the chair. "He was vanquished by the forces of evil."

Uh-oh. Jamie seemed to be getting agitated, and he was starting to sound nonsensical. I tried to calm him down.

"Take it easy, Jamie. It's okay. There's no evil here."

"Evil is everywhere," he said. "Especially here. She did it."

"Who did it? Mom?"

"For the insurance money. I heard her say it."

"What?"

His face contorted. He folded his arms in front of him and scratched both forearms simultaneously. *That's all you're worth to this family.* His voice sounded like an imitation of a gremlin.

I remembered the night my parents argued about the Opuba,

when my mother said that to my father. At the time, I assumed Jamie was sound asleep. We never discussed it, so I didn't know he had heard it and was disturbed by it. Of course he would be.

Jamie sat bolt upright, hyper-alert now. He clawed at his skin as if he itched all over.

"I saw her," he exclaimed. "She was in the house!"

"Then you ran away," I said. "To the quarry."

"No. First run to the forest, they said. Then to the caves. That's what they said."

"Who said?"

He brushed his hands over his legs and chest furiously, as if he had insects crawling on him. His cheese curls spilled all over the chair and onto the floor. I realized that I didn't have much more time to learn anything useful.

"Jamie, calm down. Remember, I found Dad in the garage. Mom couldn't have carried him up from the basement."

"She had help. They were here!"

"Who?"

"Hunding. And Hagen."

Hagen? My girlfriend Lori's last name was Hagen. Jamie thought *she* was in the house that afternoon? Besides the idea being ridiculous, I knew for a fact that she wasn't, because we were together in the quarry. Dr. Patel's letter had referred to Jamie's "delusional ideation" about my dad's death. It spooked me to think Jamie had worked Lori into his delusions.

Jamie stood up in the chair with remarkable agility, considering his size. He cupped a hand to his ear. "They're coming," he whispered.

I was losing him. "Please sit down, Jamie. Nobody is coming. Jamie, did you have something in your hands when you saw Mom?"

"Magic fire. He commanded the fire. No one can break through the fierce, flaming fire! They're coming, they're coming!"

He was gone, wild-eyed, flailing and stomping, grinding Cheetos into the chair fabric. That's when Louise and Ray came through the front door. Jamie was right, they *were* coming.

"For heaven's sake!" screamed Louise. "What in the hell are you doing?"

"Hey!" yelled Ray. "Get down off that chair."

Jamie dismounted from the chair, shaking the floor. He grabbed hold of the brass floor lamp and jerked out the plug. Then he raised the lamp over his head horizontally and hurled it in Ray's direction. Ray hopped nimbly out of the way and the base of the lamp careened off the wall, leaving a dent the size of a cruller. Jamie bolted through the kitchen and out the side door, banging it shut behind him.

Ray picked up the lamp. The harp was severely bent. "I can fix this," he said. "Honeybunch, you take it easy. I'll go after the boy."

He stopped at the entryway to the kitchen and looked back at me. "Nice going — college boy," he said.

My mother was dressed in a purple pants suit with sequins all over the jacket. She rubbed her forehead with both hands, her fingers trembling.

"I'm sorry, Mom. I was only trying to talk . . ."

"Please leave," she said. "Leave, *now.*"

I left, and I did not return for more than three decades.

o

The next morning I awoke in the "el cheapo" motel, having spent one-seventh of my net worth to put a roof over my head for one night. While shaving, showering, and brushing my teeth, I reflected on my conversation, if it could be called that, with Jamie. I realized that I probably hadn't questioned Jamie before because I was afraid of exactly what had happened. Maybe I should have trusted my original instinct to let Jamie be. On the other hand, it might have been better to question him earlier, since his disease was progressive. Impossible to say.

Had I learned anything useful? I had confirmed that Louise was telling the truth about seeing Jamie at the house on the afternoon of my father's death. I had probably confirmed that she was telling the truth about the bomb — the "magic fire," as Jamie put it.

Had I also learned that my father was killed in the basement and moved to the garage? Hard to rely completely on the testimony of someone who fancied himself a hero in a Wagnerian opera. If I'd put the "Ride of the Valkyries" on the stereo Jamie probably would have speared Ray with the brass lamp.

Thinking it might help me interpret Jamie's remarks, I went to the library and read up on the composer, Richard Wagner. Some of the gibberish Jamie spouted came from *Der Ring des Nibelungen,* a nice little choral/orchestral work that will never make it on AM radio because it's over sixteen hours long. The incomprehensible story, a mish-mash of Norse and Greek mythology, reminded me of a Tolkien story. No doubt listening to this stuff for hours on end played a significant role in Jamie's schizophrenia.

The only useful information my research turned up was that one of the villains in the *Ring* was named Hagen. It was a coincidence that my high school girlfriend had the same name as one of Jamie's imagined mortal enemies.

The disastrous conclusion of my interview with Jamie did not deter me. Next, I went to the library's telephone directories and looked up Abraham Kanter, the man who, along with my father, guaranteed the Bank of Wisconsin loan to Philip Newley. There were three listed at addresses within commuting distance of Sheboygan Falls.

Neither of the first two numbers I called belonged to an employee of Falls Dieworks. The third, a city of Kohler number, was answered by a man with a Yiddish accent, rare in and around Sheboygan.

"May I speak to Abraham Kanter?"

"Who is calling?"

"My name is Jonathan Bruckner."

"Bruckner you say? What about do you want to speak with Mr. Kanter?"

"Does the Abe Kanter at this number work at Falls Dieworks?"

"Not anymore. Why are you calling?"

"I want to talk to Mr. Kanter about something he and my father, David Bruckner, worked on together."

"I see. Kanter doesn't live here. He moved."

Click.

Well, that was productive. Two days and twenty dollars in motel bills later, on Monday morning I called Falls Dieworks and talked to Leon Bridette's secretary. She was overtly friendly, saying, "Why yes, of course I remember *you*," so flirtatiously that I was certain she wanted me to ask her out. I remembered her as an attractive, age-appropriate redhead, but I could not see myself dating Bridette's secretary, so I stuck to business.

"I'd like to make an appointment to see Mr. Bridette."

"Why, *certainly.* Could you hold for a moment?"

"Yes."

"Don't go away now."

"No."

When she came back on, her tone had changed dramatically. From honey to vinegar, and thirty degrees colder.

"I'm sorry, Mr. Bridette cannot see you this week."

"What about next week?"

"I'm afraid not."

Click.

Man was I getting popular. I took the bus to Falls Dieworks and located Bridette's reserved space in the unguarded parking lot. It was occupied by a white Lincoln Continental. The bushes there were much more comfortable than the ones in which I was accustomed to hiding. I guess the Dieworks was doing well enough to keep the shrubbery manicured. Bridette showed up around half past six.

"Mr. Bridette, I need to speak with you."

His face reddened and he held a palm out at me. "I'm not talking to you. Get off the property or I'll call security."

He moved toward his car door, but I got in his way.

"It won't do you any good to avoid me. I'm not giving up."

His face was haggard with anxiety and anger. "Haven't you done enough harm to my family already?"

"Are you kidding?" I blustered. "What I've done is nothing compared to what *you* did to *my* family."

He looked me in the eye, his expression softening. "I didn't

mean for it to end up . . . the way it did . . . for Louise and you."
His voice went gooey on "Louise and you."

"What, you expected killing my father to work out just peachy
for us?"

He shook his head. "Bud told me you thought *he* murdered
David. Now you're saying *I* did it? You're crazy, son."

"You both did it. You conspired together."

"That's ridiculous. Why would I do that?"

"Because my dad was about to find Newley and ruin your
whole scheme."

His jaw moved slowly in circles and he cocked any eyebrow.
"Oh, really? If that was true, how would I know? Would David
have told me? No. What I *did* know, because he *did* tell me, was
that David was about to pay off the bank loan, which gave me
plenty of reasons to want him alive. Eighty thousand, to be exact.
Now, please, get away from my car."

I stepped aside slowly, feeling confused. "How was he going to
pay the loan? He didn't have ten cents to his name."

Bridette opened his car door and tossed his black briefcase
onto the passenger seat. "I don't know. What I suspect is that he
sold one of his inventions. We knew he was always moonlighting,
tinkering on his own little projects when he should have been
giving a hundred and ten percent to the company. That's one of
the flaws that held him back."

Bridette plopped down into the driver's seat and reached out
to pull the door shut. He looked me up and down, repeatedly.
"David's other flaw was that he would get obsessed with solving
some problem, wasting time trying to figure it out instead of
cutting his losses and moving on. To be successful in business,
you have to care about costs and benefits, the bottom line. But
David only cared about finding answers." He pointed at me. "You
inherited that from him. You'd better try to get over it."

He started to pull the car door shut, but I grabbed it. "What's
wrong with needing to know the truth?" I demanded.

Bridette yanked the door shut and started his engine. His
power window came down and he said, "You know what curiosity

did to the cat. May have done the same thing to your father. Might do the same to you."

The Lincoln backed out of the space, swung to the right, and stopped. Bridette leaned out the window and sneered at me. "You'll find out, my boy. Bottom line–wise, the truth isn't worth anything."

III

The Bridge

23

LUKE MET ME AT THE BUS DEPOT in Antigo, about an hour's drive from Wabeno. He tossed my suitcase into the bed of a borrowed pickup truck, on top of a pile of hay. We snaked along narrow country roads through the Nicolet National Forest at dusk, surrounded by birches, poplars, and scrub oaks already showing a touch of scarlet, pre-Labor Day. We talked about Nixon's resignation, whether Ford would pardon him, and who Ford would nominate as vice president. Neither of us guessed Nelson Rockefeller.

It took all of thirty seconds to traverse the town of Wabeno — a gas station, a tavern, a small hotel, and a hamburger stand. The uncle's house where Luke was raised sat at the end of two parallel gravel ruts off an unpaved road, deep in the woods. A simple, one-story cottage of rough cedar stained reddish-brown, the place was surprisingly tidy and surprisingly basic. The walls, floors, doors, and ceilings were unstained pine, and all of the furniture was unupholstered hardwood. Both heating and cooking were provided by means of a black, cast-iron wood-burning stove, which Luke stoked upon our arrival, after he lit the kerosene lamps.

The weathered outbuilding with the quarter-moon-shaped hole in the door worried me until Luke pointed out the bathroom. Indoor plumbing makes all the difference. Luke had to teach me how to use the marine toilet, which, among other inconveniences, involved fetching water from an outdoor well with a hand pump. No wonder Luke was so strong. He got all the exercise he needed chopping firewood and pumping water.

Luke deftly whipped up a half-dozen fried egg sandwiches and even more deftly popped open a couple of quart cans of Old Milwaukee. The sandwiches were glazed with a spicy homemade sauce with hints of horseradish, turmeric, and jalapeño pepper. Luke was the only college guy I knew who could cook at all, probably as a result of having no mom. How alien Luke's Thoreau-like self-sufficiency and isolation seemed to me. It made my family life seem simultaneously much better than I had thought it was, and far worse.

As we ate I told Luke about my visit with Jamie and Jamie's assertion that he found my father dead in the basement.

"Maybe," said Luke. "Maybe not. More likely, Jamie thought your dad was dead because he wasn't moving. If he was dead in the basement, he wouldn't have been breathing in the garage. How would he get such a high concentration of carbon monoxide in his blood?"

Good point. Luke also expressed skepticism about the man who told me Abe Kanter, the other "patsy" who, with my dad, guaranteed Phillip Newley's loan from the Bank of Wisconsin, had moved away. "More likely," Luke said, "you were talking to Abe himself, only he didn't want to talk to you. Could be he doesn't want to talk to anybody but his own lawyer about David Bruckner, loan guarantees, or the Bank of Wisconsin. With Bridette up on charges, would you?"

Another good point. I described the encounter with Leon Bridette, and how he had claimed to have no motive to kill my father because my father was on the verge of paying off the loan. To this, Luke simply replied, "He's lying."

We ate, talked, and drank until the din of the nocturnal insects outside subsided and gray dawn disclosed outlines of the forest through the bare windows. Luke let me have the one bedroom, while he opened an old convertible sofa that I assumed he had slept on every night before his uncle died.

I slept fitfully for about two hours and awoke to the sound of sizzling bacon and the smell of strong coffee. In the chill morning, the wood-burning stove drew me like a magnet.

"Hey, ex-Roomie," said Luke. "How do you want your coffee?"

"Intravenously," I said, yawning. "What's on the agenda?"

"Fishing, swimming, and tripping," said Luke. "In that order. Once we drop, we won't leave the cottage."

"Why not?" I asked.

"'Cause we may not find our way back. The sunshine I scored is some heavy shit."

I had smoked pot with Luke several times. Once he talked me into trying some peyote buttons that were as subtle as herbal tea, but otherwise I had always sidestepped his attempts to recruit me into trying psychedelic drugs. Wendy disapproved of them, and I figured the demons in my head didn't require feeding. Plus, there were rumors that LSD damaged your chromosomes.

"Fishing and swimming sound good," I said. "Now might not be such a good time for me to be tripping. I've been sort of depressed lately."

Luke cracked an egg with one hand and emptied it onto a cast-iron frying pan. "*Sort of* depressed? Man, ever since Lehman dumped you, you've been lower than a snake's asshole. That's why we're dropping. They've done studies that show one LSD trip relieves depression better than six months of conventional medication." He flipped the egg with a wooden-handled spatula and applied two drops of Tabasco to it.

"Who did those studies?" I asked. "Timothy Leary?"

"A university hospital in England. It's legit. Besides, it might open the old doors of perception, if you catch my drift."

I didn't believe LSD would help with either my depression or my perception. But part of me said, "What the hell, why not?" It wasn't like I had school or a job or anything else to get up for the next day, or the next week, or the next month. It wasn't like I had a future to protect. What was I saving my chromosomes for?

"All right," I said.

We used the pickup truck to haul a rowboat to a public landing on Archibald Lake and fished all morning. Luke caught a bass as big as a watermelon, and we swam off the boat in water that was clear, cold, and smelled like moss after a rainstorm.

Back at the cottage, Luke took a ceramic salt shaker out of the cupboard and unscrewed the top. He poured a profusion of pills into the palm of his hand, selected two orange ones the size of saccharin tablets, and handed one to me.

"Down the hatch," he said. After I swallowed, he smiled wryly and said, "Fasten your seatbelt."

I remember some parts of the trip vividly, others not at all. Some of the hallucinations scared me so bad that I was never tempted to mess with LSD again, while others were mesmerizingly beautiful and deeply comforting. The beautiful and comforting visions were the ones that stayed with me.

At the beginning, all of the grain in the pine walls, floors, and ceilings organized itself into intricate, angular patterns of perfect symmetry, like the ones in Native American blankets. Next, all of the knots in the wood marched around in orderly rows, and danced in Busby Berkeley kaleidoscope formations. Then, my surroundings went berserk. The air in the room effervesced, the floor undulated like an ocean, and the sky outside flowed into the room through the windows like electric-blue lava.

For a long time I was absorbed in surreal dramas that I watched passively, like movies, except that I was in them. My father led me through a labyrinthine underwater cave. A black woman dressed in tropically colored batik sang lullabies to me, and offered me fruit from a wicker cornucopia. I held Lori in my arms, not as she was when last I saw her, but elderly, gray-haired, and frail — Lori as she would look and feel in sixty years. Holding her filled me with exquisitely sad and tender feelings.

Near the end of the trip, just before I crashed, an epiphanic vision appeared and with it came a profound insight, a crystal clear understanding of my predicament and how it fit into the entire human condition. From this profound insight I realized what I had to do. I boldly told Luke that in the morning I would leave Wisconsin and travel to the Florida Keys, and I did not know when I would return, if ever. The next day, I followed through. Luke dropped me off at the bus depot in Antigo, and I began a voyage south that would last several months.

About the profound insight: I don't remember what it was. I wish I did.

oo

The House, Day Twenty-Two

The house on Foxglove Lane moans and rattles in the merciless wind, its decrepit windows and doors letting in a draft strong enough to extinguish a candle flame. I spent nearly an hour talking and drinking with Bill Sorenson, so I figure one more brandy at this point doesn't count as drinking alone.

Where is that damn letter from my brother's psychiatrist, Dr. Patel, that my mother confronted me with that night on the shores of Lake Michigan? It's been agitating me all afternoon; I can't relax. As is almost always the case, I am agitated because some part of me knows that I have been shirking an unpleasant task. In this instance, I have been side-stepping the most loathsome part of the clean-out — excavation of the darkest, ugliest recess of all, the cavern under the basement stairs.

I glanced in there once, a couple of weeks ago. It's crammed full of boxes black with mold and crumbling under their own weight. The sump pump is adjacent to the stairs, its motor obviously inadequate. The boxes sit in a puddle of black, putrid water. Anything under those stairs is ruined, of course, but I know that I must examine it all nonetheless. There might be some precious artifacts.

To do the job right, I need a flashlight, rubber gloves, plastic buckets, bleach, drying racks, and a heat lamp or a hair dryer. But I don't bother with all that. I used to do things right, and where did it get me?

I grab hold of the first box and carry it to an open area under a bare lightbulb. The bottom falls out and the contents splat onto the concrete floor. Two centipedes the size of hamsters scurry away. The inside walls of the box are slimy and infested with silverfish. Can leeches live in a basement? I hope not.

Spilled on the floor is a pile of newspapers. Mildewed, rotting, stinking newspapers. Now that's something worth storing under your basement stairs for years, isn't it, Mom? Much as I hate to do it, I sit down cross-legged and leaf through the papers. I could use a clothespin for my nose.

They are ordinary newspapers — Sheboygan *Press-Gazettes,* Milwaukee *Journals,* Sheboygan North *Talismans* — that seem to have nothing in common except that they're old and stinky. Why save a *Press-Gazette* with a headline about a proposed new park for the lakefront? Or a *Journal* from the day Nelson Rockefeller was sworn in as vice president?

The second time through the pile I take one page at a time, and I discover the theme. *Viking Harriers Take Regional Championship. Falls Dieworks Names New Manager. Monroe Junior High Shot-putter Sets Record.* Each of these papers contains some reference, however small, to some accomplishment, however miniscule, by my brother, my father, or me. Ha. Here's a picture of Jamie with his grade school class and a fireman. *Jackson Elementary Students Learn Fire Safety.* Not well enough, evidently.

My mother bothered to find and save every newspaper that included an item about one of her boys, even if it was only my name in fine print listed with a hundred other participants in a track meet. Gosh. Did I really run a mile in 4:38 back then? I can't run a mile at all, now.

Here's a story about an achievement of mine that I never realized Louise considered to be an achievement. A small item in the Milwaukee *Journal* from the day Rockefeller became vice president. *Sheboygan Falls Executive Pleads Guilty in Bank Fraud.* The article isn't as satisfying as the headline. Bridette pled guilty to making a false statement to a financial institution, a bland-sounding offense that didn't expose him to the public contempt he deserved. He got six months suspended and was ordered to make restitution to the bank.

I doubt he ever made restitution. My mother also kept a *Press-Gazette* containing an article about Falls Dieworks' multimillion-dollar expansion project, financed by the Bank of Wisconsin. There was the payback. A later issue described how the project included a generous donation of lakefront land to the county, which was to be improved with hiking trails, picnic areas, and baseball diamonds. So there was something in the deal for the good citizens of Sheboygan County. It was to be named "Bridette Park." In the margin next to the article, my mother has scrawled in ballpoint: "Should be Bruckner Park."

Doesn't matter. The park never happened. So in the end, Bridette skated, bottom line–wise, as he would say.

The second box I lift with my hands underneath, but the bottom disintegrates anyway and the contents plop onto the damp concrete. More photos. Man did she hang on to photos.

These are water-damaged and faded. How can mold grow on glossy prints? More black and whites of long-deceased relatives. More school pictures. Polaroids of Ray and Louise at a New Year's Eve party wearing pointy paper hats and blowing noisemakers. Looks like they're having fun.

Oh, wow. Here are some pictures from my family's trip to Florida when I was fifteen. Fading has only made the azure sea and pink clouds in the pictures look more tropical and sunny. Parrot Jungle. A water-ski show. The Everglades. The four of us together on the beach at Bahia Honda. We all look so cheerful. I remember my mother saying it was the most beautiful place she had ever been. Although as far as I know, she had never been anyplace outside of Wisconsin except Illinois, Iowa, and I think she once mentioned a trip to Los Angeles.

Here's a picture of my mom and dad alone on the beach, in swimming suits, golden-fringed clouds billowing on the horizon behind them. They are in a tight embrace, kissing. His arms around her waist, hers around his neck. Eyes closed, mouths open. I wonder who took this. I have never seen it before.

The night my father died, my mother came to my room. She told me that she had once loved my father very much. Actress or not, you can tell from this picture she wasn't lying. Only two years before the letter from the Bank of Wisconsin came, these two people are holding each other like nothing else in the world matters. Such a waste. I wonder: when my parents got that letter, if instead of spending the rest of the night accusing and blaming and insulting and yelling, they had done what they're doing in this picture, how differently might things have worked out for all of us?

I shuffle through the rest of the Florida pictures until I find a shot of my father and me aboard the *Sombrero,* a thirty-foot white wooden cruiser. We're decked out in our scuba gear — black wet suits, fins and orange buoyancy vests (the old-fashioned kind with the horse collar), crotch straps, and dangling plastic tubes for inflation by mouth. This was before the advent of BCDs — the buoyancy control devices that make diving much easier. The drawbacks of those old vests piqued my father's interest in scuba gear. On that very trip, he told me how scuba diving could be safer, simpler, and vastly more popular if divers could adjust their buoyancy without taking the regulator out of their mouths. People are afraid to remove the mouthpiece when they're under water, he said. He sketched a device that would hold the air tank, inflate the jacket automatically from the tank, and even carry weights, making the weight belt unnecessary.

Three years later the so-called "stab jacket" — the forerunner of the modern BCD — would be introduced, bring about a boom in scuba diving, and make somebody a pile of money. I think my dad's preoccupation with the Opuba was his attempt to make up for not pursuing his hunch about the BCD.

Scuba training was quite different back then, too. I remember they made me swim two lengths of a swimming pool under water, and tread for five minutes holding my weight belt above my head. They dropped a full set of gear — tank, jacket, weight belt, regulator, mask, fins, and snorkel — into the deep end of the pool. I had to jump in, suit up correctly, and clear my mask before surfacing.

Now we certify anybody who can swim and pass an easy written test. No money in it if only guys who could be Navy seals can do it.

In this picture, the wind sock on the *Sombrero* is wide open, standing straight out; it was a gusty day. Now, as a dive boat operator, I wouldn't take recreational divers out on a day like that because certification doesn't mean a diver can handle challenging conditions. But my family was flying back to Wisconsin in two days, and my dad said we couldn't fly the day after diving because we had to give our lungs time to adjust to normal pressure or we would risk developing arterial gas emboli. So if I wanted to take my first real reef dive, it had to be that day. He called around until he found a dive boat operating in spite of the weather. My mother took Jamie to Key West for the afternoon while the captain of the *Sombrero* took me, my dad, and two guys from Miami out to a dive site near Marathon known as Coffins Patch, so named because a boat carrying a cargo of coffins once sank there.

The sky was overcast, the sea was choppy, the water was cloudy, and the current was so strong that the *Sombrero* couldn't hold anchor. It was a thoroughly lousy day for scuba diving.

It was the best day of my life.

24

April, 1969

"I CAN'T KEEP A HOOK IN," said our captain, referring to the anchor. "I'll pick you up at the far end of the reef, by dat buoy. It's directly soudeast of here." He pointed at a red and white dot bobbing in the whitecaps. My father and I slid our masks into place, our faces sopping wet from sea spray. Waves whumped against the side of the *Sombrero*. Noisy gulls swooped and cawed, seemingly amused to see us out on such a day.

Captain Charley was old and wiry, with leathery skin, gray stubble, and a bunch of missing teeth. Gabby Hayes with tattoos. He didn't get in the water, nor did he check us to make sure we put on our gear correctly, like I always do with the divers on my boat. The only safety advice he gave the four of us was "Stay together."

I was glad to get out of the violently bobbing boat and under the waves. The visibility beneath the surface was poor, less than twenty feet, but the sight of live coral all around me — fan coral, brain coral, pillar, and elkhorn — was nonetheless wondrous to my inexperienced eyes. The weightlessness, the feel of the warm brine on my face and hands, the rhythmic gurgling of my regulator against the deep silence, were all soothing and hypnotic.

The Miamians, thirty-somethings with military haircuts, paid the captain's advice no heed, taking off on their own as soon as we got to the bottom. My dad and I worked our way slowly along the sea floor, frequently checking our compasses to be sure we were moving southeasterly. The depth gauge read twenty-five feet — a shallow, beginner's depth — but I felt like Jacques Cousteau.

In the first few minutes down I saw barracuda, lobsters, a moray eel, and more exotically colored tangs, angelfish, and wrasses than I could count. A four-foot-long nurse shark swam past my nose so closely I could have reached out and touched it. My dad used his snorkel to gently prod the sandy sea floor. I didn't know why until a wedge of the bottom five feet across rose up and fluttered, revealing the stingray that had been hiding under a blanket of sand. It gave one flap of its wings and vanished into the murk.

It was my first reef dive, but I felt completely at ease at the bottom of the sea and knew right then that I wanted to spend a lot of time there. I am not a brave person. Many things scare me. Heights, fire, guns, and really good-looking women, to name a few. But for some reason water never made me nervous in the least. It always felt like a welcoming friend. After that first dive, when grownups asked me what I wanted to be, I stopped saying "doctor" and started saying "marine biologist."

We had been down almost forty minutes when we chanced upon a green sea turtle, a real rarity in the Keys, or anywhere else. I had never even seen one in an aquarium before. It was nearly four feet long, mottled brown rather than green, gently cruising along with winglike beats of its huge, unwieldy fore-flippers. I cruised along with it, fascinated and delighted that it tolerated my presence instead of darting away like the stingray. It took me awhile to realize that we were no longer amidst the coral. The sea floor had flattened out into sand and bare rock. We were off the patch.

My dad and I huddled up and read our gauges. I had about 1000 psi left in my tank, but my dad was down to 700. You're supposed to surface at 500 psi. He checked his compass, pointed in the direction he wanted me to go, and hand-signaled that I should lead. The swimming became much harder because we were fighting the current. I was relieved to get back to the coral and began working my way along the margin of it, hoping to find the buoy line that marked both the southeast edge of the patch and the spot where the *Sombrero* was to pick us up.

I swam hard for several minutes, not seeing a buoy line, an anchor line, or any trace of the *Sombrero* or the other two divers. My pressure gauge read 700 psi so I knew my dad was below 500. I looked up, but the water was too cloudy to see the surface. The only way I could think of to locate the *Sombrero* was to surface. I turned around to give my dad the "thumbs up" signal.

He wasn't in sight. I spun around three times; he was not there. As I retraced my route along the periphery of the reef, my pulse and respiration accelerated, even as I told myself nothing could be seriously wrong. We were less than thirty feet down.

Through the branches of a formation of elkhorn coral I saw a tempest of brown sand rising from the sea floor. Something powerful was stirring up the bottom. I cautiously swam closer. Ten feet away, I made out human limbs flailing. I swam nearer and saw my father inside the cloud of sand, kicking his fins and grappling with his hands madly, but not moving through the water. Obviously, something had hold of him.

To get his attention, I had to swim up and tap on his mask. He looked at me, his eyes as wide as saucers. A look of pure terror. He stopped flailing and fixed his gaze on the mouthpiece of my respirator. His face was chalky white, his lips pale blue. He grabbed for my mouthpiece. I let him take it.

The regulators we use nowadays all have alternate air sources — an air hose and mouthpiece other than the one used by the diver. They're called octopuses, and they eliminate the need for "buddy breathing," the maneuver in which two divers pass one mouthpiece back and forth when one of them runs out of air or a regulator fails. Octopuses are good devices. My father was right, a lot of people are scared to take the regulator out of their mouths when they're under water. As I was about to learn, my father knew this because he was one of them.

As he clutched my regulator to his mouth, I checked his air gauge. Zilch. No wonder he looked terrified. He must have burned through the last of his air supply fast, the way he was struggling.

What had him tethered? I looked around as well as I could,

my movement limited by the length of the air hose. Strands of translucent spider web radiated from his back. I moved around behind him to get a closer look. Monofilament fishing line was looped over his tank valve and behind the tank and snarled in the straps of his backpack. Apparently some thoughtless fisherman poaching on the dive site had gotten tangled on the elkhorn coral, broken his line, and abandoned it. My father, swimming by, had hooked his tank valve on the line and, with his panicked flailing, gotten his tank and backpack thoroughly snarled. In places the fishing line looked like wads of Thai noodles.

I picked at the line with my fingers, quickly realizing I could not loosen the knots. Neither my father nor I had a scuba knife strapped to our legs, and I firmly resolved at that moment never to dive again without a good, sharp one.

Perhaps I could free the fishing line at the other end, wherever it was hooked on the reef, but with my father dependent on my air supply I could not move more than a yard in any direction. I would have to remove my tank. This was actually made easier by the old-fashioned equipment because the tank was carried on a backpack rather than a BCD, so even without the tank I would still have buoyancy control. Even so, it took so long for me to get out of the backpack that I was completely out of breath.

I gave my dad the hand signal to buddy breathe. Frozen with fear, he didn't react. He wasn't going to yield the regulator voluntarily. If I pulled it out of his mouth, he might start flailing again, so I emptied my lungs into the inflator tube on my vest and I rose to the surface.

Bobbing like a cork in seven-foot waves, I spotted a buoy marking the dive area about fifty yards away. That fisherman who abandoned his broken line should be shot, I thought, fishing so near to a marked dive site. A white dot a quarter mile beyond the buoy looked like the *Sombrero*. That captain should be shot, too. If he had any doubt about his ability to hold his position at the buoy, where he said he'd pick us up, he should have called off the dive. While I was breathing deeply to load my blood with oxygen, a breaking wave caught me by surprise. I swallowed a mouthful of brine and coughed spastically. As soon as I recovered, I emptied my buoyancy jacket and dropped to the sea floor.

Twenty seconds on the surface and the current had moved me so far that it took at least another twenty seconds to locate my father again. I checked the tank pressure. Under 100 psi. That wouldn't last him much longer than the lungful I was holding would last me.

I wrapped my fingers loosely on the fishing line and traced it back to where it was tangled in the branches of a stand of elkhorn coral. Impossible to unsnarl in the time I had. I tried to cut the fishing line first with the buckle of my weight belt, then with my teeth. Not even close. This was high-test monofilament, made to handle a thrashing tarpon, marlin, or shark. I found a rock on the bottom, removed my mask, and attempted to break the glass, figuring I could cut the line with a shard. But with the water buffering the force of my blows I could not shatter the tempered glass. I put the mask back on, cleared it, and traced the line back to my father.

Feeling nearly out of breath, I didn't stop to check air pressure or anything else. I unbuckled my father's backpack and pulled it off of him, being careful not to get snared in the fishing line myself. A piece of line was caught on the crotch strap of his buoyancy vest. I would have to remove that, too, which meant his weight belt had to come off first. As soon as the weight belt dropped he would float away like a balloon, making it much harder to remove the vest and avoid getting us both tangled in the line. Quite a predicament. I was completely out of breath and needed to surface for a moment before I could deal with it.

But I couldn't go to the surface, because of something I heard. Silence — hollow, deep, and ominous. The rhythmic gurgle of air bubbles from the regulator had ceased. The tank was empty. No time to surface. My father began to struggle again. If he did not remain still, we had no chance.

I grabbed his wrists and looked into his eyes, which were still wide with fear. His face was no longer pale, it was reddish-blue. I shook my index finger in front of his mask, not an official scuba hand signal, just a stern parent telling a child, "No!" He stopped squirming.

The air tank, gauges, and hoses were useless and only in the way now, so I ripped the regulator out of his mouth and pushed the whole contraption out of the way. My diaphragm lurched in my chest repeatedly, letting me know that I could not hold my breath much longer. I opened all the buckles on his jacket, pulled the front of it open, and yanked his arms out by the elbows. Then I got behind him and simultaneously flipped open the buckle of his weight belt with my right hand and pushed him clear of the ensnared jacket with my left. I took hold of the collar of his wet suit, dropped my own weight belt, and we floated up.

We broke the surface and my father gasped and coughed and gasped some more, while I towed him to the buoy that marked the dive site. We clung to the buoy as a flotation device while I waved and screamed my throat raw for several minutes. Eventually the *Sombrero* putt-putted up and Captain Charley, with help from the Miami guys, fished my dad out while I struggled aboard.

Captain Charley apologized for being out of position when we surfaced, even as he chided us for being down too long and told us we would have to pay for the lost rental equipment. My father sat stiff, gray-faced, and silent until one of the Miamians offered to go back down and recover the stuff, at which point my dad said, "Take us in right now."

On the boat ride back, my dad got violently ill and vomited all over the deck. The captain whistled while he hosed it off. My father shook like he was freezing to death. I thought he needed to get to a hospital, but the captain said he was "just a little green around the gills," and that he'd be okay, "once he get some dry land under him." Captain Charley gave me a free Coke, and I said, "Thank you."

o

The captain was right about Dad. Two hours after the *Sombrero* docked in Boot Key Harbor he was in fine fettle, thanks to dry land, dry clothes, and a dry martini. We sat at a weathered wood table on an outdoor deck at a waterfront establishment called the Pilot House Pub & Grub. The clouds had broken up and the late afternoon sun shimmered like gold dust on the Straits of Florida. The Pilot House was decorated, as befitted its name, with gaffs, harpoons, tackle, fishing seines draped like bunting, and a cordon of nautical rope as thick as an elephant's trunk. Our table had a magnificent view of Seven Mile Bridge, which connected Boot Key, the westernmost of the Middle Keys, to Bahia Honda Key, the easternmost of the Lower Keys.

"Quite an endeavor," said my father, speaking of the bridge, as he sipped his drink and squinted into the sun, his face rosy and animated. "Built in nineteen-oh-nine by Henry Flagler to connect the Florida East Coast Railway to Key West. Incredible feat of engineering for the time. Every bit of that bridge had to be brought in by boat, even the fresh water to mix the concrete. Can you imagine?"

I tried, but I could not imagine. Also incomprehensible to me was how my father had so quickly relegated to the past his brush with death. I felt more shaken sitting on the deck at the Pilot House than I remembered feeling while I was freeing my father from the fishing line. In fact, I didn't remember being shaken at all during our ordeal on the reef, just strangely calm and focused. Very weird.

"It was the greatest railroad construction feat of all time," continued my father. "A lot of people thought it was impossible." He pointed at me. "It shows to go you, there's no telling what you can accomplish."

"Railroad?" I said. "I haven't seen any trains."

"The railway was destroyed in the Labor Day hurricane of nineteen thirty-five. Hundreds of workers lost their lives when the emergency train they had been promised by the railway officials didn't arrive in time to rescue them."

Shows to go you, I thought. No telling what you can accomplish if you're willing to run the risk of getting a few hundred people killed. I was more ambivalent than my father about what the bridge had accomplished.

"What's the matter, Jon? You look all atwitter."

I glossed over my post-traumatic shakes. "Too much Coca-Cola," I said. "This is my third one today."

"Shame on me, getting you sody pop." He toasted me so vigorously a bit of his martini sloshed over the rim. "Today, you are a man. Waitress!"

The waitress came over and my dad ordered a beer for me. I was only fifteen, but the waitress didn't bat an eye. Most bars in the Keys have really tightened up on underage drinking since then. The beer came in a green-glass longneck bottle and the waitress poured it into a frosted mug.

"You happen to be serving a very special young man," my dad said to the waitress, a brunette in braids and hot pants who didn't look like she was more than five years older than me. "Today, he saved his own father's life." My dad proceeded to regale the waitress with the tale of the underwater rescue on Coffins Patch, exaggerating a little, I thought, both my courage and my skill. "His first reef dive and he kept a cooler head than most dive masters would have! Can you imagine?"

It occurred to me that my father was overstating the danger and my bravery to make his own panicking seem less blameworthy. But I didn't blame him. He didn't do it on purpose. When it happened, I tried to handle his loss of control as just another part of the underwater environment, like the skittering stingray or the Elkhorn coral that anchored my father to the sea bottom. As many years as a dive master have since confirmed, if you panic, you panic.

The waitress acted so impressed that my dad repeated the story to three men who were eating fried fish sandwiches at the next table, only this time he embellished it a bit more. Now there were menacing mako and hammerhead in the vicinity. The listeners acted highly impressed, and one of them insisted on buying me another beer.

My initial embarrassment gave way to exhilaration as it sank in that I had finally achieved something that I had been striving for with all my heart since my earliest memory — my father's esteem. Whatever parts of his yarn were false, the admiration he expressed was genuine. I felt triumphant and whole, as if my entire childhood was now a success.

Of course, these ecstatic feelings were all mixed up with my first taste of alcohol intoxication. Some of my joy was probably beer reacting with virginal brain cells. Certainly, that was what was causing the deck of the restaurant to tilt.

"Do you understand what you showed me today, Jon?" He swept the air with his hand. "Unlimited potential. Intelligence. Tenacity. Grace under pressure. A person with those qualities can accomplish anything." He bottoms-upped his martini, and my eyes were drawn to a brown pelican plunging into the aquamarine surf beneath the bridge.

Unlimited potential. Seven Mile Bridge stretched out before me, a concrete monument to the achievement of the seemingly impossible. At that moment, I believed my father's lofty assessment of my future, and I accepted it as a precious gift.

Later in life, I would come to view it as an unwanted burden.

25

THE NEXT TIER OF BOXES ROTTING under the basement stairs brings a smile and a pang of nostalgia. Christmas junk. Strings of multi-colored lights, a tree stand, plastic reindeer, giant felt stockings with the image of Santa barely visible through layers of mildew. These glass ornaments that Jamie and I used to hang on the tree are so familiar. The round silver ones covered with pink and white snowflakes. The red and green ones partially coated with the spray-can flocking that was a fad for one year back in the '50s.

The Polish grandmother ones that were supposedly worth a fortune. Those are all cracked and chipped. What a pile of crap.

Hours of digging in mold and dust is wreaking havoc with my sinuses. My head aches, my eyes itch, and my nose runs like a Vermont maple. The cold weather has chapped my lips and cracked the skin on my sore knuckles. I'm a mess. I throw my filthy jeans and sweatshirt in the washer and hop in the shower, remembering too late that when you run the washer in this house, the shower is reduced to a tepid trickle.

Two extra blankets piled on my sagging old bed break the breeze from the window, but also add dust to the air. Stuffy and mouth-breathing, I sleep fitfully, waking frequently from disturbing dreams or the sound of my own snoring. In the early morning I wake from a recurrent dream, one I have had at least a dozen times. In it, I hold Lori in my arms. Filled with bittersweet longing, I try to tell her something. When I look into her face she is old and frail. The dream is a subliminal remnant of my LSD trip, I assume. A Freudian would interpret it as wish fulfillment. To entertain any more paranormal explanation of the dream would be slightly ridiculous.

I pad downstairs and squint through the storm door window. While I was having strange dreams and mangling blankets, Sheboygan picked up a couple more inches of snow. Agnes Atkins has her holiday decorations out — the wreath, the plastic angel, the tavernlike lights around the windows — same as thirty-five years ago. It's beginning to look too damn much like Christmas. Time is running short if I don't want to miss the entire season in the Keys.

My last, best hope to gather any useful information at this point is Leslie Rozner Jr., the attorney who addressed my dad as "David" and mentioned Audrey in the letter he wrote back in 1956. He was the lawyer who recommended that my parents file for bankruptcy. The tone of his letter suggested he may have been a friend. His name was vaguely familiar to me.

Here's a lucky break — his number is still in the phonebook. No office, just residence. I call and ask for Attorney Rozner.

"Speaking." His voice is faint and crackly. "Who's calling?"

"This is Jonathan Bruckner."

He pauses a moment. "David and Louise's boy."

"That's right. Happy holidays."

"Same to you. It's good to hear from you. I'm surprised you remember me, Jonathan. You were a toddler last time I saw you."

I don't remember meeting Rozner, if I ever did. He asks me how my mother is, and sounds genuinely sad when I tell him.

"She was a lovely woman," he says. "And such a talent. I saw her perform when I was in law school. I revised her will for her when her second husband died. Roy."

"Ray."

"That's right. Heart attack, wasn't it? So young."

Ray died at seventy, which probably seems young to Rozner. His voice sounds ancient, which he must be if he was in law school when Louise was in college. I must have seen his name on my mother's will. That's why it was familiar when I read his letter to my father.

I ask Rozner if I can have an appointment to meet with him. He says he's not practicing law anymore but he would be happy to meet with me, I don't need an appointment, come right on over. He sounds desperate for some company. I tell him I'll be by around noon.

As I recall, my mother's will is now filed with what I call the "second tier" documents, those that I need to save but which are not precious artifacts. My attention has been so focused on my father's death that I have not even bothered to read the will yet. Sure enough, it is stapled in a blue cover with Rozner's name and law office address at the top. That I failed to realize I had seen Rozner's name on the document tells me I should take a closer look at it. What else might I have missed?

"I, Louise Warchefsky Moldenhauer, being of sound mind . . ." Blah-de-blah-de-blah. Hmmm. If she was of such sound mind, why did she leave ten grand off the top to the United Theater Arts Fund? I'm no judge of mind-soundness, sitting here bothered that my mother's name at the end of her life paid homage to both her father and Ray, while my dad's name had been expunged. But give me a break—The United Theater Arts Fund? Given the condition of the house and its contents, ten large will put a real dent in the estate. I'll be lucky to come away with gas money for the drive back.

"I give, devise and bequeath the entire residual, rest and remainder . . ." Attorney Rozner apparently studied at the Redundancy School of Law, which seems to have more alumni than all other law schools combined. Ah, here's the payoff. Half to me, half into a trust fund for Jamie. God, I hope I'm not the trustee. I don't want to think about how difficult and painful it would be to have the permanent, long-term responsibility for controlling my brother's purse strings, granting or denying his requests for money, feeling either like a stingy ogre or an enabling doormat. Where is the trust document? Probably in the same place as the copy of Dr. Patel's letter.

Somewhere in this house must be a portal into another dimension, and it is strewn with socks, keys, homework assignments, and baseball cards. Yeah, what happened to my baseball cards? Now those actually could be worth a fortune. I had Willie Mays, Hank Aaron, and Mickey Mantle for seven consecutive years. If I could find those cards it might make up some of the ten thou my mother gave, devised, and bequeathed to the United Goddamn Theater Fucking Arts Fund.

Being as how I am now an heir to the Warchefsky Moldenhauer estate, on my way to see Attorney Rozner I treat myself to coffee and a muffin at one of those chichi joints where they sock you three bucks for a cup. The muffin is as big as a cauliflower and cost more than I usually pay for a full breakfast. Tasty, though.

Les Rozner lives in a painted lady Victorian with an expansive front porch near the center of town, about three blocks from the lakefront. His appearance surprises me. From his voice I expected a shriveled, hunched-over old man. But Rozner is tall, erect, and clear-eyed, with a firm handshake, a full head of white hair, and a broad smile of natural teeth. Quite a specimen, considering he must be in his late eighties. Maybe that perfect posture keeps one healthy. I stand up straighter for a moment, then resume slouching.

We sit in a formal parlor amid nineteenth-century lithographs, antique Queen Anne furniture, and authentic Persian rugs. The antiques are all as well-preserved as Rozner.

"Your mother was something of a celebrity in college," he tells me. "We all thought she would be famous someday."

"I know she was in some plays," I say.

He shakes his white head. "Oh, that is an understatement. She was quite something to see on stage. She packed the house." He chuckles as his eyes drift off in reminiscence. "Quite something to see *off* the stage, too. Louise was sort of the campus Bohemian. Very arty and flamboyant."

I was certain he was remembering the wrong Louise. "My mother? Really?"

"Oh, yes. Your father, too. He was this wild genius type who wrote futuristic essays for the school newspaper and rode around on a motorcycle. I was a bit in awe of the two of them. I was very saddened when I read of his death."

He pauses to massage his knuckles and looks at me slyly with pale blue eyes. "The paper said he committed suicide. Excuse me for saying so, but having known the man, I found that very difficult to believe."

I try to comment, but something is poking me in the throat. All I can get out is, "Me, too."

Rozner settles back in his chair and lifts his white eyebrows. "Oh, I see," he says, and I get the feeling he sees a lot. "How can I help you, Jonathan?"

I hand him a copy of the letter he wrote to my father a half-century ago, the one about the case of *Johnson vs. Bruckner,* and wait while he reads it. I ask if he remembers anything at all about the case.

"A calamity for all concerned. Louise's sister was in the hospital for an extended stay and her husband was an invalid, so Louise and David took care of your cousin Audrey for about a month. You all went up north to a cabin on Fence Lake. Do you remember?"

"No. I was only a year and a half old."

He nods. "That's right. You had poison ivy."

Now I'm skeptical. Perfect posture and good teeth notwithstanding, there's no way this geezer remembers I had a case of poison ivy fifty years ago. "You don't say."

"On your feet. Louise and you were at the cabin and David drove into Woodruff to buy calamine lotion. On the way back, he stopped to make a left turn off Route 51 and a truck hit him from behind, pushing his car in front of an oncoming vehicle. Audrey was in the front passenger seat. She was killed instantly. David suffered only minor injuries."

I guess a story like that might stay with you for fifty years. I picture the demolished interior of a 1950 Oldsmobile, the body of the little girl from the "Lake/Audrey" picture crushed and lifeless on the passenger seat, her little fingers clutching Jiminy Cricket, while my father averts his eyes in horror. The image in my mind is in black and white, like a police crime scene photo.

"If the accident wasn't my father's fault," I say, "why did they sue him?"

Rozner shrugs. "No one else to sue. The truck driver was uninsured and judgment-proof. The driver of the other vehicle was completely blameless. David was contributorily negligent, as we used to say."

"How?"

"In anticipation of making the left, he turned his wheels. If he hadn't, when the truck hit him he would have gone straight ahead, not in front of the oncoming traffic. Not much negligence, I grant you, but just enough for your uncle's lawyer to hang his hat on. The claim exceeded the policy limits on your father's insurance, and State Farm was willing to let the case go to trial, gambling that they could win outright by disputing that your father was negligent. A long shot, and if the plaintiff won, the award might have exceeded the insurance limits and forced your parents into bankruptcy. The case settled on the courthouse steps when David magically came up with half of the final demand in cash, giving State Farm a chance to get out for less than the policy limits. David said he got an advance on some business deal he was working on."

Sounds more like the kind of spin my mother would have put on it. "Advance on a business deal" is so much more hoity-toity than "loan from a neighbor." I figure the money came from Tom Atkins. That was the loan my father told my mother had saved them from bankruptcy.

Rozner yawns and his eyelids droop. My visit is tiring him; he's about to drift off. Better make it snappy. "I found my mother's will," I tell him. "It refers to a trust for my brother, but I couldn't find the trust document."

He shakes his head. "All of my office files were tossed out long ago."

"Do you remember who she named as trustee?"

His eyes trace a slow arc across the ceiling and he rubs his knuckles one at a time. "I'm sorry, I don't. But St. Rita House could certainly tell you. The trust was initially funded to pay St. Rita's for your brother's care."

I should have realized the trust was already up and running, paying for the home where Jamie lived. That means somebody has been acting as trustee, which means it's not me. Good, at least that one came out my way. I tell Rozner I'm on my way to St. Rita House right now and I get up to leave.

"So soon? Won't you stay for lunch?"

I beg off and he escorts me to the door. He sustains our handshake so long I have to fight an impulse to pull my hand away. He doesn't want to let me leave. That's the problem with a healthy old age. All your friends are dead or in the home and you don't even have nurses to talk to.

He puts a hand on my shoulder and thanks me for coming. "You know, Jonathan," he says, "your parents were remarkable people. You must feel very blessed."

Oh, yeah. Blessed as hell.

o

The highway to Port Washington is freshly plowed and the early afternoon sun blares like a chorus of trumpets on the crisp new snow. Here and there Interstate 43 rises ever so slightly and a slice of glacier-blue Lake Michigan floats on the white edge of the eastern horizon. I pop on the Ray-Bans and mull over Rozner's description of my parents in college, seemingly two entirely different characters than the straight-laced people who raised me.

Or were they? Even as a child I had a vague sense that my folks were fundamentally different from my friends' parents, that somehow their hearts weren't in suburban parenthood to the same degree. I only got to know them as people after they had spent years forcing themselves into the square holes of PTA meetings, Cub Scout outings, and Little League games. Hard to do that and remain Bohemian. I, on the other hand, was as straight and conventional as a high school kid could get, but I never had children and I ended up bumming around the Caribbean for years. I once passed a joint with Bob Marley. Hey, I'm even an artist. I collect hunks of barnacled metal from shipwreck sites, weld them into interesting shapes, and sell them as souvenirs in my dive shop.

Salty sculpture from Jonathan Bruckner, Survivor.

Port Washington is a small, quaint city with the look of a New England fishing village. It had a robust commercial fishing industry until they finished the St. Lawrence Seaway and let moray eels into the Great Lakes, which in a few short years wiped out Lake Michigan's entire population of walleye, bass, and northern pike. On a hill with a bit of lake view, but a better view of the great heaping mountains of coal next to the lakefront power plant, sits St. Rita House. It is a converted private home in a quiet neighborhood that appears to have once been wealthy, before the executives and professionals moved to the suburbs. In a larger city, a neighborhood like this would be undergoing gentrification by now. These houses are in need of paint, carpentry, new roofs, and landscaping, but the residents no doubt have enough pride of ownership to resent having a so-called Community Based Residential Facility in their midst. Especially one that caters to junkies and schizophrenics, like St. Rita House, named for St. Rita of Cascia, patron saint of the sick and desperate. You know, you let in a few dozen sick and desperate, there goes the neighborhood.

The administrator of St. Rita House is a fortyish woman at least six feet tall with short, dark hair and glasses with big wire frames. Janet Reno in dungarees. She introduces herself as Edith Curtin and shuffles me into a tiny room with two metal folding chairs and a molded plastic table. She tells me Jamie is taking a nap, but he will be very happy to see me, he talks about me all the time. I ask what she knows about Jamie's trust and she says the trust has been paying Jamie's fees for as long as he's been a resident.

"Who signs the checks?" I ask.

"The trustee, I assume."

"Do you have a copy of the trust?"

Edith leaves the room and I walk to the window. A ten-foot stockade fence surrounds the snow-covered yard like a prison wall. The window is reinforced with wire mesh. Nice, homey place. I pick up a brochure from a plastic rack on the wall. It tells all about St. Rita House, its mission, its recreational programs, its highly trained personnel, its home-cooked meals, its monthly fee. Holy moly! If this isn't a misprint, my mother was shelling out several times more to keep Jamie here than she ever spent on herself, or even on all of us put together. I could live six months on this monthly fee. Where did Louise get the scratch to fund this?

The administrator returns with a document in a blue cover like the one on my mother's will. She is reluctant to show it to me.

"Can you at least tell me who it names as trustee?"

Flip, flip, flip. She uses brown fingernail polish. "Louise W. Moldenhauer."

"That's our mother. She died recently."

Flip. "The successor trustee is Jonathan Bruckner."

Shit. Permanent responsibility for my brother's assets. One of those gifts that keeps on giving. Thanks again, Mom. Edith, who has apparently decided it's okay to show the new trustee the document, leaves to make a copy of the trust for me. When she returns, she tells me Jamie is up, waiting in the Activities Room, and he's so excited I'm here.

I follow her through a large kitchen where several St. Rita House residents sit at a long table eating white-bread baloney sandwiches with tomato soup. Quite a crew. One with shoulder-length dreadlocks and wicked needle tracks, another with a shaved head, but an unshaved face. A guy with tattoos completely covering both arms and his neck, another with multiple nose rings. I get suspicious, shifty-eyed looks from two of them, a snarl from a third. It's like walking into Nick's Pub in Key West.

In the hallway we squeeze past a black guy in a wheelchair who smiles at me like I'm his best friend. The Activities Room bunch is as strange as the diners in the kitchen. A man in bright orange sweats moves chess pieces at a table, with no opponent and no board. Two sprawl on the floor in front of the TV, watching Jerry Springer. From the looks of the face of one of them, he was once in a hell of a knife fight.

The most bizarre-looking character of the group is the one in the bathrobe dozing in a rocking chair, his huge head resting on a pillow of double chins. His gray hair is matted like a loon's nest and he has a sparse, scraggly beard. Folds of his Jabba-the-Hut body hang over the sides of the chair. He slowly lifts his head and his droopy red eyes meet mine. He gives me a lopsided smile, and speaks.

"Hey, bro."

26

"HOW'RE THINGS ON FOXGLOVE LANE?"

"A shambles."

Jamie smiles. "Some things never change." He sounds placid and seems to be in mildly pleasant humor. I don't know how the administrator could have described him as "excited." Bovine is more like it.

"Did you find my albums?"

"No, not yet." I forgot about Jamie's Mahler and Wagner LPs. Louise didn't throw them out, I'm sure of that. They must be with my baseball cards, through the portal into the other dimension.

"That's okay," he says. "They don't have a turntable here. Just a CD player."

I make a mental note to pick up some CDs to send Jamie for Christmas. No Wagner.

"How's the food in this joint?"

He regards his orbicular waistline. "Ample."

We small talk for twenty minutes, then I tell him I'm his new trustee. "Do you need anything?" I ask.

"Not at the moment." One eyelid closes and his head rolls to the side. "I'm surprised mom made you trustee. You were sort of on her shit list. Ever since you moved away."

"That was a long time ago, Jamie."

The solitary boardless chess player gives us an annoyed look and storms out of the room. Sorry to break your concentration, Boris.

"Why'd you go there?" asks Jamie.

"I had to leave. For a lot of reasons."

"No, I don't mean why'd you *go*. God, I know why you left. I wish I could've. I meant why *there*. Why the Keys?"

I have wondered this many times myself. When I announced my destination to Luke, I was quite definite. I bounced around the South for a long time before I got to the Keys, but I knew that was where I would land. Was it because I heard my mother say it was the most beautiful place she had ever seen? Or because I heard my dad and Tom Atkins, when they were both blasted, daydreaming out loud about retiring there, as if that would be some sort of panacea?

Maybe I was drawn to the Keys because it was the site of my glory, my big success, saving my father's life on Coffins Patch. Sometimes I think I became a dive master so I would have opportunities to perform more underwater rescues, to try to recapture a little of the exhilaration I felt that afternoon near Seven Mile Bridge. Perchance save someone who wouldn't undo my achievement by dying so soon after, possibly by his own hand. It seems to me our motivations are buried so deep we never really know why we do anything.

"It's nice there," I say.

"Have you got a girlfriend? You always had a girlfriend."

"I have some women friends I see from time to time. Nothing serious."

He bobs his gray eyebrows twice. "Whatever happened to that really hot girlfriend you had?"

"Lori?"

"No, the *really* hot one." He makes a lecherous, comical growl from the back of his throat. "Rrrrrowww."

"Wendy?"

"Yeah, yeah, yeah. Wennnnndy." He seems to float off into a reverie for a moment, then he says, "The one who talked about Frrranz Boas. What happened to her?"

My stomach somersaults and my cheeks burn like sirloin on a hot grill. "Last I heard, she was fine."

"What was the last you heard?"

Nosy bastard. I almost get up to leave, then I almost ask him if this is the Spanish Fucking Inquisition, then I grit my teeth and say, "I bumped into her in Islamorada eight years ago."

"How'd she look? What was she wearing?"

Easy boy, or I'll have them up your dose. "She looked good," I say. Then something releases inside and I let the mortification wash through me. It hurts less if you don't fight it. "She looked great. She introduced me to her two beautiful daughters. Her husband was at the Pennekamp Marine Sanctuary that day giving a symposium. He's a prominent ecologist at Princeton University."

"Did you meet him?"

"Not then, but I knew him from before. We roomed together, in college."

The administrator comes over and asks if we'd like a glass of juice or something. I say how about a triple bourbon Manhattan and she laughs politely as she looks around nervously. I guess it's bad taste to make booze jokes within earshot of recovering addicts. She gives us each a plastic cup of orange juice. Mine's watery.

Jamie looks like he's about to nod off. So did Rozner — my conversation must be scintillating today. Jamie's eyelids flutter open and he fixes his gaze on me. "Are you glad Mom's dead?" he asks.

"No. Are you?"

"No. I forgave her a long time ago."

He seems so serene, I decide to risk sailing into the hazardous waters of that unseasonably warm afternoon in October of 1971 when Dad died. "Why are you so sure she did it?"

"She was there. She said that was all he was worth. She lied to the police."

"Are you certain Dad was dead when you saw him in the basement?"

"He was dead."

"Where was he, exactly?"

"On the floor in front of his desk."

"What did he look like?"

"Red. He had sleep lines on his face, like he dozed off at his desk. I checked his pulse. Dead."

Jamie fidgets and shifts his corpulence in the rocker. He seems calm enough. I ask, "Why did you have explosives in your hands when Mom saw you?"

His eyes shift and he grips the arms of the rocking chair. "To make the fire."

"Why make a fire?"

"They . . . told me . . ." He closes his eyes. "I *thought* they told me . . ." He shakes his head.

I try a different angle. "Why would someone tell you to make a fire?"

His eyes pop open and he says, "To protect us."

"From what?"

He looks at me with a sheepish, lop-sided grin. "Honest to God, I don't know. Dad looked so ugly lying there. I thought sure Mom was going to get caught. They'd take her away. I think I just wanted to destroy all the evidence, so no one would ever know what happened, except me and her."

Jamie thought he was shielding Louise, while she thought she was shielding him. I doubt they ever spoke to each other about it. "How would you feel if we found out Mom wasn't guilty after all?"

He chews on this for a full minute, closing and opening his eyes, then he cocks his head and says, "Different."

At the other end of the Activities Room sits a ping-pong table with paddles and a ball at the ready. Jamie asks if I'd like to play a game. I doubt he can get out of the chair on his own, let alone play ping-pong. To my astonishment, he rocks himself up, waddles over to the table, and proceeds to return my first three serves so fast I can't get a paddle on the ball. It looks like he's going to beat me going away, but after winning eight straight points he's sucking wind like a sled dog. The administrator materializes and says Jamie needs to rest now.

We wait at the door while Edith enters a security code on a keypad to let me out. Jamie gives me a weak high-five and says,

"Maybe I'll come down and visit you in the Keys sometime."

"I'd like that," I say, knowing it will never happen.

○

The message light is blinking on my mother's answering machine for the first time since I got here back in November. I had assumed it was broken. Man, was she isolated toward the end. At least she got one message.

No, she didn't. It's the file room clerk from the Sheboygan County Courthouse calling. The file from *Johnson vs. Bruckner* is in. Perfect timing, since I just talked to Rozner and don't need it anymore. Thanks, anyway.

The message reminds me that I have been lax about picking up messages from the answering machine in my dive shop. I hate using the remote message pickup, it's so damn complicated and I use it so infrequently I forget how. A card with the instructions nestles between a credit card and a PADI certification card in my overstuffed wallet. Jesus, that print is tiny. Where did I leave those reading glasses? Here they are, on the table next to Dad's chair.

Step one is easy, dial the number.

"We're sorry, the number you have reached has been disconnected . . ."

Great, that'll be good for business. I was only a couple of months late paying the phone bill, for crying out loud. Okay, three. The point is made, I absolutely must finish up here, pronto. Next, they'll repo my boat.

Louise doesn't get phone messages, but she gets lots and lots of mail. It's piling up like snowdrifts on the kitchen counter. Nothing but bills, junk mail, and Christmas cards from people who don't know yet that she's dead. A responsible person would take the time to write all these folks and let them know. Fortunately, I'm a screwup.

Uncle Stan sent her a card from Scottsdale, Arizona. Of all my relatives, he's the only one from that generation still alive. Remarkable, considering his war injury and the wheelchair always made him seem frail. Hats off to the V.A. Hospital.

Son of a bitch, I don't believe this. A card from Leon Bridette. I rip the envelope open. Currier and Ives picture, "Warm holiday greetings to your family from ours at Falls Dieworks," Bridette's name preprinted, no signature. This one I might answer. Warm this, you scum.

Whether he was in on my father's murder or not, I always felt Bridette got off too easily on the bank fraud. A suspended sentence and mild public embarrassment that was quickly washed away by Dieworks' philanthropy and its PR department. The only scintilla of justice done was that he lost his retreat on the Cisco Chain. But they let him stay on as president of the Dieworks, and he cleaned up when the company was sold to Rocksmith International.

Newley, on the other hand, didn't fare so well. He went on the lam, but a cop in Cable, Wisconsin, pulled him over for a rolling stop and made him. Newley resisted arrest and the cop applied a nightstick in the same location Luke had found with the anchor, which was not good at all for Newley's subdural hematoma. In a small jailhouse in northwestern Wisconsin at 3 A.M. on September 4, 1974, Philip "Bud" Newley, formerly of Oostburg, found peace.

Time's a-wastin'. Back to work. There are drawers here in the kitchen stuffed like Thanksgiving turkeys. Out they come, onto the floor with the contents. Get down on your hands and knees, you lazy bum, comb through this crap. Phonebooks, cookbooks, address books, matchbooks. Ray and Louise's collection of bar souvenirs — swizzle sticks, tiny umbrellas, a bumper sticker that says "I Closed Wolski's." Key chains loaded with keys to which no one could ever find the lock. Dozens of road maps, at least half of them Wisconsin. Ashtrays of all shapes and sizes, most of them cracked and chipped, except the metal ones, which are dented.

A drawer of linens, packed so tight I have to pull with both hands to open it. I toss linens over my shoulders left and right, high-speed excavation. Napkins, tablecloths, doilies, placemats. Aprons — here's the frilly yellow one she wore at holidays. The hand-embroidered linens from Poland. Careful, they're worth a fortune! A girdle — yikes, how did that get in here?

The kitchen's finished and I'm off to the attic. I'm getting overheated from the exertion, but that's good because the attic is an icebox. Here I encounter towers of hatboxes, legions of wardrobe boxes, countless shoeboxes. Heaping hillocks of hosiery. And fad exercise equipment galore: an Ab Roller no ab ever rolled, a Bullworker no bull ever worked, a NordicTrack nobody Nordic ever tracked. Ha, here's one of those vibrating belt machines from the '60s: effortlessly melt away those love handles.

Did the stamina of my youth seep away gradually, or did it desert me all at once some years ago, and I didn't notice at the time? Two hours in the attic and I'm done in, weary to the marrow of my bones. On my way down the stairs, I can almost smell the Jack Daniels awaiting me.

Mmmm. It tastes even better when you're exhausted, does it not? Ahhhh. Feels better, too. The second one feels better yet. Ditto, the third. Let's see if there's anything on the old TV. *Time/ Life presents 100 of your all-time favorite holiday recordings. Perry Como. Patti Page. Nat King Cole.* Your all-time favorite recordings if you're a hundred years old.

Curious emotions stirring. Driving through the snowy countryside, spending the afternoon with my brother, opening those Christmas cards, topped off with a dose of this music, and I find myself feeling a little Christmas spirit for the first time in many years. Not authentic good-will-towards-men spirit, more the artificial-holly-and-tinsel spirit, rusty and arthritic from long dormancy. It never feels like Christmas in Marathon. No snow. No Jack Frost nipping at your nose. The lighted plastic trees in the Kmart look like zoo animals, sad, skittish and out of place.

Bing Crosby. Bing might be home for Christmas, but let's face it, I won't be. At the rate I'm going, Christmas Eve will find me sitting in this dump alone, snorting bourbon and watching Jimmy Stewart beat a rap for bank fraud cleaner than Leon Bridette did. I'll never be in Wisconsin in December again, what the hell. I'm going to bring some of those decorations up from the basement and hang 'em one more time. I'll just freshen up this drinky a little first.

Fa-la-la-la-la, la-la-la-la. Boxes one and two fall to pieces as I pull them out from under the stairs into the brash light from the bare bulb. Don't be afraid, Mr. Centipede, I won't hurt you. This string of lights looks serviceable. Hey, what do you know? There's still one unbroken Polish grandmother ornament! Whoops. Oh, well.

Behind those two boxes is a big black one that looks sturdy and intact. My eyes adjust to the dark and I see it is not a box, it's a trunk, with brass fittings on the corners, a hasp, and a padlock. I remember it, sort of.

Three small boxes are in the way. I heave them in the direction of the sump tank — each lands with a splash. The trunk has a leather handle on the left side. It breaks. So does the handle on the right side. I grab hold of the padlock and drag the trunk through the puddle water, black as coal tar. The muscle I sprained in my back hoisting my dead father in October of 1971 badgers me from time to time, and I know when the whiskey wears off I'm going to pay for this.

There were a hundred keys in the kitchen drawers; one of them has to open this padlock.

Wrong again. After forty keys, I give up and get the crowbar I used on my father's desk. I stick one end through the padlock and put all of my weight on the other end. The trunk walls are rotted and the hasp pops free from its moorings.

I flip open the lid.

Joy to the world. I have found the portal.

27

The House, Day Thirty-Five

NEW YEAR'S EVE USUALLY FINDS ME at Nick's Pub in Key West, not in front of the tube watching Dick Clark. The formerly ageless Dick stays indoors now, and that guy from *American Idol* handles the outdoor work. Amazing, isn't it, how many people want to cram into Times Square in the freezing cold to stand around waiting for that stupid ball to come down? Imagine the traffic and bad parking, the drunk drivers.

I myself haven't touched a drop since Christmas, because I wanted to devote all my energy and faculties to the contents of the black trunk I found under the basement stairs last week. But I am going to pop a bottle of bubbly tonight, even if it is only bulk-processed domestic crap that set me back all of five dollars. Not to celebrate New Year's, but because I am almost finished going through the stuff in the trunk, which will bring to a conclusion the excavation phase of this expedition. Next comes the packing, hauling, and throwing-out phase. When that's done, I'll spring for some real French champagne, not this cheap swill.

My mother apparently packed the trunk a few years back, when she still had both oars at least partly in the water. Unlike the files in my room and the kitchen drawers, there was a discernible order to the trunk's contents and organization. It was a place to put items for preservation. Too bad she shoved the chest under the stairs, where dampness, insects, and fungi have corrupted like absolute power.

In the top layer I found collectibles. Jamie's LPs were still intact, but the liners and jackets had disintegrated. My baseball cards had decayed so badly you couldn't tell Willie Mays from Whitey Ford. Some ancestor of mine — probably the Polish great-grandmother — was a needle pointer *par excellence.* Jamie had collected stamps, filling three albums with postage from six continents, each colorful rectangle carefully affixed in place with a gossamer hinge.

It's all garbage now.

Also ruined were the certificates and awards that made up the first substratum. There I unearthed blighted diplomas from my elementary, junior high, and high school graduations, Jamie's graduations, and my parents' graduations from high school and college; Louise's collegiate drama awards; David's Employee of the Month award from Falls Dieworks; my National Merit Scholarship Finalist letter; my certificate of participation in the Sheboygan High School Science Fair; my University of Wisconsin admission document; a certificate Ray got for driving a truck 60 consecutive months without an accident; and so on and so forth.

She organized the certificates thematically, rather than chronologically. One batch consisted of baptismal, confirmation, and marriage certificates — all the sacraments together. When I looked those over, it struck me as odd that my mother had Jamie and me confirmed. You can't have your kids confirmed unless you belong to a church, and that costs money. Why would a woman as frugal as Louise spend dough on confirmations? She hardly ever went to church. When I was ten I asked her if she believed in God, and she said she never thought about it.

My mother's theological apathy seemed normal in comparison to my father's religious viewpoint. He never went to church at all and described himself as a "relativistic pantheist." When I asked him the same question I had asked my mom, he told me that he believed the "unified space-time continuum" was God.

"Infinite time, space, matter, and energy undifferentiated, an endless nothingness with such creative power that the entire universe precipitated out of a singularity. When we die, we simply lose the illusion of time and space and individual consciousness and merge with the continuum. We separate ourselves from our selves. Can you imagine?"

No, I couldn't imagine. I was ten years old. It seemed to me that while my mother didn't think about God at all, my father thought entirely too much.

My best guess is that Louise had Jamie and me baptized and confirmed to satisfy Aunt Melanie and her other relatives, and otherwise stayed away from the whole religion thing to avoid a clash with Dad.

The lower layers of the trunk pleasantly surprised me. With uncharacteristic foresight, Louise had packed some of the cards and letters into Tupperware bins before stashing them away. She had her own notion of what constituted precious artifacts, and these were preserved in plastic boxes with lids that burped. I didn't find very much in those letters that shed light on my father's death, but I became absorbed by the light they shed on his life.

The first plastic box I opened was full of love letters. David was one heck of a romantic guy. Even as a grown man I was initially embarrassed reading his mush. How he yearned for the rose-petal softness of her touch; how his heart burned like the flames of a million torches for her, on and on, *ad nauseum*. Then after a while I got into it. What he lacked in poetic talent he made up for with enthusiasm. And exclamation points!

By far the most interesting and perplexing letter in the collection was in an envelope postmarked in Chicago. In it, along with the usual over-the-top *amorata*, my father wrote of a recruitment interview he'd had at "the U. of Chi." with a "rep. from the Army Corps of Eng.," to work on a project that was

> " . . . totally hush-hush. All I can say is, by the time the interview was done, I knew I didn't want to have anything to do with it. Insanity! They only talked to me because of that absurd Physics paper I wrote, which was mostly malarkey. By Saturday, I'll be back in your arms. I can't wait! Let's have cocktails and stay up 'til the sun rises!"

In the Tupperware box, the letter was in a pocket folder with a ten-page typewritten paper by David Bruckner for a class called Physics 812. The paper was entitled, "Magnetic Isolation of Uranium Isotopes."

What didn't you do in the war, Daddy? I knew you avoided the draft, thanks to having had a kidney removed. What else did you dodge? It looks like you weren't even willing to support the war effort as a civilian working on a weapons project. You would have fit right in as a student in the early '70s, but you must have been an odd duck in the '40s.

Louise held on to love letters from other guys, too, most notably Ray. He was an even worse poet than David. And he used! Even more!! Exclamation points!!! Nonetheless, I'm sure some historical society would be interested in his letters home from the Pacific front. He fought in the Philippines and landed on Luzon in January of 1945. He complained more about the bugs than the bloodshed.

She also had a couple of letters in there from another soldier boy, a guy named Ted who was in the European theater. Nothing romantic — his letters talked about David as if they were all good friends. Ted's letters were in a folder with his obituary from November, 1944. Twenty years old. Reading it, I felt thankful that my dad had only one kidney.

I still haven't completely recovered from seeing the three letters in there written by Leon Bridette. In one, he gushed a little too much about how "charmed" he was to meet David's "bride" at the dinner party celebrating David "joining the Falls Dieworks family." In another, he offered condolences on David's "untimely passing" and offered to help in any way he could, closing with, "Love, Leon." That one reminded me of how he tried to act paternal towards me at my dad's funeral, and how it pissed me off.

The third Bridette letter offered condolences when Ray died. He opened with, "Dearest Louise," and didn't merely offer to help, he enclosed a check. I don't know for how much, the letter didn't say, but it gives me the creeps to think Bridette may have seeded Jamie's trust, even in part. I wouldn't want to soil my hands managing any money that came from that slime.

Was that check the work of a guilty conscience? Or was it

a clumsy come-on by an admirer, waiting in the wings, who had missed his first chance, and didn't know how to go about gaining a woman's affections other than to use his money? Either way, it confirms motive. When I confronted Bridette in the Falls Dieworks parking lot, he appeared to be emotionally stirred when he told me he didn't intend things to work out the way they did for "Louise and you." I didn't ask him how he did intend for it to work out. Nor did I ask myself why the tender way Bridette spoke Louise's name sounded so dissonant to me.

My worst shortcoming as an investigator, I suspect, is that I don't pay enough attention to my own gut reaction to details. I depend too much on logic. In fact, I have believed for years that some part of my brain I can't seem to access has processed all those feelings and details and figured out long ago who killed my father and why. I just need to excavate my brain the way I did this house and pull the black trunk of subliminal memory across my *corpus callosum* into the left hemisphere of my brain, so I can use words to explain it all to myself.

Reading the box of letters from Aunt Melanie was as boring as reading cooking recipes. In fact, a lot of her letters contained recipes, along with the dullest possible recitation of what she and Stan did all day. The only interesting letter was the one Melanie wrote in the hospital in 1956, and it was only of interest because I never knew what she was hospitalized for. "Nervous breakdown," they called it back then. Now I finally understand why Louise seemed so relieved when Deputy Detective Adams asked her if my father had any mental illness in his family. It meant she could stop blaming her side for Jamie.

In a box of formal white cards, I found an invitation to Wendy and Luke's wedding. "Professor and Mrs. Walter P. Lehman request the honor of your presence . . ." I didn't go. Clipped to the wedding invitation was one to Luke's bar mitzvah. Didn't go to that, either. Both invitations were addressed to me at Foxglove Lane, so I never received them. No matter, I wouldn't have gone anyway.

I found the copy of Dr. Patel's letter collected with other correspondence pertaining to Jamie's illness. My mother wrote to so many doctors and facilities before placing Jamie at St. Rita

House, it must have been like a part-time job for her.

This morning I opened the last of the plastic boxes. A melange of cards and letters, the contents included what I imagine was my mother's most precious artifact — a letter from an assistant casting director at RKO Studios. He congratulated her on her screen test and said a contract offer was forthcoming. The letter was dated six months before the day I was born. It's not hard to figure out what happened. When she got this letter, my mother was over thirty, late in the game for an actress to be starting in movies. Having a baby and raising it to school age didn't mean postponing the RKO deal, it meant passing on it.

If my mother was displeased with me when I was little, she would often say, tongue in cheek, "How sharper than a serpent's tooth it is to have a thankless child." Sharper still, I guess, if having the little ingrate scuttled your motion picture career. Downright piercing.

She never told me a Hollywood studio made her an offer, even though it was no doubt a big event in her life. Probably, she didn't want me to feel sorry for her, and blame myself, that she passed on the opportunity so she could stay in Sheboygan, live in this crummy house, and raise a couple of crummy kids. If so, her instincts were sound — I do feel sorry for her, and I do blame myself, a little. I'm good at that.

Now, after spending an intimate week with the contents of the black trunk, I'm cross-legged on the living room floor, going through the last of the Tupperware-preserved letters. My middle-aged knees object to sitting in what we used to call "Indian-style." I haven't heard the term in a long time, either because it is now considered politically incorrect, or because people my age hardly ever sit like this. The muscle I sprained in my back doesn't approve either, but all of the chairs and table are now repositories of artifacts.

They've started the countdown in New York. Time to take a break and uncork the so-called champagne. Feh. A modest little wine, with much to be modest about. How dare they call this sugary swill "brut"? Well, what do you expect for five bucks? Maybe it's not so bad, once you get used to the cloying aftertaste that makes your diaphragm shudder like a gaffed tuna. This stuff is so bad, I don't know how it is that I'm on my third glass and they haven't even finished playing "Auld Lang Syne."

Good night, Dick. I'm into a batch of letters now that all pertain to my dad's inventions. Some of these I never heard about or don't remember. Here's a letter my father wrote describing a device I could use, for people with sensitive sinuses who wear glasses: a clip that attaches to a headband, to hold eyeglasses up off the bridge of the wearer's nose. He called the gadget "Spec-spenders." His letter says seventy-five percent of the test subjects reported their noses were less stuffy when they wore Spec-spenders with their glasses. Here's a picture of my Aunt Melanie modeling them. They're quite dorky-looking. May have had a shot at selling in the '60s when headbands were in. I also find an eight-by-ten black and white glossy photo of a vending machine, paper-clipped to a drawing of the coin mechanism, in which several small discs are labeled "magnet."

Why is this in here — a carbon copy of a letter to Frank T. Shriner, Vice President for Business Loans at the Bank of Wisconsin?

> October 21, 1971
> Re: Guaranty of $80,000 Loan to Philip J.
>   Newley
> Dear Mr. Shriner,
> This is to memorialize our telephone conversation of this morning, in which I advised you that I will be tendering payment in full of the entire principal amount of the above-captioned loan, prior to the end of this month. You have agreed that if payment is so made, the Bank of Wisconsin will release me from liability for interest, penalties and other charges. Please confirm this agreement in writing.
> > Very truly yours,
> > David Bruckner
> > cc: Leon Bridette
> > Abraham Kanter

It is paper-clipped to a letter from Frank Shriner, dated the next day.

> Dear Mr. Bruckner,
> I am writing to confirm our agreement that, if you pay $80,000 to the Bank of Wisconsin on or before October 31, 1971, the Bank will release you from your guarantee. If you pay by any form of check or draft, please bear in mind that the funds must be actually received by the Bank before the close of business that day.
> Sincerely,
> Frank T. Shriner

I stand up slowly, looking at the letters. Then I bend over and pick up the half-empty bottle of champagne, which I think I am going to need. So Luke was wrong, Leon Bridette wasn't lying when he told me my dad was about to pay off the loan. Somehow, my father thought he was going to come up with eighty grand, within a week before the day I found him dead in the garage.

If that was so, Bridette was right, he had no reason to want my father dead, and every reason to want him to stay alive, at least to the end of the month. The same would have been true for Newley, only more so. The timing of my father's death couldn't have been worse for Kanter, who was about to get out from under $80,000 of his debt to the bank.

And what about Louise? If my father was right, she had no motive, either. Assuming, that is, she knew he had a deal in the works to get out from under the debt to the bank.

The memory of the day my dad died blotted out almost everything from the far more mundane days that immediately preceded it. Who remembers what they were doing the day *before* JFK was shot? But I have retained a few memories from the day before I found my dad in the garage, only because that day was also intense for me, in a different way. That was the day Lori and I made our plans to consummate our young love on the morrow. Lost in fantasy, checking the weather report hourly, practicing with the prophylactic, I got no homework done that evening. Fixated as

I was, I barely noticed when my father came through the door and announced, "Louisie, I'm home!"

My parents shared a bottle of wine with dinner. I was so distracted, I didn't ask what the special occasion was. What I should have zeroed in on, but with my head full of Lori did not, was that my mother didn't ask, either. One of those gut-tweaking details I never managed to drag up to the conscious level before.

She knew something was up, or she would surely have criticized the extravagance.

"I will be tendering payment in full . . ." Not I hope to be, or I expect to be. I will be. If true, he had no reason to take his own life, at least no reason I know of.

My father never made an idle boast. He found a way to pay the loan. Good for him. Swell. Only thing is, every theory I have ever had about his death has just been knocked into a cocked hat.

28

LOOK AT ALL THESE LETTERS, CARDS, PAPERS, and mementos piled up around me like barren desert mountains. I've read a thousand documents, sifted and sorted and categorized all manner of sludge and dross while the hours and days and weeks have slipped away. I've never worked so hard in my life, and the upshot is, I know less now than I thought I did when I started.

I down the rest of the sparkling wine, which has lost its sparkle, straight from the bottle. This godforsaken house and the goddamn refuse in it have bested me. I am profoundly fatigued, utterly fed up, and above all, frustrated beyond tolerance. It is the climax of three and a half decades of frustration. In a twist on the old tradition of tossing champagne glasses into the fireplace, I get a good grip on the neck of the champagne bottle, rear back, and with a bestial grunt, let it fly right between the andirons.

God that felt good. The green shards rest in black ashes like emeralds on a field of volcanic cinders. The last time I smashed anything in frustration I was eight years old. I had nearly completed assembling one of those made-in-Japan plastic model airplanes using the sort of glue teens use to damage their brains. A piece was missing from the kit, and the model wouldn't go together without it. I smithereened the bastard with a ball-peen hammer. My mom yelled at me.

Well, she's not yelling now. The stemmed champagne glass follows the bottle into the fireplace, shattering like a childhood illusion. Then, in goes the ashtray I previously bounced off the wall; it splits in two against the sooty bricks.

Next, to the china cabinet. It's chock-a-block with worthless, breakable trash. *Crash!* goes a Hummel. *Smash!* goes a punchbowl. *Crash-tinkle-tinkle* goes a Polish teacup.

But why am I wasting energy on china and crystal, when the real enemies are these four-flushing, time-stealing, good-for-nothing documents? I kick a pile and it spills across the floor, reminiscent of a losing hand of cards. Another pile I heave into the air and the pages flutter down like giant confetti. Handfuls I rip, tear, crumple, and mutilate. The living room is littered worse than Times Square an hour after midnight.

I get hold of the brass floor lamp — the one Jamie flung at Ray on the occasion of my last visit to the house — and I grip it like a baseball bat just above the base. Preparing to take a mighty swing at a tower of letters atop the coffee table, I recite, "And now the air is shattered by the force of Casey's blow."

Apparently the champagne has gone to my head more effectually than I realized. I miss the tower entirely and plant the harp of the lamp in the flimsy drywall. The bulb breaks with a blue spark and the room goes dark. "Strike one," I say.

Feeling I have accomplished enough for one day, I plod upstairs to bed. The fifth stair tread squeaks more loudly than ever, apparently caught up in the party spirit. I fall onto the dusty, sagging bed, too spent to brush my teeth, change into sleepwear, or even take off my shoes. Above, the crack in the ceiling grins at me sardonically. The house knows it has won.

"Happy fucking New Year," I say, and pass out.

o

Why can't I find my locker? I go there every day, right after homeroom, to get my books for morning classes. Funny, I can't seem to remember what course I have first period, but I think I have an exam today and I'm not prepared. The hallway is dark, endlessly long, and deserted, as if everyone except me has been evacuated. I feel frightened.

A picture of Lori exactly like the one from my yearbook is taped to one of the lockers; I think it must be mine. I turn the lock, but I cannot get the combination right. Bill Sorenson is standing beside me. "You lost it, man," he says. "You lost it." He lopes away with long easy strides. "Wait," I call out, "where are you going?"

"Fire drill," he shouts back.

My eyes open; my nostrils flare, an acrid odor biting them. I sit up and drop my feet on the floor. A slate-gray ghost drifts past the bedroom door. Smoke?

I clomp clumsily to the bedroom door and look down the hall toward the stairs. On the wall, shadows cast by the banister spindles wiggle like a row of belly dancers. There is a flickering light emanating from the living room. *Fire.* The hiss of a chorus of angry snakes comes at me from behind. I turn to see a shower of sparks splash out of the doorway to Jamie's bedroom. Fire there, too. I am surrounded.

How did this fire get so far along while I slept? Didn't my mother have a smoke alarm? Oh, yeah, I took the battery out and put it in the automatic thermostat.

There is a telephone in my parents' bedroom. Should I run to it and call 911, or just get the hell out of the house? The question is answered by a report like that of a detonating grenade. I feel the explosion on my skin and through the soles of my shoes.

Christ, I did too good a job jamming magazines around the window in order to keep out the cold; they shred when I try to pull them out. Finally, I free the sash and open the window to a blast of arctic air that brings tears to my eyes and makes me think twice about leaving the house. Twenty feet to my right, the window of Jamie's room shatters and a flaming projectile streaks over the moonlit snow. All right, I'm leaving.

I grab the windowsill and work my feet slowly down the roof, using the crusty snow for traction. My feet dangle over the edge as I slide on my knees and belly until I am able to grab hold of the gutter, first with one hand, then with both. The gutter miraculously holds my weight, and I lower myself until my arms are extended, my feet suspended a couple of feet above the snow. I let go.

Pain shoots through my knees and up my back. My hands ache. To think I used to jump off that roof for fun, forty years ago. Through the kitchen window and the arched passageway into the living room, I can see sparkling showers of embers spraying in bursts. A bizarre-looking house fire, sort of like indoor fireworks. It's not a conflagration yet, but with all that paper scattered around on the floor, it soon will be. Most of those documents were damp from the basement, or the place would have gone up like dry kindling.

A siren in the distance announces that the Sheboygan Fire Department is on the way, apparently summoned by a neighbor. It's obvious to me what happened. My brother must have continued to make gunpowder and homemade bombs as long as he lived here. Under threat of harsh punishment from Ray, Jamie developed ever more covert places to hide his cache, including, apparently, in the wall spaces. I set it off when I put the brass lamp through the drywall.

The fire marshal won't buy this explanation, I'm afraid. Gunpowder, fuses, crumpled paper, in a dilapidated old house that any heir would be happy to trade for the insurance proceeds, and a smoke detector with the battery pulled. Yep, it will look exactly like arson to him. I should hop in the car and flee to Mexico, but I don't have the energy.

Whizzzzzz-bang! That was impressive. Do I know how to celebrate New Year's Eve, or what?

I crunch through the snow to the front of the house where a hook-and-ladder is parked and a half-dozen men in black slickers are already hard at work. In front of the fire truck two uniformed cops get out of a squad car. The husky, ruddy-faced driver approaches me with his hand on his nightstick.

"You live here?"

"Yes. No. It, it's my mother's house. Was my mother's house, I mean, before she died. I'm just . . . visiting?" I sound like an idiot.

"Do you want to get in the squad, sir?"

Do I have a choice? I'm freezing out here, I might as well get in the squad. Unless I want to go warm my hands on the house.

Pop! Pop! Hissss. Pop! The husky cop is talking to a fireman. Now he's tapping on the window next to me.

"Yes, officer?"

"Do you have explosives in the house?" He has a distinctly unfriendly tone.

"No. I mean, yes? I don't. Maybe my brother . . . I don't know."
Idiot.

"Have you been drinking, sir?"

I should refuse to answer that question on the grounds that it's New Year's Eve. "A little."

The cop talks to the fireman some more. They look extremely displeased. The fireman scratches his head underneath his metal hat, then he shouts something to the other firemen and they all back away from the house. Chickens.

I watch the house through the window of the squad car. The flames cast silhouettes across the crisp, cobalt-blue snow — spectral images of my crumbling childhood home, shadow puppets of a fairly happy family that failed.

o

Here I sit in my car, cold, hungry, bone-weary, and woozy, having spent the morning at police headquarters answering questions. I am grateful that the cop didn't hold me, although he did tell me not to leave town until they "get this sorted out." I'm also grateful for this blanket the police loaned me, even though it smells like they took it off an alcoholic goat.

The Fire Department acquitted itself well. Once they got the explosives expert out of bed, they brought the fire under control quickly. They saved the detached garage and, as a result, my car. The house stinks, and it smolders a bit, but it's still standing. The policeman warned me not to go inside. Too dangerous, he said, but I think they want to keep me out for other reasons. The yellow tape over the doors says, "Crime Scene."

It occurs to me that the smoke damage from the fire has spared me the packing, hauling, and throwing-out phase. Quite a silver lining. That would have been motive enough for arson. I saw a homeowner's policy in the insurance folder. Maybe my mother kept up the premiums, maybe not. If not, it would help clear me on the arson, but it would be a blow to the United Theater Arts Fund.

If there was an item in the house that might have given me the answer I was hunting for, it has undoubtedly been destroyed, along with anything else worth saving. Driving up from the Keys, abandoning my dive shop for the holiday season, spending myself on the search — it was all for naught, all pointless. My precious artifacts, my mother's souvenirs, everything is gone. All I have to show for my efforts are two books resting on the passenger seat — my high school yearbook and the volume of inspirational poetry Lori gave me when my father died.

Shame on me, leaving this book of poetry to rot in the basement. I have never even taken the time to read all of the poems. The first one is "Winter for a Moment Takes the Mind," by Conrad Aiken. How seasonally appropriate. I know I am in a foggy, funky mood, but this poem seems much deeper, much heavier than I thought any of the verse in this book was. I never heard of Aiken, but a brief biography follows the poem. Pulitzer, National Book Award — his accomplishments were major. I am an ignoramus for not having heard of him. Hmmm. When Aiken was a child, his father committed suicide. Aiken found the body. Was Lori trying to tell me something with this gift that I didn't pick up on for thirty-six years?

Now that I look more closely, I see pertinent, personal messages in many of these poems. How much time and thought she must have put into selecting this book. Here's the one she circled.

> . . . *Your anguished tears are*
> *mingled with my own.*
> *I walk unseen beside you*
> *Up the hill.*

What a stupid clod I was not to appreciate this gift more. I have never been comfortable with sentimentality, but for some reason it is getting to me now, big time. Must be extreme fatigue.

I pick up the yearbook and find her picture. Absolutely

gorgeous. And her inscription — the frilly femininity of her handwriting is enough to turn me on all by itself.

> Jonathan,
> Can you believe high school went by so fast? Now we move on. No one can say what the future holds in store, but I know that with your intelligent mind and beautiful soul, you will go far. But remember that wherever you go, whatever you do, life holds for you one certainty — I will always love you.
> Up the hill,
Lori

Lori's inscription embarrassed me at the time. One of the guys on my school bus read it, and got laughs calling me "soul man" for the rest of the year. The inscription makes me abashed now, too, but for a different reason — I never told Lori how I felt about her.

I turn to the passenger seat as if she were literally there, unseen beside me. "Can you believe it?" I say. "Thirty-six years later, and I'm still not up that damn hill."

A crazy thought pops into my befogged brain. Maybe my trip to Sheboygan was not in vain, after all. Maybe I didn't come all this way and spend all this time and energy to find out what happened to my father. What if the point of the trip was for me to find Lori? Just to tell her. To set the record straight.

Not that I have a prayer of starting anything up between us. On the contrary, I hope she is happily married and that life is giving her everything she wants and deserves. Really.

But we never actually said goodbye to each other. The last time I saw her, I didn't even know it *was* the last time. I never realized I was missing the chance to tell her how much I appreciated her loyalty and how she helped me get through senior year, how much I cared for her and admired her. How I would always love her, too.

I decide to make a new plan, to change entirely the purpose of my expedition to the north.

The streets are slushy, gray, and deserted. Everyone is watching bowl games or sleeping it off. I drive a little out of my way to cruise past the quarry. Gone are the meadow and the folksy barbed-wire fence with the hole in it. A self-storage warehouse squats there now, with a fascistic twelve-foot chain-link fence behind it, guarding the quarry. The teens who live around here now don't know what they're missing.

There's the house where Lori lived, a red brick ranch with a black asphalt shingle roof, green shutters, and a *faux* Colonial portico. A wooden sign swings from a cast-iron bracket on a black lamppost: *Ronald and Ruth Hagen.* Her parents still live there.

I turn my rearview mirror to the left. The guy looking back at me needs a shave, a haircut, and about ten gallons of Visine. Ah, what the hell, I'm not going to a fancy dress ball. Just the same, I'd best lose the smelly wool blanket.

The doorbell sounds like chimes. The green door opens, and I see Lori, not young, not middle-aged, but Lori as she appears in my recurring dream — wrinkled, white-haired, and frail.

$$29$$

SHE PLACES HER DAINTY, WILTED HAND on the middle of her chest. "Jonathan? Jonathan Bruckner. Lori's friend."

"That's right, Mrs. Hagen," I say. "Happy New Year."

"Come in, come in. It's ten degrees out with the wind chill, don't you have a jacket?"

Lori's mother is no more than five feet tall, less than a hundred pounds. Her skin is that of a withered pear, and an expression of chronic pain resides in the furrows around her soft brown eyes. But her voice is sweet and youthful, and the lineaments of her face are balanced and fine. She is a lovely woman, just as I imagine Lori will be when she is eighty. DNA rules.

"Please sit down, Jonathan. Can I get you something to eat?"

"No, thanks."

"Some fruitcake? I have a nice strudel."

"No, thanks." What am I saying? I'm famished. "On second thought, strudel sounds good."

Ruth shuffles into the kitchen. She's wearing open-heeled slippers, stretch pants, and a sweatshirt with red roses and the word, "Grandma" embroidered on the front. If she's Grandma, there must be some grandkids. I wander around the living room and foyer, inspecting pictures. Two small children, a boy and a girl, frolic in a backyard above-ground swimming pool. A handsome, fair-haired man who might be Lori's older brother poses with a woman I don't recognize hanging on his elbow. I see school pictures of the swimming pool kids, older.

Oh, my God. Lori with the fair-haired man. She looks about thirty years old and is wearing a formal black dress, pearls, and heels. She is beautiful. My stomach flips and my face gets warm. I'm trying to figure out who goes with whom in these pictures when Ruth scuffles in carrying a silver tray. The coffee smells first-rate and the strudel smells like heaven.

Ruth says it's so nice of me to drop by, and asks how my mother is. When I tell her, she says she's sorry and nods knowingly, as if she is accustomed to hearing that someone her age has passed on. I ask about Mr. Hagen. When she tells me, I say I'm sorry and nod knowingly.

"How long has it been since the last time you were here?" she asks.

"About thirty-four years," I say. "Lori and I sort of lost track of each other after high school." Man, that's some good strudel. I hope I don't make a pig of myself, but I probably will.

"I remember she went out to Madison to visit you one weekend, when you were in college. She was very upset when she got back."

"That was my fault," I say. "I said the wrong thing. I didn't mean it."

Ruth wrinkles her nose at me, exactly the way Lori used to. "I hope you told *her* that."

Let's get off this subject. "How long did she work at that accounting firm in town?"

"Only a few months," she says, pausing to sip coffee from a china teacup. Her hands are as fragile as the china, but they haven't the slightest tremor. She must have an exceptional nervous system. Maybe that's why her teacups aren't cracked and chipped. "She stopped working there when she married one of the partners."

Of course. I feel a sagging in my gut. My stomach, which has been in my throat the entire visit, sinks back into its normal gully.

"He left the firm, too, and took a job in San Francisco. Lori didn't care much for California. Too crowded."

"Did she have children?" I gesture at the "Grandma" on Ruth's sweatshirt.

She touches the embroidery. "No, no, this is a Christmas present from Ron Jr.'s children. Lori's niece and nephew." Her voice becomes wistful. "Lori never had children."

I don't know what to say to this. That's too bad? A little part of me hears it as good news. I despise that little part.

"Probably for the best that she didn't," Ruth continues. "The marriage didn't last long."

That evil, selfish little part of me, the part cartoonists portray in a devil costume, rejoices. But I really want Lori to be happy. Honest.

"Did she remarry?"

"No, she never did." My internal devil clicks his heels. "In fact, she moved back to Wisconsin and enrolled in college. She got a teaching degree at Steven's Point, with honors."

Good for her, I think. Guess she showed me who's stupid.

"She taught public school in Wausau for fifteen years. Elementary. Then she moved to Milwaukee."

My mouth is dry. I can't seem to swallow the strudel crumbs. "Mrs. Hagen," I ask, "where is Lori now?"

The furrows around her eyes deepen. "Oh, Jonathan," she says, tilting her head. Her lower lip quavers. That tremble of her lip is an ice pick through my sternum.

"Jonathan, I thought you knew. We lost our Lori to ovarian cancer three years ago. I'm sorry."

You're sorry? She's your daughter, why are you telling me *you're* sorry? Is it because my face has gone clammy, and I can't breathe, and I'm struggling to stand up but I don't have enough blood pressure in my head to get out of the chair? Is my face as pale as it feels?

"I'll get you a glass of water," she says.

She brings a plastic tumbler full of ice water and a box of Kleenex. The Kleenex is for herself. She dabs at her eyes.

"Are you all right?" she asks.

Yeah, I'm okay. Or am I? Hard to say. I'm numb. I finish the water and clear my throat.

"Thanks for the coffee and strudel," I say. "I have to get going."

She follows me to the door. "It was nice to see you again, Jonathan."

I turn to face her. Do I have anything to say to her that's worth saying? Do I ever have anything to say to anybody that's worth saying?

She reaches out her hands, steps toward me, and hugs me around the waist. Her head does not reach my chin. I wrap my arms gently around her frail shoulders and feel a familiar sad, tender, bittersweetness for a moment, along with a sense of déjà vu and a need I can't define.

"I . . . loved your daughter, Mrs. Hagen."

"I know."

"Do you think she did?"

Lori's mother steps back and places her hand on my cheek. "I'm sure she did." She smiles.

o

Finally, I get it. I see what happened at a level deeper than logic, deeper than intuition, deeper even than profound insight. Now, I understand what happened to my father at the cellular, genetic level.

Whatever it was he was counting on to rescue his finances, save his marriage, and turn his life around didn't come through. Fate laid a body blow on him, and he couldn't trick himself into believing he would ever again waste his effort trying. Whichever gland it is that produces the false hope hormone became depleted. No more juice left for plans, inventions, or struggling. Not when you have the perfectly good alternative of merging with the continuum. And a painless way to do it.

Sometimes, the Freudians say, a cigar is just a cigar. We Bruckner men have a tendency to overthink. Sometimes a suicide is just a suicide.

The numbness is familiar to me, and comforting, like brandy on a cold, dark night. I feel eerily calm and focused, as I was that day on Coffins Patch. Able, when one plan falls apart, to quickly improvise another.

The battery in my mother's portable garage door opener is dead. Each time I come and go, I have to get out of the car and enter through the side access door to open the overhead door with the inside, hard-wired button. The garage door moans and squeaks and stalls out a couple of times on the way up. It stalls once on the way down, too. Then I settle into my Dodge, parked in my dad's space in the garage, the center of the vortex of negative energy at 5451 Foxglove Lane.

For two and a half years after my father's death, before I was tricked by vapors into believing he didn't kill himself, I wondered constantly what it was like for him. A thousand times I imagined myself going through it. What did it feel like? How hard was it to sit there, waiting? What thoughts went through his mind? Did he think about me at all? Did he start to bail out at any point, perhaps more than once, or was he resigned and unequivocal?

I could never get a clear picture because I couldn't truly put myself in his place. I hadn't been dealt so many losing hands. I didn't feel defeated by life. I didn't feel like I didn't matter. I wasn't certain that no amount of effort would ever get me up the hill. I was seventeen, he was fifty. We were different, at the cellular level.

But now I'm just like you, Dad. Except my headline will say, "Out of Town Man Found Dead in Garage."

Carbon monoxide is supposedly odorless, but car exhaust is acrid and nasty. It burns my eyes and coats my tongue with a foul resin. Did David cough like this? I suppose he did. Did he feel nauseated and frantic? Probably. Did his chest feel like it was in a vice? Painless, my ass.

If my father was anything at all like me, about now he was saying to himself, this ridiculous melodrama has gone on long enough, it's completely stupid, who are you kidding, enough already. Then he would have planned an escape route.

How about the access door?

Now that door is a perfect example of one of those nettlesome details I shouldn't have filed away in the back drawer. The evening I found my father I noticed that someone had locked it. Neither my father nor anyone else in our family would have done that, because we all knew the door was too warped for the lock to hold — the door just popped open anyway. One of the many idiosyncrasies of the house that only we were familiar with. Every old house has them.

But somebody locked it — the person who put my father in the garage to conceal his murder. I know it, just as at some level I have always known it. The door was locked. Ergo, he was murdered. It's as simple as that.

I shut off the engine and open the car door. The fumes are thicker outside the car. In a house fire, you're supposed to get low to the ground. Is it the same for carbon monoxide? Who the hell knows? I bend over at the waist and stride as fast as I can to the button for the automatic garage door opener, holding my breath. I feel weak and light-headed. There's the opener button. I straighten up and reach for it.

Dark purple dots fill my field of vision, as if I have gotten up too quickly out of a hot bath. Emotional exhaustion, sleep deprivation, and toxic fumes have sapped my blood pressure. Oh, Jesus, I am going to faint. My knees buckle and I feel myself descending into a murky hole

The world dissolves into grainy blackness, and I am gone.

30

ABOVE ME, A BRIGHT LIGHT APPEARS in a shimmering haze. Is this heaven? I look to my left. I don't pretend to know anything about heaven, but I am fairly confident it does not have grease stains and hunks of rusted metal on the floor. This is my mother's garage — a far cry from heaven.

Afternoon sunlight fills the garage and the clouds of car exhaust have diffused and lifted into the rafters. Apparently, I hit the opener button before I blacked out and for once the door didn't stall on the way up. Dumb luck has saved me from my world-class stupidity. I am, however, suffering from the worst headache I have ever had in my life. It feels like I hit my head on the concrete when I went down.

I sit up and touch the back of my head. There's a big goose egg and a lot of blood; I must have split the skin. I'll probably need stitches. The puddle of blood on the garage floor is uncoagulated, so I haven't been out very long. I lie back down to quell the suggestion of nausea in my throat.

Have I punished myself enough for being such a bastard to Lori? Did I level my karma? No? Maybe if the gash on my head gets infected . . .

Supine on the cold concrete floor, I remember why I resisted telling Lori how crazy I was about her, besides the typical awkwardness around romance that afflicts teenage boys like acne and athlete's foot. Had it not been for our decision to meet in the quarry that afternoon, I would have been home, and my father wouldn't have died in the garage. Not that I blamed Lori, I just mistrusted my ability to resist her allure. My feelings for Lori became intertwined with my guilt and grief over my father so that I couldn't relax and wallow in my feelings for her anymore. They were always accompanied by an internal knot of wariness and disapproval, and every time we returned to the quarry the knot got bigger and tighter.

There's a lot of stuff up in the lower rafters of the garage. Folding lawn chairs, garden hoses, shovels, rakes, a fertilizer spreader, skis, my old Flexible Flyer sled. Rummage I haven't rummaged through, perhaps because I'm uncomfortable in the garage. Lying on my back, I can get a good look at all of it. A lot of worthless junk that my parents stuck up in the rafters because they were either too frugal or too lazy to throw it out.

The bright light in the haze is sun glinting on a metallic object tucked in the upper rafters. It's cylindrical, about a yard long, and lying lengthwise on a four-by-eight wooden beam. If you didn't know it was there you'd never notice it, unless you happened to be lying on your back on the floor of the garage, along the wall. I would say it has been deliberately concealed. Why?

My legs are weak and wobbly as I pull myself up by the rear bumper of my car. Mercy, my head hurts worse than a thousand hangovers, and I speak from experience.

How am I going to get that thing down? How did somebody get it up there? If I stand on the roof of my mother's car, I think I can reach it with a rake or a broom. Climbing up on a car roof is way harder than I remember. Curse my traitorous knees. Why are my hands so stiff and sore? Oh, yeah, twelve hours ago I was hanging from a steel gutter.

The rake should do nicely. It's not quite long enough, unless I get up on my toes and stretch. Purple dots, fuck, I'm passing out again. No, I'm okay. I can just barely hook the tube with the teeth of the rake. Now, a little pull, and . . . here it comes, headed straight for the bridge of my nose.

Thanks to my catlike reflexes the metal tube only catches my cheek a glancing blow. I lose control of the rake and it leaves a deep dimple in the hood of my mother's car, but I don't care. What's a little dent in her car, after I burned her house down? The tube rolls under my car.

I climb down and use the bow rake to recover the metal cylinder. It's an aluminum tube with a screw top that looks exactly like the one my dad used to store the plans for the Opuba. The fall to the floor has dented the cap, and I struggle with my sore hands to open it. Rolled sheets of heavy paper nestle inside.

The documents are unwieldy. They are three feet long and have been coiled up for so many years that they resist unfurling. I hold them down on the trunk of my Dodge and gradually unroll them. The first two inches of the top sheet reveal an identification box containing my father's signature in blue ballpoint ink. I put a knee over the bottom of the sheaf and use both hands to unroll it.

At first glance, the top sheet looks like an elaborately detailed, oversized comic strip featuring robots, or perhaps space aliens. It takes me a moment to realize that what I am looking at is a set of schematic drawings of the fronts, backs, sides, and insides of parking meters.

And now I know.

o

Leaving the garage, I rip the yellow police tape from the back door and enter the house. The place reeks of wet ashes, and the walls, floors, and ceilings are as uniformly gray as the Wisconsin sky in January. The caustic air in the house prickles my sinuses and bites at my lungs.

By comparison, the dank fustiness of the basement is pleasant. There is little damage down here, except for the black parabolas of carbon that trace waves along the top of the cinder block wall, where the fire ate through the floorboards.

Somewhere above me a charred timber moans and settles with a thump. Having so recently decided that life is worthwhile, I hope the house doesn't collapse and trap me down here. This basement would be a singularly lousy place to die.

My father's desk, or what was left of it after I finished working it over with the crowbar and saws, squats in the same spot it occupied thirty-plus years ago. According to Jamie, Dad was right here, in front of the desk, with no pulse. I found him in the garage a few hours later. The police report said he had toxic levels of carbon monoxide in his blood. If he was already dead when Jamie found him, he wasn't breathing in the garage. He died of carbon monoxide poisoning right here, in front of the desk. His murderer was surprised when Jamie came home early. When my brother came downstairs, the killer hid — probably over there, under the stairs, until the house was empty again. Then, he moved the body to the garage.

I pace off the distance to the window in the back corner nearest the garage. Thirteen steps, approximately forty feet. The window is about eight feet from the floor. I say goodbye forever to the basement, ascend the stairs, bid adieu to the rest of the house, and leave by the back door.

From the rear corner basement window to the place next to the garage where Dad kept our boat is only ten crunchy paces through the icy snow. The total distance is seventy-eight feet. The air supply hose for the Opuba would have reached easily.

My father had something you wanted badly, didn't he, Tom? Something you may have even felt entitled to after the investments you made and the hours you put in. You were smart enough to see its value, even if you weren't smart enough to invent it yourself. And you were desperate, ruthless, and clever enough to get your hands on it.

You and my father had spent so many hours in our basement, drinking and confabulating about business schemes and inventions, my father didn't suspect a thing when you proposed an early afternoon toast and followed your well-worn path to our liquor cabinet. Once he was three sheets to the wind, he easily fell for your suggestion to give the Opuba a dry run in the basement. So what if the water in Lake Michigan is too cold in October? We can drop the outboard's prop into a trash barrel filled with water, run the air supply hose through the window down into the basement, and test it right here in the comfort of your home. What a great idea!

My brother said he saw "sleep lines" on my father's face. Those weren't sleep lines — they were marks from the face mask. Did you feed the paraldehyde down the air supply tubes, Tom? No, that would have left evidence. You put the stuff right into the mask. I can see you helping my dad on with the mask after starting up the outboard, then holding it firmly in place with those Popeye-the-Sailor forearms of yours. You got him good and soused first, probably poured the drinks triple strength, so he didn't even struggle much, did he? Besides, you had the element of surprise — he'd have never guessed what was up.

Once you had him knocked out with the paraldehyde, you could have just hauled him up to the garage, closed the doors, started the car engine and left. But then he might have come to or been discovered before he was dead, and you weren't taking any chances. You had to be sure he was dead before you left, yet still make it look like suicide by carbon monoxide poisoning.

It was a simple matter of shoving the air intake tube into the exhaust outlet, and waiting a few minutes while your trusting friend and neighbor paid his debts to nature and to you simultaneously. Pretty slick, Tom.

Did it cross your mind that David might have a duplicate set of signed plans for the Bruckner Parking Meter stashed away someplace? Or that he may have already talked to a patent lawyer about the device?

Sure, he probably showed you the letter from Stewart Sassoon praising the invention's commercial potential when he got you to agree to invest in it. Your investment was what he planned to use to pay off the Bank of Wisconsin. Is that why you bided your time before you peddled the invention, because you were afraid the patent lawyer might have seen the article about his client, the local man who was found dead in garage? It took a lot of patience to sweat it out for a year, waiting for your $400,000 ship to come in. Or maybe it just took that long to find a buyer.

I can't wait to see the look on your face when I shove these drawings in it.

31

HEAD DOWN AGAINST THE BITING WIND, I sprint across Foxglove Lane to Old Lady Atkins' house and ring the front bell. I stand on the stoop and hop up and down for a few minutes trying to keep warm. She finally comes to the door in a quilted floral-print robe over sweats and a pink turtleneck.

"Oh, Jonathan," she says, "I'm so relieved to see you're all right. What a terrible fire! Come in, come in. Can I get you something to eat?"

What is it with women of that generation and food? Something to do with growing up in the Great Depression, I suppose.

"No." Her foyer and living room are architecturally identical to my mother's, but the decor is totally different. Agnes's place has frilly lace curtains, Jesus pictures, a petit-point settee, and the smell of potpourri, as opposed to ashes, charred timbers, and the smell of a doused campfire.

"I woke up in the middle of the night, and I thought, good heavens, what *is* that? It sounded like a gunfight, right here on Foxglove Lane. I looked out the window and saw flames in your living room, so I called the fire department."

"Sit down, Agnes."

My brusqueness startles her, but she recovers and leads me

into the kitchen. She sits down at a clean butcher block dinette table.

"I could heat up some coffee. . ."

"Don't bother." I unroll the parking meter plans on the table and pin them open with a cookbook and a sugar bowl snatched from her counter. Agnes stares at the drawings blankly. I point at the signature, rapping the tabletop hard with my index finger. Agnes jumps a little. Her eyes move back and forth from the drawings to the signature.

"Oh, dear," she says. "Oh, my. When did you find these?"

"Just now, in my mom's garage. Do you remember Tom's phone number at work, when he was still at the plastics company?"

She recites it from memory. Gee, that's nice. I guess wives call their husbands at work a lot. I wouldn't know.

I dial the number and get a recording that says Northrup Plastics is closed for the holiday. Without a word to Agnes, I bolt through the door that connects her kitchen to the garage.

I flick on the lights, three bare 100-watt bulbs, each suspended on two thick wires coiled around each other like strands of desiccated DNA. Agnes's garage has as many years' accumulation of junk as my mother's, but unlike the disorder at Louise's place, Agnes's junk is lined up neatly on rows of sturdy wooden shelves, presumably constructed by handy old Tom when he lived here. I see an impressive assortment of power tools, rusty and gathering dust, machine parts, obsolete office equipment and small appliances, ancient copies of *Popular Mechanics* in bundles bound with hemp twine, and lots of fishing tackle — I'm surprised Tom didn't take that with him when he ran off to Florida with his new squeeze.

Along the back wall are row upon row of paint cans, each with a splotch of the color dabbed on the label for easy identification, in case Agnes wants to touch up a room with the color it was painted, say, forty years ago. Next to these are Ball jars and tin canisters of chemicals with hand-printed masking tape labels curled at the corners, followed by metal containers of turpentine, linseed oil, paint thinner, carbon tetrachloride, and some stuff I have never heard of, like ethylene glycol and pyridine. Here's one I have heard of: paraldehyde.

That private detective who swindled me thirty-four years ago, Herb Tierney, said that paraldehyde was used in the manufacture of synthetic resins. I hate myself for not realizing back then that the plastics company where Tom Atkins worked probably made synthetic resins. I knew Tom pilfered from work — that's how he got the tubing for the Opuba for free.

I can't resist the temptation to unscrew the top and take a little sniff for old times' sake. Tom screwed the cap on so tight it aggravates my sore hands to open it, but not tight enough to have prevented the contents from evaporating over the years. Just as well. I'm not certain I could have handled the feelings that smell might have stirred up.

I carry the can back inside and plop it on Agnes's kitchen table.

"My dad's autopsy showed paraldehyde in his blood. It's a sedative. Tom got it from work."

Agnes's cheeks are wet and her face trembles. "Oh, dear. Oh, my."

"Where is he, Agnes? Where is Tom?"

She rubs her hands together, as if she's cold. "Florida."

"Where in Florida?"

She rises slowly and fetches a book with a purple cloth cover from the cupboard. "I haven't heard from Tom in twenty-five years. His brother sent me a Christmas card list with the addresses for all the family a few years ago, and Tom was on it. I don't know if he still lives there." She hands me the book opened to the "A's."

Christ, I don't believe it. Palmetto Road, Big Pine Key. I know exactly where this is. It's less than forty minutes' drive from Marathon. I pass within five miles of it every time I drive to Key West.

"Goodbye, Agnes," I say.

She reaches a shaky, purple-veined hand toward me. "What are you going to do?"

"Right now, I'm going to visit my brother."

o

"Jamie's in the Activities Room," says Edith, the St. Rita House administrator, who obviously does not appreciate surprise visits from family. She probably wouldn't let me in at all if I wasn't the trustee now and in a position to turn off the tap. "He just ate dinner. He'll be ready to go to bed soon, so your visit will have to be brief."

I assure her I only need a few minutes with Jamie and ask to use the private meeting room with the folding chairs. I wait while she gets my brother. She escorts him in with a hand under his elbow as if he's an invalid, which he clearly is not.

"Don't tire your brother out, now," she says.

I give Jamie a sly, conspiratorial look, cueing him to respond, "Don't worry, I won't." The administrator doesn't laugh. I tell her to leave the room, and I don't say please.

"I didn't think you'd visit me again so soon," says Jamie, slowly. "I don't see you for years, then twice in two weeks. Cool."

"I have something to show you," I say. "Jamie, do you remember Tom Atkins from across the street?"

"Sure. He hung out with Dad in the basement all the time. His wife used to yell at us if our ball rolled into their yard."

"Do you remember when he made a bunch of money on an invention?"

"Yeah," he says without hesitation. "The Atkins Parking Meter. He hit the big time." The medication apparently hasn't damaged Jamie's long-term memory too badly. "I always knew," he says, mimicking my mother's voice and delivery, "Tom Atkins was a really smart guy."

I unroll my father's mechanical drawings on the plastic table. Jamie helps me hold the corners down. "I found these up in the rafters in the garage," I tell him. "Look at the signature. Tom didn't invent the Atkins Parking Meter. Dad did. Tom stole the plans."

Jamie studies the drawings, the muscles beneath his scraggly gray whiskers and thick facial adipose twitching and contorting. He bites his lip. He is catching on; I see it in his eyes.

"Tom Atkins used a chemical called paraldehyde to knock

Dad out," I explain. "I smelled it on him when I found him in the garage. They use it at the plant where Tom used to work."

Jamie's jaw muscles tighten. He closes his eyes. His brow gathers. "I smelled it, too."

"The marks you saw on Dad's face were from a scuba mask. Tom used the Opuba to asphyxiate him. That's how Dad died from carbon monoxide in the basement. You came home from school early, before Tom was finished. He hid in the basement until you ran off, then he moved the body to the garage."

Jamie clenches his fists and his eyes dart back and forth beneath his eyelids. "I saw the tubing coiled up next to Dad's desk," he says, his words flowing out now in a rapid cadence instead of his usual drugged drawl. "The outboard motor was stuck in a metal barrel."

"It all adds up, Jamie."

He stands up and looks around, more confused than furtive. His breathing is labored, his face pinched and twisted. "So, so, so . . . that means they were all wrong. Dad didn't commit suicide."

"They were wrong. He didn't commit suicide."

"And, and," he swallows hard. His mountain of a body quivers, his chest heaves. "And Mom didn't do it."

I stand up and clamp my hand on his shoulder. "No, Mom didn't do it."

His head hangs down, his fists unclench, and his breathing eases. When he looks up at me, his face is soft and imploring, gently expressive in a way I have not seen since before Dad died.

"And, and . . ." His voice is a whisper.

"And what, Jamie?"

He looks into my eyes. "And *I* didn't do it, either."

This has never crossed my obviously inadequate mind — that years of living with a mother and stepfather who suspected him, being treated by a psychiatrist who suspected him, combined with the Bruckner propensity for self-doubt — of course, Jamie would come to suspect himself. With the delusions and the drugs and everyone treating him like a lunatic, how could he trust his own memory and perception?

And I thought *I* was carrying a burden. I haven't been any

kind of a brother for the past thirty-four years, so I feel a sense of undeserved privilege leading Jamie to a conclusion someone should have led him to long ago.

"No, Jamie. You didn't do it, either."

He grabs hold of me and breaks down. His body quakes, and his sobs when he inhales remind me of a humpback whale. Yes, he's my brother, but nevertheless, he *is* heavy. My knees and back are greatly relieved when he straightens up, sniffing and rubbing the tears off his cheeks with his giant mitts.

"Sorry," he says. "Didn't mean to slobber all over you."

"That's okay." We sit back down.

The administrator opens the door and tells Jamie it's time to wash up.

"Do you mind?" says Jamie, moving his upturned palm back and forth between us. "I'm talkin' to my brother here."

Edith looks startled and indignant, but she leaves.

"So what's next?" says Jamie. "You goin' back to the house?"

I tell him the house isn't habitable anymore, but spare him the details. "I'm going down to Florida. Tom Atkins lives there."

He bobs his wild gray eyebrows. "Gonna pay Tom a visit, eh? What're you gonna do to him?"

"I'm not going to tell you," I say. "I don't want to make you an accessory."

Jamie narrows his eyes and gives me a wicked lopsided grin. "Gooood," he says. "Just don't get caught."

32

I HEAD SOUTH ON INTERSTATE 43 and stop at a gas station just north of the Illinois border to call Attorney Rozner. He recommends that I not leave the state against the instructions of the police, but I tell him I need to, in order to track down my father's murderer. I tell him about the drawings I found in the garage, and that I believe they prove Tom Atkins copped and cashed in on my father's invention.

"Incredible," he says. "I'm surprised your father would have shared the plans with Atkins. David was idealistic, but I never thought of him as naive."

I explain how Tom originally bought into my father's inventions. "Remember," I say, "when we talked about the lawsuit you handled for my dad, when my uncle sued over the accident that killed Audrey? My father planned to file for bankruptcy because of it. You told me the case settled at the eleventh hour when my dad came up with the money from some business deal."

"Yes, I remember. It was quite startling."

"The deal was Tom Atkins, fronting the money to settle the lawsuit and save my parents from bankruptcy. In return, he got a piece of the action on my dad's inventions. For years, none of them panned out. By the time my dad came up with the parking meter, he had another enormous debt, from a loan he guaranteed at work. Tom apparently wasn't satisfied with his cut."

As I explain my theory to Rozner, the biting wind seems to get colder and harsher. The horizon to the north glows eerily orange from the urban aura of Milwaukee. To the south, where the much larger Chicago metro area is equally proximate, the sky is black, suggesting the approach of a winter storm.

"It's a shame there's no other evidence the invention was David's," says Rozner.

"There might be," I reply. "I found a letter from an attorney named Stewart Sasson telling my father his invention had significant commercial potential. I had thought Sasson was talking about an aquatic device my dad invented, but now I'm certain it was the parking meter."

"Sasson passed away a few years ago," says Rozner, "but his practice was merged into a larger firm. They might have warehoused the documents. I'll look into it for you."

"Thanks." A semi rolls by on the interstate, drowning out some of Rozner's words. In the wake of the eighteen-wheeler, a few stray snowflakes swirl in the halos of the tall streetlights.

" . . . and you know, Jonathan, I still have a couple of old chits to call in with the police. I'll take care of your temporary absence from the jurisdiction."

"Thanks again."

"Glad to help." Rozner doesn't ask what I plan to do when I find Atkins. He might think I won't tell him, or maybe he just doesn't want to know.

It's after midnight by the time I hit Indiana. The flurries have picked up and snow is accumulating on the highway. From Indianapolis to Louisville I fight a full-fledged Midwestern snowstorm, driving twenty miles an hour in second gear at times. In Murfreesboro, Tennessee, I stop for a couple hours of sleep, three submarine sandwiches, and about a half-gallon of coffee.

An ice storm slows my progress from Chattanooga to Atlanta, but I keep rolling. At the dawn of my third day on the road, the Sunshine State fails to live up to its name. Having stuck it out through a northern blizzard and a southern ice storm, I am finally forced off the road by a subtropical downpour, rare in January. I pull off south of Ocala, fall asleep sitting up in the driver's seat, and awaken with a pain in my neck that feels like somebody stabbed me with a cold chisel. The wound on the back of my head sticks to the headrest, and when I pull it off, starts to bleed again.

The rain stops around Kissimmee. Driving alone for thirty hours gives one a lot of time to think. Maybe too much. I start to wonder whether subconsciously I always knew it was Tom, and I moved to the Keys because I figured he would retire there, like he said he would. Have I just been waiting all these years for the plodding, logical part of my mind to connect the dots? It's a crazy idea, and one that makes me feel anxious all the way from Yeehaw Junction to West Palm Beach.

Between Homestead and Key Largo runs a straight, flat stretch of U.S. 1 where passing lanes are only provided at intervals and frequent signs advise motorists to otherwise refrain from passing. I have always respected those signs, until now.

As I hop the series of bridges that connect the Matecumbes to Long Key, Long to Conch, Conch to Duck, Duck to Grassy, and Grassy to Vaca, the green Florida Bay on my right and the blue Florida Straights on my left gather me in a welcoming embrace.

Finally, I pull up in front of my dive shop, joints creaking, eyes bleary, stomach growling, happy as hell to be home.

Shit, what's this? My landlord, the son of a bitch, has slapped a plug-lock on the door to my dive shop, a cute little device used on tardy tenants that's about as subtle as a blackjack to the kneecap. Good thing I have this large, decorative conch shell beside the stoop, big enough to protect the hand, hard and pointy on one end, the perfect tool for breaking and entering.

Behind the front door I find a pile of paper on the floor beneath the mail slot. On top of the pile some nasty-looking legal process sneers up at me. What have we here? Aw, damn it, the finance company has repossessed my boat.

The shop smells the same, but it looks very different. My landlord has collected some of the back rent without resort to legal process. A lot of my more valuable inventory is gone, along with my glass pelican light fixture and the cash register. Hey, he didn't take any of my wreck salvage sculptures. I'm hurt.

He also didn't take my personal scuba gear, because you can't get peanuts for used wet suits and such. Fortunately, the reason I stopped at the dive shop is right where I left it. I pull up my pant leg and strap on my diving knife. I promised myself on Coffins Patch I would always have one on me when I needed one. She's a beauty — a Beluga skeleton-handle tactical dive knife, made to the specifications of the German military Special Forces. Double-edged, curved blade, serrations along one half, very sharp point. I could gut a large, live bull shark with it if I had to, and one time, I had to.

God, I'm tired. If I could just close my eyes for a few minutes . . .

I climb the stairs to my living quarters and collapse onto my bed. It smells of salt, sand, and iodine, like the beach.

When I wake up it's dark outside, and even darker inside, because the electricity has been shut off. The lighted dial of my dive watch says I've slept for three hours. I still don't feel rested, but it's time to go. I say goodbye forever to my dive shop, climb into the Dodge, cross over the dark, struggling waters of Moser Channel on Seven Mile Bridge, and descend into the Lower Keys.

○

The address on Palmetto Road is a trailer park, and a rather shabby one at that. No double-wides, lots of rusted siding, small pads, chicken wire fences. What the hell did Tom do with his four hundred grand, blow it on jai alai? I drive around killing time until 3 A.M. to minimize the likelihood that anyone in the park will be up and about. Then I leave the Dodge two blocks away and approach Tom's place on foot.

His doorbell is mechanical, not electric. I hear shuffling from inside and a grotesquely hoarse voice saying, "Criminetly, who the hell?" The lights go on, the door opens, and there behind a walker is a desiccated, liver-spotted, hunched version of the man who used to live across the street from me.

"Who's that there?" he rasps, squinting behind thick, square lenses. "What time is it, for cryin' out loud?"

I step through the doorway into the light. "I'm Jonathan Bruckner. Remember me, Tom? From Foxglove Lane?" I close the door behind me.

"What? Jonnie Bruckner? Holy smokes, it is you. What are you doin' here? What *time* is it?"

"Sit down, Tom."

His living room is tidy but tacky, with plastic paneling, sculpted turquoise carpeting, and artwork from Kmart. "What is that you got there?" He points at the metal cylinder in my hand.

I grab hold of the walker and shake it, hard. "Sit the fuck down, Tom."

His face blanches, including the age spots. He regards me warily as he creeps his walker to a brown vinyl reclining chair, into which he shakily lowers himself. A long white surgical scar traverses the sagging flesh on his neck, suggesting that a partial laryngectomy is the cause of his raspy voice. I remember Tom smoked a pipe.

"What're you doin'?" he says. "Criminetly, it's the middle of the night. I could call the police."

"Good point," I say. I pull up my pant leg, unsheathe my dive knife, stroll over to his phone and slice the cord as easily as it if were made of tissue paper. Love the Beluga.

Tom's stunned, horrified facial expression tells me he has figured out I'm not here for a friendly visit. His mouth opens and flutters futilely for a moment; then he says, "Jonnie, I got no beef with you. Whatever you're doin' this for, you're wrong. I never did nothin' . . ."

"Shut up, Tom." I pull the drawings from the metal tube and toss them on his lap. He struggles to open them, but they keep rolling back up, so I reach over the walker and hold the top of the drawings for him while he holds the bottom and studies them for a minute. I let go and the drawings curl up in Tom's lap like a roller shade. He looks off to the side, biting at the corner of his mouth.

"This don't prove nothin,' " he says. "Dave coulda signed a set of copies."

"Did he?" I tap the knife blade on his walker. "I've got a lawyer going through the old records of Stewart Sasson."

His gaze moves from the knife to my face. "The patent expired years ago. The statute of limitations . . ."

"There's no statute of limitations on murder, Tom."

His jaw jumps around like he's lost control of his dentures. He swallows with great effort, the scar tissue in his voice box emitting a loud click. I think he's about to say something, but then his eyes wander off to a corner of the ceiling and his expression goes blank, the face of a patient who's just been told he's going to die and he can't cope with the news.

"You came over to celebrate my dad's new invention, and your investment in it. But the share he had offered you wasn't enough. You wanted a hundred percent. So you came prepared with a can of paraldehyde and a perfect plan. Get him drunk, put him under with the paraldehyde and use the Opuba to kill him with carbon monoxide. Then dump him in the garage with the doors closed and the engine running. Very clever."

Tom seems to shrink in his reclining chair, crushed under the weight of the accusation. It's obvious I know too much for him to construct a lie that will explain it all, and he must sense that if he tries to deny it, I will fly into a rage. He looks at me pleadingly.

"Jonnie, you can't do this."

"Sure I can."

"You don't know everything that went on, Jonnie."

"What don't I know?"

"Why, you were only a year old when I gave your dad the money that kept him out of bankruptcy. You would have been out on the street."

"You gave him nothing," I say. "You made an investment, and you expected a return."

Tom straightens in the chair and his eyes animate. "Yeah, sure, what's wrong with that? But I was getting a screwing, because of the bank loan he guaranteed. You don't know about that."

"Yes, I do, and it doesn't make a damn bit of difference. Your investment was speculative. It's no excuse."

The pale, scarred flesh in Tom's neck quivers as his eyes and lips twitch. I thought I would enjoy seeing him squirm, but it's only sickening and fatiguing me.

"I helped your dad develop his ideas. I got him parts and tools from my company. I believed in him, you know?"

Tom watches me reflecting on this, and it seems to embolden him. He perks up in his chair. "He never would have invented anything without me."

I plunge the knife into the headrest of the vinyl chair, an inch from Tom's ear. "Enough! It doesn't matter." I pull the blade out of the chair and press the tip to the bridge of his bulbous, purple-veined nose. The room fills with the smell of urine. "Do you have any idea what you did to my family? Do you ever think about it at all?"

I step back and turn away, wondering whether it's worth the karmic debt to waste this piece of garbage, when Tom lets out a sigh that sounds like cardboard being dragged across pavement. Then I hear him say, "Have you ever been in love, Jonnie?" I turn to face him.

Tom slumps, deflated in the chair, head down, shoulders drooping. "Her name was Lydia," he says. "I would have given everything I had in the world to be with her. But everything I had wasn't enough for Lydia." His eyes cloud behind the fat lenses. "She was a greedy gold digger, and I knew it at the time, but I couldn't give her up. That's why I did it. In the end, it was all for nothin'. She went through half the money in two years, then she took most of what was left in the divorce."

He looks up at me with more shame and remorse on his face than I would have thought him capable of. "So the rest of the money from your dad's invention ended up with Lydia and some Cuban gynecologist I never met. If it makes you feel any better, the so-called Atkins Parking Meter brought me nothin' but misery."

It's not Tom's misery, but something is making me feel a little better, or at least different, more than I anticipated. With his confirmation of my suspicions, a large part of a weight that I have become accustomed to carrying seems to lift, taking with it a lot of confusion and anger. The certainty that I am, after all, not the brother or son of a murderer, and not the fruit of a bent, sapless tree, obliges me to reorient myself. The strongest urge I have at the moment is to get away from this place. I have better things to do.

I'm halfway out the door when Tom croaks my name. "Jonnie!"

I look back at a shrunken old man who now strikes me only as pathetic and irrelevant. He says, "You need to see a doctor about that gash on your head." His mouth moves soundlessly and tears dump from his hazy eyes onto his crinkled cheeks. Then he says, "The other thing you need to do is to forgive. Can you do that?"

Without a word, I close the door behind me.

o

Above the tips of the red mangroves on Bahia Honda Key, a quarter moon casts its sheen on the Atlantic, dark and rippled like broken slate. The windows are open, and the cool, moist air, redolent of salt, shellfish, and tropical flora, feels as soothing on my skin as a spa filled with baby oil. A night heron creeping through the mangrove prop roots caws as I pass by, sharing a secret, or perhaps warning me not to get any ideas about poaching on his hunting grounds.

It is beginning to penetrate that the resolution I have been hoping for my entire adult life is no longer a doubtful part of an uncertain future; it already belongs to the unchangeable past. My father was not a failure who committed suicide, nor did he abandon us. He was a gentle, accomplished man who was the innocent victim of a mugging. I rewrite his obituary in my head: *"Brilliant Inventor Senselessly Slain."*

My brother was not a homicidal maniac, he merely had an illness that wasn't properly treated, that was exacerbated by the sort of stress no one should have to bear. Now that I'm certain he wasn't guilty, I realize I always got a kick out of the guy, even if I didn't share his musical tastes.

My doubt had its most corrosive effects on my attitude towards Louise. How I underestimated her strength and sacrifice. My ingratitude would make a serpent's tooth, by comparison, seem as blunt as a molar. I resented her skimping, her stubborn pride, her harsh practicality, her dependence on Ray's brutish tactics, the way she leaned on me. Part of me even resented that she directed so much more time and energy towards Jamie than she did towards me. But I understand that these were her survival techniques, and they worked, for all of us. Perhaps all she, Jamie, and I did in the wake of my father's death was survive, but with the breaks we had, and with the likes of Tom Atkins and Leon Bridette lurking about, that was a pretty fair accomplishment.

Leslie Rozner Jr., was right, I was blessed. But until I heard Tom's confession, I could never let myself believe it.

On the east end of Ohio Key is a place to pull off the road near a small patch of beach. Louise said the Keys was the most beautiful place she had ever been, and I didn't know until a few days ago that included Hollywood, California. It may be awhile before I'm back here, so I stop the car, open the trunk, and take out a plastic canister about the size and shape of a motel room ice bucket.

Lori's book of poetry might come in handy. I leave my shoes on the sand. The water is cool this time of year, but still gracious and welcoming. In the shallows the sea bottom is as soft as custard.

At mid-thigh depth, I feel the pull of the current, driven by the tide through Moser Channel. I hold the last remains of Louise Warchefsky Bruckner Moldenhauer in the crook of my elbow and open the book of poems. This one by Charles Mackay seems apropos for a woman who never thought about God or heaven. I read by the moonlight.

> *There is no such thing as death.*
> *In nature nothing dies.*
> *From each sad remnant of decay*
> *Some forms of life arise.*

I pour the sandlike pebbles and powder into the sea. The current draws a gray trail into the path of the reflected moonlight, heading out toward the reef.

Lots of good forms of life arising out there. Nice resting place for sad remnants.

And I should know. I've been something of a sad remnant

myself for the past thirty-four years, and I thoroughly enjoyed every single minute I spent out there on the reef, squandering my academic gifts to be a scuba guide. If tragedy hadn't befallen my family, or if my mother hadn't been driven by circumstance to forgo nurturing an extended childhood for me, I'd have surely graduated from college with honors and in all likelihood ended up spending the balance of my youth in some urban glass box pushing pencils and sorting paper for guys like Leon Bridette.

That's the thing about survival. It usually works out better than meets the eye.

Sitting on the beach, pulling on my shoes, I stop and look out over the moonlit channel. "Thanks, Mom," I say, but for once, I'm not being sarcastic.

Seven Mile Bridge rises over the channel and the lights of Marathon shimmer in the distance. This is the new bridge built in the early '80s, which replaced the one my dad told me about after our dive on Coffins Patch. It's as impressive a feat of engineering as the original. The first suggestions of dawn sharpen the edge of the horizon, and the sky behind Boot Harbor fades from black to purple. Beyond the harbor I think I can make out Fat Deer Key, Sombrero, and a whole continent of possibilities I never saw over there before.

"Have you ever been in love, Jonnie?" The answer to Tom's question is yes, twice. In love, Tom and I were both fools, but at opposite ends of a spectrum. I wasn't willing to do enough to hang on to it. Tom was willing to do way too much. There has to be a happy medium.

I feel a lightness under my wheels as I pass over the crest of the bridge, and I glance to my right, certain at this moment that Lori is there, unseen beside me. She is wrinkling her nose at me teasingly, because she always knew, as I did not, that every hill has a summit, and the higher it is, the more exhilarating the view.

"You need to forgive. Can you do that?" Now, Tom, that's a tall order. But I think that what I have needed for the past thirty-four years is not someone to blame for what happened to my family, nor someone on whom to take revenge. What I've needed is someone

to forgive for it. It was impossible when I wasn't sure who was to blame. Now, it's possible.

"I forgive you, Tom," I say, with a grandiose sweep of my hand. Not so hard after all.

Hell, if I can do that, I can forgive Newley, Bridette, and everybody else who had a hand in the disaster. It shows to go you, as my father said, there's no telling what you can accomplish. Maybe someday I'll even be able to forgive myself. If I could do that, then who's to say what I might find over there on the other side of Seven Mile Bridge?

Unlimited potential. Why, I may even be able to find someone who can take this slightly ridiculous, fifty-four-year-old survivor and care enough that he actually matters, just a little.

Here are some other novels from Pineapple Press. For a complete catalog, write to Pineapple Press, P.O. Box 3889, Sarasota, Florida 34230-3889, or call (800) 746-3275. Or visit our website at www.pineapplepress.com.

Conflict of Interest by Terry Lewis. Trial lawyer Ted Stevens fights his own battles, including his alcoholism and his pending divorce, as he fights for his client in a murder case. But it's the other suspect in the case who causes the conflict of interest. Ted must choose between concealing evidence that would be helpful to his client or revealing it, thereby becoming a suspect himself. (hb)

Mystery in the Sunshine State edited by Stuart Kaminsky. Offers a selection of Florida mysteries from many of Florida's notable writers. Follow professional investigators and amateur sleuths alike as they patiently uncover clues to finally reveal the identity of a killer or the answer to a riddle. (pb)

Nervous Water by Wil LaBossier. Six short stories that explore the spirit of fly-fishing. The author uses tales of stalking fish to examine environmentalism, philosophy, fishing as entertainment, the nature of celebrity, the meaning of relationship, and the importance of fishing to our identities. (hb)

My Brother Michael by Janis Owens. Out of the shotgun houses and deep, shaded porches of a West Florida mill town comes this extraordinary novel of love and redemption. Gabriel Catts recounts his lifelong love for his brother's wife, Myra—whose own demons threaten to overwhelm all three of them. (pb)

Death in Bloodhound Red by Virginia Lanier. Jo Beth Sidden raises and trains bloodhounds for search-and-rescue missions in the Okefenokee Swamp. She is used to dealing with lost kids, prison escapes, snakes, bugs, macho deputies, and her abusive ex-husband. But now she is suspected of murder and has to choose between betraying a friend and proving her innocence. (pb)

A Land Remembered by Patrick D. Smith. This well-loved, best-selling novel tells the story of three generations of MacIveys, a Florida family battling the hardships of the frontier, and how they rise from a dirt-poor Cracker life to the wealth and standing of real estate tycoons. (hb, pb)

The Honor Series of naval fiction by Robert N. Macomber. Covers the life and career of American naval officer Peter Wake from 1863 to 1907. The first book in the series, *At the Point of Honor*, won Best Historical Novel by the Florida Historical Society. The second, *Point of Honor*, won the Cook Literary Award for Best Work in Southern Fiction. The sixth, *A Different Kind of Honor*, won the Boyd Literary Award for Excellence in Military Fiction from the American Library Association.

Confederate Money by Paul Varnes. Two young men from Florida set out during the Civil War to exchange $25,000 in Confederate dollars for silver that will hold its value if the Union wins. They get mixed up in some of the war's bloodiest battles, including the largest battle fought in Florida, at Olustee. Along the way, they meet generals Grant and Lee, tangle with criminals, become heroes, and fall in love. (hb)

The Bucket Flower by Donald Robert Wilson. In 1893, 23-year-old Elizabeth Sprague goes into the Everglades to study the unique plant life even though warned that a pampered "bucket flower" like her cannot endure the rigors of the swamp. She encounters wild animals and even wilder men, but finds her own strength and a new future. (hb)

Black Creek by Paul Varnes. Through the story of one family, we learn how white settlers moved into the Florida territory, taking it from the natives—who had only been there a few generations—with false treaties and finally all-out war. Thus, both sides were newcomers anxious to "take Florida." (hb)

For God, Gold and Glory by E. H. Haines. The riveting account of the invasion of the American Southeast 1539–1543 by Hernando de Soto, as told by his private secretary, Rodrigo Ranjel. A meticulously researched tale of adventure and survival and the dark aspects of greed and power. (hb)